USA 2.0
Freedom's Resurgence

Also by W. C. Augustine

Shades of Green

Atlas Rising Series:
Atlas Rising
For the Common Good

USA 2.0

Freedom's Resurgence

Third in the Atlas Rising Trilogy

W. C. AUGUSTINE

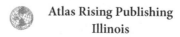

Atlas Rising Publishing
Illinois

USA 2.0 -Freedom's Resurgence

Published by Atlas Rising Publishing.

Cover and interior design by Carol Davis, www.tolgraphics.com

Published and printed in the United States of America

Library of Congress Cataloging-in-Publication Data is available upon request.

ISBN: 978-0-9864355-5-3

1.Fiction, Suspense
2.Fiction, Political

Acknowledgements

Among others, I especially want to thank my editor, Ginger Griffis, and my cover designer and formator, Carol Davis.

Ginger was invaluable not only correcting my numerous punctuation and spelling mistakes but giving focus to my story keeping it on track.

Carol, in addition to her tireless work advocating adherence to the constitution, captured the essence of the story with her cover.

And, of course, a thank you to my first proofer, my wife, Sue.

Yes, young people familiar to me, have in the future become instrumental in reviving freedom in America after the present generation squandered it.

Forward

Atlas Rising

Andrew Collier had no inclination to make a difference, even if he was capable or knew what cause was worth applying himself toward. Politics he knew or cared little about. He heard rattle about the loss of liberty in the country, but it did not affect his life. All politicians he considered to be self-serving egomaniacs who should be ignored as much as possible. A robotics engineer with a passion for astronomy with comfortable means, Andrew abided his nation's laws.

But he did care about the planet, humankind and everything that had been placed on earth. Although he formally practiced no religion, his mother instilled in him a belief in something bigger than himself. Perhaps that was why astronomy became his passion. Maybe he was looking for something out there.

For humankind, it was not a fortuitus coincident that his expertise as a robotics engineer was applied to astronomy. He was first to discover an asteroid trajectory would be altered sending it on a deadly march to earth. Bureaucratic arrogance refused to give credence to his discovery. Indecisiveness, rigid regulations, and inflexible union contracts delayed effective action.

After receiving an illegal health care procedure, Andrew was rescued by Julie Marcus, his future wife. Andrew's apathy toward the current direction of the country was broken by Julie's passion. His remaining indifference was squelched by the murders of a businessman he admired and a former girlfriend.

For the Common Good
After marriage, Julie and Andrew hoped to live a quiet, peaceful life, she providing corporate security, he adding to robotic advancement. They brought two children, twins, into the world endeavoring to provide them with a normal life. It was not to be.

Connections from their past, warning them of a clandestine plan to alter and spread a virus, forced Julie into action. Again, Andrew was apprehensive about getting involved. For their children's sake, he believed they must stay off the radar. When an altered virus killed one of their children, he realized indifference would ultimately protect no one.

Most of the population was either invested in state control or lived in fear from thousands of drones tracking the movement of everyone. The ability of the government to analyze the who, what, when and where was increasing exponentially. It would soon be too late.

Paired with expatriates making their home on a former cruise ship in international waters, a plan was devised. A rebel military force liberated American dissenters from a Guantanamo, Cuba gulag. Only by extreme measures could the 1984ish yoke of surveillance and repression be lifted. Three mini-nuclear devices neutralized the eyes, ears, brains, and database of the National Security Agency. Although a degree of liberty was restored, the fight had only begun.

> "Life should NOT be a journey to the grave with the intention of
> arriving safely in an attractive well preserved body, but rather sliding
> into home sideways, totally worn out, shouting 'Thank you God,
> what a ride!'" –*Author unknown*

Chapter 1

March 15, 2050

It was a quiet, uneventful night for most everyone in the country. Scattered thin clouds danced with the moon in the nighttime Iowa sky. Clouds sometimes obscuring but not completely hiding the moon. Julie and Andrew looked to the south expecting to see lingering evidence of a fission event fifteen miles distant. They could see none but knew it had happened twenty minutes earlier while they were inside their bunker hideaway. Perhaps they should have come outside earlier to visually validate their effort.

It was as if nothing had changed, certainly not in this nighttime sky. Unobstructed by clouds, the Big or Little Dipper hadn't moved in the sky. When a lone heavier cloud covered the crescent moon, some with imagination thought they detected a faint glow to the south. Good news—-they had not destroyed the country, but hopefully they had changed it. Upon reflection, perhaps *restored* would be a more appropriate word. Regardless of the static sky above the clouds, they knew that much had been shifted in the country. Just how much and to what end, they could not foresee.

Only a few miles away a small, low radiation fission device had obliterated the Federal Drug Administration's (FDA) manufacturing plant for nano-machines which were intended to be injected into people's blood stream. The microscopic devices would have been instrumental in the final measure of population control.

That evening, similar fission devices also destroyed the mega National Security Agency (NSA) data storage unit in Utah and the analytical ability of the NSA in Maryland. Knowledge of everything about everyone could no longer be transformed into actionable arrest warrants, non-ignorable invitations to re-education camps, and downgraded citizen scores. Every measure had been employed by Resistance members to assure the doomed facilities were vacated, but regrettably there was loss of life.

Julie and Andrew were leaders of the Resistance Movement. Although other leaders and volunteers were spread throughout the country, for security the base of operations was a former cruise ship in the Gulf of Mexico. Mason Trotter, leader of the Resistance movement in Texas, had given two employees, Kelly and Eric, leave to assist the Iowa operation. They had achieved their objective in Iowa. It was now time to leave.

"It is as if we have lit a grass fire. Where it goes, we do not know. But we do know the undergrowth needed clearing before it choked us all to death," said Kelly, a Texan volunteer.

NSA's drone spies-in-the-sky using facial recognition software had caught Kelly wearing a T-shirt with the inscription *"1984- It was **not** meant to be an instruction manual."* His name had been on a list stored in Utah to be picked up for re-education. The list was now a pile of silicon.

Tens of thousands of what were officially called Personal Protection Units (PPU) 2.0s scanned the country from above, two-thirds in the air at any time while others took on an electric charge. They were sold to the citizenry as a measure of security, a means to identify criminals.

In the earlier part of the century—because of a few bad cops— police were handicapped by an avalanche of strict new guidelines. Local and state police budgets were cut dramatically, which cut the non-federal police force in half. Consequently, crime of all kinds spiked. Citizens demanded that something be done. It was the government's obligation to protect citizens.

Technology offered a new alternative to police enforcement. Citizen surveillance drones sent data to the National Security Agency (NSA) which analyzed the data using face recognition software.

In 2013, NSA opened a gargantuan data storage unit in Utah. The 1.5 million square foot facility could store a Yottabyte of information, a unit of information equal to one septillion (1024) and perform 100,000 calculations per second. It had the capacity to store every word ever spoken by all humans since they started grunting. The storage was underutilized until thousands of PPUs started feeding information into the unit.

With eyes-in-the-skies, crime rates did go down. The Federal Bureau of Investigation (FBI) was expanded and became a national police force charged with carrying out directives from the NSA. Bureaucrats now decided which laws would be enforced. As the NSA came to know citizens' every who, what, when and where, activity that was not necessarily illegal— but incorrect by the overseers' standards— was tracked.

Because the PPUs were the size of turkey buzzards and gave people an eerie feeling, many citizens came to call them vultures.

"Well put," said Julie, commenting on Kelly's remark while looking deeply into the sky above the clouds and moon—for why and for what she did not know. But she did know a greater force guided her.

Reflecting on these thoughts, Julie continued. "As a young girl studying for my bat mitzvah I learned Moses said to God, *Who am I, that I should go to Pharaoh and bring the Israelites out of Egypt?* And God replied, *I will be with you.* Let us hope He is with us now."

Andrew encircled an arm around his wife's waist and said, "I'm sure He is. We were taught by the addition to that Bible that if Caesar's soldier asked you to carry his pack for a mile, you were to carry it for two. But we were not taught that we should become slaves like beasts to bear the burden of supporting the privileged. We did what we were called to do."

Among items they were evacuating from their temporary headquarters was a sketch of the Founding Fathers his mother had framed in walnut with her own hands years ago. Andrew held it up and said, "He was with them also."

They pulled a white van close to the gigantic twenty-acre Environmental Protection Agency (EPA) railroad tie dump. The dump's purpose was to keep carbon bound in the organic molecules of the discarded railroad ties to save the environment. Contrary to its intended purpose, the dump hid the temporary headquarters of the Resistance inside the country. With their fingerprints and DNA throughout the facility, they could not chance their hideaway being found.

Electronic files were concealed under the van's floor. In case they were searched, they filled the back with clothes and miscellaneous items expected to be taken by a couple moving. The Texas volunteers also hid copies of files in their vehicle. The Texas vehicle with stolen Iowa plates had the mandatory vehicle tracking device removed. The van did not, but it was assumed the ability to track citizen movement had been destroyed by their efforts that evening.

Nevertheless, they installed an incendiary device in each vehicle— as well as others spread throughout the railroad dump. Julie and Andrew were a mile from the headquarters when she set off the devices planted in the railroad tie dump. Ten miles into their escape, the sky glowed red behind them. Tens of thousands of railroad ties burning overshadowed only in spectacle what had happened at the FDA plant fifteen miles away.

The volunteers from Texas headed home, while Julie and Andrew took a different route.

Eric said as they viewed the conflagration behind them, "In a generation that site will either be a national monument or erased from all memory."

"Yes, and it's up to our generation to determine which," Kelly observed.

They had completed the job in Iowa. Andrew and Julie felt confident the van could not be tracked after NSA's information and analysis systems had been destroyed, but the roving eyes of NSA's vulture drones remained. Although the drones were not blind, the brain in Maryland which received signals from the drones had been destroyed, rendering their signals worthless.

After six months in Iowa, Julie and Andrew would have preferred to head for their condo in Midland, Texas, and live an uneventful peaceful life— but it was too dangerous. Perhaps someday they could return to Texas with their daughter. At lease they would soon be with familiar, like-minded people and their daughter in safety.

At the end of a five-hour drive to St. Louis, they stopped in a residential area and tossed two garbage bags of clothes, a flash drive, and the walnut framed drawing beside a pile of residential garbage. Before the garbage pickup arrived, a nondescript blue car loaded the garbage bags.

After leaving the van in a State-Mart big box parking lot, they briskly walked five blocks. On the walk, they dropped a yellow envelope in a mailbox. It contained a second antiquated flash drive back-up. It was addressed to a post office box in Texas. The inner envelope was programmed to destroy the flash drive with acid if touched by an incorrect finger. The irony of using a government arm to cut off over-reaching arms was not lost.

As Julie and Andrew walked a residential street, a blue car with the garbage bags they had earlier dumped pulled beside them. The driver lowered the car window and asked, "We've lost our golden retriever. Have you seen one loose?"

"Yes, a couple blocks that way," Julie pointed.

"Get in and show us," the driver replied.

With passphrases exchanged, the driver took them ten miles north to Alton, IL—the junction of the Mississippi and Illinois Rivers. They got out at a large grain elevator aside the river. Safely hidden on a tugboat delivering barges of corn to New Orleans, they headed downriver.

The Previous Evening in Maryland

Ellen Herwick and her life partner of ten years, Traverse Jones, unloaded a common electronic/mechanical carrier pigeon from their pickup truck. The carrier pigeon, as they were called, delivered packages by air to residential and commercial businesses. It was common to see a number in the air. The pigeon's wingspan was five feet and easily distinguished from NSA's spy vultures.

Ellen and Traverse's pigeon carried a three-pound fission device which engineers on the former cruise boat had miniaturized by separating a Russian nuclear device. The pigeon— sporting a Liberty Bell that Ellen had painted on its side— took off for the NSA headquarters in Fort Meade, Maryland, ten miles distant.

They had not spotted the new 3.0 version of NSA's PPU surveillance drone overhead which had followed Ellen's every movement for a month. New technology allowed its belly to change colors based upon the sky's condition making it nearly invisible from the ground. The chameleon drone also contained noise cancelling equipment, rendering it nearly silent. It was a test version operated out of a secret location.

The 2.0 spy drone version in common use was manufactured at a converted gun factory in Massachusetts. When local regulations threatened to shut down the last manufacturing facility in the state, NSA chose to have the new 3.0 version manufactured by a quasi-government company in Georgetown, Texas. The Georgetown plant would be in full operation within a year.

Only twelve 3.0 versions had been built and were being tested around Ft. Meade, Maryland. Data from the twelve PPUs were not yet fed into NSA's database but kept offsite. Someone at NSA foresaw the danger of having all data and analytical abilities centralized.

Ellen worked at the NSA Ft. Meade facility for fifteen years as a mathematician. She was good at her job. She knew it, as did her colleagues. But four times she had been passed over for promotion because of her lack of enthusiasm at agency political meetings. Meritocracy had ceased to be. She was not a rabblerouser— complying to new social mores, never marrying Traverse— as marriage was considered an antiquated religious custom.

Ellen and Traverse attended the same high school and had known each other since Traverse's parents moved to the area the last year of pre-school. Friends throughout school, but never more, they each dated someone else in high school. All were friends, and often they double dated.

Traverse had always been a rebel. His high school biographical essay about Andrew Carnegie, depicting him as an innovator revolutionizing the steel industry and funding 2,509 libraries around the world was not well received. Proper thought considered him among 'robber barons' of the age. A note was made in his file.

Although he had excellent grades and high-test scores, level 1 through level 3 universities shied from his record. He was accepted at a level 4 college, but his letters to the editor of the college newspaper caused his expulsion. He ended up at a trade school for welders.

It was through her family that Ellen learned Traverse had moved to the area. Their meeting for coffee turned into dinner. Within a week, they were together all of their leisure time; within a month, Traverse moved in with her. They both knew they would be together forever and discussed marriage; but they were aware of the stigma it now carried, and they wished to keep all they had.

Algorithms developed at NSA identified that Ellen, having been passed over for promotions, could have a propensity for errant behavior. Adding that to her relationship with a man known for anti-social thoughts, she needed to be watched. An NSA computer algorithm sort identified the twelve highest security risks among fifteen hundred employees at the Fort Meade NSA headquarters. Ellen had been under constant observation for a month by a 3.0 drone when Traverse and she launched the carrier pigeon. Had Ellen and Traverse spotted the airborne voyager, they would not have altered their plan.

The Previous Evening at the White House

The White House reception for entertainment celebrities had ended early the night before. People receiving messages on their grapes started to leave before the president agreed to abandon the latest Hollywood heartthrob for an update. She was enjoying proximity to his unbridled power, as he was the sexuality spilling from her. Few but Hollywood women could be glaringly feminine in these asexual times.

Before his chief of staff could give him the news, the president lamented that grapes should be banned from White House functions. These personal electronic devices had become much more than cell phones and were commonly called grapes, as other electronic devices took on other generic fruit names.

It was 2:00 in the morning when the presidential order came down that all state borders be closed and airline traffic halted. State patrols closed interstate highways first but lacked the personnel or will to close most country roads. The attempt at isolating people responsible for the bombings was futile. The Texas volunteers were traveling only back roads and soon were safely back in the Lone Star State.

Before the NSA facility in Maryland was destroyed, technicians had determined that an inordinate number of suspicious coded signals had been emanating from an Iowa EPA railroad dump site. Sending coded signals was illegal. Before the bomb hit the Maryland NSA headquarters and ended his texting, the NSA director messaged the Iowa discovery to the president's chief of staff. The president acted quickly.

Offutt Air Force Base, south of Omaha, was closer than Whiteman in Missouri to the Iowa railroad tie dump. The stealth of the B-3 was not needed. Offutt was home to the century old B-52. The bombardier was surprised to find the site already a burning inferno as they overflew it. But as ordered, he dropped a 21,000-pound MOAB (Mother of all Bombs). It landed in the middle of the firestorm, buried itself deep into the loess Iowa soil before blasting a crater.

Eric's question about the future of the site was answered in the near term. The site would no longer be an 80-feet tall eyesore of a dump on the Iowa landscape, but a hole in the ground.

New Orleans

Along with corn, Julie and Andrew were transported to a Polish grain freighter on the Mississippi River near New Orleans. They were a few miles into the Gulf of Mexico when they felt safe tuning to news broadcasts. Reception of broadcasts could be tracked, and interest in American news by Polish speaking seamen would be a red flag. The news was sketchy. The powers-that-be had not decided upon a course of action, but the couple's fears were confirmed by news speculation that a foreign power had launched an attack on the country.

Eastern European countries, with a vivid memory of total state control, were the biggest antagonists of the current US policies. They desired to be where America had been. Even in international waters, being on a Polish freighter was dangerous— given the news spin.

Julie and Andrew met the captain, Pawel Bartosz, in his quarters. "I believe it prudent to offload the boat and put us on it now," Julie stated.

"My order was to keep you until we were within a hundred kilos of the cruise ship. And a storm is approaching."

"I understand, but a terrorist attack of some sort has occurred; and my country is blaming your country. It would be better for you and your crew if we were not found on this ship."

Captain Bartosz thought for some time. He was not one to recklessly veer from the company's instructions, but the company was giving captains more flexibility to make immediate decisions. Why would Americans finding two fellow citizens on his freighter be a problem? They were not kidnapped. Then he tied it together. He would ask no questions.

"Give us a few minutes and we'll have the boat launched. Be aware you are five hundred kilos from the ship you are headed toward, and the sea will be rough."

The boat, powered by two 135-horsepower outboard engines, was only a few miles over the horizon when a submarine surfaced near the freighter. The freighter captain had no choice when it was demanded he stop and be boarded. Sensing danger, the captain had moved two seamen into the former quarters of Julie and Andrew after it had been cleaned.

"Can we proceed?" The freighter captain asked the submarine captain in broken English after the ship had been searched.

"My orders are to hold you until I'm told otherwise."

For hours they sat in the headhouse of the freighter. Bartosz offered the American captain food; the American had sailors bring food from the submarine. It was all cordial, for they were not at war but fellow seamen.

"What do you do to pass the time on these long journeys?" the American asked.

"I think you Americans call it Sudoku."

"I love the game. Can I see your version?"

The captain opened a cabinet door in the headhouse and pulled out a paperback full of the Sudoku games. While the door was open, the American caught a glimpse of a colonial drawing of the American Founding Fathers signing the Constitution.

"What is that framed drawing?" he asked.

Bartosz had found Julie and Andrew left the drawing in their haste to leave. He knew any hesitancy showing it would raise suspicions. "Here," he handed it to the American captain. "I bought it at a… what-do-you-call-it— *flea market* in Ama, Louisiana."

"That looks very old," the American said. Knowing that he had an ensign and chief petty officer with him whom he could not trust, the American captain made eye contact with Captain Bartosz. In that moment holding each other's eyes, they came to an unspoken, unexplainable understanding recognizing they were on the same side.

Finally, the American captain said matter-of-factly, "Well, you better keep it. It'd not be good if it were found on my sub. Holding representations of discredited Americans is frowned upon."

Out of the corner of his eye, the captain detected a smile on both the ensign and petty officer. He was relieved. Later he asked the ensign, "Are you okay with how I handled the situation back there?"

"Yes, sir," the ensign answered, then added, "Absolutely, sir." Now the captain returned a knowing smile. Maybe he could trust his ensign and petty officer.

The trip was rougher than Andrew and Julie imagined. They soon understood the Polish captain's advice to tie themselves onboard. More than once, they nearly abandoned hope of seeing their daughter who was on the cruise ship. It had been six months. Between brutal waves, they attempted to tie themselves shorter. Although they were not in danger of washing overboard, they were taking a terrible beating being thrown around the deck. For two days and three nights they were without bathroom facilities— but more importantly without food, water, or sleep.

A board meeting was held on the cruise ship about what action to take, given Julie and Andrew's predicament. With the storm, their three hundred mile trip to the cruise ship was perilous. Everyone knew that changing the ship's course would be noticed by satellites and bring more scrutiny. It was not an option. As an alternative, they remained on course at a slower speed and sent a boat to intercept Julie and Andrew.

The storm had passed by the time the rescue vessel found the couple's boat, dead in the water. It had taken a pounding, but Andrew and Julie were alive. The damaged boat was sunk—its occupants given water, food, and medical attention. The parents' spirits rose quickly upon seeing their daughter, Sandy, standing on the ship's rail waving as they docked.

Chapter 2

Washington, D.C.

At 4 pm General Jerome Martinez, the Chairman of the Joint Chiefs of Staff (CJCS), was headed back to the Pentagon for the second time in a day. A National Security Council meeting scheduled for 11 am had been postponed until 4 pm. Now it was postponed again. Each time it was postponed with little notice. Trips to the White House for postponed meetings were preempting what would have been a busy day at the Pentagon.

Traveling to and from the White House, he could not help thinking about the family argument that had broken out with his sister at the spring holiday, no longer called Easter. His sister argued that Jerome was lending support for the usurpation of liberty in the country. She nearly begged him to resign and move back to Wichita—reminding him that he had purchased their childhood home—hoping to return at retirement.

The CJCS, who had risen through the army ranks from college ROTC (Reserve Officers Training Corps), was considered an outsider by many in the service. He was frustrated by the lack of communication from the White House. Unilaterally, he had put all forces on high alert after the NSA explosions. For what ends he did not know, he sought direction.

The president continued to meet with his chief of staff (COS), the FBI director, the attorney general, and that morning's newly appointed head of the NSA. There was consensus to declare martial law.

Martial law usually means subjecting citizens to military rule. And as the president is Commander-in-Chief, it gives the president unchecked powers. Historically, martial law is only applied temporarily when civil rule fails. Although the definition is fluid, civil liberties are suspended—such as allowance for searches and seizures without warrant, freedom of association, and freedom of movement. The *writ of habeas corpus* (the right to a trial) also may be suspended. The most often noted examples in US history were the internment of US citizens of Japanese descent a century earlier and warrantless wiretapping and torture after the 9/11 attacks at the turn of the century.

"Let's go through our proposed actions again and not forget we will have this opportunity but once in our lifetime," the president said.

"I think a ban on public mask wearing is frivolous," stated the attorney general. "What end does it serve when our capacity to manage the citizenry through facial recognition is nearly destroyed?"

Although a few decades earlier mask wearing had been mandated to repress the spread of a virus, now mask wearing was discouraged. Those wearing masks in public either retained virus paranoia from the past or were seeking to avoid recognition and most often up to no good.

The COS responded, "The ban would serve a purpose. We know our ability to process information is compromised, but the public does not realize the extent. Let them assume the worst, or in our case the best."

"She's right," said the president, surprising no one because he usually agreed with her.

He then turned his attention to the new NSA director. "I know our 2.0 PPU fleet is neutered. I argued that centralizing all information and analysis was dangerous. It put all our eggs in a single basket. I know you were with me in the debate; that is why I promoted you over others. Nevertheless, the former president was more concerned about hacking if things were spread out. She was wrong. But the drone fleet can still serve us; leave it all up as if nothing has changed. It will still serve a purpose, creating doubt as to whether they are impotent."

The attorney general (AG), who previously had been a senator from Florida, had another issue with the proposals outlined before them. "What does the National Tax Equalization (NTE) bill have to do with this terrorism?"

The NTE had been proposed for years, but given the power of smaller states in the Senate it could never be passed. Proponents argued that it was not fair that people in some states with lower taxes paid less total tax than in other states. The bill would set federal taxes higher in low tax states than in high tax states to equalize the total tax burden across the country.

The COS, formerly a senator from Illinois, took issue with the AG. "You must remember that you no longer represent only the people of low tax Florida— but the whole country."

"I'll remind you that people in low tax states already bear more of the federal burden by the deductibility of local taxes granted people in high tax states," retorted the AG.

"Enough, enough, break it up," interrupted the president. "You two have done this battle often in the Senate, no more. It is decided, we will equalize taxes. We must take advantage of the crisis."

"In addition to outlawing masks, National Guards in all states will be called up. Initially they will seal the border of states, and permits will be required for interstate travel. Anyone associated with the terrorist attack will be tried for treason."

"You had a good idea," he looked at the new NSA director. "We will say crude explosives made from hydrocarbons were used on the three facilities. Acknowledging nukes were used portrays them as technically savvy. We will paint them as the ragtag group of wacko discontents they are."

"Attributing the explosions to a derivative of oil allows us to take another step needed for years. By martial law, the Department of Energy will take over all oil refineries and oil drilling operations—

new drilling will be prohibited. Eventually, we'll shut it all down; something that should have been done years ago."

"What about ethanol?" asked the AG.

"We'll lump it all together."

"What about electricity?" the COS asked.

"Oh yes, the Department of Energy will also take over and control the electric grid to assure an equal distribution of energy. No more brownouts in some states while other states gloat on electricity. And yes, that means we'll tell Texas they must hook up to the national grid or else!"

"What's the else?" the AG asked.

The president ignored the question and said that the National Security Council would meet in thirty minutes. The CJCS's car was near the Pentagon when it turned around again. The last time, he hoped.

The vice president, the CJCS, and secretaries of defense, treasury and state joined the others—who had already made the decisions. The directives of martial law were outlined.

The CJCS sat silent as the agenda was laid out until the president said the activated National Guard units would be required to take an oath to follow the directives of the president.

"All National Guard members have already pledged allegiance to the US Constitution and the state they represent. Requiring them to pledge allegiance to your directives under martial law is overkill in my opinion. It will needlessly raise the ire of many governors, as states have borne the cost of their training."

With a stern look, the president cut him off, "I want there to be no doubt to whom their allegiances lie. Chief, your responsibility is to carry out my military orders, not second guess us on political issues."

He then turned his attention to the director of the FBI, "I want someone arrested for these bombings within forty-eight hours. Remember civil liberties are suspended; it is imperative that we make an example of someone. I do not care what you must do. We will cut through lengthy court room BS and make it clear that opposing the common good carries an absolute and heavy penalty."

The vice president, who had been quieter than normal, took her sentiments to the next level. "Remember once there was someone in another country who successfully oversaw finding criminals. He told his leader—'Show me the person, and I will find the crime.' We should not be timid. I am telling you— this is the crime, show us the people, not just the person. Under martial law, I suggest anyone who speaks against this government's policies in Congress be immediately arrested."

The CJCS spoke up, "You are referring to the director of security in the old Soviet Union. Is that where you would take us?"

"Enough, enough," declared the president. The CJCS and VP were like water and oil. The president had made an effort many times to rein in his VP, but ignoring her worked best, and he did not have time for a lengthy ideological argument. "I need to prep for my national address; the meeting is over."

Gulf of Mexico

Julie and Andrew had been riding bucking seas when the president's martial law address was given. After receiving medical attention, their priority was spending time with Sandy.

Sandy had passed her sixth birthday in her parents' six month absence. Although Julie and Andrew could not bring her a gift, Melissa—a longtime friend on the ship— had a gift for them to give her. Melissa had migrated to the cruise ship with other Atlas employees after her husband, Dan, was murdered in prison.

Given that Sandy was immersed among many highly intelligent people with several participating in her schooling, her verbal skills were beyond her age.

Noticing bruises on her parents, she asked, "Mommy, the bad people I hear talked about, did they beat up you and Daddy?"

"No, honey. It was the sea. We were in a small boat with big waves."

"I remember there was a storm here, too; the ship rocked back and forth."

"Well, you have nothing to worry about. Your mother and I aren't planning on leaving you again," Andrew added. He caught a hopeful but uncertain look from Julie which he ignored. In his opinion, they had done enough. Now their only priority was to become anonymous.

Although others summarized the president's remarks, the couple watched the recorded speech in their ship room. He held a Q and A afterwards, but Julie shut off the monitor as questions from reporters had not been probing for years. It surprised them that the president attributed the explosions to crude explosive devices rather than nukes. They expected him to use anything—true or not—to scare people and build public support for his mandates.

The fatality exaggeration at the three facilities surprised the couple. The death tolls at the Fort Meade, MD, Eddyville, IA, and Bluffdale, UT facilities he claimed were three hundred forty-two, two hundred sixty-seven, and one hundred ninety-four, respectively. Torrence, who handled intelligence operations at the ship, said their sources estimated deaths to be less than fifteen at each of the three sites. His sources also said all first responders at the sites were forced to sign non-disclosure documents under heavy penalties, meaning they would likely never know how many perished.

"How do you think different states will react to his directives?" Andrew asked his wife.

"About the same as always, some will grumble; but in the end, fear will cause them to cave because of possible repercussions for their states."

"What does repercussions mean?" asked Sandy.

After Julie explained the meaning to her daughter, Sandy headed for the bathroom.

Andrew said, "Well, at least we set their harassment of citizens back years; we've done our part. The world's largest data storage unit, the software and know-how to analyze the data, and a manufacturing facility for the ultimate means of control have vanished with one stroke—or three—I guess. Now it's up to others to take it further."

Sandy, now back, jumped on her mom's *(properly called birth person's)* lap. Julie's only response to her husband's statement was a smile. Andrew knew from the squint around her eyes she was skeptical they were finished. He would continue the conversation without Sandy.

Austin, Texas

Madison wore a server's apron with a nearly blonde wig pulled over her auburn cropped hair. Wig or not, her hair could have passed her for a flapper in the early part of the previous century. Again, it was the style in the mid twenty-first century. In an employee parking lot behind an outbuilding to the Georgian style mansion, she got in a small 2- seat electric car. Twenty minutes later, she parked the car on a residential street halfway across Austin, TX. Before exiting the car, she lost the apron and put on a mask and walked the sidewalk as nonchalantly as possible.

Two blocks into her walk, she heard the familiar buzz before she saw the vulture drone overhead. Rumors were wrong; they were still there. Wearing the mask was the right decision. For her, being recognized here by the beast was more dangerous than wearing a mask.

The mask was imported from Poland. It had been smuggled illegally into the country in a grain freighter captained by Pawel Bartosz. Manufacturing masks had been banned for years, and importation was illegal. Now, by the president's directives, even wearing a homemade mask in public was illegal. She had been told that wearing masks to prevent federal face-recognition tracking was no longer necessary after the explosions, but she would take no chances.

From the sidewalk, she heard the hum of an electric lawn mower. The man waved at her as he crossed his neighbor's property line and kept mowing. He was mowing two yards. *A good deed for the neighbor or an illegal bartering arrangement,* she wondered. Nevertheless, he was friendly and seemed happy. It confirmed what her husband, Carl, often said, *"Those that live by their own conscience regardless of the law are happier souls. Those bent upon toeing the line are too focused on societal guilt to enjoy life."*

Whether the man was bartering lawn services with his neighbor or being charitable, it was illegal. A tax was required for any such service. Currency had been outlawed for years. All economic activity was conducted in United Nation Credits (UNC). Yes, people did exchange gold, silver, and valuables as currency—but only discreetly. As happened earlier in the century in a South American country, toilet paper—often in short supply—was also used as currency.

It had been a major controversy at the United Nations over what to name the monetary units. Some nations wanted to name it *UNU (United Nations Unit)*, but *credit* was preferred by the majority as *credit* insinuated it was an economic blessing from the government. Some nations balked and maintained their own currency—including Poland, Hungary, Romania, Ukraine, Australia, many Latin American nations, and China.

Madison crossed the street into a commercial area filled with factories and warehouses. Before she stepped into a pillow factory warehouse, she saw two cars pull into an adjacent warehouse. Inside, she was met and escorted to a basement and tunnel to the nearby warehouse. Four men and three women rose as she entered the room. They said in unison, "Good evening, Governor."

Governor Madison Archibald was in her second term as governor of Texas. She was the daughter of a woman who decades earlier had been arrested for courageously keeping her hair salon open against emergency shutdown orders. Had it not been for her mother's ordeal, she likely would have taken no interest in politics.

With her cabinet assembled, she asked, "We've all had time to ponder the effects of the martial law edicts. What will be the consequences for the people of Texas?"

The Texas railroad commissioner was the first to speak. With more responsibility than the name suggested, this commission regulated the exploration, production and transportation of oil and natural gas in Texas.

"A federal takeover of the oil industry in this state would put an untold number of people out of work and wreak havoc on state revenue streams. There is no doubt the long-term goal of the Feds would be to shut us down."

"Didn't you once tell me that the Department of Energy gets all their data about the oil industry from your commission?" asked the governor.

"Yes, they do. They don't have the manpower or logistics to acquire that information."

She next turned to the director of ERCOT (Electric Reliability Council of Texas). Three electric grids existed in the lower 48 states—the Eastern Interconnection, the Western Interconnection and Texas.

"What will it take for the Feds to tap into our electric grid?"

"No major feeder line lies within ten miles of a border. Consequently, heavy lines would need to be built on our side of the border and who knows how far on the other side. The president didn't address who would pay for the extensions and how soon it would need to happen."

Smiles broke out around the table when she said, "I expect the permit process for any new lines out of Texas to be quite burdensome."

Only a look from the governor prompted General Tate, the commander of the Texas National Guard, to speak, "As you know our guard has already taken an oath to defend the United States Constitution as well as the state of Texas. Theoretically, if the question came down to following the order of the president or defending the Constitution, it is clear as no mention is made of the executive branch in the oath.

A subsequent pledge to follow a president's directives under martial law would take priority over any prior pledge according to legal experts I have consulted. You must also realize that once such a pledge is given the guard is, in effect, no longer the Texas National Guard."

His analysis created a buzz around the table, "All right, all right, one subject at a time," the governor said, raising both hands and bouncing them lower to defuse emotions.

She looked at the Texas state treasurer, "We've discussed this NTE thing often, and we've been successful blocking it. Again, give us a brief summary of what it will do to our economy."

The state treasurer was a slight man, often looking like he had lost more weight as his jackets were always too large. His glasses were more than big enough to serve the purpose and looked like they were more about protecting his face. His voice was soft and unrattled. But there was nothing slight about his answers—a simple sentence answer he normally stretched to a multi-paragraph lecture in economics. Hence, she asked for a *brief* summary.

"Federal tax for most Texans will increase by 20-22.5% if total taxes here are to match taxes in Illinois, California and New York.

My analysis suggest that will translate into a huge decline in discretionary consumer spending of 11%. People will pay the mortgage, utilities, buy gas to get to work and put food on the table— but entertainment, restaurant, recreational and non-essential spending will be curtailed hitting those industries hard..."

"Thank you," the governor cut him off.

"But Madame Governor, there is another important consequence of this move which we haven't discussed."

"Go ahead."

"As the general games out military strategy, in our field we game play the ramifications of a change in clothing styles and what it has to do with the price of cotton, or price of tea in China." He paused for effect hoping to add levity, but as always, he failed.

"Please," the governor said.

"We are confident the NTE would set off an endless spiral of state spending. What is there to stop Illinois from raising taxes again, sending a rippling effect throughout the country, then New Jersey ups the ante as they have nothing to lose?"

"We get the point, and it is well taken. Let's meet tomorrow and develop contingency plans, but now I'm open to discussion on all topics on the table."

The discussion went on for an hour before the governor laid out a plan. "On the question of connecting our electrical grid to the rest of the country, let us quietly research what delays and hazards may pop up before that could take place.

On the Department of Energy access to our database of the oil industry in this state, let us make sure that information is as secure as possible. Nothing gets shared unless I give authorization.

I will be meeting tomorrow with the treasurer to discuss further the ramifications of the National Tax Equalization order and how we might prepare for it.

All preparations and contingencies we develop must be done quietly. We do not want to give cause for the Feds to be concerned. It is our hope that after the shock of these bombings wear off, cooler heads in Washington will prevail. Regardless. we must keep our options open."

"What about the Guard and the demand for the pledge of allegiance?" asked General Tate.

"Deploy the Guard to roads leading into the state as directed by Washington, but I expect your border closings to be very lax. Only refuse entry of suspicious vehicles. We don't know how this will all play out but having a force at our border seems prudent. As to the new pledge...delay, delay. The pledge is only to be administered with my authorization."

Carl Palmerton, the governor's husband, was an attorney. When his wife was elected governor, it was decided any law work he performed would be considered a conflict of interest; hence he suspended official legal work. One of his major clients was Trotter Electric Company owned by Mason Trotter. Over a period of years Mason and Carl had become good friends.

Although Mason's company was headquartered in Austin, he also owned an electrical company in San Antonio and Dallas. The company was started by his grandfather and expanded by his father and him.

Mason was the leader of the Texas Resistance Movement. He had one of three secure grapes in Texas. The electronic devices were encrypted, allowing private conversation with acting national leaders Julie and Andrew Collier and the cruise ship. The phones were bogey trapped such that if the wrong fingerprints touched them, acid destroyed the grape.

He was privy to planning the triple attack on NSA and voted to authorize it. Mason had personally driven his employees, Eric and Kelly, to Iowa. It was the first time he met Julie and Andrew at their hideaway tucked inside a railroad tie dump.

In a company van covered with Trotter Electric advertising, Mason parked at the governor's mansion and knocked on the door wearing an electrician's tool belt. Carl let him in and waved security away. He took Mason on a tour of the governor's mansion with Mason waving his grape around which contained an electronic eavesdropping detection app.

In the study off the governor's bedroom, Carl locked the bedroom door. Confident no staff members were nearby, Mason said, "No evidence of bugs, but you should check the house daily."

Mason pulled a second secure grape from his tool belt, punched a code in the grape and had Carl place his right ring finger on the device. It was now programmed to only allow use by Carl.

"This one is now yours," he told Carl as he explained the secure grape's use.

They soon had Julie, Andrew, and Torrence—the ship's information director—on the secure grape phone.

Later that evening the governor wore a powder blue camisole to bed. She needed to be distracted. Any other night Carl would have taken advantage of the opportunity, but he needed to talk.

"While you were gone, Mason was here."

"Do you have any idea how dangerous that is?"

"He was in electric garb. We hooked up with others on the ship including Julie and Andrew, the national leaders. He left me this device so we can be connected." Carl pulled the grape from under his pillow and showed Madison.

"I don't want to know about this. We have discussed it; it is much too dangerous for me to know anything. And by the way, the drones are still up."

"I know they're up, but now nothing more than decoys to keep people living in fear. The explosions were completely successful; the vultures are nothing but eyes floating around without any brain to which connect."

"Okay, but I can't abide the loss of life in the process."

"It's propaganda. Although there were numerous injuries in the parking lots, *we've* only been able to identify eight people who were killed in those explosions. Fire alarms were set off first, then small explosions moved people further from the facilities."

They both lay in the king-sized bed on their backs with ample room between them, staring at the ceiling in silence for some time. Both had lost thoughts of other activity.

Her husband's use of the pronoun *we've* kept bouncing in Madison's head. He was committed, which would mean for anyone looking in from the outside— she would be considered compliant at the least.

It was her responsibility to be abreast of what was happening in her state. It was now unavoidable, and most likely meant to be.

"Okay, tell me everything you know and don't leave anything out."

Chapter 3

The Texas Department of Economic Development was created in 1997 when the 75th Legislature abolished the Texas Department of Commerce and transferred its functions to the new agency. Its function was to promote Texas as a location for businesses and provide economic incentives to lure businesses into the state. Although the agency liked to receive credit for business growth in Texas, it was actually other states' anti-business policies that was the major contributor to Texan economic growth.

The department director was summoned to the governor's office on short notice. As instructed, he had familiarized himself with a new factory near completion in Georgetown.

He addressed the governor, "The company owning the factory is EYE, Inc. Fifty percent of the stock is held by the federal government and fifty percent by a consortium of other companies. It is, in effect, a quasi-government entity."

"What about the non-government interest?"

"One large shareholder is the Princeton University endowment fund, another a conglomerate that owns two cable companies, and another company also holds many shares of a major social network site. And you should know two percent of the stock is held by a Chinese company."

"I understand the factory will make a third generation PPU. What kind of incentives have we offered them?"

"The regular ten-year fifty percent tax abatement and we laid two roads for access to the plant and extended the sewer system nearly a mile to accommodate the development."

"How soon will the plant be operational?"

"Last I heard mid-summer, two to three months."

"Have the sewer lines we're paying for been finished and inspected?"

The director was surprised by the question. The governor was known to get in the weeds with detailed questions, but this? He thought he was well prepared, now he knew not well enough.

"I can't say for sure; if they are finished, I don't believe the final inspection has occurred yet." He was fumbling, she could tell.

"I can get you the answer soon."

"Please do."

With the information the governor had received from her husband, she agreed to a safe grape conference call under the condition that she would only listen. On the call were department heads on the Resistance's cruise ship and Resistance leaders from most states including Mason Trotter. Governor Archibald was surprised at the attendance and organization of the meeting. Julie started the meeting by disclosing what was known.

"As we reported before, the three facilities we targeted are completely out of commission. Nothing remains worth salvaging. It will be easier for them to rebuild from scratch. Any data transmitted by the 2.0 drones today is gibberish and useless. Only systems at NSA headquarters were able to decipher their transmissions. To our advantage, they thought a centralized system was the safest. Hopes of maintaining a level of fear in the population is the only reason the 2.0 drones are still flying.

The problem we need to discuss is the 3.0 version PPU which will go into production this summer in Texas. As you know, they are testing a dozen around DC now. It's a given, they will have learned a lesson and the new drones' data will not feed into one place."

"We can't let the plant in Texas start production," stated the Missouri leader.

"Don't we have three remaining miniature nukes on the cruise ship?" asked the Georgia leader.

Julie responded to the state leaders, "Agreed, and yes. However, do we want to give the Feds more reason to crack down? As a last resort, absolutely, we will not let that plant become operational. But we need to pursue all other means first."

"Why not, the nukes have proved effective? The more they clamp down and come up with these ridiculous directives, the more resistance it will encourage," an Ohio leader said.

Julie reminded the group that earlier agreements gave the state leader veto power over any action within their state. Governor Archibald realized Julie meant Mason instead of her. Although she had promised herself to only listen, she needed to allay their concerns to dispel any crazy actions."

"This is the governor of Texas speaking. I hear your concerns, but you need to realize we are working on a plan to delay the plant."

Three other governors at various times had been on conference calls, but this was a big state governor. Participants were quietly delighted. Their reach was expanding.

"Could you give us a hint of your plan?" asked the Missouri leader.

"The Feds are experts at tedious regulations. Let's give them some of their own medicine. The county owns the sewer system to the new plant, but the state is responsible for inspecting it. The plant cannot be opened until it is approved. It is possible the system was put in incorrectly and will need to be completely replaced which will take months. It will give us time. And we will always have the other options you discussed."

Everyone on the conference call caught the significance of the governor using the pronoun 'We.' Some state leaders might have been offended by the governor effectively taking Texas leadership, but not Mason. They had gained full endorsement of a major elected official.

After discussion, two things were agreed upon. The plant would never be allowed to become operational, and sewer inspection would be used to delay it.

White House

The NSA director was anxious to meet the president and FBI director in the Oval Office. It was good news, the president hoped.

"We got them," he said.

"Got who and what?" the president asked.

The NSA director pointed his grape toward the room's large wall monitor. The screen showed a man and woman unloading a pigeon carrier from a pickup truck and sending it off.

"What are we looking at?"

"Ellen Herwick and Traverse Jones sending the explosive device toward the Fort Meade headquarters but fifteen miles away." As instructed, all references even in conversation characterized the destructive instruments as *'explosives.'*

"Ellen Herwick is employed at NSA headquarters as a mathematician. With her being passed over for promotions and in a relationship with Traverse Jones, a man with an anti-social history, Ellen was on the PPU 3.0 watch list."

"Great, pick them up immediately."

"Mr. President," answered the FBI director, "Teams are on their way at this moment to arrest them."

"There's more, Mr. President," interjected the NSA director. "We have a connection, although loose, to Jayden Samuels, a janitor at the building."

"By all means, we need to set an example. Get someone to talk, I don't care what you must do."

SWAT teams from DC to Baltimore were called in and assembled. The arrests would be made Wisconsin style.

Decades earlier Milwaukee County authorities, with assault weapons drawn, arrested people who allegedly violated campaign laws—hence the arrest description. The military garbed teams awakened them from bed at 4:00 in the morning. They were all cleared, but most were forced into bankruptcy with their reputations destroyed. The arrest tactic was soon adopted by the Feds to use on those dubbed anti-social.

Jayden Samuels was on no watch list. He completed his training in a two-year vocational school for building maintenance and sanitation after the compulsory one-year social training. His grades were average, his social adjustment score was above average. Never in any trouble, he could have been considered a model citizen.

The 3.0 PPU tracking Ellen logged who was in proximity to her. It identified Jayden's vehicle in the same park as Ellen and Traverse when they launched the pigeon, although the tree canopy did not allow the PPU to witness him fishing with the proper license.

Two evenings earlier, the PPU identified Jayden entering a pizza parlor where Ellen and Traverse were dining. They worked in the same section of NSA headquarters, and a week earlier they were both seen at a local flea market and were caught greeting each other. Too many coincidences existed, given that pressure was immense to name co-conspirators. He did not understand why his apartment door was broken down in the middle of the night and he was roughly roused from bed. He never would.

Georgetown, Texas

Jane worked for the Texas Commission on Environmental Quality (TCEQ) in the commercial sewer inspection and certification division. Her husband, Kelly, worked for Trotter Electrical. As her husband did his part for the Resistance in Iowa, she would make her contribution in a sewer inspection. Unlike what some friends thought, she never roamed in a dirty sewer. Her job was to collect evidence that new sewer connections were done properly.

She inserted the recording circuit into the robot and lowered it in the culvert at the junction of the main sewer line and the branch to the new plant. It took over an hour for the robot to cover the distance looking for any cracks or flaws in the line. On its return, she hoisted the robot out and removed the circuit. The circuit recorded the time and GPS location of the inspection. Inside the circuit, she pulled out a chip which contained the inspection video. She placed it in her pocket and inserted another, then put the circuit in a sealed box. In route to the Austin office, the chip she had taken from the circuit ended up on Interstate 35, soon to be crushed by traffic.

Jane turned the circuit board in for inspection at the TCEQ's main office when a new office inspector was on duty. The office inspector was appalled at the mess. Multiple fractures were evident through-out the branch line. The sewer contractor had obviously not properly bedded the sewer line. Soil settling had rendered the line a potential environmental disaster. Repairing it would be more costly than put-ting in a new parallel line. The general contractor was notified.

The new office inspector did not know he had evaluated a sewer branch line inspection circuit board containing a chip from a sewer line than had been rejected for flaws three years previous.

Maryland

Ellen, Traverse and Jayden were held in a secret prison run by the NSA outside of Baltimore. They were not allowed to see each oth-er, and each were told the others had confessed and been released. Although not used for decades, the maximum-security facility need-ed few tools for water boarding.

General Martinez, chairman of the Joint Chiefs of Staff, discov-ered what was happening at the NSA facility and called the presi-dent. "Mr. President, under martial law the military is charged with handling and the trial of prisoners. Why are the prisoners being held in an NSA facility?"

"As president, that determination is mine alone. I can assure you the trial will be speedy and the punishment swift."

"How soon do you wish to convene the military trial? Our lawyers will need preparation notice."

"I don't think you heard me. It will be taken care of," the president answered before hanging up.

Although the water boarding was continuous for days, Jayden knew nothing to reveal. Ellen and Traverse gave up all they knew on the second day. They revealed their connection to others was a hid-den grape. The package containing the miniature nuke was delivered to their house from where they did not know. They stole a carrier pigeon from the postal service for the delivery. And they never met or knew the identity of anyone in the Resistance.

FBI agents working with the NSA surrounded three tennis courts a few blocks from Ellen's home. Once the area was secure, an agent pulled the top cap from a pipe set in concrete which held up the net in the middle court. As described by the prisoners, a string was found. At the end was a grape inside a plastic bag. The agent carefully handled the grape turning it in her hand as pictures were taken of it. Fortunately for the agent, she was wearing gloves. The phone did not detect the saved fingerprint within ten seconds of being handled, bursting an interior acid sack which melted the inside and spilled over the agent's hand.

Texas

Although Texas National Guard General Tate understood the reason and inconsequential act of instructing a platoon of twenty soldiers to recite a pledge of allegiance to the president, he had complained heartily to the governor. A platoon of National Guard soldiers was hastily organized including ten retiring within a week and ten others who were about to be asked to leave the guard for various reasons. The platoon was filmed pledging alliance to the president with audio and circulated with scenes of other guard units around the state reciting the original loyalty pledge to the Constitution and Texas without audio.

In the office with the governor were Carl, General Tate, and Mason Trotter. On Mason's secure phone were Julie and Andrew. The president's call was scheduled for 2:00. He was late.

"Have you been in contact with other governors?" asked the governor.

"Yes, directly with the governors of Nebraska, North Dakota, Missouri, Oklahoma, and Georgia. Through a third party with Kansas, Arkansas, Wyoming and Indiana."

"Wow, that surprises me."

"Why should it? We have sympathetic feedback from many other governors. With these outrageous presidential directives, what is the point of maintaining states? They feel threatened."

It was nearly 3:00 when line one on the governor's desk phone rang.

"Good afternoon, Mr. President."

An hour previous, the president had completed a call with the governor of Nebraska. The call did not go well. He prepped for the call with the Texas governor by reviewing videos of the Texas guard pledges.

"That is good news," he told his Chief of Staff (COS) as he slipped his arm around her.

Usually preferring business first, she cautioned him, "You should see this film taken from a drive around Georgetown, sir."

The film was of an abbreviated drive around Georgetown, TX, and surrounding areas. Political yard signs had long since been outlawed; these were legal as they did not promote a candidate. The president was taken back by the preponderance of identical yards signs showing a picture of a turkey vulture with a red circle around it and a diagonal slash mark through.

He quickly covered his disgust. "So what... what power do these people have? There is a reason they are stranded in backwater towns, living pathetic lives and we are here. They do not understand the world, nor do they want to. Make life too comfortable for them, and they get crazy ideas. If they had less warmth in the winter or air conditioning in the heat, and a smaller choice of diet and less gadgets to play with, they would learn to appreciate what we allow them to have."

He would vent things with his COS he would never reveal to other staff. Their relationship was special, and she knew when he was just blowing off steam.

"Now that's out, I feel better. Go ahead and get her on the phone."

"Governor, I appreciate you following my directive to turn over allegiance of the guard to me. I was afraid you were hesitating."

"Not at all, Mr. President. It just took longer than it should have."

"Hopefully, the reports I've gotten about the guard not enforcing border closings are exaggerated."

"As far as I know they are only letting through essential trucking, but I will check on it."

"Thank you, governor. One other favor, with the PPU's information logistic system somewhat partially handicapped by the treasonous acts, we need to get a new generation in production as soon as possible. It has come to my attention that final work on the plant in your state has stopped because of some sewage line inspection problem."

"Let me look into that, Mr. President. I'm sure some way can be found around whatever the bureaucratic delay."

Neither the president nor the governor were into long conversations filled with small talk.

"What did you think?" the president asked his COS once the conversation ended.

"I don't think we can trust her."

"I agree, too conciliatory," said the president. He looked at the NSA director, "I think a better use for those dozen new PPUs would be protecting the new plant in Texas. We cannot risk having that plant sabotaged. How soon can we get them there?"

"They will not fly that far, but they can be on the road tomorrow morning."

Off the phone in the governor's office, the governor said to Julie on the secure grape, "I understand you had a conversation with the president before the attack on the NSA sites."

"Yes, he was in the middle of a White House party and didn't appreciate my interruption. Our conversation was not as cordial as yours."

"It's the big downside of being a politician, sometimes you must bite your tongue until it hurts."

Julie commented, "I found it telling that the president referred to the vultures as being *somewhat partially handicapped* after we effectively put the NSA out of business. Two adjectives describing a word that speaks for itself is usually an indication of a lie."

"Before the call, you were about to talk about intelligence you received from the army base in Fort Hood?" the governor asked.

Julie answered, "Some of our contacts there say about a thousand soldiers are ready to move somewhere, once given the order."

"Any idea where?"

"No."

Guessing where they might be headed, the governor turned to General Tate, "Well General, I don't think we have any choice. How soon can you have a brigade of soldiers to the Georgetown plant?"

"I can have five thousand soldiers there by tomorrow morning."

Torrence walked into the ship's conference room and joined the conversation, "We are ready to patch other governors in now."

Introductions were made with the governors of North Dakota, Nebraska, and Oklahoma. They had met at governor conferences.

Julie asked the governor of Nebraska to summarize his earlier conversation with the president.

"The president's directive to take over the ethanol industry will be devastating to our state, and I told him so. Over 40% of our corn crop is used to produce ethanol as it is in other midwestern states. If the Feds take over the ethanol plants, management will be replaced with incompetent political hacks. Only God knows how many inconceivable ridiculous regulations they will come up with. Our economists estimate that the operating and administrative costs of ethanol plants will at least double. And who will bear the cost? Demand will only stand so much. So, we would expect the price of corn to plummet. Add to that the new tax he has proposed on meat products, there goes the major uses of grains. Farmland values will tank. My assessment of the impact on our state did not seem to faze the president, but he did not refute my analysis.

And I am sure you all heard that ridiculous statement by the Secretary of Agriculture yesterday that people should eat more sweet corn that has been genetically engineered to have a higher protein content. You could grow all the sweet corn that could be eaten in this country in one Nebraska county."

"Isn't Iowa the largest corn producer? Does the governor of Iowa have similar thoughts?" asked the Texas governor.

"Yes, and she is also under pressure from the insurance industry, Des Moines being an insurance hub. The proposed changes to the insurance industry are not just new management controls but complete takeover. The governor will come around."

The conference call continued another hour with the governors of Oklahoma and North Dakota concurring with the Nebraska governor's assessment.

Maryland

Hung high inside an eight-foot diameter storm drainage culvert under a road was a carrier pigeon. It had been placed days earlier. A motion detector turned on a recording of a rattlesnake giving warning if someone approached. The culvert was fifteen miles from the former NSA headquarters. Suddenly the pigeon dropped, exited the culvert, and took off into the sky—tripping the snake warning to no avail. The pigeon had no fear— neither did the people who placed it.

The charging stations for the 3.0 PPU fleet were temporary. One third of the fleet was always taking on electric charge while the other eight were in the air. The charging drones were each hooked to a charging station inside a sixty-foot truck trailer. The truck was decaled as a US Postal Service truck. It was not.

Four mechanics inspected the drones as they were hooked to the chargers. They changed shifts with the drones. Unless a problem was found after a 30-minute inspection, the mechanics were idle. Three NSA armed security guards completed the shift. They periodically walked the perimeter of the vast empty parking lot surrounding the remains of NSA headquarters.

It was a humid late spring day, the kind of day that usually preceded a thunderstorm. Charging the drones produced heat; no cooling system existed in the trailer. Although PPU charging task protocols written by a desk jockey at the temporary NSA quarters required the door to the trailer always be closed, it was not practical.

From the pigeon carrier's view overhead, the drone charging detail looked like an oasis in the vast empty parking lot. A semitrailer, two vans, three umbrellas covering tables and chairs where men sat were all that occupied the ten-acre lot. A guard hardly noticed the carrier overhead until it fell to six feet above the parking lot, then turned back toward them. They were not expecting a delivery.

He drew his sidearm as the carrier pigeon neared them, but its oncoming profile was a small target to hit. His second shot struck a wing which tilted the pigeon as it disappeared inside the back of the trailer. Concussion from the small amount of C-4 explosive the carrier delivered knocked the guard off his feet and toppled umbrellas.

No one was seriously injured, but the PPU 3.0 fleet was now down to eight.

Chapter 4

White House

It was evening when the president received word of the PPU loss. He was furious.

"Why weren't those PPUs headed for Texas as I ordered?"

"They were scheduled to be gathered and to leave after dark. We thought it would be safer," answered the NSA director on the phone.

"Have them taken immediately to the Marine Base in Quantico. We'll have them sent to Texas as soon as an escort can be assembled. You people cannot secure an area, perhaps they can in Texas."

"Do you wish for our people to help with the escort to Texas?"

"No, I'll hand pick who I want to escort the PPUs."

Fort Hood, Texas

Although it only took an hour for the convoy to reach the Georgetown PPU factory from Fort Hood, the colonel in charge of the unit was not as prepared as he had indicated to his superiors. Organization and efficiency were not high on the list of reasons the *lieutenant* was dropped in front of *colonel* in his rank.

When the convoy neared the parameter of the future PPU manufacturing plant, they discovered a checkpoint had been set up and soldiers were stringing wire in both directions from it. Armored vehicles were spaced at intervals, and sandbags were being placed.

The colonel was unaware that another unit had been assigned to the plant. He walked to the checkpoint and asked a sergeant at the guard post, "What unit are you with?"

"Texas National Guard, 79th Brigade, sir."

"Well, you can stand down now, Sergeant. We are here."

The sergeant did not respond to the order but picked up a phone, "Sir, you better come to the front gate checkpoint." His tone conveyed urgency.

The colonel's back straightened when a vehicle pulled up. He expected to assume command from a National Guard part-time colonel. As the man approached, the colonel saw stars on his lapel.

"General, I was sent to take command and secure this facility."

"Great, we're glad you are here. Your regiment can set up a half mile over there," he pointed.

"But sir, I'm regular Army."

"And let me introduce myself. I'm General Tate, commander of the Texas National Guard."

Tennessee

Word spread to state leaders that the PPU 2.0s were neutered. From state leaders, it spread to others. A natural skepticism existed about information coming from the top of any organization. But the probability of not being spied upon made Ronnie more eager to carry out his mission.

Ronnie did not tell his wife what he planned. In a storage shed behind the house, he raised two flooring boards. It had been a year since he lifted his 243 caliber Winchester with the 4-9X variable scope from the hiding place to clean and oil it. Ten miles from home he parked, pulled on a camouflage mask, and walked a mile in the moonlight to an industrial park. It was known for heavy PPU surveillance. It was not long before he heard buzzing. By moonlight, he put the crosshairs ten feet from the vulture and shot twice. The shots did not alter its path. Soon a pickup truck stopped at a stop sign, he jumped in the back. The driver and he waited behind the driver's business warehouse two blocks away until dawn. No influx of other PPUs, police, FBI or ATF units arrived. Normally, shots fired at a PPU would draw an avalanche of attention. It was true— the PPUs were blind.

When Ronnie got home, Karen was up. "What do you want for breakfast?" she tersely asked. He knew what she suspected. He had an affair five years previous; it had been a mistake he would never repeat. Counseling by their pastor put their marriage back on solid grounds, but she had to have doubts at some level. He told her where he had been and that he had not told her for her protection—in case he was caught.

She understood. Her sister had been imprisoned a year for swinging a baseball bat at a home intruder, breaking his collar bone. The jury found that, given she had an escape route through the back door, the confrontation was not necessary. She was in violation of the *"retreat, do not confront"* laws. Consequently, Ronnie's wife was more active in the patriot resistance group than he.

White House

The president had a direct call made to a major at Quantico Marine base. The major was a second cousin of his COS. She had long lobbied the president to help her cousin; it was the way things were done. The president described the mission to the major and his immediate commander, then said, "I know you've been a major too long. With a successful mission you will get the promotion you deserve."

When word traveled up through the ranks to the Pentagon, the CJCS was infuriated that the president did not go through the proper channels. He would not forget the slight.

By the president's order, only the major and the lieutenant colonel he reported organized the delivery of the PPUs to Texas. Leaks were too common, according to the president. The major sent a V-54 Osprey helicopter to Nashville to be refueled and ready. He picked out four of his best from the ranks and placed two in each of the leading and trailing armored vehicles to escort three semi-trucks. The first truck contained the hardware and software necessary to interpret encrypted signals from the PPUs. The second truck held eight version 3.0 PPUs. The third truck was an empty decoy. The major assumed any attack would target the 3rd truck as the most important. He could have added many more escort vehicles but doing so would draw attention. He had a better plan. The major wished the caravan well when it left.

After the gate was closed, the major headed for a waiting Osprey helicopter. His crew would circle the caravan out of sight. Because fuel would not allow a sixteen hundred mile trip, a relay copter was waiting outside Nashville near Interstate 40. If any trouble developed, the late model Osprey had fifty caliber guns and air-to-surface missiles. His preparation was overkill, he suspected, but he knew his career depended upon its success.

Corporal Davis was in the trailing armored vehicle. The sergeant who was driving caught Davis texting on his grape. "We had orders not to make contact with anyone. Put that thing away."

"I was just letting my girlfriend know our date was off tonight, nothing more."

"Okay but don't do it again."

Before they left, Corporal Davis used the restroom and texted his father in Cookeville, TN about his mission. Denzel Davis was with a group having coffee with Ronnie and Karen when he received a text from his son that read, *We're leaving.*

Denzel and Ronnie were neighbors. They both were fascinated by history. Their conversations about *'what ifs'* in alternative history went on for hours. Research into their family backgrounds found they had much more in common than they could have imagined. They were certain it was what drew them together as close friends. Many generations ago, Denzel had an ancestor who had been a slave on the farm of Ronnie's ancestors.

With the plan in place, Ronnie retrieved an old Model 94 Winchester 30/30 from its hiding place and handed it to Karen. His 243 he had left out since firing at the vulture. He had nearly begged her to stay, but she was a strong-willed woman and would not be denied a chance to strike a blow for the Resistance. Although his deviance five years prior was the biggest mistake in his life, with counseling from the pastor, they both admitted their marriage had never been stronger.

Denzel, Karen, and Ronnie parked their cars under a large oak tree, walked a mile, joined four others, and walked another mile to a cluster of volunteer trees and bushes. The woody plants in the hedgerow were as varied as the seven people and the arms they carried. Beyond the green partial barricade lay a highway. The seven lay in wait behind the hedgerow along Interstate 40 a few miles from Cookeville. Most were better armed than Karen and Ronnie. Two AR-15s and one AK47 were among the weapons. In one man's backpack were Molotov cocktails intended for the interior of the second truck. The major's assumption was wrong— they would target the second truck.

Traffic was light on the highway because of the ban on interstate travel. When they received signal from an observer that the caravan was five minutes away, two vehicles stopped on the highway. One car parked half blocking the right lane and the driver got out while the second car broadsided it. Leaving just enough room to be passed on the shoulder, the drivers scurried for the hedge row. Now nine were lying in wait.

The lead armored vehicle stopped, assessing the situation. Once the lieutenant determined they could safely get by, she radioed the others to cautiously drive on the shoulder past the wreck. Their mission was too important to offer assistance at a wreck; that was a job for locals.

As the second truck passed the wreck, a line of fire erupted from the hedgerow. Half directed their fire toward tires to disable the truck; others sprayed the trailer. Seeing what was happening, Corporal Davis and the sergeant passed the last truck and drove through tall grass down the road ditch and jumped out. Mostly hidden in the grass, the sergeant raised his weapon to fire on the ambushers. Corporal Davis reached for his sergeant's automatic rifle and pushed it into the grass, saying, "They are not firing on us."

Before the sergeant could answer, they heard thumping of helicopter blades followed by the bone chilling chatter of 50-caliber cannons. Tree limbs shook and leaves fell to the ground as if a hailstorm from hell had come down. The helicopter made two passes before Major Miller's voice on their radios surprised them, telling them the threat had been eliminated and ordered them back to the road.

The sergeant jumped in the vehicle and hollered *"Now!"* at the Corporal to jump in. Davis turned and walked toward the hedgerow.

"Shoot me if you must," Corporal Davis replied. The sergeant raised his weapon at the man's back but could not fire.

Major Miller was more concerned with preventing further attacks and getting back on the road than pursuing a deserter or dealing with survivors. The Osprey hovered in lookout over the roadblock as he instructed men to move the PPUs from the second truck to the decoy truck.

Karen and Ronnie laid in the prone position side-by-side when the shooting started. They never heard the helicopter coming. Ronnie struggled but turned toward his wife. She managed to roll on her back. Her hand clutched an exit wound on her chest. Blood oozed between her fingers spreading darkness over the sweater he had bought her for her recent birthday.

"I've always loved you," he said before light-headedness overcame him.

"I know," she whispered.

They were soon in greener meadows.

Although he knew, the shock nearly overwhelmed Corporal Davis as he stepped over the fence. Nine bodies, including the drivers of the wrecked cars, lay strewn in no order; the grass was red with blood and splatter. He saw neighbors holding each other in death. Then he caught movement. It was his father bleeding from the shoulder and leg. He discarded his weapon, picked his father up and made his way through a corn field to his dad's truck.

Back on the road with two trucks, Major Miller was confident no attack would take place around the high traffic area of Nashville. He swapped the helicopter for a fueled one loaded with ammo. They traveled on with no other incidents on I-40 and switched to I-30 in Little Rock.

With the growing realization that the NSA no longer had the ability to track phone calls, word spread fast among patriots of the massacre in Tennessee.

Arkansas

Ben taxied his Air Tractor AT-502b crop duster to the fueling area at the Hot Springs airport. It had been nearly a year since he had been there for fuel. He was surprised the young attendant remembered him.

"Nice to see you again in that antique plane, forty gallon like last time?"

"No, fill it up."

"Going on a long flight, huh?"

A smile appeared on Ben's face, "Yeh, a really long flight."

Normally, it grated Ben when someone called his crop-dusting plane an antique. No doubt, they thought the same of him. At eighty-two years, he guessed he was an antique. After the crop spraying business dried up, he closed what had been a successful business but kept his favorite plane. Most of his time was spent tinkering with welding equipment in his shop. He quit renewing his pilot license before they could deny it. What were they going to do if they caught a man his age flying, lock him up? At least twice a year he took the plane for a spin from the grass runway on his farm.

Ben had been lonely since his wife died the previous year. It was ovarian cancer. They said it was very treatable, but they had not factored in her age. When she was due for her second chemotherapy treatment, the doctors could no longer ignore her age. She had turned seventy-five. Her HCI (Health Care Index) was lowered to forty-nine with the age turn. An HCI of less than fifty downgraded her treatment status from a two to four grade, which was basically no cancer treatment. They said they were sorry. Turning seventy-five relegated people to minimal health care—unless you had been a government worker or attained privileged status other ways.

She had never been the same since their son died three years previous. Reckless, he had always been. A rebel in high school, they should never have let him go off to college in Iowa. He had fallen in with the wrong group, was nabbed at a protest rally and sent to a US government-leased detention camp at Guantanamo Bay, Cuba. When it was liberated by patriots, it was found he died of a virus the government had altered and used on the camp's population for testing.

But all was good, Ben was at home now flying again, up in the air away from all the heartache and turmoil below. Crop spraying was among the most dangerous occupations, but he had been careful, keeping his planes serviced well. Now they said he had prostate cancer—no treatment, of course—at his age. A year left they said. It had been a good life. He pushed the throttle full ahead exceeding cruising speed of 154 mph.

From the helicopter, Major Miller saw a crop plane making low passes over a soybean field adjacent to the highway. Had he been familiar with modern agriculture, it would have struck him as odd. He was not, and the plane was soon out of sight.

Ben turned and headed down the highway behind the caravan. The driver of a car stopped, thinking the plane was going to make an emergency landing on I-30. In front of the crop duster were two trucks sandwiched between military vehicles. Ben had always been interested in game theory. He knew most people would assume the lead truck to be running interference for the more valuable cargo in the second truck. A wise strategist would do the opposite. His landing wheels passed but a few feet above the second truck when Major Miller saw the plane.

Miller had no time to react before the plane disappeared into the back of the lead truck and exploded in a ball of flame. The combination of one hundred seventy gallons of fuel and a five-hundred gallon sprayer tank filled with oxygen from torch bottles in his shop left nothing of the PPU 3.0 operating system.

Ben was welcomed by his wife and son at the end of a light tunnel.

Hours later, Major Miller delivered eight PPU 3.0s to the US Army regiment outside the Texas National Guard encirclement in Georgetown. Four were damaged by gunfire that penetrated the truck in Tennessee but could have been repaired. They were not because they had no value, as the gibberish they transmitted could not be interpreted. And as they were nearly invisible, they could not instill fear in the citizenry. Major Miller never got a promotion.

Back in Cookeville, the county coroner was called to the scene and the bodies were transferred to the county morgue. The FBI spent days putting evidence together to recreate what happened in the shootout along I-40. However, the FBI statement at a briefing and news reports did not reflect their findings.

Five of the eight dead Resistance fighters and Mr. Davis who got away went to the same church as did the coroner. The coroner ran into the pastor at a grocery store.

"Rumor has it that you are not conducting services for those killed along the Interstate."

"It was a difficult decision, but I must think about the future of the church. What they did with those truck drivers was reprehensible. The FBI station chief told me this morning if we conducted services, the church would be destroyed."

"What about the truck drivers?"

"I understand they stopped the trucks, made the drivers get out, then shot them in cold blood. Perhaps the FBI station chief was right. The church should be closed. I, obviously, am a failure that six in my flock would do such a thing."

"I don't know what you're talking about. I was the coroner at the scene. There were only eight dead, and I talked to the truck drivers—they were fine. There were no bullet holes in the tractor cabs they were in."

That evening, the pastor was at the altar praying for guidance when he heard a knock on the back door. It was Denzel Davis and his son. His son had used his Marine medical training to treat his dad's wounds. The reverend called a doctor in the congregation. They sought sanctuary and got it.

The pastor always attempted to moderate the anti-social fire within some members of his congregation. He sought the best in everyone and told his congregation the Bible directed them to follow the nation's leadership. But the events forced him to reconsider his *go-along-get-along posture.* Nevertheless, he compromised and conducted services at a funeral home outside the church.

Trotter home, Austin, TX

Mason Trotter had been single for ten years. His wife had desperately wanted children. But with the couple's low Prodigy Suitability Index (PSI), an authorization for the antidote to the drinking water infused male contraceptive was unlikely. Mason's anti-social activity caused their low score. She divorced him and married another man whose score would allow her to have children.

It was late when his grape rang. He welcomed the late calls from Damon, his brother, in Chicagoland.

Both brothers had been very bright in school but because of antics as a youngster Mason was assigned to a trade school, while Damon was admitted to the University of Chicago, a level four university. Damon was particularly pleased because their grandfather attended the university.

Universities were ranked from one to four, based upon how coveted their degrees were. The ranking categories had little to do with the quality of the education they provided but reflected a combination of their reputation and the level of their social awareness programs.

Mason often ribbed Damon about attending a university founded by a man now labeled as an evil robber baron, oil magnate J. D. Rockefeller. Damon graduated with honors and was awarded a professorship across the city at Northwestern University.

When their father—who started the electric business— passed, Damon wanted no part of the electric repair and installation business. He acknowledged Mason had been responsible for its growth, and ownership in a business would negatively tint his status at the university. They reached an agreement, and Mason bought Damon's interest in the business.

They were cordial and respected each other as brothers but differed in the way they viewed the world.

"It looks like equality will finally come to taxation with the mandate of the National Tax Equalization," observed Damon.

"I hardly think so," replied Mason. "What is equal about requiring Texans to pay more federal tax than Illinoisians?"

"You will not pay more total tax. Total taxes will be equal across the country."

Mason came back, "Why should Texas taxpayers be penalized just because voters in Illinois and other high tax states choose to elect spendthrift, corrupt leaders?"

"You don't get it; it is all about fairness."

"I guess then that Texans have nothing to lose by spending money like drunken sailors and letting other states foot the bill."

The argument went on for some time until each ran out of points to make or maybe because they tired. However, as always, the conversation ended affably.

Chapter 5

Nebraska

Blair was a small town with a population of eight thousand, lying about thirty miles north of Omaha. The biggest employer was an ethanol plant which produced two hundred ten million gallons a year. Ethanol, for years, was added to gasoline to stretch the supply of fossil fuels. The Blair plant was not the biggest ethanol plant in the country but among those.

The president demanded management at the facility relinquish control to his representatives from the Department of Energy. The governor advised management to refuse and promised he would back them up. Officials from the Energy Department entered the company's office complex with three FBI escorts and demanded executives surrender their offices and leave the building. They refused.

The Feds were in the process of handcuffing the management staff when sirens were heard. With guns drawn, twenty Nebraska state patrolmen entered the building and demanded the federal agents leave. After tense moments of heated arguments, the federal agents left.

The intended new federal manager of the plant, who nothing of corn or chemistry, said "You'll regret this." He was as furious at the

FBI agents for not fighting as he was at company employees. The local FBI agents out of the Omaha office were outnumbered. Without a vested interest in the outcome, they were not going to resist the overwhelming odds against them. They had followed orders but would not go a reckless step beyond.

The president was receiving a briefing on the disastrous attempted transfer of advanced PPUs to Texas. His COS received a text message, left, then came back with news.

"Oh my God, I can see it is more bad news; what is it?"

"Our energy department people have been thrown out of an ethanol plant in Nebraska, and the governor ordered two hundred fifty National Guard troops to the plant. Nebraska is one of the states whose National Guard has not taken the pledge to you."

"Get that Neanderthal governor on the phone."

As per the norm, a presidential secretary got the governor on the phone, then put him on hold for the customary ten minutes. The hold produced one of two advantages for the president. It either established with an exclamation mark that the president was dominant and his time was more valuable, or it aggravated the governor which caused him to speak more bluntly and avoid political posturing BS—which was good.

"Governor, I believe there has been a misunderstanding concerning control of an ethanol plant in your state."

"How so?" the governor responded.

The president struggled to hold his temper upon hearing the governor's tart response. "You know what my directives are, and you know I have the power under martial law. Let's avoid any conflict here, it would be better for everyone."

"What do you suggest?"

"I suggest you remove the National Guard from that ethanol plant and allow my people to take over. And I also demand that the guard pledge allegiance to me."

"Or what?"

"I'll cut off funding to the guard, and I'll have you arrested."

"That's ridiculous! In the first place, a state National Guard is funded by the state unless the governor calls it up for federal use. And for what charge would you have me arrested?"

"Treason," the president said, very deliberately drawing the sounds out before he hung up.

The governor immediately notified the commander of the state's National Guard to add another two hundred fifty soldiers to those in Blair and send two hundred fifty to Lincoln."

"Where in Lincoln?" the commander asked.

"The capitol grounds."

The president also made a move. An example had to be set. The response needed to be overwhelming. If he dawdled, other governors could be tempted to chart their own course. He ordered the 82nd Airborne division out of Fort Bragg, NC to deploy two thousand soldiers and supporting equipment to a small town in Nebraska within twelve hours.

"Perhaps filling the air with parachutes will get the message across," said the president to a room of advisors. No one responded.

Cargo planes were always loaded with small tanks, artillery, and vehicles for rapid deployment. The operation was delayed a few hours until sunlight reached Nebraska to enable full media coverage. The cable, newspaper, social media, and TV network industries, whose executives moved back and forth between public and quasi-public positions were given a heads up. Anyone close to Blair would never forget the spectacle of a sky full of parachutes. Media technology allowed people throughout the country to witness the new power of the president in a changing world.

Once on the ground, the airborne division was efficient gathering equipment into offensive formation. Formed up as in training, they moved forward with tanks and armored vehicles leading, artillery and foot soldiers trailing. There was excitement throughout the ranks, officers were impressed with how well they organized themselves.

The columns stopped a couple hundred yards from defensive positions five hundred National Guard troops had taken. The guard had a few armored vehicles. But they were deployed without tanks, artillery, or anti-tank weapons.

The 82nd could see sandbags formed into walls and what appeared to be machine guns deployed. Those with binoculars could see American soldiers behind the sandbags. Exhilaration from a perfect landing and maneuvering soon dissipated.

"What do we do if we're ordered to shoot, lieutenant?" asked a sergeant. The lieutenant avoided an answer by shaking his head and walking away. But the sergeant could see in the eyes of a corporal in communications from Nebraska, one mind was made up.

The general commanding the 82nd deployment had attained his rank by religiously following orders without question. His mind was conditioned to not even think about alternatives to orders. Experience taught him following a bad order had no repercussions. Hesitating to follow orders froze people at lower ranks.

Following a phone conversation with the National Guard Colonel, the 82nd's General was soon inside the plant to peacefully end the confrontation.

"These are the conditions— surrender all arms and lead your soldiers in pledging allegiance to the president in this national emergency. Those that comply are allowed to return to their bases. Those that do not will be arrested."

"Sounds good to me, but give me time to call the governor," replied the colonel.

"You've got thirty minutes," the general said as he left.

The colonel told the governor their situation was hopeless. The governor was not impressed by his eagerness to surrender. After discussion, the governor ordered the colonel to call their bluff and sit tight until the Feds made a move before conceding.

It had been an hour with no response. The general's calls to the colonel went unanswered. The general called an artillery unit. "See the National Guard equipment truck a half mile to the south parked broadside to us in an open field? Strike it with a shell."

"But sir, do we know it is uninhabited?"

"You have your orders."

The artillery captain ordered gun number 7 to hit the truck. The soldier responsible for laying the gun *(aiming)* was from Missouri. He had cousins who lived in Nebraska. Was he to be responsible for starting something that should not be? Once he had the gun on target, he turned it two degrees to the right and fired.

The shell missed by a hundred feet. The captain ordered his best crew, winner of the last base competition, at gun number three to fire. The shell whizzed over the truck and plunged into a farm field.

Cheers could be heard from the National Guard side of the sandbags. The general was livid.

"What the hell is going on? We do not tolerate misses like that at five miles!" He yelled at the captain from his command post. "The next crew that misses gets court-martialed."

Soon the truck exploded into a cascade of pieces.

The general's phone range. "We concede."

"I want to see a white flag to signify it," demanded the general.

The general had five hundred members of the Nebraska National Guard assembled and led them in the pledge. It was short.

"For the establishment of a more perfect union, I solemnly
pledge my allegiance to the President of the United States."

The general was frustrated that the majority of the men and women in the assembly did not raise their hand, and could not be heard, but signatures were what counted. With media cameras rolling, he thought better of making an issue of their reluctance to verbally pledge. They would sign or be arrested. Tables were set up in front of the group for written affirmation. The general felt better about the process when he noticed many guardsmen had smiles on their faces. It was good that no hard feelings lingered. Once signatures were secured, the members of the National Guard left without weapons in the vehicles in which they came, minus one truck.

"Well done," said the president on the phone personally thanking the general for his handling of the incident.

A captain was waving at the general while holding the signed pledges in his hand. *"I'm talking to the President of the United States, you idiot,"* the general thought.

"Just doing my duty, sir," he responded to the president.

"Well, the footage I've seen is marvelous. You have a great future."

Off the phone, the general asked the captain, "What was so important that you tried to interrupt my conversation with the president?"

"The signatures, sir."

Examination showed the pledge had been signed five times by George Washington, fourteen by Martin Archibald King, six by Clint Eastwood, ten by Susan Anthony, Donald Duck, the Sandman, and the Tooth Fairy. The most signatures were sixty-four of Jarmal Green.

"Who is Jarmal Green? If he is a Resistance leader, I'll have them all arrested," demanded the general.

"I don't know," replied the captain.

The communications corporal from Hastings, Nebraska, who was checking phone lines overheard and meekly said, "He was the Heisman trophy winner on the Cornhusker's last football team." *American football had been banned a decade earlier as it promoted aggressive behavior.*

The governor of Nebraska was appalled by the media's ongoing hammering coverage of the Blair incident showing a white flag waving and happy looking National Guard members lining up to sign the pledge. Although the media had long since lost credibility, it was still humiliating to the governor.

Upon his request, the colonel in charge of the National Guard in Blair entered his office. The governor was tempted to remove him.

"I gave you permission to concede if they made a move but not make a spectacle waving a white flag."

The colonel explained he was simply making sure misunderstandings did not get someone hurt. Then he explained in length that very few guardsmen signed the pledge. It was enough to save his job.

Texas

Carl, the governor's husband, checked the first floor of the governor's mansion before the conference call. Those that worked in the mansion were gone for the day or retired to quarters on the other side of the building. The governor had gone to her closet after she got home from the capitol. He was sitting in the governor's study when his wife walked in.

She wore a white blouse with ruffles around the sleeves. The top two buttons of the blouse were not buttoned, showing a pearl necklace. She wore a gray charcoal skirt, the hem struck her in the middle of her knees. Her shoes were black with two-inch heels. She was dressed anything but seductively, it was a turn-of-the-century women's business look.

"You look great," Carl commented.

"Thank you, it just feels right to look like a woman at times."

In the mid twenty-first century, women wearing dresses or skirts were frowned upon—not taken seriously—and considered throwbacks to less progressive times. Erasing any signs of gender was the way of the times.

The governor took the chair behind her desk when the secure phone rang. Julie briefed Governor Archibald and six other governors on what had really happened during the PPU 3.0 relocation.

"We thank the volunteers in Tennessee and a gallant senior citizen in Arkansas for ensuring that the vultures arrived in Texas neutered. Their sacrifice will long be remembered in Texas," offered Governor Archibald.

The Governor of Tennessee asked Julie, "I understand some of your people on the ship have made contact with Denzel Davis. For what reason?"

"Torrence Jones, our director of intelligence and Barry Bradley, our IT guy, are producing a video of Denzel telling what really happened in Cookeville. Barry will hack and splice the video into the network feeds when we are ready."

"That will be great," the Tennessee governor said, then added for the Texas governor, "We appreciate the thank you for taking care of the PPUs, but we expect something in return."

"Okay."

"What happened in Nebraska can't be allowed to happen in Texas. If the plant becomes operational and those new vultures are produced in numbers, everything that has been done will be for nothing."

The Oklahoma governor jumped in, "If necessary, we'll send national guardsmen to help."

"Thank you all, but I think I'll let General Tate, commander of our National Guard, who is in the Georgetown area, address that offer."

"I, too, appreciate the offer. But know we have a battalion surrounding the Georgetown plant, and the governor has authorized me to deploy six more battalions in the Georgetown area, including an armored unit. They will be stationed ten miles north of the plant which will allow flexibility of attack. Our total strength in the area will be around nine thousand. I assure you if any white flag is raised in Georgetown, it will not be ours."

"That is all good, but the commander of our National Guard says there are around forty-five thousand federal soldiers in Fort Hood, only an hour away from Georgetown," responded the governor of Missouri.

Governor Archibald spoke, "That is correct. If we had not acted immediately, I suspect many more than a thousand federal troops would be near the Georgetown plant. To the Feds, our pretense for placing soldiers around the plant is to protect it from Resistance terrorists. The destruction of NSA facilities demonstrates the need. Instantly sending soldiers to guard and protect the plant validates our purported intention and puts soldiers under my command in closest proximity to the plant. I think we can all agree that it is preferable that our National Guard soldiers surround the plant rather than Feds."

After a pause, the governor added, "But be assured we do have a plan. No PPUs will ever be made in Texas."

The White House

"Good news, Mr. President. Satellite images show that Texas National Guard civil engineers are digging in a sewer line parallel to the flawed one. Also, the eight truckloads of necessary tooling shipped from Pennsylvania to the plant are no longer kept from entering the plant. One by one, the trucks are inspected for contraband, then let in. Once the sewer line is in and the equipment is installed, the plant should be operational in thirty to forty-five days."

The president gloated, "See, our show of strength in Nebraska sent a message. If the governor of Texas had other ideas, she has thought better of it. Then again, perhaps her original stated reason for securing the plant was genuine."

He was interrupted by the vice-president's entry. "Am I late?" she asked.

"We're about finished," he answered, as the VP glared at the COS who had given her the wrong time for the meeting.

The president continued, "How successful has the Department of Energy been acquiring oil and gas data from the Texas Railroad Commission?"

Without the secretary of the DOE on hand, the FBI director answered, "They are still claiming their database was hacked and cannot access the data themselves. We doubt that and are sending anti-viral experts from NSA to assist them. They will be accompanied by a combined ATF and FBI swat team."

The president responded, "The oil and gas industry are important to the state. They are attempting to protect it. Let's keep our eye on the ball; our number one priority is getting that Georgetown plant operational. Right now, our power is defined by fear that the PPU units in the air are still useful and new more sophisticated ones are on the horizon. That fear will ebb as the public discovers otherwise.

Good behavior deserves reward. Stop the NSA people and that swat team. Let them assume we have backed off taking over their oil and gas industry. It will encourage more good behavior. Once a new fleet of PPUs is in the air, the energy issue will be addressed."

"It all sounds like capitulation to me," the VP said.

"Thank you for your input. The meeting is over."

Dallas

Mason, leader of the Texas Resistance, guided a semi-truck as it backed into a warehouse at his electric service company's Dallas location. It was from the national common carrier's fleet that carried tooling for the Georgetown plant. This truck was empty. Once the warehouse door was closed, Texas license plates were exchanged for Pennsylvania plates. Four pallets were loaded on the truck and covered with canvas, leaving room for one pallet in the rear. Mason purchased a used CNC machine from a machine shop a block away.

The owner found it strange an electric service company would need an outdated CNC machine. Computer Numerical Control (CNC) machines were robotic parts makers, not used by electric service companies. But given the price, the owner asked no questions. He had an employee carry it on a forklift to the electric company's warehouse. Mason had the employee put it on the back of the truck. The employee was not curious.

A squad of twenty National Guard soldiers was given the task of inspecting trucks carrying tooling into the Georgetown plant. For each truck, they asked the driver to get out, while they inspected the cab and pulled the trailer tailgate up. They uncovered any cargo to verify it contained machines. The same procedure was used on all the trucks until the last one. A private entered the back of the truck and pulled up a canvas exposing a CNC machine.

He started forward to the next pallet when his hastily returning sergeant yelled at him, "We've seen enough."

The private assumed the sergeant, having been summoned to the officer's quarters, had been dressed down for something. He would not aggravate his sergeant.

The sergeant helped him out of the truck and said, "Let's go; the chow line will close in ten minutes."

The colonel commanding the Fort Hood army detachment entered an observation area they had set up a half mile from the Georgetown plant. High-powered lens on a scope allowed them to monitor unobstructed activity by the guard.

"Notice anything unusual about the trucks going in, particularly the last one that arrived?"

"We had a good view of guards inspecting the trucks. With the tailgates up from this position, we could see in the trucks. The last truck, like the others, had several pallets. We saw a CNC machine in back as the canvas was raised."

Mason Trotter's home

Mason had not talked to his brother in Chicagoland for a couple weeks. He was curious how Damon was interpreting events, although Mason assumed his brother was taking the Fed's explanations.

"What are you teaching in summer classes?" Mason asked.

"A fun new course I've been working on—*How Twentieth Century American Imperialism Thwarted Growth in Central America.*"

"Sounds interesting," Mason responded, trying to sound interested.

"I'm happy none of the nonsense in parts of the country is happening in Texas. Some feared Texas could be a trouble spot but looks like the craziness is limited to Nebraska, Arkansas, and Tennessee."

"Yes, crazy things have been happening. Hopefully, the country will get back to normal soon," Mason responded, careful not to define normal.

Damon was relieved at Mason's reaction, "I know we have our disagreements, but it is nice to know you have no sympathy for the crazies. Soon they will be back in the box where they should be."

Mason gritted his teeth and answered, "Isn't that the truth!"

Chapter 6

Tennessee

Denzel Davis and his son, Corporal Darius Davis, moved from the Cookeville church to a remote cabin on Clingman's Dome near the border of Tennessee and North Carolina. A member of the church congregation, whose family had owned the cabin for generations, offered it as a hideaway. The family never used the cabin but were not allowed to sell because of National Park encroachment.

All network cable and broadcast feeds traveled through the Department of Accurate Information (DAI). The department delayed passing live feeds on from five to thirty minutes allowing monitoring and censoring inappropriate transmissions. Caution had to be taken in case a citizen said something out of line on a live broadcast.

On June 26, 2039, Barry Bradley hacked the system and directly fed an interview with Melissa Barnmore to outlets. It took five minutes for the censors to become aware of the hack and shut everything down. Melissa was the wife of the man whose company saved the planet from an asteroid catastrophe when NASA failed. He was thrown into prison with hardened criminals, setting the stage for his murder. In the five-minute interview, she revealed the real story.

At the time, Bradley had been employed at the DAI for 10 years. He was one of the most able computer whizzes ever employed. However, his social index score and his membership in a church relegated him to a low-level position with no chances of promotion. At his small cubicle, he was assigned low level coding tasks. While lamenting the insignificant use of his talents at a bar, a man struck up a conversation with him. They soon discovered similar beliefs. Barry became a member of the Resistance because he believed in the cause. Working with the Resistance gave him purpose and an opportunity to use what God had given him.

Karen Ryerson, a DAI sub-department head, was married to the Maryland governor. Karen was the antithesis of femininity—not unlike most serious women of the day—loose fitting slacks, short hair, a unisex style blazer and shoes that tied. She bristled when someone called her *Karen,* saying she hated the given name from her bourgeoisie parents. She preferred to be called Director Ryerson. She knew little about coding. Public administration was her forte, although it was her spouse who gave her position and status.

Barry's cubicle was the only one in the office in a position to see the hallway from which a door led to a storage room. At least once a week, he witnessed Karen enter the storage room. Within minutes of her entry, a man entered who worked in another department. He witnessed someone try to open the door once, and it was locked from the inside. One day he saw her leaving the storage room more disheveled than normal.

Barry had always been an out-of-the-box guy. He had a need to delve into the unknown, and the boredom of his job only exasperated his fidgety nature. He placed a miniature camera on a shelf in the storage room directed toward four chairs that were stored side by side. He was not a voyeur by nature, but he was resourceful.

Nearly a month later, Karen opened her emails to find a very compromising picture of herself in the storage room. It was from an encrypted address that had been rerouted through seven servers around the world. The next day, another picture of her and the man arrived with a different time stamp. In the next day's picture, a different pose accompanied by a one sentence note which read:

I need the department third level access password.

Barry could hack through the department's first level code, whether he worked there or not. His sub-department's code was neither a problem. But the third level administrative code was unbreakable. It allowed access to all information and gave the user the ability to alter material.

Karen found herself in a quandary. If the pictures were revealed, her domestic partnership would be destroyed—and she would be lucky to get a job sweeping floors in a despicable small business. Same outcome if she was caught revealing the code. Attending parties as the governor's mate she would not give up. Her only chance at maintaining the lifestyle she had become accustomed to was compliance.

In his cubicle across a maze of other cubicles from Karen's luxurious office, Barry received an email with a code of seventeen letters, numbers, and symbols which in the middle contained six blanks. The next day the email was as short: *Moon position today: 14*

The next day's mail: *This hour's temperature in Stuttgart, Germany*

The third day's mail: *This hour's temperature in Middlebury, Vermont*

His online search soon found the present temperature in those cities. With the moon position number placed in the order of the emails, he was in. But the password was constantly changing. The following day, the password did not work. It took him two days of investigation to discover astronomers designated the night's moon position from one to twenty-eight. Finding the temperature in those cities was easy, but he found on even numbered days it needed to be . entered in Celsius, and odd-numbered days Fahrenheit.

Without Karen succumbing to her natural God given instincts, the Resistance might never have gained a foothold. She was never revealed, and Barry eventually left the department. Barry Bradley was now IT director on the Resistance cruise ship.

Although Barry had hijacked the media feeds nine years earlier, it could only be done sparingly. Frequent use of hijacking could jeopardize their link to information. However, at this critical time, an arrow could not be left in the quiver.

For connection with the audience and credibility, they sought an interviewee untrained in media savvy—without the glamour of Hollywood looks— from middle America. The Davis's fit the bill and had firsthand knowledge of an event that had been distorted. At 9:00 prime time EDT, normal programs were hijacked. Denzel Davis and Corporal Darius Davis appeared on screens and monitors across the country.

Interviewer: *Mr. Davis, you were part of a Resistance movement that ambushed a convoy of trucks and a military escort from Fort Bragg, correct?*

Mr. Davis: *No, we did not ambush any soldiers. We directed our fire only at a truck carrying a new generation of vultures capable of taking the level of snooping on citizens to the next level.*

Interviewer: *In the ambush, did your group direct fire and kill two truck drivers?*

Mr. Davis: *We did not; that is propaganda. Ask yourselves, have they revealed the names of the drivers who were allegedly killed? Have they revealed the names of hundreds of people supposedly killed by explosions in Idaho, Maryland, and Iowa?*

Interviewer: *Corporal Davis, you were with the escorting soldiers from the Marine base in Fort Bragg. Tell us what happened.*

Corporal Davis: *Fire came down on a truck from behind a hedge row. We were ordered to return fire. I refused, as we were not fired upon. No truck drivers were killed. But the citizens attempting to eliminate the new vultures were strafed with 50-caliber machine gun fire from two helicopter passes. I ran to survey the damage and* (there is a pause as the Corporal tries to compose himself) *the grass was covered with blood and human debris. All were dead except my dad who was hit twice… Bottom line* (the Corporal looked intensely into the camera) *the older version vultures flying today are now worthless without support; do not fear them…*

This time only three minutes of the interview got through before all mass communication was shut down.

For a quarter of citizens, the video clip reinforced what they already knew or suspected. Another quarter refused to believe anything that did not protect their status and job. The third quarter considered the video believable and something to consider. The remaining quarter could not care less about it—or anything for that matter.

White House

The president intended to get to the bottom of the media hacking. He summoned the Director of the DAI and all relevant department heads to the White House. It was the third time Karen Ryerson had been in the White House, previous times as spouse to a governor.

The president growled at the group, "It is not only the deceitful video that was hacked into our system, perhaps hacking into your department's database is the primary source of the traitors' information. I demand all measures be taken to secure your data systems. Let it be known that anyone working in your department who either negligently allows information to escape or is purposely feeding information to the mutineers will be tried by military court for treason. Any questions?"

Seeing none, he said, "Now get the hell out of here!"

Back at department headquarters, the sub-directors all sat at the at the director's conference table waiting for the director. Usually, Karen marveled at the exquisite long oval solid teakwood table. It was rumored to have cost more than any two of their salaries. This day she did not notice the table.

"Are you okay?" a colleague asked.

"I guess I'm a little upset."

"I'm sure we all are," the colleague answered.

The director entered and instructed someone to close all the window blinds, then wrote two city names on paper and passed the paper around the room. He then dumped a snack of dried kale in the conference room sink and burned the paper in the empty bowl. He took no chances that the room had been bugged—audio or video.

Back at her office, Karen's mind spun. Treason, wasn't the penalty for that execution? But surely in post-modern times it would never happen? It had not for decades. The following day, she received another graphic storeroom picture that she had not seen before.

If she ignored the implied request and the pictures were revealed, she would be uncovered—it was treason. If she was caught giving the altered code, it was treason. She had stepped into a trap, and it was getting deeper with the door locked.

Barry soon received an email with an article about universities in Wuhan, China. The next day an email about the long-outlawed rodeo in Cheyenne, WY. The cities to search for current temperature to place in the code had been changed. He was soon back in at the administrative level.

In mid-afternoon, the president met with his close advisors—COS, NSA Director, AG, and the FBI Director. The Chairman of the Joint Chief of Staff had also been summoned to the meeting. As the meeting was about to start, the vice-president showed up uninvited.

"We need to do something big to divert attention from that contemptible video they hacked into the system, any ideas?" the president started the meeting.

"No kidding," interrupted the VP, "I suggest we have an Army division search the backwoods of Tennessee until the Davis's are found and shot. And why did it take so long to get them off the air? Perhaps some network executives should pay a price."

While some people had to work at political correctness, the vice-president was born with a leg up. Her paternal grandfather was African American, grandmother Caucasian; her maternal grandfather was Arab, grandmother Chinese. The rumor her paternal grandmother was part Native American she did not deny, but fed.

She was schooled in China while her mother served as U.S. ambassador. Although she had tutors, she attended regular Chinese schools and was an expert in Chinese Communist Party (CCP) doctrine. She felt comfortable in a room with a portrait of Mao Zedong, not so much George Washington.

After graduate school in the US, her first domestic partnership with a man lasted only five years. Her later partnership with a woman lasted ten. During her second term in Congress from Delaware, she entered a domestic partnership with a man and woman. It was working well for her.

She was a necessary addition to the political ticket, but otherwise a thorn in the president's side. The president decided to speak his mind.

"Madame Vice-President, while your views are always interesting, this is politics. It involves give and take. We do not always get what we want. You have no defined role in the Constitution other than presiding over the Senate. I suggest you go there."

She snorted but did not budge from her seat at the table.

His other advisors batted around several ideas while she remained quiet. Come up with names from nowhere of those who died in the explosions? Invent a treacherous past for Corporal Davis? Claim the video was a Polish and Russian production?

None of the ideas had shock value in the president's opinion. They simply answered a ridiculous charge giving it legitimacy. He wondered at times why he needed advisors.

The CJCS reluctantly spoke up, "Mr. President, as the topic of this meeting is political in nature, I'm not sure why my presence is needed."

"General, everything everywhere at all times is political," the VP butted in.

The president ignored her, "General, I'm getting there. Under martial law, it most definitely concerns the military."

He turned to the NSA director, "Have you been able to glean any information from the three prisoners?"

"Terrorists Herwick and Jones divulged the use of an encrypted phone to communicate with the misfits and its location, but it was booby trapped. We've got nothing from Samuels."

"What are the odds of getting more from them?"

"Slim to none, after what we've put them through. We had to back off to keep them alive."

The president took a deep breath. "Martial law means military rule. And who is Commander in Chief of the military?" He paused but got no response, as it was obviously intended for the CJCS.

"I am. Those three should have a military trial— and as I am Commander in Chief, I will set the rules for the trial. The trial will take place in this office two days hence. Get a prosecutor ready, and find some podunk lawyer to defend them. They will be tried remotely. The trial will be broadcast live in their absence. Their pictures will appear on a split screen. They will be seen behind bars in prison garb. It will not only grab the attention of the country— it will also spread fear. Let the population know severe consequences await anyone who defies the common good."

The CJCS spoke, "But Mr. President, two days will not be enough time for military prosecutors to properly prepare the case. All the evidence is held by the NSA. And military law dictates the accused are represented by military counsel. In two days, how can someone properly defend their clients if charges have not yet been formally filed?"

"General, perhaps you missed my earlier assertion of the chain of command. I suggest you get to work."

General Jerome Martinez had grown up in Wichita, Kansas. He was a third generation American. His grandfather immigrated in the 1980s and started a landscaping business in Wichita.

The business became remarkably successful and put his father through law school. Everyone expected Jerome to also become an attorney. His intent was to study law while at the University of Kansas; but after he enrolled in ROTC, his interest in law dissipated. Although he did not attend West Point, his rise in the military was steady. He had an excellent knack for balancing efficiency in military organization and tactics while not stepping on any political toes. He had been Army Chief for three years and CJCS for four.

The general's wife was a partner in an Arlington, Virginia, medical practice where they lived. She did not share her patients' maladies with him, and he—not only for security reasons— did not discuss military matters with her. Their marriage was strong. They continued to call it a marriage rather than a domestic partnership.

During dinner that evening he said, "We need to talk."

He outlined what the president expected him to do and his lack of comfortability with it.

After hearing him out, she asked, "So what are you thinking?"

"I'm sixty-three. We bought my sister's share of my parents' home in anticipation that someday we would retire there. How many times has your brother asked you to come and join his practice in Wichita?"

His wife, Camila—always the practical one—said, "We have some savings. I'd be working, and you have a pension; but you realize, we'd get nothing from this house?"

"I can handle that, can you?"

They had purchased the Arlington home fifteen years previous. Ten years ago, they had forty percent equity in the house. But single family home prices had declined twenty percent— primarily because they were targeted with high property taxes. By selling the house, they would incur another fifteen percent exit tax, leaving them virtually nothing in the house.

Although they were never officially called exit taxes—in effect, they were. In the early part of the century, Chicago and suburbs levied a property transfer tax, initially two percent of the home's value meant to compensate for the administrative cost of title changes. Some people actually believed that explanation. Metro areas losing population around the country adopted the idea and slowly increased the tax in an effort to retain their taxpayers.

The general and Camila pondered their future from all the angles they could imagine until well after midnight. He was up fixing breakfast at 6 am. The COS delivered the general's letter of resignation at 8 am.

After two military service chiefs knowing the president's directive declined appointment to Chairman of the Joint Chiefs of Staff, the second ranking member of the Navy accepted. The change delayed the trial for three days.

Texas

It was decided by committee that having the Resistance national leadership, intelligence, and expertise in many disciplines centralized at one location was dangerous. Detection of the ship would spell doom for the Resistance.

Again, it was difficult for Julie and Andrew to leave Sandy, but she was in good hands. They promised within thirty days they would come back to the ship to stay or to get her. Ultimately, what they did was for her future. Their goal was solid—more freedom and liberty for citizens and return to the fundamental principles the country was founded upon. What form that would take, they did not know. What challenges lay ahead; they could not visualize. But their calling could not be denied.

Julie, Andrew, Torrence, and Barry exited a boat in Galveston Harbor and were taken to Austin. The next day another boat arrived at the harbor—this one carrying their personal effects, copies of software, and communication hardware.

Through a third-party, Mason leased a vacant warehouse two blocks from his electric company. By the time the group arrived, three bedrooms had been set up. A large supply of electronic equipment —including satellite dishes— had been delivered in boxes. Barry and Torrence each carried a briefcase full of software and specialty electronics.

Jeanie Rowlett had been a junior partner in an accounting firm for two years. She was happy where she was and hoped to make full partner within five years. The firm's specialty was tax work for small businesses. She had walked clients through many IRS audits—some successful, most not.

She was stunned getting a call from an associate director of the IRS. Normally, contacts were made through a local IRS office.

"I'll be at your office in an hour," he told her.

Her shock level rose, "Can you tell me who the client is so I may be prepared?"

"No, we'll discuss that when I arrive. And keep our meeting to yourself. Tell no one in the office, understand?"

Mentally, she went through her client list wondering if anything had been done to get her in trouble. She could not think of any tax dodging that would bring an associate director to her office. An associate director had never been in their office. She was glad a partner with an office close to hers was gone for the day, as she greeted the man and led him to her office.

In total command and not waiting for her to ask what the visit was about, he sat without being offered a seat and said, "Our local office has been watching you. I have heard good things about your work. Face it, you deserve to be somewhere other than this place." He looked around and pulled his shoulders in as if he could get germs in her office.

"I'm offering you a position as a level 2 IRS accountant in DC. You will start in a week. We have a place for you and your husband to stay until you get settled."

The assistant director did not know why he was offering her the coveted position. To his knowledge, it had never been done before to someone of her status. He knew there was a reason, but he never asked why. He had become assistant director by following orders, not questioning them.

Flabbergasted, she was nearly speechless. "Wow! I need to call Steven."

"No need, we have a position for him at more than he is making now. Here are your plane tickets, and this number is for a moving company that will pack and move you at our expense."

Jeanie took her time looking at the first-class plane tickets, moving voucher, and a deposit slip for twenty thousand United Nation Units.

Reading her mind, he answered, "That is a signing bonus. It has been deposited in your account. And, of course, your HCI will go up by ten points as a federal employee."

She knew a level 2 IRS accountant earned over twice what she did. She would not earn that much as full partner in the firm. Not having gone to the right university, she had never even bothered to apply for an IRS job. Steven and she were applying for a permit to have a child. This position would assure them a permit to have a baby and get their child into the right university.

His look demanded an immediate answer.

"We'll be there in a week."

The Texas governor had two administrative assistants—the policy assistant whose office was in the capitol building and the social assistant who handled all of her trips, social events, and the governor's mansion. His office was in the governor's residence.

As Jeanie was being offered a highly sought IRS position, Steven, the governor's social assistant, was offered a position managing activities in a federal office building in DC. They both turned in their resignations the next day and moved within a week.

Chapter 7

Texas

The governor and Carl were both disappointed upon learning of Steven's resignation. They were happy for him but never surmised the reason. Carl headed for Steven's office to tell him goodbye but stopped in the kitchen to get a pastry. He did not know Madison had left early for the capitol and saw a tall, medium built woman with auburn hair cut three inches above her shoulders reaching in the refrigerator. She wore a black knit top like his wife normally wore. He intended to surprise his wife, sneaking up from behind her, until the woman said, "There are croissants covered in the basket on the counter."

He caught himself before he touched Audrey, the cook who had served three governors. Besides hair and body build, Audrey had many of the same features as the governor- broad forehead, full pouty lips, high cheekbones, and wide-set eyes. More than one person had mistaken them for sisters.

Audrey was an amicable woman, a few years older than Madison; she was always friendly and her pastries a treat. But polite society did not look kindly on her for having three children all with the same man. Two were sanctioned, the last was not. It was fortunate that the family was healthy because with an oversized family, their Health Care Indexes (HCI) were reduced.

It was not uncommon in the mid twenty-first century to mistake someone's identity, whether it be in appearance or gender. Both genders wore similar hair styles. Women wearing shoulder length hair were considered of frivolous character—as were blondes. Women's hair styles had gone full circle back to the flapper look over more than a century before. Long gone were the days of women choosing to be blonde. Naturally blonde women most often darkened their hair. Flashy clothes were taboo—as were heels, skirts, dresses, and tops exposing collar bones.

As women's hair styles had shortened, men's hair had lengthened to join them. The unisex look was the norm. Anything outside the uni-look indicated an outdated belief in gender difference. Accordingly, separate clothing sections for men and women in department stores were outdated. Walking down a city sidewalk, it was often difficult to distinguish men from women from behind—let alone similar-looking women.

Texas State employment positions were effectively filled by the Texas Public Union (TPU). The TPU had become the human resources arm of state government, although it was much less stringent and dogmatic than the American Public Union (APU). Often the unions disagreed on policy, but the TPU owed the APU a favor for the independence they allowed the TPU.

The president of the TPU received a call from the APU president.

"I understand the position of social assistant to the governor has opened. We have a great candidate. It would be a lateral move for this person. She may be overqualified, but a personal situation makes her desirous of a move. I'll send you her resume."

The Texas union president did not wish to jeopardize his relationship with the APU and would take his word on her resume.

"How soon can she be here?"

"Later, the TPU president found her resume in his e-mail box. It was awesome. Perhaps it was the APU doing the favor.

White House

In the days leading up to the trial of the Maryland trio, a producer and a director from Hollywood met the president in the Oval Office often. They would orchestrate the production of the trial. The message to be conveyed to the citizenry was plain— hiding from PPU eyes was fruitless, all citizen actions were tracked, and certain and swift justice awaited those who violate the common good.

The president's degree was in law, but he never practiced after failing the bar examination. It was straight into politics for him as an assistant to a congressman. When the congressman unexpectedly died, he ran in a special election. It was unlikely that he would have won the first time in a regular election, but his political career was launched. Now he was sitting as a judge, a position he could never have obtained through regular channels.

Five attorneys who specialized in the defense of high-profile criminals declined appointment to represent the Maryland trio. They preferred mild sanctions for refusing an appointment to stigma in proper society for representing traitors. The last appointee was given no choice.

In the morning pretrial conference, the defense attorney sought to enter as evidence the illicit interview tape of the Davis's. The president ruled he would consider it if the Davis's were produced for his questioning before the day was over. It was physically impossible that day, even had the Davis's been naïve enough to comply and face charges themselves.

The prosecution previewed the video evidence they would be presenting. As they had no witnesses, the PPU video and two defendants acknowledging possession of an illegal encrypted grape constituted the evidence. The defense attorney sought to have experts examine the videos to insure they had not been tampered. The motion was denied by the president.

After the pretrial conference, the president was on the phone with the NSA retention and interrogation facilities where the Maryland trio was held.

"That's right, the orders delivered to you by the director of the NSA are mine. You will get it done and have everything in place by 10:00

am the day after tomorrow; or we will find someone who will, and you can spend the next twenty years minding prisoners at the NSA camp in Rampart, Alaska."

The trial took place in the evening at prime time. The trial would be limited to one hour at the president's order because of concern more time would lose audience. All networks, cable and grape feeds covered the trial. The video feeds were split-screened, showing on the left side the president—on the right-side small, stacked pictures of the three defendants wearing oversized orange prison jump suits. The images of the prisoners were behind bars and looking alternately fidgety and detached. The prisoners noticed their dinners that evening had an unusually sour taste.

The prosecution's evidence was primarily video. A film clip of Ellen and Traverse greeting Jayden at a flea market was presented at the trial. The defense attorney protested that it was not the same clip the defense had been presented, and he accused the prosecution of withholding exculpatory evidence. The clip had been edited to lengthen their simple greeting into a conversation, but he was overruled by the president.

In closing arguments, the prosecutor spoke over a slide presentation of the damage to NSA facilities in Maryland, Utah, and Iowa. He ended his pleas with a question, "Ask yourselves, where will this end if perpetrators suffer no consequences? Will the building where you work be next, the school where your children learn, or the restaurant where you eat?"

The defense's closing argument was twofold. First, he centered on the government's failure to present evidence substantiating multiple deaths that it claimed. "If the defendants intended to murder workers, why were the fire alarms tripped? Why were small explosions set to scare people away? If murder was the intent, why did they try to minimize it?"

His next appeal was to nature. It was an appeal to the secular, materialistic view of humankind. The prevailing view of those in power was that people were but the product of their genes and environment—both of which they had no control— rendering their actions outside their conscious control. If someone stole a turnip, raped a teenager, or murdered a spouse, it was some random, unexplainable, tragic conflagration of their genes and experiences for which their consciousness should not be held responsible. The argument switched the question of guilt from what the person did to what the person could control. In another respect, it switched blame from the individual to society as a whole. Why hold the individual more culpable than the culture which molded the person? The argument used in the right situation often brought an acquittal.

"I'll have my verdict in short order," said the president to the camera before coverage broke for a commercial espousing the value of new health protocols.

Back on camera, the president wore a solemn face. "Fellow inhabitants of the boundaries of this country, this has been an arduous decision. Easy as ignoring my duty might be, I cannot fulfill the responsibility in which you entrusted me by ignoring a treacherous act that endangers us all. You elected me to make tough decisions for the common good—as distasteful as it may be sometimes, it is my duty.

The evidence is overwhelming. It is not circumstantial or witness based— which can be faulty— but real, hard, and irresistible."

The president turned his head as if looking at the defendants, "I regrettably hereby sentence you—Ellen Herwick, Traverse Jones, and Jayden Samuels— to the punishment traditionally given to the worst kind of criminals. Tomorrow at 10:00 am under the powers of martial law, at the NSA detainment center in Maryland, I sentence you to be hanged by the neck until dead."

The facial expressions on the defendants did not show any emotion. Audio had been turned off in their cells. But by the sober expression on the president's face, Ellen and Traverse assumed their sentence would be long. Jayden was sure his innocence would ultimately prevail.

The president turned away from the defendants, giving eye contact to the camera in front of him. "And let this be a lesson to any others with insidious leanings. Rebellious actions against the accepted common good will bring disaster upon you and your families."

Austin, TX

The governor and Carl were taken back by the president's resolute tone in sentencing the three to death. Although they did not expect an execution would take place, both silently contemplated the line they had crossed.

Across town, the reaction of Julie and Andrew to the trial and verdict was not one of surprise. "Staging a trial as they did could hardly result in a not guilty verdict," observed Andrew.

"What time in the morning do you expect commutation of sentence to come down?" Julie asked.

"I'd guess early, the verdict will have served its purpose as people ponder an execution all night. And it will soften his perception in some quarters," Andrew answered.

"I disagree. I expect him to wait until the last few minutes. I can still remember the brutal underlying personality I sensed, talking to him on the grape before we ordered those facilities eliminated. But what is particularly disturbing is the plight of Jayden Samuels. No one in the Maryland Resistance or anywhere else has any recollection of him being involved at any level. In fact, no one knows him. They cannot have any real evidence against him; he must be a framed scapegoat. Such a shame, he will likely spend years at that social adjustment gulag in Alaska."

Julie and Andrew's room in the warehouse had been hastily built. The walls to the bedroom extended eight feet high, the warehouse ceiling fourteen. A bathroom separated the couple's bedroom from Barry and Torrence's rooms. None of the bedrooms had a window, but plenty of natural light filtered in from above. The bedrooms sat ten feet from the outer wall. The space between the bedrooms and outer wall was office space and storage for their communication hardware. The only access to the offices was through closets in the three bedrooms.

In the event of a search, the offices could easily be found; but a cursory inside look at the warehouse would not reveal where they spent most of their time.

Julie and Andrew's mattress was not the most comfortable, but they agreed it beat the cot they sometimes shared at the Iowa railroad tie dump. They lay asleep, covered by an old quilt someone likely picked up at a secondhand store, when pounding on the closet wall woke Andrew.

Andrew knew neither Barry nor Torrence would have attempted to wake them unless it was important. He hollered into the closet, "We'll be right there."

Julie pulled a robe on as they moved through the closet, "What's up?"

"I couldn't sleep and found on a Fed website someone other than General Martinez is now listed as CJCS. A little digging found that he resigned, and his house is for sale," said Barry.

"Okay?" said Julie in a questioning tone.

"There's much more," added Torrence. "Our cruise ship received word from a source in a Maryland lumber yard that the NSA detention facility put a rush order in yesterday for 12-foot 4X6 posts, a good deal of deck planking, and get this... a hundred feet of one inch hemp rope."

"Oh my God!" exclaimed Julie. "As tight as restrictions are on the use of wood— particularly in government facilities— I can think of only one use for that mix of materials."

Maryland

Ellen, Traverse, and Jayden continued to be held in separate cells, unaware if the others were also locked up or had been turned loose. In fact, Ellen and Traverse had no idea Jayden had been picked up. The three woke earlier than normal, disturbed by pounding somewhere in the facility. Breakfast came at 8:00, later than normal; but they were pleased finding it was more than the normal day-old stale pastries. The eggs, toast, and imitation fruit jam went down easily; it was an indication of better conditions or release, they were sure.

At 9:45, four guards appeared at each of their cells. "Use the toilet now if you have need, you'll be gone awhile," said a guard timidly. Jayden thought it was because the release paperwork would be lengthy.

They were handcuffed and escorted down a hallway. Traverse noticed one of his guards looking pale before he trotted away. Coming from another hallway, he saw Ellen also escorted by four guards. Although he had hoped she was not in prison, he was glad to see her. She did not look well. It struck him that he probably did not either. He tried to move toward her but was restrained by a guard. Then he saw a man escorted by four guards following her; he looked familiar, but Traverse could not place him.

At the end of the hallway, light shone through a door window. It was refreshing, seeing sunlight, the first they had seen in weeks. Someone opened the door from the outside, and they were walked into a courtyard. Ellen took a deep breath, exhilarated to be outdoors on such a fine day. Hopefully, they would be given ample time in the courtyard.

At a Y in the sidewalk, they were turned around. Ellen blinked her eyes again and again, not believing what she saw. Traverse stared blankly as if he could will the scene away. Jayden jerked his tied hands away from a guard and took off in the opposite direction. Two guards were hesitant to chase him, others were not.

TV cameras and large lights were set up on both sides of the sidewalk they were marched down. At the end of the sidewalk were new wooden stairs. It struck them the stairs and platform were the source of pounding throughout the night. It must be a dream from which they would soon awaken was the dominant thought the Maryland trio clung to. For the guards, it was a nightmare they would not forget.

Jayden's knees weakened midway up the stairs and had to be helped.

They were each held beside a noose as guards tied their legs together. A guard whispered to Ellen, "Sorry about this, nothing personal, but I have a family to think of."

Traverse could feel his heart pounding in his chest as they stood. He turned to Ellen and said, "I love you and have no regrets."

Jayden was silently mouthing the few Bible verses he could remember.

Hope the three had that it might be an elaborate charade to scare them into revealing more information evaporated when they saw three members of their guard scurry away and lose their breakfasts.

Execution by hanging resulted in strangulation which caused death by asphyxiation or breaking of the neck. The traditional method was suspending a criminal from gallows and dropping them through a trap door. The length of the rope determined how the person died. Strangulation took some time before death came, a sufficient jerk that severed cervical vertebrae was thought to bring an immediate loss of consciousness.

Although used throughout ancient history, hanging became the most common method of execution in Germanic culture from where it spread to Britain, then the colonies.

The pacing woman on the platform who appeared to be in charge kept glancing at her watch as three minds were racing through their lives summarizing all in the fast forward mode. Suddenly she stopped and said, "It's time."

Small red lights came on the cameras, and flood lights were turned on. "Aren't you going to let us say anything?" Ellen courageously asked.

Her answer was a black hood pulled over her head as she gave Traverse a 'goodbye' look.

Traverse's legs were quivering, they could hardly hold him up. Then from somewhere came a faint breeze; it brought him an inner peace but also strength. He stood straight— almost stiffly— realizing the cameras were recording, Traverse was intent on one last act of defiance. He yelled through the hood, "FREEDOM!" The second time he repeated it, Ellen joined him. Not knowing why, Jayden also joined them before they felt the floor falling beneath their feet.

The public saw an edited version of the executions. A statement was read by an announcer of the charges against them—unheard by the prisoners, as they stood while their legs were tied. One by one, cameras gave a closeup of each prisoner's face as it was covered with a hood. A wide-angle view of the three prisoners was shown, all standing stiffly. Hoods could be seen puffing out as they yelled 'Freedom,' but no audio was transmitted from the gallows. Many viewers at homes, offices, and shops had left their screens—unwilling or unable to watch the morbid ordeal. Those that watched assumed the puffing hoods were the condemned breathing in terror.

When the traps opened, the condemned fell from the view of the camera. Momentarily another wide-angle shot showed them hanging below the scaffolding, necks at an odd angle, legs twitching in death. Most viewers did not realize they saw only three masses of carbon-based molecules, their souls were gone.

A third of the population refused to watch the ordeal. A quarter killed their monitors before the traps were sprung. In the aftermath, the hangings pushed a quarter of the country further toward rebellion; a quarter became even more fearful of the government. Another quarter—who generally for self-interest supported a strong government—were appalled at the barbarity of it but accepted it as necessary.

Austin, Texas

The governor and Carl were in her capitol office when they received notice that something major was in the works. As usual, Carl closed the heavy gold drapes to limit window reflection on a large screen opposite the governor's desk. They soon wished they had left them open. The repulsion at what they saw left them speechless. Madison had left the room for the restroom when her phone rang. Carl answered. It was the governor of Oklahoma.

Yes, we'll be on," the governor heard her husband say.

"Who was that?" she asked.

Carl had pulled his secure grape from a jacket pocket and was reading a text. He answered her by waving his grape toward the hallway leading to the bathroom and a library extension of the governor's office. They entered the library. Two walls were lined with books in Texas walnut built-in cases. In the center of the room set a small conference table that would seat eight. For bigger conferences, a larger room was used outside the governor's office. The library had no windows and was seldom used.

Carl circled the library, holding his secure grape which contained an electronic surveillance finding app. Confident it was clear, he said, "That was the Okie governor; there is a conference call in ten minutes, and this room is secure."

"I thought we were going to confine these calls to the residence."

"We must make a decision whether we're going to use what we saw to further motivate us or live in fear."

Julie convened the conference call meeting. All but two state leaders were on the call, as well as Resistance board members on the ship and nine governors. The governors of Louisiana and Wyoming were new to the conference calls.

"As you know, I've been authorized to make day-to-day tactical decisions for the group with the approval of the state leader of any state where an action is to take place. If twenty-five percent of the board calls for discussion on a topic, a vote will be held. The other provision for a vote is if I request it. I am requesting a vote because there needs to be consensus on the topic of retaliation."

The Missouri Resistance leader summed up the feeling of many; he was adamant, "If we do not retaliate, we will look helpless."

"Who would you have us kill?" asked Andrew.

Maryland's leader: "Our martyrs were from my state. It is our responsibility to take revenge. We know where the warden of that detention center lives. She almost seemed to enjoy the ordeal; it gave her a chance to be on national TV."

Several leaders agreed; one suggested that the Resistance take tenfold the three martyrs to let them know a price would be paid.

Another leader said, "So then, they take down ten times those numbers? Where will that get us?"

Barry took the conversation in a different direction. "We know that General Martinez has resigned his CJCS post. We are picking up reports that he is moving to Kansas. Since normally an execution under martial law is carried out by the military, it is safe to assume the general may have refused an order. I think it is important to encourage people like the general to stand up—and at the same time, draw sympathy from the martyrdom of the Maryland Trio. Retaliating now may squelch any sympathy we gain. We should honor the sacrifice of the three patriots and not waste their martyrdom in reckless revenge."

The Tennessee leader spoke, "The murder of our three compatriots will strike fear in many; that was the purpose of the execution and making a public spectacle of it. We need to show that costs are to be borne by those who implement such orders and strike fear into those who would carry out such orders by the State."

The debate went back and forth. Julie had an opinion but chose to not express herself. When asked what she thought, she refrained.

But Andrew spoke, "We were all shocked beyond belief at what happened. I know we all want revenge, but will it do us any good? I expect that is what they would like us to do. Barry was right. Violence, if necessary, should be directed toward alleviating control they have over the citizenry, not lustful revenge. Our actions should be directed toward winning back liberty, not giving them an excuse to squeeze more from us.

We should realize that our activities will most likely put us on the gallows if we are caught. Perhaps anyone unwilling to take that chance should step back. Myself, I prefer to not go to the gallows for useless vengeance. If I must go, I would prefer it be for something that advances our cause."

Governor Archibald spoke, "I think nearly three hundred years ago our countrymen were faced with the same choice. They remained focused. They did not back down—and neither will we, but we must avoid being reckless."

Julie had heard enough, "It's time to vote. All those who favor immediate retaliation press #1 for *yes* on your secure grape; those opposed #2 for *no*.

The tally read 21 *yes,* 42 *no;* no retaliation would be taken.

Chapter 8

Camila and Jerome Martinez had moved numerous times as his rank in the army rose. Their residence in Arlington, Virginia, had been the longest. But they were excited about the move. If any place felt like home, it would be Wichita—where they grew up.

Unlike the very distant cousins of most Americans in Europe, Americans moved. Moving trucks, trailers and van rentals were almost non-existent in Europe. Perhaps Americans inherited the proclivity to relocate from ancestors who made a dangerous trip across an ocean. Like the Martinez family, those whose ancestors came from Latin America also had the adventurous moving gene. Cruelly, those who by force came from Africa adapted to the move; if they did not, their genes were not passed on.

The country was not settled by people who liked taking orders. By nature, those who ventured here were a self-reliant people. Many left the security of their ancestral homeland to worship God according to their conscience, rather than the dictates of the State. They were a hypomanic, adventuresome lot. Genetically, they had a much higher prevalence of D4-7 allele—the risk-taking gene—than the genetic pool they chose to leave. Those who came here involuntarily learned to take care of themselves, often for survival, and developed an aversion to taking orders.

Most importantly was an underlying predisposition that caused most Americans to move when necessary, the desire for freedom and little fear of the unknown. Those of European and Latin ancestry were descendants of those who had fled tyranny, lack of economic opportunity, religious persecution, and the remnants of a feudal system. African Americans still had memories of slavery, the antonym of freedom. A century earlier, immigrants fled the national socialist movement in central Europe. Later they fled another form of socialism, the oppression of communism around the world.

Americans by nature were always seeking greener pastures. The lure was articulated by the song *"Home in the Meadow"* in the near century-old classic movie *How the West was Won*.

> *Come, Come*
> *There's a wondrous land*
> *For the hopeful heart, for the willing hand.*
> *Come, Come*
> *There's a wondrous land*
> *Where I'll build you a home in the meadow.*

Although movement was a norm of American life, migrating from state to state had increased in the preceding decades. Steps were taken to slow the movement. States imposed exit taxes; the federal government forbade corporations from relocating without federal permits. However, midsized companies that were trapped in high tax and high regulation states often went bankrupt, while new companies emerged in other states. As some states increased taxes to compensate for their lost tax base, more people were forced to leave.

However, migration was not in one direction. A few decades earlier, citizens and residents were given a monthly stipend from the government. The stipend progressively declined for people who earned between one and a half and two times the national average, where it ended. As jobs moved to other states and out of the country, the stipend encouraged people to stay in place. States which lost population had excess housing. To support collapsing home prices, states bought vacant housing and offered subsidized rent—often at less than the original property taxes had been. To collect something was better than nothing.

Those who chose to live on a stipend, subsidized housing and other enticements caused a cross migration of people moving to housing surplus states. Those dependent on the stipend became a reliable voting bloc which pushed for frequent increases in the stipend.

Another migration congested the District of Columbia area. Most of the super big conglomerates moved their headquarters closer to the seat of power, Washington. They found proximity to the power that protected their status and threw regulatory roadblocks in front of smaller competitors advantageous.

Previous generations of corporate America found innovative products and services key to growth and success. Later generations of companies emphasized marketing. Now corporate fear of the State and the necessity of huge lobbying efforts influenced board decisions.

Texas

Governor Archibald was scheduled to meet her new administrative assistant for social affairs in the morning but received a call indicating the new assistant would be late.

"Honey, if I wait longer, I will be late. Would you mind meeting the new assistant? After all, you will be dealing with her more than I."

Carl had a hard time from succumbing to the use of 'Honey'. "Sure, I'll take care of that for you."

The governor's term was not up for two years. However, the need to campaign was continuous. She endeavored to tour the state periodically. It made sense to fly to destinations in a state the size of Texas. But with commercial airline fares at prohibitive prices for middle America and private aircraft considered a luxury of the privileged, she avoided air travel because of the political optics. Two mid-sized diesel-electric buses took her around the state. The buses rolling through a small town made a connection a plane overhead would not. The bus in which she rode had a traveling office and twin beds. Usually, her husband traveled with her on one bus, staff the other bus. Carl would not be traveling with her on this trip.

Although vultures in the sky were no longer a threat, it was assumed the FBI had agents tracking the governor. Hence, her riding partner boarded at the bus garage on this three-day trip before it picked up the governor.

"I'm very glad to finally meet you," said Julie as the governor boarded the bus.

"And I you. I've never heard where you are from."

"I grew up in various cities on the east coast, lived in Idaho with Andrew for a time, and was in Iowa during the effort to stop the mass nano-machine injections. But my home, a condo, is in Midland. And I voted for you two years ago."

"Thank you. I'm thinking, what is wrong with this country when two strong Texas women must sneak around like this?"

"Isn't that the truth, but that is why we are here. If it were a free and open society, we would not be meeting. In the big picture, you are here for a reason—as I am. I don't believe in coincidences, do you?"

"No, I'm sure a greater force is at work. But speaking of work, will we be able to connect with everyone while traveling?"

"Yes."

The planned route was a big circle— Wichita Falls near the Oklahoma border, then Texarkana on the Arkansas border, then Beaumont on the Louisiana border. At each stop, they would meet the governors of those states and be brought up to date on Fed's effort to link into the Texas electrical grid. From Beaumont, they would stop at a fundraiser in Houston; then on the way back, visit the National Guard encircling the Georgetown plant.

The governor was looking out the window at traffic, "My, my, the traffic has picked up. People are getting out."

Julie offered explanation, "In my last conference call with state leaders, they indicated seeing the same thing. Word is spreading that the vultures are blind; people knowing they are not tracked are making trips which would be dubbed unnecessary before. Driving to see that elderly aunt or to a favorite restaurant they quit because rumor was a Resistance member had been there is not seen as dangerous now... "

Julie lost her train of thought as she peered through the window. "Did you see that homemade sign? I couldn't read it."

"I could. It read, *Remember Ellen.*"

Carl received word that Zoe Barnett, the governor's new social assistant, would be arriving soon. He scanned her resume. She was well-qualified. What struck his eye was the notation in the confidential resume of her reason for relocating —boyfriend problems.

"You must be Carl," Zoe said, bright and beamy as the Texas sky.

Her hand reached out for his. Her handshake was ladylike. He noticed her hand was moist, but not clammy. She wore gray slacks and a periwinkle top that was not bought at a federally subsidized big box store. The slacks he guessed were size eight, and the top two buttons of her blouse were unbuttoned. Her hair was a light brown, not blonde, but on the light side of the narrow bell curve of proper women's hair shades. If she tilted her head slightly, hair ends flirted with her shoulders. Some would consider the length provocative.

"I must show you my updated resume," she said as she turned and pulled it from the bag she had laid behind her. The slacks looked tighter from behind, *perhaps part of her was not a size eight,* thought Carl before he shook the thought from his head.

Zoe Barnett was born Olivia Bidwell, but she had used several aliases. Her employer was the Central Intelligence Agency (CIA). Her parents had a long-term career with the government which got her into a tier one university. Influence or not, she was gifted in many ways. She spoke four languages, had an IQ of one hundred fifty, was a black belt in Karate, and an expert in Taekwondo. Her most recent assignment had been undercover in Poland. Her favorite movie was the old classic, *"Hunger Games."*

Espionage took many forms— satellite, electronic, drones and human contact. Zoe was an expert at gleaning information from targets by contact. She employed no electronic means. Most of her targets were keen on those methods, and planting devices ran the risk of being exposed.

Carl was correct. The moisture he felt in Zoe's handshake was not sweat from new job jitters, but a skin-absorbed agent that boosted testosterone production and lowered inhibitions.

"I'm very much looking forward to working with you," Zoe said, as he started showing her around.

When Zoe was settled, Carl left Austin and headed to a former hunting resort. The only shots taken at wildlife on the hunting grounds were from a camera. Killing of animals had been banned as barbaric a decade earlier. The hunting lodge was still a go-to place for guys who liked to get away. Carl was joined by Andrew, Mason and Torrence at the lodge. Connecting by secure grape with the governor and Julie on the road, they in effect had a three-day planning conference all the time patching in leaders from other states and the ship.

Later that evening Torrence asked, more than stated, "I understand the governor has a new social assistant?"

"Yes, I met her today."

"Tell me about her."

"Given today's narrow range of women's looks, Grandfather would have put her on the *wolf whistle* side."

"You lost me there. What do you mean by *wolf whistle?*"

"Growing up, I would often visit my grandparents for a week during summer vacation. One evening we were going out to dinner and grandmother came downstairs, after spending much time getting ready. Grandfather whistled at her. It was a distinctive two-note glissando sound that I had not heard before but couldn't forget. Grandmother thanked him.

Later, I asked him what the whistle was about. He said in his time it was a form of flattery to a woman. He said the whistle was common; and if a woman spent time to look nice, it was almost seen as an insult not receiving a wolf whistle. He said he and friends often whistled at a girl less than attractive to avoid hurting her feelings.

He told me in later years it became considered an aggressive sexual gesture and was frowned upon. Had not men quit using it because of the social stigma, it would have been outlawed.

I researched the origin of the wolf whistle years ago and found it originated in a 1943 Tex Avery cartoon called *"Red Hot Riding Hood"* where the wolf whistled at a female character called *Red*. As grandfather said, the whistle eventually came to be considered offensive and was outlawed in some European countries.

Then grandfather lamented a bigger social change. He said growing up it was common to hear people, mostly men, whistling popular tunes. Many were quite good, walking down the street in a gay, joyous mood. He had a neighbor who whistled in his backyard, and people would talk about his song selections and look forward to his one-man band. In his old age, grandfather bemoaned that carefree, happy spirit had disappeared from society."

"All interesting," responded Torrence. "Wolf whistle material or not, I'll check her out."

The hunting resort where they were staying was run by a patriot, and it had become a meeting place for the Resistance. On the group's stay, the lodge's security cameras were out of service. It was not the first time they failed to record who the guests were. The second day, General Tate, commander of the Texas National Guard, joined them in civilian clothes. Later joining them was what appeared to be a married couple. They looked the part— she in a skirt, which was appropriate for the lodge—and he, escorting her as if they were married. Contrary to what patrons in the dining room assumed, they were not a couple. Anyone but her husband—or a partner in a necessary charade— touching her would not fare well.

Colonel Nancy Everett and Colonel John Conner each commanded a brigade of five thousand soldiers at Fort Hood. She was from Florida, he Alabama. The six met in a conference room. It was a strategy session—planning moves, discussing contingencies, and developing a plan to submit.

At stops in Wichita Falls, Texarkana, and Beaumont, Governor Archibald found electric line construction at the same point in the neighboring states. Contractors working for the Feds had constructed grid hookup lines to the state borders. With small detachments of Texas Guard at the border, construction had halted.

At each border stop, she met with the governors of the respective states while Julie stayed hidden in the bus. The governors all supported hooking to the Texas electric grid but had their concerns about the possibility of energy being drained from their states to help energy deficit states. An agreement was reached.

When the bus left Beaumont, the governor reached General Tate at the hunting lodge. She instructed him to remove guard units from border locations where grid connections were to be made. The action fit into the plan that was being developed. Within days, construction workers were extending the lines into Texas. In route to Houston, the governor and Julie saw more *"Remember Ellen"* signs along the road.

After they left the fundraiser in Houston, a conference call with the ship, those at the hunting lodge, and state leaders around the country was held. A plan was submitted. Julie stated that as it was a Texas plan to be carried out in Texas, leaders from other states could voice their concerns, but it was a Texas issue. The leaders gave input, but none objected. Some offered assistance, but the prevailing thought was that moving many people across state lines early would draw attention. The plan was adopted.

A few miles from Georgetown, the governor received a call from the president. "I've been notified that guard detachments have been removed from the border at electric line construction sites. I applaud your cooperation. Nice to know we are all headed in the same direction for the common good. What are you, a third of the way back to Austin now?"

The governor noted the president pointed out that he knew where she was. She was not surprised at his subtle intimidation. "I had a campaign fundraiser in Houston on the way. Then I'll stop in Georgetown to support our guard defending the factory against terrorists before I'm back in Austin."

"Well, fundraisers I understand, just a nasty diversion of our efforts protecting the common good. I will be looking forward to hearing your remarks to the Guard. Enjoy the rest of the trip. I'm tied down to a boring conference on state aid the rest of the day."

The governor smiled at the overt coercion.

General Tate was back from the hunting lodge. He and members of his staff met with the governor at the Georgetown plant. An empty area in the plant, which would store finished PPUs, was set up for the governor's address to the Texas National Guard unit. For security, no national media were allowed in the plant; but a communication contingent of the Guard would record the speech and submit it to the media.

Hundreds of Guard members were in attendance as the governor gave a perfunctory pep talk to the guardsmen. Cameras were set up to record the event but not turned on. Audio recorders captured crowd applause. The speech emphasized the state's tradition of being leaders in the quest for freedom and a reminder that their duty was to follow ranking officers' commands as they followed hers.

Once the guardsmen had left, the doors were locked, the cameras turned on and the governor gave another speech. This time her audience was not in Georgetown, but in Washington.

"Guard men and women, we are citizens of Texas, but also citizens of the United States. Our duty is to defend the Constitution, and the Constitution establishes who our leader is, the President. In these trying times, we must strive to support the policies he has implemented for our common good. This plant will produce the means to fair, harmonious society without vicious discord. ..."

Submitting the video to the president was enjoyable for the governor. However, the media airing the speech to the public was a tough pill to swallow, but necessary. Julie, Andrew, Mason, and the governor herself were soon busy on their grapes assuring leaders around the country that the speech was a charade and to ignore it.

On the trip back to Austin, the governor said, "Well, I guess we've set things in motion. I'll have to be honest with you, I'm a little shaky at this moment."

"Governor, I understand. How do you think I felt when I ordered the destruction of three NSA facilities? In the end, we do what we must. Or I should rephrase that, we do what we are guided to do."

"Look, there is another *"Remember Ellen"* sign," the governor said.

"How does seeing the sign make you feel?"

"Like we are doing the right thing."

"Perhaps the signs are there to support you," offered Julie.

The bus stopped at a stop sign, and Julie looked out the window at a grisly sight on the shoulder of the road. She pointed and said, "Look I see a dead possum on the shoulder. Maybe the possum is there to remind us of something."

"Of what would a dead possum remind us?"

"It carries two messages. Notice the possum was lying on his back when he was run over. Most likely he heard a vehicle coming, feared being struck, rolled on his back, put four legs in the air and over-played dead. What good did fear and playing possum do him? Perhaps, if he would have taken action by running instead of faking death, he would be alive.

If we let fear dictate our actions, we too will end up like the possum.

The other message is deeper. At one time it was believed that enough study of the human body would reveal what makes us tick. If we only had a more powerful microscope, we would see the answers. But we did not find the answers with the electron microscope, we only found more questions. Later Watson and Crick discovered DNA. It would not be long now before we had the answers, again only more questions.

Unimaginable powerful computers at the time mapped our DNA only to find we share eighty-five percent of our DNA with that possum on the side of the road. Still, life could not be explained—the more we know the less we can explain. Now the talk is epigenetics, quantum theory, string theory, multiple universes, etc., etc. Although we have a hard time admitting it, the more we know, the more we realize we do not know.

Scientists tell us that the odds of all the amino acids coming together in the right order to form one of many proteins in our body by chance is ten to the 164th power. That is about same as the odds of you finding one tagged atom in the Milky Way. And we are to believe we are here by coincidence?

I passionately believe there is something we cannot empirically grasp. We are all given certain talents and desires for a reason. One of the biggest failings we can have is never figuring out why we are here or ignoring it. We have abilities far beyond that of a possum; if we fail to use them, we revert to the eighty-five percent of the genes we share with that possum. In that case, we just as well be a possum.

Imagine the guilt one might encounter someday realizing you were at the right place, the right time with the tools you needed to make a difference and you tarried. That could be our hell."

Mason Trotter home

Mason received a call from brother Damon that evening. He had heard clips of the Texas governor's speech to the guard.

"Mason, I have to apologize about everything I've said of Texas and your governor. The state is taking a very sensible position."

"What do you think about the executions?" Mason asked.

"Frankly, I think they were an overstep, but hopefully it will save future lives."

Chapter 9

Austin

Carl learned that Barry had intercepted internal FBI mail expressing concern that the heavy drapes in the governor's capitol office were most often closed. It could only mean that laser beams outside the human visible range were focused on the windows. Technology had been developed to allow conversation to be picked up by reflection of laser beams off glass panes vibrating from voices. The Austin FBI Office, half a mile away, had a window with an unobstructed vision of the governor's office window. The governor often kept the drapes closed as sunlight reflection made monitor and screen viewing difficult. Carl had an idea. Before the governor returned, he directed the capitol's equipment manager to rearrange the governor's office.

At the residence, Carl explained his rearrangement of her capitol office and the reason to Madison. The rearrangement would allow her to feed the FBI what they wanted while using the secluded library for safe communication. The next morning, she found the sunlight in her capitol office refreshing with the video screens usable.

At the residence that evening, the governor took a call from Julie.

"We are set to launch them in an hour—if you have any second thoughts, now is the time to express them."

"Mason, Carl and I discussed it again this afternoon in my library. We are on board. We will have a couple opportunities later to stop the plan if something goes wrong, but like you said, it is our calling."

Georgetown

The Texas National Guard soldiers immediately surrounding the Georgetown plant had surface-to-air laser batteries, capable of downing subsonic aircraft or drone pigeons from the ground. However, because drones traveled at low altitudes, their area of protection was small. They had purposely deployed the batteries to the north and east of the plant.

At 9:45, a carrier pigeon took off from fifteen miles northeast of the plant. The pigeon drone was the same make and model that the postal and other delivery services commonly used. Restricted airspace had been declared in a five-mile radius of the plant. The restrictions covered delivery drones, to the objection of residents within the circle.

Five minutes later, another pigeon took off from north of the plant. Radar picked up both drones immediately. Guard batteries guided by radar were always charged ready for hostile targets in the sky.

At 9:55, a pigeon took off from southwest of the plant.

When the pigeons from the northeast and north crossed the five-mile perimeter, the batteries launched focused lasers. Within seconds, two drones exploded in the nighttime sky. On a clear, dry Texas night, the explosions could be seen for miles. Explosives that the pigeons carried were rigged to go off if they were struck by anything.

The colonel commanding the federally controlled brigade from Fort Hood stationed south of the plant was on his second shot of rye whiskey when he heard explosions. He was outside before he could be summoned.

The pigeon coming from the southwest, encountering no batteries, reached the manufacturing plant and exploded on roof impact. A hole was torn in the roof above an intended warehouse section of the plant where the governor had spoken. The damage was minimal, but the shock waves were major.

The Army colonel immediately notified the Pentagon, then connected with the National Guard commander at the plant.

"What happened?"

"We had three incoming drones, got two of them and the third did little damage."

"How did one get through?"

"Our intelligence told us of a potential threat from the north. We do not have enough batteries to protect three hundred sixty degrees. If we were to spread our batteries out surrounding the plant, gaps would be left between coverage. The three pigeons they sent could not carry enough common explosive to do substantial damage to the plant. Our engineers will have the roof hole fixed before the day is over."

Both colonels knew they had not spoken of the major concern. What if the drones carried a more powerful weapon?

Austin

The governor had followed the evening's developments in the study off the bedroom. She sat at a small desk with her grape linked to a monitor.

"It all went well, you should be relieved," Carl said to his wife.

"I know, but just so much to think about," she answered.

He walked up behind her and massaged her shoulders. She groaned as his fingers dug deep. He continued the massage while slipping the robe from her shoulders, her nightgown fell with it to the chair's low back. His hands started working lower.

"No, please not now with all that is happening."

He backed away and said he was going downstairs for a nightcap.

Adjacent to the first floor bar was the social assistant's office. A motion detector placed years earlier warned Zoe someone was coming downstairs. As Carl walked by her office, he noticed the door was open, he discreetly peered inside. Zoe sat at a chair wearing a less than correct gray skirt. The side view showed her leaning with her head in her arms on the desk whimpering. Her legs were crossed, and the skirt had ridden up.

He quietly walked past her office and poured himself a double. On the way back to the stairs, he glanced in her office. Her reddened eyes were looking at him. "I'm so sorry, it's just that I can't get over how abhorrent he was to me."

He stepped into her office. Zoe reached for him while seated and pulled him to her. Her arms were around his waist. He patted her back lightly with short taps, body language indicating he was not comfortable. Without words, he left.

The next morning, the governor left early for the office. Carl finished a late breakfast and used the kitchen exit to avoid Zoe. But she was near that exit door when he stepped outside.

"I'm so sorry about last night. It just gets to me at times. Will you forgive me?"

"Of course," he replied.

"Only about business, right?" she said extending her hand in a business manner rather than a hug. Her hand again was moist.

At 10:00 am in the Capitol building, the governor asked Julie, "Do you still think we'll hear from the president before noon?"

"Yes, our intelligence says the new CJCS, and the FBI and NSA directors all arrived at the White House before 8:00."

"I won't ask about the intelligence source," responded the governor.

White House

The consensus was immediate that another drone could not be allowed to penetrate the area surrounding the Georgetown plant. Getting the new version PPUs produced and in the sky was imperative for maintaining control of the population. Reports kept surfacing that people were traveling more as they discovered they were not being watched. In the president's mind, people traveling more at their own volition could only lead to more aberrant behavior.

On the ground, intelligence found traffic in and out of the homes of medical doctors who had previously skirted the law had increased. The population could not be allowed to bypass the public health care system (PHCS).

Every person in the country was tagged with a Health Care Index (HCI). The index determined the level of health care you were allowed. An index of under twenty allowed you to receive only minimal health care—penicillin at the most, no resuscitation, no internal surgery. You were, for practical purposes, on your own.

A coveted HCI of over eighty afforded you the best, most up-to-date healthcare. Factors that determined whether you were a twenty or eighty were age, the amount of money the government had invested in your education, your status as a victimized group, whether you were a public servant, your Social Index Score (SIS), and an unspecified factor which generally meant your political correctness or who you knew.

Determination that you made an unnecessary trip or were caught speeding above the forty-five mph speed limit would lower your HCI by ten points. Attendance at a paganistic church service cost you fifteen points, as would being caught using tobacco by a PPU. Being caught twenty pounds over your ideal weight without a genetic predisposition exclusion cost ten points. Habitual patronizing with people holding lower SIS scores would result in your HCI lowered.

As a person's SIS was a major determinant of one's HCI, you lived a longer, healthier life playing by the rules. If circumventing the public health service by seeing a doctor on the side was allowed, soon the government would lose a major facet of control.

The president barked in the Oval Office, "Bypassing the PHCS cannot be allowed to get out of control. And these *Remember Ellen* signs,—I want anyone who has these signs on their property arrested."

The attorney general responded, "Mr. President, the problem is these signs do not appear on home yards, but in farm fields. And there is no reason to believe the farmer placed them."

"Well, let's set an example. Farmers should be patrolling their land. To allow such signs is to condone it. We need to rid the countryside of the rabblerousers."

His advisors were unsure of whether he was talking about farmers or those who put up the signs. Before they could ask for clarification, he said, "Get the Texas governor on the phone."

Carl laid his grape on her desk, enabling Julie to hear the conversation between the governor and president.

"Governor, I want to thank you for that wonderful address you gave the guard in Georgetown."

"It is the least I can do, Mr. President. We are all in this together."

"Let me get to the issue, we cannot allow another drone to penetrate the *no-fly* zone around the Georgetown plant. My intelligence tells me your National Guard's nearest other surface-to-air batteries are in the Houston area."

"That's correct, Mr. President, we need help to keep the plant secure."

"Since your guard surrounding the plant is in place and appears capable—but shorthanded—I suggest we leave them there and augment them. You have five thousand guard soldiers twenty miles to the north in reserve. I suggest you move those held in reserve closer to the plant. I have ordered five brigades, around twenty thousand soldiers from Fort Hood to complete the encirclement of the plant to the west, east and south.

My Pentagon people assure me this will allow complete control of a twenty-mile radius surrounding the plant. We will expand the *no-fly* zone to twenty miles. We cannot tolerate another drone hitting the plant."

"Sounds like a good plan, Mr. President."

"I'm glad you agree. But we do need a central command. I have contacted General Martinez, who recently retired as CJCS, and he has agreed to command the operation."

General Martinez had been contacted by the president. He was reluctant to take the position, but under martial law he could be called up, and refusal would have negated his pension.

"How soon will those units be deployed, Mr. President?"

"Deployment will start within twenty-four hours and be completed in forty-eight. It is imperative that we not leave an unprotected window of opportunity for the hooligans. One more issue needs to be addressed. It has come to my attention that homemade signs which attempt to make a martyr of those traitors have been appearing. Hopefully, that problem can be attended to locally."

"I'll get on it, Mr. President."

When the president was off the phone, Carl pumped his fist into the air and mouthed the words, *"they took the bait."* The governor raised her hand, cautioning him not to make a sound. She then said with a wink, "Get the head of the Texas Rangers on the phone."

Carl, who in practice was the governor's administrative assistant, stepped into the designated administrative assistant's office and dialed the governor's phone. When she answered, he disconnected.

"Ranger Darrien, we have a problem in the Georgetown area. It has come to my attention that signs are appearing glamorizing the executed traitors. A major deployment of Fort Hood soldiers will soon take place there."

She paused as if listening to a response. "Those signs will not help morale. I want your people to get them down and arrest anyone placing them." Another pause, "Thanks for getting right on it."

The governor left her desk and headed for the library, Carl picked up his grape and followed. With the door closed, she got Ranger Darrien on the phone for real.

"Ranger Darrien, here is what I want you to do......"

Ranger Darrien contacted a local TV station and asked for a broadcast crew to meet him at a rural Georgetown location. With the satellite van sending the signal to the station, Rangers lifted a *Remember Ellen* sign from a farm field while Darrien told an interviewer such signs would not be allowed.

The video was sent to national news outlets. But all knew that it would never be shown. To show the video was to admit that such signs were becoming common.

Three realities would prevent the video from being shown: Government censors would not allow it, networks would fear government retribution if they tried to air it, and the ideological bent of journalists opposed acknowledging opinion divergent from what was prevalent in Washington

With Julie on speaker connected to Carl's grape, Julie said, "Well done with the president, Governor. You almost convinced me we should be leery of you."

The governor and Carl stayed in the library and went over her travel calendar for the next month, although both knew events would alter it.

"Would you go back to the residence and coordinate it with the new social assistant? Frankly, I don't have time," she asked her husband.

"Sure," Carl said and leaned in to kiss her; but a phone ring caused her to turn, and he only connected with her cheek.

Carl entered Zoe's office and took a seat opposite her desk. She surprised him when she got up and sat on the desk in front of him. At least she was appropriately wearing slacks, he thought.

When they finished discussing business, Zoe asked, "I saw an unamerican sign today that said *Remember Ellen.* What does the governor think about such signs?"

"She has ordered the Rangers to get them down."

"That's good," Zoe said as she started to get up but stumbled. He reached out to catch her, but she first grabbed his neck to steady herself.

She thanked him and smiled. Their eyes locked momentarily as he smiled back. In the hallway he noticed his neck was moist where she touched him.

White House

Before the morning White House meeting convened, the president asked his COS, "I heard you on the phone with the VP, what did you tell her?"

"I told her the meeting started at 1:00 pm."

"Good, we don't need her saber-rattling."

When all were assembled the FBI director announced, "We just got a laser feed from the governor's office after your phone call with her."

The president listened to the recorded conversation and said, "We may have had and still have our political differences, but it's nice to see when it comes down to saving the country, she is with us."

"I agree, sir, but I suggest we keep our plant in the governor's mansion," added the CIA director.

"Oh, I'm not saying otherwise. The CIA should continue with the plan."

Fort Hood

Fort Hood is the most populous U.S. military base in the world. It is located southwest of Waco and about fifty miles north of Georgetown. The base, with training area, covers over two hundred thousand acres. It is the headquarters of two Army armored divisions. Forty-five thousand soldiers are assigned there, and over eight thousand civilian employees work on the base.

General Martinez arrived at Fort Hood and immediately assembled the top officers including all brigade commanders. The assembly included Colonels Nancy Everett and John Conner, who under cover had attended the Resistance briefing at the hunting lodge.

He described the mission, "We will send five brigades to encircle a factory near Georgetown. Our mission is to protect the plant while it comes online producing the latest version of PPUs. We see no need for heavy armor; armored brigades will stay here. The perceived threat to the plant is from carrier drones and possibly local Resistance fighters.

Light infantry brigades led by Colonels Dewitt, McAlister, Everett, Donnelly, and Fairview will deploy immediately. By immediately, I mean before the day is over. Highways leading to the facility are being closed to civilian traffic as I speak. A brigade of Texas National Guard is deployed closely encircling the plant. They are well dug in, and we will leave them at that position; but I will be taking full command of the guard units including the guard brigade held in reserve a few miles north of the plant. Are there any questions?"

"How serious do you think the threat is?" asked Colonel Dewitt.

"The Resistance may send a dozen to ambush a truck on the interstate or send an armed drone in a sneak attack, but attack twenty thousand of our best trained, plus ten thousand guardsmen? I do not think so, our deployment will squelch any ideas."

Colonel John Conner caught a slight smile from Colonel Everett as she left to assemble her soldiers. His armored brigade had not been ordered to move which they hoped and expected, while her unarmored brigade had. Although left at Fort Hood, his armored brigade would not be idle.

General Martinez called General Tate of the Texas National Guard in the presence of the general in command of the fort. The commanders of the National Guard brigades in the Georgetown area were patched in the call.

"I know that you are apprehensive about losing your autonomy, which I can understand. Although I will oversee this operation, I will leave operational control to you. You understand the capabilities of your units. The command structure of your brigades will remain intact."

The guard officers were relieved.

The Fort Hood general was not. "Sir, I think you made a mistake not interspersing our officers with theirs. Not doing so may hamper a coordinated effort, and if I read the president's directives correctly, he has instructed us to take charge of the guard units."

The Fort Hood general came from a family of civil servants in Massachusetts. He was not pleased that General Martinez had been sent to take charge of the operation. It was his to handle. Below the surface, he lacked respect for a general who had come up through the ranks from a mid-level 2 university's Reserve Officer Training Corps (ROTC) program.

Even more frustrating to the Fort Hood general was the way Martinez blew him off, "I think the success of the operation is more important than making a political point by stripping the guard units of command."

The Fort Hood general reluctantly bit his tongue.

Austin

The governor and Carl were in the capitol office library on the conference call. Most state Resistance leaders were on the call along with several governors. Both Julie and Governor Archibald gave everyone an update on what was happening around Georgetown.

"To date, all is going according to plan," Julie said. "The only surprise may be a good one. Former CJCS Martinez has been sent to command all operations in the area. He is not with us, but he has indicated reluctance to follow the president's directives. At the very least, he is more preferable leading federal troops than the alternative general."

The newly elected Kansas governor added, "General Martinez's sister is with us. We can contact her and see what she may be able to do."

"Great to hear that," said Julie.

Governor Archibald interjected, "Welcome aboard the governor's circle, Governor. Carl tells me you are from McPhearson. He had a client there."

"Well thank you, but it's McPherson, there is no fear in McPherson."

"I like that attitude," said Julie. "I'm not ignoring Kansas, but I'm traveling by plane for the next few days in a big circle. The hectic agenda is packed with brief meetings. State leaders will give me an audience with the governors of Missouri, Arkansas, Iowa, Indiana, Tennessee, Alabama, Kentucky, Mississippi, and Louisiana.

If all goes according to plan, we are ten days from *FR Day*," Julie tossed the last statement out knowing she would be asked.

"And what is *FR Day?*" asked the governor of Oklahoma.

"It is *Freedom Restoration Day*."

Two evenings later from a hotel room in Des Moines, Julie contacted Governor Archibald in her study off the bedroom. The governor asked, "How did it go in Iowa?"

"Well, I think they are ready, but like many states it will take success on our part to get them to act. A huge amount of dried kindling lies throughout the country, but it is not going to ignite itself. It needs a spark, and Texas must supply that. And how did the meeting with the finance people go this afternoon?" Julie asked the governor.

"I met with our treasury secretary, economic development director, and the president of the former Texas Independent Bankers Association. Much is to be done, but we have a plan. Next week when I get off-site per our plan, they will be joining me with the National Guard paymaster. We must be successful for a number of reasons."

"Yes, there is a lot at stake," commented Julie before she realized the casual over-simplification of her remark.

The governor put it in more graphic terms, "Yes, there is, including our own necks."

Carl needed a nightcap and decided to let the women talk while he headed downstairs. Zoe was in the bar area.

"Let me pour that for you," she said.

With three fingers of Marker's Mark in the tumbler, she stepped toward Carl, but did not extend her arm with the glass. She held it close to her breast. He tentatively reached for it, then stopped. She gave him a brawny, but naughty, smile—then leaned in and kissed him. He accepted her kiss, then pulled his lips from hers.

"I understand the governor is traveling tomorrow. Kind of *hush-hush*. Where is she going? It is my job to help her coordinate activities."

"She has a fundraiser she doesn't want the opposition to know about," he answered.

"Where is it?" she persisted.

Avoiding the question, he leaned into her and returned her kiss. Before she could ask another question, he was gone.

Chapter 10

Having escaped Zoe with only a kiss, Carl, still holding a tumbler, entered the study off the bedroom. Madison was sitting at the desk but staring out the window.

"Where have you been?" she asked.

He tilted the tumbler over his mouth and seemed to squeeze the last drop from it contemplating an answer. "I picked up this drink and was on the phone with Andrew and Barry," he told part of the truth.

"What did you guys discuss?"

"Strategy. What are you doing?"

"Waiting for a call from Julie. Four skeptical governors have agreed to joining in a conference call and Julie wants me to repeat thoughts I spoke to her on our trip."

Carl pulled a chair up to her desk when the conference call started. Introductions were made with the governors of Indiana, Ohio, Idaho, and Utah when the conference call was made.

The Texas governor spoke not as much as a politician, but a philosopher.

"Recently, I thought much about how we got into this mess in the country. Many in our generation may be together today in a quest to restore freedom as have a number of generations who fought for and preserved freedom. Unfortunately, one generation dropped the ball."

"What do you mean by that?" asked the Ohio governor.

"The first generation in this country secured our freedom. Succeeding generations settled the country, built roads and railroads, innovated new technology, and built the most efficient manufacturing plants—all while preserving our liberties.

A generation fought a terrible bloody civil war to extend freedoms to everyone. Generations after that worked to ensure that newfound freedom for some was real. We persevered an economic depression without handicapping the most productive economic system the world has ever known.

We saved the world from the tyranny of national socialism in Europe and simultaneously stopped a military dictatorship in the East. Then we beat back the spread of another form of socialism—communism. We were triumphant. Democracy was spreading around the world, and our economic system spread—raising billions of people from poverty. The adaptation of free markets fostered a large middle class the world had never known.

Then what happened? Our preceding generation got fat and lazy. A little freedom given up here and there, but for security. It was incremental. Most knew better but did nothing. We slowly traded an economic system that worked for one that never has.

Although stifling freedom with authoritarianism has never worked, we would make it work—we were told. American exceptionalism would carry the day. But the irony is those who advocated more government were the least inclined to believe in American exceptionalism. It was progressive we were told; but in the history of the world, moving toward authoritarianism is regressive. It is moving back to the norm when few people make decisions for many before our brief period of liberty and freedom.

I remember my father complaining about encroachments of freedom, but he did nothing. What did his generation do to preserve what they had inherited? They did not have to fight external threats or make strides for more freedom. They only had to preserve what they had been given—they failed. I loved my dad— but damn his generation!

The house we grew up in had a small cedar tree near a sidewalk. A neighbor warned dad that it should be taken out before it heaved the sidewalk. My dad was a do-it-yourself kind of guy, but he also procrastinated. Years later, after I left home the cedar tree had tripled in size and started to buckle the sidewalk. Too late, Dad attempted to take the cedar tree out with a chainsaw, axe, and a shovel. Mother came home and found him dead with a half-dug hole around the tree. Was his life cut short by a heart attack, or his putting off what he knew needed to be done for years?

Now we are challenged to dislodge the creeping vine of authoritarianism from the house that the previous owners have ignored. It will not be easy, but it will be done. Our generation must pay the price for the apathy of the preceding generation. It is our calling."

"Are you insinuating it may be too late to cut the tree down and save the country?" asked the governor of Indiana.

"No. Not at all, but we must decide whether we will ignore the tree squeezing liberty from the country or whether we will act."

With the call ended, Madison said, "How about a glass of wine before bed?"

Carl soon brought her a glass, bypassing Zoe's office on the way back from the bar. His wife's ability to think deep and rationally was what Carl loved about her. Carl was different, he often went with his instincts. Some say opposites attract. Their different personalities meshed well.

Wearing his usual boxers, he hoisted himself onto the king bed beside her and asked, "Are you dreading the call with the president tomorrow?"

"Of course, it will be crossing a heavy line; but we've been crossing smaller ones. However, crossing this line will not allow retreat."

He reached over and held her hand, "Do you wish to preserve the option of retreat?"

"No, we can't. We have no choice."

"Good, we're all in this together, you know."

Finally, Carl felt her hand twitch in his.

"Enough philosophizing, want a distraction?" he asked.

"Absolutely."

The next morning Carl was heading to the capitol to join the governor who had left early. The governor left a suitcase for her trip in her closet to avoid questions among the staff. Carl carried her suitcase to his car and thought he had avoided Zoe until he heard a voice from behind him, "Why the intrigue about the trip?"

"I told you earlier, it's about not revealing too much to the opposition." Immediately, he realized how true his statement was.

Zoe was looking at the suitcase. Carl answered her unspoken question, "She forgot her suitcase. Oh, and I'm sorry about last night."

"Why? I'm not." Her smile made him nervous.

She continued, "By the way, someone I met at breakfast this morning said the Texas Rangers are busy arresting people placing signs, is that true?"

"I don't have time to talk, perhaps later," he answered, tossing the suitcase behind the front seat. "I'll be back alter in the day."

A driver and state vehicle moved the governor between her residence and the capitol. Carl drove himself to avoid criticism that he had too much influence with the governor.

On entering the governor's office, Carl asked, "Did you get the request for a call placed?"

"Yes, they said he was busy but would get to me before noon. I hope so, otherwise it will...." She cut herself off remembering they were likely being overheard.

Noon had passed when she received the callback from the president.

"Thanks for reaching out to me. I saw the video of the Rangers taking down a sign, but my information tells me, other than what is seen on the video, not much is happening to rid the countryside of that hobbit dung."

"I'll contact the Rangers again, but that is not the reason I wanted to speak. We are working together very well on this Georgetown plant protection. I got the sewer approved, our National Guard protected the plant when the Army wasn't there, our National Guard has taken the new pledge, and we are cooperating with interstate electric grid hookups…"

The president interrupted her, "Yes, I'll give you that, but the Department of Energy tells me information about the oil industry in your state has not been forthcoming."

"I'm told it is being worked on. It seems the data is stored in different digital languages."

"So, what is the reason for your call?"

"Although we come from different political backgrounds, we are working together; and I would hope you would cut us some latitude on the National Tax Equalization (NTE) directive."

"And why would I do that? Fairness dictates that citizens in all states pay the same in taxes."

"But citizens in high tax states have put politicians in state offices who spend and waste much. Whereas, states like Texas have been frugal. We are already paying more federal tax, why should we be penalized by paying disproportionately even higher federal taxes? It seems to be penalizing good government and subsidizing spendthrift government."

Except for a few years earlier in the century, federal taxpayers could deduct all their state and local taxes from their income before the federal income tax was calculated. A taxpayer in a high tax state who reported one hundred dollars of income might deduct twenty dollars for state and local states. In which case the taxpayer would only pay federal income tax on eighty dollars.

A taxpayer in a low tax state might only be able to deduct ten dollars for local taxes, so that taxpayer would pay federal income tax on ninety dollars—- twelve and a half percent more federal tax than the taxpayer in the high tax state.

"Governor, there is another issue here— the migration in this country is out of control. We are seeing a separation of people which over time will Balkanize this country economically and politically. The NTE is not as much about raising taxes on people in Texas as it is about controlling migration."

"I get that, but what can you do to cut us some slack on the NTE?"

"If I delay implementation for Texas, what about other states?"

"I only speak for Texas. But it would be helpful to all if we continued to cooperate, rather than the alternative."

"I'll consider it, have a good day," the president said as he ended the call. He fumed, sending an empty coffee cup across the room.

"What's wrong?" his COS entered, carrying a fresh cup.

"I was just given an ultimatum by a governor."

The governor put another fake call into the Rangers about the signs before they went to the library.

"You were wonderful," Julie's voice came from Carl's secure grape, surprising the governor.

"What do you think, Julie? Any chance he'll pull the NTE for a year?"

"If he pulls it, it will only be until the Georgetown plant turns out an ample number of PPUs."

"I'll see you shortly, we'll talk more then," she told Julie as Carl interrupted.

Looking at his watch, Carl said, "I'm leaving now."

Carl held his wife. He could feel her heart throbbing. "You did great."

"Thanks, I'm nervous, but I feel like we've crossed another big hurdle."

He left the governor's office and waited in his car. The car was parked behind the governor's campaign bus, blocking a view of his car from the Capitol.

"It is time to hit the road campaigning," the governor told her staff and a few legislators as she left the capitol building. She walked around the campaign bus as if to enter the bus door but got into Carl's car and left. Within a minute, the bus left for El Paso via a long route— without the governor. FBI agents tracked it on a planted GPS device, and two CIA agents followed it.

Madison turned, reached into the suitcase side pocket, and pulled out a gray wig. Carl, trying to lighten the mood, said it had been years since he had driven his mother around.

"Aren't we a smart aleck today?" she answered, giving him a half-hearted punch on the arm.

A few blocks from the capitol, Carl pulled into a big box parking lot beside a dull white minivan. Torrence jumped out and grabbed her suitcase. Madison kissed her husband goodbye. Julie, Torrence and the governor headed to a hunting lodge— while Carl went back to the residence.

Most of the rooms in the Hunting Lodge were in the main building; but for families who wanted to get away, a few three-bedroom cabins were spread around the premises. The governor, Julie and Torrence would stay unseen in a far cabin while they received visitors.

The following day, the Texas Treasury secretary checked into an adjacent cabin. He would later be joined by the representatives of the former Texas Independent Bankers Association, the state economic development director and National Guard paymaster.

Washington

The president contemplated what to do with the governor's request for delay in implementing the NTE. His advisors were split. Some argued that it would be little to give for the governor's continued co-operation. At the end of the year before tax season, the Georgetown plant would be putting many new PPUs online. Implementation could be delayed until then.

Others argued that it would set bad precedent allowing extortion by a governor. "Where does it end?" one asked. "Does Maine get exemptions on cod fishing, or Iowa on soybean fertilizer?"

Regardless, the decision was his. Making decisions was why he was president instead of them. He often said that a bad decision is frequently better than no decision, but this was not one of those situations.

"Who says we must make a decision and answer her? As part of the declaration of martial law, I decreed implementation of the NTE. No answer is no variance. Let her think we are considering her request. Nothing to lose. If she pushes us for an answer, we are considering her request. The ball is in our court, time is running down, and we will stall.

In the meantime, as martial law commander-in-chief, I have sent an order to General Martinez. It will make a point. She may soon reconsider playing tough with me."

The president looked at the CIA director, "What have you learned from on the ground personnel at the governor's mansion?"

"We've learned that the governor is going on a fundraising trip, but we do not know where."

"Find out."

Fort Hood, Texas

Colonel Conner, commander of a full heavy armored brigade, arrived back from a trip to the Hunting Lodge where he had met the governor, Julie and Torrence. He left with more confidence than ever, particularly after his discussions with Torrence. The Resistance's knowledge of what was happening in Washington was reassuring. Back at Fort Hood, he instructed his brigade to ready themselves in the morning for a weeklong full armor training session around the perimeter of the base.

General Martinez felt comfortable at Fort Hood. Many enlisted men remembered him fondly. Prior to being assigned to the Pentagon, he had spent more time stationed at the base than the two-star major general that presently commanded it. The air continued to be tense around the major general. Minor disagreements about how Martinez deployed soldiers around Georgetown continued to fester. More than once, General Martinez was tempted to remind the general that he wore four stars rather than two.

They were tolerating each other over dinner when a lieutenant orderly to the major general entered the dining room carrying a note, "It's from the president, sir."

Now it was General Martinez who felt slighted when the note was handed to the Fort Hood General, "I see the president continues to shortcut military protocol, bypassing the new CJCS and me."

The two-star general ignored him and read the note out loud after skimming it.

"Under the powers of martial law, I must use all available
means to preserve order. The placement of signs celebrating

a traitor will not be tolerated. No measure is too extreme to protect the common good. I hereby order anyone caught placing one of these signs to be *summarily* executed under martial law."

Both generals sat mulling over the directive from the president in their own mind. How would they implement it? *Summarily* meant without trial, didn't it? How much manpower would it take? How aggressively should they seek out the planters of signs?

No US military procedures had been established for executions in a *summary* manner. In the last century it had been only socialists who had used it, both the national (Nazi) and communist kind. Hoping to find an out, General Martinez pulled out his grape and checked synonyms—at *once, on-the-spot, promptly, arbitrarily, and without delay.*

The major general broke the silence, "Lieutenant, get all the colonels in the field on the phone."

"What are you doing?" asked General Martinez as the lieutenant stood beside them typing a message on his grape.

"We have our orders."

General Martinez motioned to the lieutenant, "Give me that grape."

"But sir..." he answered glancing at his commander.

"That is an order." General Martinez took the grape and dropped in a pitcher of water.

"Sir. are you violating a direct order from the president of the United States?" the major general asked.

"Martial law or not, I took an oath to the Constitution of the United States. Where do we stop? Should you be shot because you part your hair on the wrong side? This order is so outside our traditions, it will be ignored."

"Sir, I may feel bound to report your insubordination to a presidential order."

"I would think twice about that, you are here. The president is not."

General Martinez headed for his room. He stopped at the sentry to the officer's quarters. "How are you tonight, sergeant?"

"Fine, sir."

"Is there anything I should know about this camp that I haven't heard?"

"No, sir, have a fine evening." From the sergeant's tone, General Martinez knew the 'no' was not unequivocal. He would pursue it later. The sergeant regretted not venting about the discord among officers.

From years of deployments around the world, General Martinez had developed a habit of checking his room daily. With an app on his grape, he scanned the room. No surveillance devices were found.

While the general was checking his room, Colonel Everett, stationed around Georgetown, received a frightening order from the two-star base commander. She immediately contacted Mason Trotter.

General Martinez had finished reviewing Fort Hood personnel files and was thinking about bed when his grape vibrated, and a picture of his sister appeared on it. He pointed the grape toward the monitor on his small desk, and a better picture of her appeared.

"How is everything in Kansas, Sis?"

"Fine, I talked to Camila today and she seems thrilled to be in her brother's practice."

Martinez's sister was five years younger. She looked up to him, and it was earned. In school she had been picked on for wearing glasses. Perhaps their parents placed more emphasis on function than style in choosing her glasses. The teasing stopped after her brother's frank discussion with her provocateurs. Sympathetic to the Resistance, she had discouraged him from taking the assignment in Texas.

"You told us that your taking command of the situation in Texas would mitigate those with more extreme tendencies. I respected that," she said.

"Yes, that is right, but I know you have more to say."

"We know about the appalling order you received. Last week, I placed a sign on the farm near the road. Should I be worried? Am I to be shot?"

General Martinez was taken back that his sister in Kansas knew of the order within a couple hours of it being delivered to him.

"I don't know how you found out about that order, and I won't ask. But A—-it only was directed to the Georgetown area, and B—- it will not be carried out."

"Are you sure about that?"

Before he could answer, she continued, "Do you remember the guy from Idaho who warned NASA about the asteroid back in '38?"

"Vaguely, he kind of disappeared; Collins, or something like that."

"Collier, Andrew Collier, I'm going to patch him in."

Suddenly the monitor screen was split—his sister on one side, Andrew on the other. "General, we have received intelligence that your orders to ignore the presidential directive have been circumvented. Thirty minutes ago, orders were given by the base commander to start looking for sign placers in the morning."

Barry, Torrence and Andrew had studied the general's file and background with psychiatrists on the Resistance ship. His family connections, his resignation because of the mock trial, and other personality traits determined he was a risk worth taking. It was a risk, but timidity and playing it safe would not restore liberty.

"Again, I wonder how you know that, but I will check it out. I will either rescind the order or resign."

"General, we do not want you to resign. Plans are in the works. American liberty will not again be the prey of vultures in the sky."

"That is a bold statement, how do you plan to do that?"

"Did you meet Colonel Connor?"

"Yes, he is in maneuvers with the 137th armored brigade in the field."

"Are you right or left-handed, General?"

"Left, why?"

"Pull up your aerial status map of the brigade and watch for a few minutes."

Martinez could see Andrew talking to someone at his side. The app showed one hundred twenty tanks of the 137th in formation heading due south at twenty miles per hour. Within minutes they all made an abrupt turn to the east.

"Okay, they turned left, coincident? The general tried to ignore the message.

"And I also assume you meant Colonel Everett. Her brigade you deployed to the Georgetown area. Do you see three lights in a triangle shinning upward from the brigade formation?"

"Yes."

"Are there now six lights in a hexagon?"

"What do you want from me?"

"We need your help."

The general took a deep breath. He tilted his head back, looking up at the blank ceiling, hoping to see something, perhaps writing—he did not know why. He lowered his head, still searching for answers. Finally, he looked inside himself, gut maybe. He felt a warmth. Camile often told him he should rely on instincts when he contemplated major decisions. Was his allegiance to his commander or something greater? Who was his commander? Perhaps we are connected by conduit to something greater. The warmth became a fire giving him the answer.

"Okay, I'm with you, but I need to know everything."

"Great, let me start from the beginning."

"No, not now, I have an order to rescind."

When General Martinez reached for his jacket, he caught movement under the door. As he pulled his jacket on, he partially covered his face and discreetly saw a snakelike appendage out six inches from the bottom of the door. He knew immediately that someone had inserted a lens and was watching him.

He headed toward the bathroom then hugged the wall out of the lens's view and skirted toward the door. Reaching from the side, he carefully turned the door handle. Once the lock disengaged, he leaped in front of the door and kicked it with all his might.

The lieutenant tumbled backward toward the opposite hallway wall. The general's hand grabbed the stunned lieutenant's collar as his heel ground into the grape attached to the lens appendage.

"You are under arrest," the general spit at him.

The lieutenant was the son of second-generation university teachers in California. As factory workers turned out precision machines, universities had turned out tuned, sculptured minds for a generation. His grandparents would have abhorred his decision to join the military. The military had changed. Influence gained him a position as orderly to the commanding general of the Fort. He was on the fast track.

The general marched him to the sentry at the end of the hallway and told the sergeant, "He's under arrest, take him to the lock up."

The sergeant gladly followed the order. He had too often been treated like a serf in a better's fiefdom by the lieutenant.

General Martinez stopped at an MP station and gathered three to follow him. He found the two-star general in his office with another orderly. "Have you circumvented my orders?"

"The question is, did you circumvent the president's orders?"

"You are under arrest, general. Take him away," he directed the MPs. Like the sergeant, they were happy to take the arrogant man who had treated them like lower life forms.

"Lieutenant, get all the field commanders on the phone immediately," demanded General Martinez.

Chapter 11

White House

The president was livid. The Pentagon could not reach the Fort Hood general, and General Martinez would not answer his grape. Neither could the White House staff reach either.

"Must I go down there myself to see what's happening?" the president challenged the new CJCS.

"We are picking up reports, sir."

"What is it. Can't anyone here be straight with me?"

"No one has seen the commander of Ft. Hood for twenty-four hours, and there have been no reports of anyone caught placing signs. Indications are your order was not passed on."

"What about that blasphemous governor? The timing of her attempt at coercing me and this mutiny cannot be coincidental."

The CIA director added, "I wouldn't call it mutiny; we don't know enough. And our source in the governor's mansion has been told to find out where the governor is, whatever it takes."

"The good news is there have been no more drone attacks on the Georgetown plant, and intelligence has found no evidence of plots," said the CJCS. The general learned early in his career to always finalize any report to superiors with good news—no matter the stretch.

The president turned to the FBI director, "I understand Martinez's wife is a doctor in Wichita. Have her picked up for questioning. I suspect she knows why the general will not answer his grape. Perhaps he will when he discovers we've picked her up."

While the president was fretting about his lack of control, Andrew was detailing the plan with General Martinez. The general's wife, sister, the Kansas governor, and the state's Resistance leader were also on the call. The general was impressed with the planning but also skeptical. Bottom line, he figured it was too late to back out; he lived in Kansas now and as always was a Kansan. At the end of a conference call, Andrew suggested the general's wife, his sister and her husband leave Wichita. Later that day, they left Wichita for a mountain cabin of a friend in Colorado.

Austin

The study off the bedroom was Carl's workstation at the residence in his wife's absence. He kept abreast of happenings on his grape tuned to the small desk monitor. Occasionally, he toured the mansion, careful that no one was checking on him. Doing so, he ran into Zoe often. She was wearing a black pencil skirt and white blouse. Not something a correctly dressed woman would wear in public. But she was not in public, and her dress was fine with Carl. He also noticed that her legs glistened, she was wearing nylons— a throwback to an earlier time. He was careful to only pass the time-of-day with her.

His secure grape looked like any grape, but the secure ones had been modified at the Resistance ship in many ways. Their transmissions were in code, and in addition to their failsafe destruction mechanism, they contained a small storage chip limited to five hundred megabytes of data. The non-modified grapes everyone carried had no storage capacity. Private data storage had been outlawed. All data storage was on the cloud to which the government had access. Although in theory, the government still had access to all data in the cloud; in practice, the destruction of NSA facilities eliminated their ability to analyze citizen data.

Engineers on the ship had provided the means to back up data outside the secure grape's limited capacity. They used an antiquated storage device that had been called a flash drive. Carl saw that his grape storage was near capacity.

In a small closet off the hallway to the bathroom from the bedroom, he retrieved an eight-foot step ladder. In the ceiling at the foot of the bed was an access hole and cover to the attic. The mansion's maintenance man had said the ladder could be stored elsewhere, but Carl insisted that it stay available to him.

With the downloaded flash drive in his pocket, Carl climbed the ladder, set the hole cover aside, reached across a ceiling joist and retrieved a ziplock sandwich bag from under twelve inches of blown in fiberglass insulation.

After adding the flash drive to the bag and putting it back in place, he heard someone say, "What are you doing up there?"

He looked down and saw Zoe standing beneath him looking up. His surprise that she had entered their bedroom without knocking, added to the shock of being caught, caused him to stammer an answer before he thought, "Just checking the traps. Madison thinks rats are up here."

"Don't we have exterminators for that?"

"Yeah, but I'm a do-it-yourself guy, and" he stammered again, "Madison doesn't want it known that she may have a phobia."

Uninvited, Zoe was now sitting on the edge of the bed, and he was off the ladder.

"How are the governor's fundraisers going?"

"As well as can be expected."

"When will she be back?"

"This is not a good place to talk," he said nervously as his eyes had trouble avoiding her nylon-clad legs.

She reached down, coyly smiled at him, and slowly lifted the hem of her skirt until the top of her nylon stockings and the garter straps to which they were attached were exposed. "I know these are so passe, but they feel so good on my legs. Why shouldn't people do what feels good?"

Now knowing their plan could not be delayed, he composed himself, took a step toward her, and ran his hand over her knee, leaned in and kissed her. The short kiss was meant to step up his question, "Do you have a more private place where I might answer some of your questions later?"

"Sure," she whispered.

She left the room once they had settled on 8 pm. It was already 4 pm, and he had a lot to do.

When she was safely gone, Carl used a washcloth and soap to remove the moisture she had put around his neck and contacted Mason.

Georgetown

In the plant, machinery movers were finished, and all CNC machines and tooling were set in place. Electricians had completed all wiring. Computers containing the software to build the new version 3.0 PPUs were connected. Next week, the machines would be tested. The following week, software engineers and machinists would train operating the machinery. In another week, they would be producing the new eyes in the sky.

Plant inspectors had gone for the day. Everything was in order; all boxes on their inspection sheets had been checked OK. In Texas, bribery tips were not required to pass perfunctory inspection checks as they were in many states.

Texas National Guard Captain Michaels handpicked a few men to work in the plant that evening. A forklift entered the building and placed a pallet in the middle of the floor. The next trip another pallet was placed beside it. The pallets were from the ninth truck delivering machinery to the plant.

Once the pallets were placed, a small rubber-tracked dozer entered and started pushing machinery and tooling toward the pallets. In the process, machine anchors to the floor were torn loose. Conduits of electric wiring and fiberoptic cable were ripped and torn like spider webs. Sounds of tearing and the screeching of heavy machinery scrapping on concrete as it was pushed echoed in the plant. The dozer continued until all CNC machines, lathes and presses were piled in a tight circle around the pallets. What had earlier looked like a state of the art, new machining factory now looked like a giant pile of rubble.

The dozer left, and the forklift returned carrying other pallets. They were placed along exterior walls. Thirty men entered, members of both the Texas National Guard and the Texas Resistance. They broke the pallets open and placed the contents of cardboard boxes ten feet apart around the interior circumference of the building while others wired them together.

As work was going on inside the plant, the brigade surrounding the plant was packing up. Only the positions that could be seen by a federal army surveillance post stayed in place. Everything else was loaded on trucks and ready for departure. By sunlight, 5,000 guardsmen were ready to move.

Austin

Carl left the governor's residence in his small electric car and parked in the parking lot of a bar where he sometimes met friends. Instead of entering the bar, he moved to another electric car left there by Mason, drove to the warehouse, and met Barry and Mason. Barry gave Carl two different colored capsules; he swallowed one and put the other in his pocket. Mason left soon.

Zoe was in her rented townhome. The tracking device she had planted on Carl's car showed him at a bar. *That was good*, she thought, *liquor would loosen his tongue.*

Assured by Mason all was clear, Carl left and drove back to the bar parking lot, returned to his car, and drove to Zoe's. Zoe saw that he had left the bar and was headed toward her— all was good. Carl saw Mason parked in a Trotter electric van across the street from Zoe's place. Mason nodded to him as Carl passed. The driveway to her garage was empty, as they had hoped. He parked in the street.

Carl rang the doorbell. "It's open, come in," her voice came from the doorbell monitor. He entered but did not see her, then a voice came from another room, "I'm in here." He entered her bedroom. She lay in bed under a comforter. He stood with one hand in his pocket, pondering what to do.

She tossed the comforter from her. She was wearing only the nylons she wore earlier.

"Do my nylons look better this way?"

He hesitated. Mason and Carl had not envisioned this scenario.

"Don't be bashful, join me."

He pulled his hand from his pants, stripped to his underwear, and crawled into bed with her. As he lay beside her, his lips found hers. She missed his hand moving to his mouth as he lost his clothes.

Once Carl was in the townhouse, Mason backed the van up to the garage door and waited. He did not have any way to verify Carl was ready. It had been decided he would only wait five minutes. He held a universal door opener and watched the van clock move five minutes.

With Carl's lips firmly meshed to hers, he pushed a capsule between his front teeth, crushed it and blew its contents into her mouth. She struggled tasting the sour liquid and pounded his shoulder with her fist, but not for long. When she quieted, Carl got up and spit multiple times, hoping the antidote was effective. He was relieved that her struggle did not last long.

Weeks earlier, Carl sent her resume picture to Barry. Facial recognition software could not find a match in the Resistance's data base but linked into the Polish database she was found. They had identified her as a CIA operative, who had been uncovered after her martial arts skills killed two Polish agents.

Mason entered the bedroom, asked Carl if he was okay, then saw Zoe passed out on the bed. "Wow," he said to no one in particular.

They rolled her up in the comforter and carried her to the garage. Mason lifted the garage door and walked around the van. Seeing the street was clear and no one was on the sidewalk or peering from windows, he opened the back door to the van, and they quickly loaded her. In a warehouse storage room, they pulled her arm from the comforter wrap and chained it to a support column.. She was starting to wake up.

"Are you going to leave me like this?"

"Yep," Carl replied as he closed the storage door. He returned later with a sweatshirt and pants of Julie's and tossed them at her.

She rattled the chain on her arm. "How do you expect me to put those on like this?"

He remembered that she had killed two Polish agents with her hands. "You'll figure something out."

Carl stayed in the warehouse until morning. No one slept there, or in the hunting lodge cabins, the brigade around the Georgetown plant, the commander's headquarters at Fort Hood, or at other connected places around the country.

At some point amongst the flurry of activity during the night, the governor asked Carl if all had gone according to plan with Zoe's abduction. He replied, "Not exactly, but the spy was silenced."

"What went awry?" she asked.

"I'll fill you in later. We've much more important things to think about," Carl answered, wondering how long the bruises from Zoe's pounding would last on his shoulder.

Georgetown Plant

It was half past six when the commander of the National Guard brigade surrounding the Georgetown plant received orders from General Tate to leave according to plan. Trucks with heavy equipment moved out first, headed north. Soldiers manning barricades around the perimeter stayed; but empty transport vehicles were left close by, so their exit could be hasty.

At 7:00 CDT, 8:00 EDT, the governor of Texas contacted the White House and requested immediate access to the president. The president received the request within five minutes.

"Since when do I bow to 'an immediate' request from a governor?" he asked his COS. "She's pushing me for an answer to the NTE declaration— we'll blow it off."

Thirty minutes later he received word from the Pentagon that the National Guard brigade around the plant was moving heavy equipment out.

"Who in the Pentagon ordered them to move?" the president asked.

"No one here, sir, we just assumed you did from the White House."

"Find out why they are moving and get back with me in five!" barked the president.

It was more than five minutes before he got an answer, "Mr. President, we finally were able to reach the colonel of the vacating guard unit," the new CJCS was reluctant to continue.

"So, what did you find out? This is not a hide the answer game."

"He said the governor had ordered them to vacate."

"They don't answer to the governor any longer, did you tell him that?"

The president slammed the phone and turned to his COS. "Get me that fool governor on the phone!"

The president was able to calm himself before Governor Archibald was on the line. "Madame Governor, why is the National Guard leaving the Georgetown plant? You know you do not have control of them under martial law."

"What did you decide about the NTE directive?"

"Governor, that is unrelated. Why did you direct the Guard to move?"

"Sir," the governor's voice firmed while her back straightened. "I will send the Guard back if you agree to no NTE, keep the DOE out of our oil and gas business, and move your vulture plant somewhere else."

He asked her to repeat what she had said, unable to accept what she had demanded and needing time to formulate an answer. The president knew the PPUs were called vultures by many Cretins, but no one had called them that to his face.

"Look, Lady, that is enough! Do you know who you are speaking to? You have obviously lost your shallow mind. You will be arrested. I hope for your sake a mental retardation defense will be successful."

He ended the conversation, with his head spinning. Governor Archibald felt amazingly better as if an anvil had lifted from her shoulders.

Phones were ringing in the Oval Office as the president's head continued to spin in shock. "What is it now?" He barked at his COS.

"The Pentagon says the rest of the brigade around the plant is leaving, abandoning their sandbag barricades."

The president himself picked up another ringing phone, "What? Who is this?"

"CIA ,sir, we want to inform you that our operative inside the governor's mansion is missing."

He smashed the receiver into its cradle. With his face reddening, he turned to the FBI director, "Send a swat team to the Texas governor's mansion and seize it. Arrest the governor, her husband and anyone they are with."

This time it was the vacating National Guard commander who called the federal Army colonel. "Sir, do not move your forces closer to the facility."

"Why, do you have any idea what trouble you are in? I've been ordered to arrest you."

"Be that as it may, keep your soldiers away for at least ten minutes."

The colonel anticipated what was to happen and put his anti-aircraft crews on high alert, but the danger was not from above. He was searching the sky for drones with binoculars when he felt the shock wave before the sound. A cloud of debris was in the air—fortunately the only soldier wounded was standing close to a sewer manhole cover when it blew off and broke his arm.

Fort Hood

Colonel Connor's armored brigade, that had been on maneuvers inside the perimeter of the 330 square mile Fort Hood base, broke out and deployed with 120 top-line tanks in a defensive position directly south of the base. The National Guard brigade deployed north of the Georgetown plant moved north and joined Colonel Connor's position. Soon the Guard brigade that had abandoned close defense of the Georgetown plant also joined in defense of the Fort Hood Army base. An armored unit and nearly 15,000 soldiers now guarded the base from the south from a potential attack by forces still under federal control.

Colonel Everett's Army brigade moved in the opposite direction of the Guard brigades. Her brigade headed south for Austin.

Inside the Fort Hood base, General Martinez assembled 2,200 officers who had not been deployed around the Georgetown plant. His address was broadcast to all enlisted soldiers, families, and civilian employees of the base.

"If you have heard rumors that the former commanding general of this base has been arrested, it is true. He ignored a direct order from me to disallow a presidential directive to execute citizens on sight for expressing their first amendment rights. I, as all of you, have taken a pledge to support and defend the Constitution of the United States. Yes, we have a commander-in-chief, but when his actions clearly violate the Constitution, it is our duty to defend the Constitution. The Constitution long predated this president.

However, I will not force my interpretation of the events upon anyone. If your conscience requires you to follow the president in his use of unlimited powers under martial law, you will not be arrested or looked upon unkindly. You may leave at once, unfettered in your exit except you may take no weapons or equipment. Those who remain here in twenty-four hours will be expected to follow my orders subject to court martial if they choose otherwise."

After the address, General Martinez had the fort commander and his lieutenant orderly brought from confinement to his office.

"I heard your address—obviously treason. I will be happy to preside over your firing squad!" growled the general through teeth that were nearly clinched.

"Yeah, well, don't get too anxious; it will not be today. Both of your wives are waiting in your personal cars. I suggest you leave immediately; otherwise, you will be taken back into confinement."

Half the officers and enlisted soldiers at the base were members of the Resistance, had family members who were, or were sympathetic to the Resistance. Many did not understand the political situation but had been stationed at the base for a long time, their family resided there, and it had become home. Some were indecisive; less than five percent left the base in twenty-four hours.

White House

The PPU plant soon to be online producing the means to keep the citizenry in line was gone. Mutiny had taken place at the largest military base in the world; and a governor was obviously opposing him, probably leading the rebels. *"What else could go wrong?"* thought the president.

Without a firm hand to guide them for the common good, oafish common people would revert to survival of the fittest mode. An unchallenged military mutiny could precipitate a universal standdown, tempting Polish and Ukrainian democratic freedom forces to confront the top down well-managed societies in Western Europe. And if one governor was successful in rebellion, others could follow.

A carrot and stick— no it was time to apply a carrot and cannon. "Get the Texas governor on the phone," the President told his COS, confident he was now under control of his faculties.

"Where are you, Governor?"

"I'm in Texas, Mr. President."

He ignored her slight. "I think we can come to an understanding here, Governor. You have my promise the NTE will not be implemented in Texas for three years, nor will the DOE take control of your oil industry in that time. However, you will not acknowledge this, and you will fully employ the National Guard to have General Martinez arrested."

"What about other well-run states and the NTE? Who's to say in three years we will not have the same disagreement? No, Mr. President, General Martinez is a hero. If you persist in restricting the freedom of Texans, perhaps someday the Texas flag will fly over Fort Hood."

"That is a full-scale rebellion. Fort Hood is national property...."

The governor interrupted him. "No Mr. President, it is now Texas property, taken as restitution for Texas paying more federal tax than others for years."

"That is ridiculous, you sound as crazy as that woman who called me before the NSA explosions."

"She's right here if you'd like to speak with her, Mr. President."

The line went dead as the receiver bounced off the Oval Office wall.

Austin

A joint FBI and ATF swat team of 200 was assembled. FBI office personnel that had previously worked in the field were also summoned. They approached the governor's mansion to find it surrounded by a Texas Ranger complement.

The mansion was encircled by a fence with brick column posts every ten feet and wrought iron fencing between. The closed entry gate with a large Texas star hung from oversized brick columns and twenty feet of decorative brick wall in each direction. A circle driveway led to the front door. Rangers had formed a perimeter around the building with state vehicles— blocking the front door—and were using the vehicles as barricades to shield themselves. FBI SWAT team members took up positions behind the brick fence columns.

From a bullhorn, the FBI station chief stated, "Please stand down. We have direct orders from the president to take possession of this building and arrest the governor."

The director of the Texas Rangers bullhorned him back, "We have orders from the governor to prevent you from doing that. Go home."

After a nudge from another Ranger, he added, "Or you may come and get her, your choice."

The FBI swat team outnumbered the Rangers but would not take the bait. They would wait them out. On the roof of a two-story building a block away, an FBI sharpshooter set his high-velocity rifle with a 9X scope on a tripod. He trained it on a dining room window.

They assumed but did not know whether the governor was inside. She remained at the hunting lodge cabin. Only Carl, Audrey the cook, and a member of the cleaning staff were inside the governor's mansion.

Assured that the Ranger contingent could hold off the FBI/ATF swat team, other Rangers away from the mansion and Resistance members headed for the FBI Austin office near the capitol. Eric, who had spent his last vacation in Iowa protecting a railroad tie dump, led the storming of the office. Two agents ignored warnings to surrender and fired at the inbound Rangers. It was their last mistake.

Chapter 12

White House

The president sat at the White House Cabinet table with a bipartisan special martial law committee of senators. He outlined what he had offered the Texas Governor to avoid any further trouble. All agreed that his offer to the governor was generous, given what had happened; but none believed he would follow through on it if accepted. Most of the senators—opposition party or not—he owned either by knowledge about their getting rich at the public trough, campaign irregularities, or bizarre sexual proclivities. None too soon for the president, the meeting ended.

With the senators gone, seven members of his cabinet remained. "Give me the status of the military situation in Texas," barked the president at the CJCS.

"It appears General Martinez has, at best from our perspective, only neutralized the soldiers at Fort Hood. At worst case, they will fight under his orders. Although he allowed those unwilling to follow his orders to leave, few left.

One armored Army brigade and two Texas Guard brigades have established defensive positions south of Fort Hood. We have four brigades around the destroyed plant. They are all waiting for orders except one brigade that is heading for Austin."

"Why is one brigade heading for Austin?" asked the president.

"The brigade is headed by a Colonel Everett. At her discretion, she is, in her words, *positioning closer to the source of trouble.* We consider her move without orders reckless and improper, Mr. President."

"Get her on a line. I want to talk to her."

How quickly she was on the line surprised even the president. "This is the President of the United States. Colonel Everett, why are moving your brigade toward Austin without orders?"

She answered, "Given the rebellion at hand and without orders to stand, I felt it prudent to move closer to the rebel leadership and meet the challenge."

The president looked around the conference room. It was obvious none wished to be in Colonel Everett's shoes, and all were thinking of ways to distance themselves from her. His advisors who, without their drab attire, sterile demeanor, and unrelenting adherence to established protocol, might have been humorless court jesters in the past, thought the president. Have we really progressed? He would make a point.

"We need more initiative from leaders like you, General!"

"Thank you, Mr. President, but it is colonel."

"No, it is now General Everett."

Boldness was one of the reasons he sat in the White House. He knew when to use audacious gestures to make an example. The point was made to others in the room.

"Okay, this is what we will do. Everett's brigade is headed for Austin, have another brigade follow under Everett's command. They are to take control of the capitol. The other two brigades will head for Fort Hood and wait for backup. How soon and how many airborne divisions can we get to Texas?"

Austin

General Everett was at the suburbs of Austin when the president called. Contrary to what she told the president, her mission was to defend Austin from potential federal attack. Her movement to

Austin had been conceived in Resistance planning sessions. The president had promoted her under the false assumption she was preparing for an offensive into Austin. She was shortly in contact with Generals Martinez and Tate. They were astonished at the fortuitous development.

"Instead of being court-martialed for sedition, I'm given a promotion and another brigade to command! Someone big is on our side, Generals!" she burst in confidence.

"I think you hit that right, General— yes, General, get used to it. But what do you know about the commander of the brigade joining you?"

"He's from Oregon, I've never discussed the Resistance with him; but he has always struck me as a *follow-the-rules* kind of guy."

"I suggest you remain in an offensive formation and wait until he joins you to assume defensive posture. No use giving him a heads up. If he balks—as you now outrank him— you can relieve him. Know though that we are not arresting anyone unnecessarily. We allow them to leave without equipment, or in his case without followers. Remember, our greater movement is about freedom of association, not coercion.

It had been a stalemate for hours at the governor's mansion. Even well-armed and trained agents would not do well storming the building guarded by Texas Rangers. The use of tear gas to remove the Rangers was not an option as they were outdoors on a windy day. Perhaps, the Rangers were bluffing, but no one on the front line hoped to hear a charge order.

The FBI sharpshooter on an adjacent roof received word that two at the regional office had been killed in a shootout. He did not know them well but had a drink with one a month earlier. In three prior hostage situations, he had been in position with the H-S Precision HRT (Hostage Rescue Team) .308 sniper rifle. Fortunately for him, he thought, he had never been given the order to fire. Little activity had appeared in the large plate dining room window his rifle was trained on. He had seen the governor's husband pass by, but no one else.

In the White House, the president was appraised of the standoff in Austin.

"The governor must be arrested. The longer this goes on, the more other governors will be tempted to do idiotic things. Stopping it now, this rebellion will die like a chopped vine."

"We must assume the Rangers will defend the mansion. Storming it would cause great loss of life, Mr. President," offered his COS.

"Test them out," ordered the president.

Three FBI agents each fired four rounds at Ranger positions, intentionally shooting high. They hoped it would be enough to cause the Rangers to stand down. It did not. The Rangers returned fire, also aiming high. A bullet from a Ranger handgun struck high on the brick column behind which an FBI agent had taken cover. The lead bullet fractured a brick on the edge of the column, sending a walnut-sized chunk of brick at the agent's shoulder above his armor vest. The wound was superficial, but he bled heavily.

Now with a man injured in an exchange of bullets without surrender of the defenders, something had to be done to maintain Federal supremacy. The order was given to use an alternative.

A maintenance worker, Audrey and Carl were in the kitchen when they heard gunfire. Audrey had a tray of her famous caramel pecan rolls in the oven. It took her mind off activities outside, and the aroma gave Carl something else to think about. The maintenance man suggested they should close all the drapes. He headed for the entryway, Carl headed toward the living room, and Audrey peeled an apron from her midnight blue top and gray slacks and went to the dining room.

The sharpshooter saw a tall, auburn-haired woman grab a drape and pull it to the center of the wide dining room window. He had never met the governor but had seen her on TV often. He knew she was tall with auburn hair. She reached for the drape on the other side of the window and stood facing him, almost daring him. He had been given his orders. With the scope's crosshairs intersecting slightly on the left side of her chest, he squeezed the trigger. When he refocused his eyes from the recoil of the high-powered rifle, she was out of view. It was just as well, he thought.

The maintenance man and Carl returned to the kitchen. They heard the shot—one this time, not many— perhaps that was a good sign. Audrey had not returned, but she would soon to mind the rolls. Slowly the tempting aroma of the rolls turned to a burnt smell. Carl pulled the tray from the oven. Blackened or not, the maintenance man cut himself a roll. It was not like Audrey to ignore something in the oven. Carl left the kitchen to find her.

Carl's search for Audrey started at the women's room off the hallway. He knocked, no answer. He headed down the hall, and at second glance saw pink splattered on the dining room wall across the table from the window. In the room, a closer look showed the splatter contained chucks of something. He turned and saw a spider web of cracks spread from a hole in the window. *'What could a stray bullet hit on the table to cause that?'* he momentarily thought, involuntarily hoping for an alternative answer. Moving around the table, a midnight blue lump on the floor yanked him to reality. Carl soon added to the mess in the dining room at the far corner of the room.

Halfway composed, Carl summoned a Ranger from the front door. The Ranger called the coroner while Carl contacted the hunting lodge. Madison was devastated, not just because she knew the bullet was intended for her; but Audrey had become a friend and she was a real person, earning a living through work with pride.

The FBI SWAT team gave the coroner's van no trouble as it went through the gate and parked near the front door. The Texas Rangers stood at attention and saluted as the body was loaded. A few members of the SWAT team also saluted the van as it drove out.

The leader of the Texas Ranger contingent walked to the front gate. He was met by the FBI SWAT team leader. The Ranger only said, "You can leave now."

"Nothing we'd like to do more, but we've been ordered to arrest the governor's husband and take any advisors the governor had inside for questioning."

The Ranger did not answer but turned and walked back to his position behind a vehicle. He radioed Ranger headquarters, "They are not finished."

It was but an hour before the media mob were all spewing the same story. A shoot-out had taken place around the Texas Governor's mansion. Hostile forces had fired upon federal forces. A federal officer had been seriously injured. Workers charged with enforcing the common good reluctantly returned fire. The governor of Texas, who was leading the assault by firing from a window, was accidentally hit by gunfire. It was unclear whether the bullet came from the rebel force or government forces.

Given experience with past distortions, few believed the reports were factually correct. Some believed the greater context of the story was true, at least they preferred it to be true. Others believed some segment of the story might bear a semblance of the truth. But a plurality of the public did not buy any of it.

The governor heard a variety of opinions about how to handle the tragedy. Some argued to let the public think the governor had been killed for as long as possible. They cited the advantage of the diversion lessening security concerns. Julie carefully avoided giving an opinion, as it was the governor's decision. Carl understood his wife well enough to know what her approach would be.

"Barry, how soon can you set up a hijack of the media cable and airways?" the governor asked.

"We could do it in a few hours, but know we cannot do it often without being shutout."

"I understand, but this is important. However advantageous it might be to let them assume Audrey's death was mine, I cannot tarnish her memory by hiding behind her death to protect myself."

"Noted," he said. "Three hours, we'll be ready."

Julie was anything but a film choreographer, and the cabin was anything but a studio. Torrence hung a white sheet over the wall so their location could not be identified. The governor sat in a chair with the small lodge cabin desk pulled in front of her. Under advice from experienced people on the ship, Julie moved closer to the governor with her grape to avoid showing more of the desk. A closeup shot gave the appearance of seriousness.

"Fellow citizens, I am Madison Archibald, the Governor of Texas. I am being filmed now in the present, as you can see, I am very much alive. To paraphrase a past American, reports otherwise have been greatly exaggerated. Beside the exaggeration, reports of what happened in Austin are outright falsehoods.

Let me first speak of the catastrophe that did happen. A wonderful lady—a cook at my residence, mother of school children— was mistaken for me as she attempted to draw drapes closed. On orders straight from Washington, a sniper brutally ended her life. The force that snuffed out her life remains surrounding the residence attempting to arrest, possibly also murder my husband and others in the building.

Whatever issues the president has with me, let us talk about it. I should be allowed to present my side of the case. That is the way it was intended to work in this country, a free exchange of ideas. As the president uses fear to keep people in line, he too fears the validity of an opponent's cause. If confident of his ideas and merit of his methods, it would follow that he would be anxious to present his case. However, the president does not want to win the argument, he wishes to end the argument. In this case, he does so cowardly with a bullet followed by propaganda."

Fort Bragg, North Carolina

Fort Bragg was known as the "Home of the Airborne." The major unit was the XVIII Airborne Corps. One of the sub-units was the famous 82nd Airborne Division in which most had recently returned from the Nebraska deployment.

Upon orders from the White House, those airborne units on continuous standby were sent to Texas in the middle of the night, but their numbers were unusually light. Of the 10,000 expected to be sent that night, only 8,000 were reported as sent. But officers fearful of the consequence of under delivery exaggerated the numbers— only 7,000 actually arrived. Armored personnel carriers and batteries were parachuted from cargo planes. Three cargo planes carrying fifteen battle tanks, unable to land at Fort Hood, landed at the Waco airport sixty miles away.

General Martinez expected tanks would join the airborne deployment from Fort Bragg. The Waco and Austin airports were similar distance from Fort Hood. He correctly assumed that the more densely populated Austin airport would be avoided.

An order from Washington closing the Waco airport to civilian traffic made it easier for two companies sent by General Martinez to lay in wait for the tank transports. A lieutenant colonel and 200 soldiers were charged with making sure the tanks were not unloaded. The transport carriers were surrounded upon landing; and after an hour of negotiation, the tanks and crews were on their way back to Fort Bragg. With the transports back in the air, the Fort Bragg soldiers had other work to do at the airport.

Mason joined Eric and Kelly on a country road south of Fort Hood. It was the first time Eric and Kelly had been together since their Iowa experience in the railroad tie dump. The three watched parachutes fall from the nighttime sky. The parachutes were falling due north of their position, but closer than they hoped. Suddenly by moonlight they saw over-sized parachutes deploy south of their position. They raced to what was being dropped.

When they reached the dropped armored personnel carriers and cannon batteries, a dozen young men were busy. The farm field soil was dry and powdery. The young men were pouring the sandy clay soil into vehicles' oil reservoirs. They had treated over half of the vehicles when Eric, Kelly and Mason reached them.

The trio heard of the plan and had come to hasten the boys' exit before they were caught. They spread out telling the young men, "Okay, enough! You've done well, but it is not worth getting caught."

Before they left, paratroopers caught Eric and four young men as they headed for their car.

"What are you doing here?" barked the sergeant.

"The boys were curious. We never see anything like this," answered Eric.

"We may want to join up someday," offered one of the young men. "It looks neat falling from the sky."

"Search them," he told two privates.

Finding no weapons or anything of concern on the young men and Eric other than dirty hands, they were told to leave.

When an engine is started cold, it is normal for the oil pump to bypass the oil filter momentarily. Dirt and sand will soon destroy the internal bearings of an engine. One third of the engines were soon inoperable. And the young men were gone.

At Fort Bragg, more transport carriers were ready for departure the next morning, and the 82nd transports were back ready to transport more soldiers to Texas. It was believed that the entire corps of 30,000 soldiers deployed to Texas would intimidate the rebels and prevent a standoff.

Soldiers not on immediate standby were given notice to be ready to move out in the morning. That evening, many huddled with their families or sat in a bar and saw the Texas governor's message. Of the nearly 20,000 expected to leave Fort Bragg that morning, only about 15,000 showed up. Rumors had spread from the Nebraska encounter about the uncomfortable predicament of facing fellow citizens and the possibility of being ordered to fire upon them. Many turned in sick, some did not acknowledge receiving notification and others ignored the order.

Of the 15,000 who loaded for Fort Hood in the second wave, only a few thousand were to be parachuted. Others would land at the Waco airport. The airport remained closed to the public. The old Lockheed Martin C-5M Super Galaxy aircraft could carry 500 soldiers plus or minus depending on the amount of equipment. The first C-5M in route radioed the Waco tower asking for the obligatory permission to land.

"The airfield is closed," was the reply.

"I know, but this in an Army transport ordered to land."

"You don't understand, the airstrip has been destroyed."

Not taking the word of the tower, the pilot lowered the monster plane for a pass over the runway. He saw trenches dug across the landing strip on both runways. The prior evening, the companies sent by General Martinez to prevent the cargo of tanks from unloading contained a platoon of civil engineers with backhoes.

The transport was diverted to Austin. It landed and was immediately surrounded by soldiers from General Everett's brigade joined by three times the number of civilian Resistance volunteers—including Mason, Kelly, and Eric. The volunteers were all armed with various firearms they had retrieved from hiding places. The cargo plane was ordered to park in the middle of the runway. The next transport found a similar fate on the parallel runway. With the runways blocked and apprehension about attempting to land at DFW or Love field in Dallas, the transports were sent back to Fort Bragg. For nearly all the soldiers, it was good news.

In addition to soldiers sent to the Austin airport by General Everett, she sent a company of two hundred soldiers in armored vehicles to relieve the siege on the governor's residence. For the safety of the FBI/ATF SWAT team, they arrived just in time. A spontaneous mob of citizens stirred by the governor's message had retrieved their firearms from hideouts. The variety of firearms they carried had been hidden many years. How many would fire, they were finding out. Most ammunition over time had lost power.

Unorganized, but agitated, citizens were firing upon the FBI SWAT team. The SWAT team had now taken protective positions on the inside of the governor's fence with their back to the Rangers. As the SWAT team no longer posed a threat, Rangers were not firing at them. In the confusion, it took skilled negotiating to convince the citizens that Everett's Army company was on their side and under order to end the siege.

The SWAT team was relieved when gunfire stopped. They thought the Army had come to their rescue. Although rescued they were, these Army soldiers were not on their side. The SWAT team leader and sniper were retained primarily for their own protection. Other SWAT team members were stripped of their weapons, loaded into vehicles, driven away from the crowd, released, and sent home.

White House

The President glared at the FBI director. "So, your people mistook a cook for the governor, murdered her, allowing the very much alive governor to make a martyr of a cook. Incompetence beyond belief. Where is the leader of the swat team and shooter?"

"We believe they are being held, Mr. President."

"By whom?"

"The Resistance, sir."

"That's just wonderful,"

He turned his attention to the CJCS. "That Benedict, Bridget Arnold, Everett! I want the turncoat court-martialed immediately. Where does her family live?"

"Her family lives in Iowa, sir."

"Have the family all picked up," he said to the FBI director.

Then turning to the CJCS, "And you failed to get enough soldiers on the ground to get the job done."

"Mr. President, I believe we have enough presence to prevail."

"We are not taking any more chances. If the Army cannot get the job done, let's bring in Marines."

"Mr. President, as you know, no major Marine bases are close to Texas—Carolina, Georgia, and California are the closest."

"I know the Marines have a base in Arizona."

"Yes, but it's pilot training. I assume bombing is not an option. And Marines in other bases do not have a large airlift capacity. They are transported primarily by helicopter."

"Well get the helicopters moving."

The FBI director jumped in, "Why is bombing off limits?"

"Really, Director, we would prefer to end this without destroying the country."

Without any military presence in Iowa to speak of, an FBI SWAT team in Des Moines converged on the Ankeny suburb only to find the Everett family home vacated.

Austin

General Everett surmised the reason the colonel of the brigade which joined her in Austin called the officers' meeting. She had been told he was furious at her dispatchment of soldiers to the airport and the governor's mansion. She suspected her promotion to *general* also riled him. The general brought MPs with her. After learning of her family's last-minute escape from federal agents in Iowa, she was not in a conciliatory mood. All the brigade's officers above the rank of captain were present.

"You called the meeting Colonel, speak your peace."

"General, I respect you and your rank; however, I and others are not comfortable defying the orders of the commander-in-chief, particularly during a time of martial law."

"What do you propose?"

"That I be allowed to take my brigade and travel north to join forces around Fort Hood. I would offer anyone not comfortable following me the option of staying with you."

"I see," said the General. "How generous, but it is I who is in position to propose an offer. You may leave at will, but only those that seek permission from my staff will be allowed to join you."

The colonel concluded, given the General's attitude and MPs in the room, he had little choice. "Okay, I will leave but will require most of my brigade's light duty tanks and armored personnel carriers accompany me."

"You will leave immediately with only what troop truck transports and unarmed vehicles you require to transport your group."

"General, I must say that is insulting—only appropriate for a defeated opponent."

She ignored his comment, "And you and whoever chooses to follow you will leave their sidearms with the MPs."

The colonel left humiliated that only a minority of his brigade's officers and less enlisted soldiers followed. The remnants of the brigade headed to the federal force controlled by the Pentagon which now faced defenses protecting Resistance-aligned Fort Hood. In route they saw many signs in which the name Audrey had been added to 'Remember Ellen.' Reporting to the general in charge, the colonel was humiliated for arriving without equipment. He soon sensed the contrast in morale between those he left and those he joined. He found himself skeptical of his decision.

Chapter 13

The 82nd Airborne Force in Nebraska which had enabled the federal takeover of the ethanol plant in Blair remained. The force of 2,000 had encountered no resistance since the Nebraska National Guard left. No intelligence had been uncovered indicating a threat was in the works.

The need for soldiers was greater in Texas. All but two companies—400 soldiers— from the Nebraska deployment were transported to augment forces preparing to retake the largest Army base in the world.

The governors of Nebraska and Iowa had been in continuous discussion about what the federal takeover of ethanol plants would do to their states' economies. They had agreed to work together if an option became available and were working on contingency plans. The drawdown of forces surrounding the Blair ethanol plant and inspiration from activities in Texas gave the Nebraska governor an opening and the courage to act.

With the federal troop withdrawal, the Nebraska governor contacted the neighboring governor. "We can retake the Blair facility without help, but working together would send a message. The Feds have drawn down their forces to augment forces in Texas. After the Blair plant is liberated, we could assist you reclaiming ethanol plants in Iowa. As we have discussed before, the Feds don't have any military bases to speak of in the Midwest."

The Iowa governor promised an answer within twenty-four hours.

The Iowa governor had invited her sister to dinner at Terrace Hill, the governor's residence. Halfway through dinner, she could tell something weighed heavily on her sister's mind.

"Maggie, I can tell something is bothering you," inquired her sister, Ava.

"Yes, something is; I have a big decision to make."

"What is making the decision so difficult?"

"Frankly, fear. Fear of the consequences if it does not go well. You've always been fearless, how do you do it?"

"Remember when I pitched in the state softball tournament? I was so scared, I nearly faked illness. People often say you should never dwell on the negative. I found the opposite more helpful. I thought about the worst things that could happen. I could hit a batter, I could walk a runner in, or allow multiple home runs. Then it struck me, the worst thing I could do was not show up. I could live with the other outcomes."

"That's interesting, I'll try to think of it that way."

"You might also look for a sign. Perhaps we are given signs from a greater energy, or our minds identify something as a sign because that is what we subconsciously desire. Don't ignore what may direct you."

It was 4:00 in the morning when the former CFO at the Blair ethanol plant heard pounding on his front door. He was scared, what had he done? But at least they were knocking instead of ripping the door from its hinges, Wisconsin style. He answered the door to find a Nebraska National Guard Major who was among those who tried to hold the Blair plant from the Feds. Now he was wearing colonel insignias.

The colonel saw the CFO looking at his insignias. "The former colonel was canned. I am now in charge, and you will soon be at your office in Blair. Be prepared to assume your former duties before the day is over."

The sun was rising behind them as a caravan of 1,000 Iowa National Guard soldiers from Des Moines crossed the Missouri river on I-80 into Nebraska. Before noon, two-thousand joint National Guard units were postured in attack formation outside the Blair ethanol plant. The Major left in command of the remaining 82nd Airborne troops was unable to reach the Pentagon to advise them of his situation.

A communications corporal appeared to be working feverishly on the problem. Actually, the corporal caused the problem and only appeared to be trying to fix it. Member of the 82nd Airborne or not, Nebraska was his home, and he would help defend it.

Unable to reach the Army major by other means, the new Nebraska National Guard colonel walked to the defender's position. The irony that a few weeks earlier their positions were reversed was on his mind.

"Major, I suggest for the good of all that you surrender your position."

"You took an oath to obey the president," he answered in a haughty tone. "Who are you to instruct me?"

"You should remember me standing in line at this very spot signing the pledge, I'm Donald Duck."

They stared at each other in the searing mid-day Nebraska sun. Each felt sweat working its way down their spinal column. Like a western style standoff, they each carried a sidearm, but their concern was that speaking next would show weakness.

The major knew that anything less than holding the plant would destroy his career. His parents had lobbied him to seek a civil service career in non-military service as they had. He argued that the military no longer carried the stigma of immoral American hegemony. As an only son, he could not fail them.

He pulled his eyes from the colonel to an MP, "Arrest this man for treason."

"I came here under a truce," the colonel protested. Before the MPs reached him, he keyed the microphone on his grape. "I've been arrested."

He was immediately relieved of grape and sidearm and taken away.

As per the agreement, the colonel from the Iowa National Guard was now in command. She ordered six armored personnel carriers to move forward followed by foot soldiers staying in cover behind the carriers. The Army major ordered a line of fifty caliber machine guns to fire in front of them. They did not fire. The major assumed they had ignored the order; but the corporal in charge of communications had sabotaged their connection, and they did not receive the order.

The major ran to the machine gun installation. The armored guard carriers were getting closer. He had no time to reprimand the battery. He pushed a man out of the way, "Let me!" he screamed and jumped behind the gun, grabbing its handle.

Civil administration had been the major's field of study in college; he was on the fast track for promotion. He had excelled in all the community service and social awareness studies that were required, but he had no training manning a machine gun or any gun. *Point, pull the trigger, how difficult could it be if those beneath him did it?*

The National Guard's armored personnel carriers were now within a hundred yards and still coming. He pointed the barrel at the center of the leading carrier. The gun would not stop it but send it a clear message. If he failed, at least he would have shown bravery. He pulled the trigger. The Dillon 503D erupted at a rate of 25 BMG cartridges per second.

The major had no idea how difficult it was to control. The barrel weaved in a circle as he tried to rein it in. When his finger finally left the trigger, the carrier had stopped, and a man could be heard screaming beside the carrier. Blood spurted from his neck on the side of the vehicle and ran down across a window as he bled out.

Another carrier continued forward. The major, successful once, was determined to stop the next carrier and sprayed it with gunfire. The machine gun was silenced when the communications corporal pulled his 45 and put a bullet in the major's temple.

In most such scenarios, the corporal would have been shot or immediately arrested— not in this case. Those that witnessed the shooting, officers and enlisted, had much more in common with the corporal. The major was lofty and arrogant, even an officer needed to relate to those he commanded. For reasons other than rank, all could feel the major's distaste at the necessity of being around *deplorables*. And the Nebraska corporal— well, they were in Nebraska.

In shock at the major's death, the two companies of the 82nd froze. They were soon surrounded by the Nebraska and Iowa National Guard. The MPs released the National Guard colonel. He found a captain, now in command of the two Army companies, and asked him to surrender.

"I guess we have," he said shrugging his shoulders.

Any Army soldiers from Nebraska or Iowa were offered the same rank in their respective guards. All twenty-one took the offer. The rest were told to leave.

"How?" the captain asked as he saw Guard members taking their equipment.

The colonel let the 370 remaining keep ten jeeps and told them to walk if they could not ride, but not to be caught within ten miles of the plant in the morning.

The next morning the Iowa Guard and half the Nebraska Guard headed north, crossed the Missouri River near Sioux City, Iowa, and liberated an ethanol plant there from bureaucrats who knew nothing about chemistry, corn, or competition. Within a week, all forty ethanol plants in Iowa and twenty-five in Nebraska were back in private hands.

Cruise Ship

Pawel Bartosz, captain of the Polish grain freighter that had taken Andrew and Julie out to sea, was in the Gulf of Mexico headed back to the Mississippi Delta for another load of grain. His navigator, who had communication equipment and know-how far beyond what was required to direct the freighter, entered the captain's bridge.

"I picked up a shortwave signal you should know about."

"Nothing unusual about that, is there?" inquired the captain.

"A number of things, the wavelength is unusually short, around twenty-five meters; it is being transmitted in short intermittent bursts and in code. But the most curious aspect is it is being bounced off the ionosphere by a transmitter pointed out to sea from that cruise ship with which we've been in contact."

"I'll let them know what you found, but they probably have several means of communication, some not known to us," the captain assured him. "Just in case, did you capture any of the transmission?"

"Yes, it was a short burst which could only be received in a small area of the sea. We are long since out of the area."

Captain Bartosz conducted much business with the Resistance cruise ship, but only at arm's length. Scientists and engineers, most from the defunct Atlas Transportation Company, had relocated to the ship after successfully destroying the asteroid in '39. On the ship, they did contract software and engineering work for several non-American companies. Many of their clients were Polish. Captain Bartosz picked up the products and hid them in his grain shipments. The contracts were very lucrative and financed much of the Resistance's activities. The captain had never met anyone on the ship, as all exchanges were done by intermediaries on small boats. For safety, he only communicated with Torrence, who was now in Texas.

Torrence, who was at the hunting cabin, attempted to figure out the ramifications of the shortwave burst. He knew that the cruise ship did not use microwave bursts for any communication. His first search was for ships within the fifty square mile area of the gulf at a time that could have received the shortwave burst. Other than the Polish freighter, there was only one, a Communist Chinese submarine.

Torrence contacted Barry to work on another aspect of discovery while he researched personnel files. He determined seven people on the ship had a combination of radio expertise and access to materials in which to build a short-wave device. Nothing in their files suggested any were suspect to breach ship security protocols. He broadened the search to include immediate family, nothing.

When he broadened the family search, he found two possibilities. One woman had parents in their sixties who were traveling in China. They had been there longer than expected.

The other suspect was a man whose brother from California serves in congress. The Washington rumor mill whispered that a Chinese Embassy worker often spent the night at the congressman's Washington apartment while his wife was in California. Of course, as his voting record was proper and gave him cover, it never made the media.

Torrence contacted his confidante, director of security on the cruise ship, and relayed his suspicion. The security director had their rooms searched while the two were working in ship offices. They did not find any electronic devices which could emit short wave radio signals. It was assumed the device was hidden elsewhere on the ship. But they did find small wire filament carefully strung out of sight around the walls in the man's cabin, a workable shortwave antenna. The Chinese had gotten to the man through his brother's mistress.

Barry was working on another aspect of the security breach. For safety, only he, Torrence, Julie and Andrew were on the call.

"Our access to communication between Washington and the CCP (Chinese Communist Party) has been particularly good, and we have seen no relay of information about the Resistance ship. If Washington were tipped off about the ship, I am sure something would be in play to silence the ship; we've found nothing."

Andrew inquired, "We must assume the CCP knows of the ship and most likely much of what we are doing there. Why do you suppose they're keeping it to themselves?"

Barry answered, "Most likely they are waiting until it is to their advantage. Should we have the congressman's brother detained?"

"No, that would tip them off and possibly expedite sharing what they know with Washington," answered Julie.

Andrew added, "That's right. Perhaps the ship has served its purpose. Without NSA's analytical abilities restored and no new vultures on the horizon, our people can return home. Most still have homes on land. Doing so will allow us to spread out, the eggs in the basket thing."

"Makes sense, vacate slowly, a few people off the ship by motorboat daily. We'll tell people on the ship it is safe to go home, but not divulge the breach. And the last to leave the ship will be the congressman's brother," concluded Julie.

"Let's do it the other way," said Andrew. "If we leave him on the ship, the Chinese will learn most of our people have evacuated. We have already determined arresting him would create a long-term burden. Confront him with what we know, tell him if any more problems arise with him, we will feed his brother's trysts to any and all outlets. Deboard him, send him home and let him assume the ship continues to operate with all aboard."

The California man was confronted, given enough money to get to California, and deboarded. It was a long boat ride to the Texas shore at Port Aransas. Fortunately, for him it was not as rough as Julie and Andrew's ride. Once it was determined he had left Texas, they proceeded with the plan and sailed north.

As it did periodically to fuel, the ship pulled near the twenty-four mile international water limit from Galveston Harbor. Daily, ship residents were taken to land. Most of the scientists and engineers returned to their homes in Midland.

On the third day Andrew was waiting to pick up Melissa and Sandy. Sandy was elated to see her dad. Andrew drove Melissa and Sandy to the hunting lodge.

In route, Sandy asked, "What do those signs '*Remember Ellen and Audrey*' mean?"

"They are heroes," Melissa answered.

"What did they do; how do you become a hero?"

"Someday you'll understand," answered Andrew.

Hunting Lodge

As expected, Sandy was elated to see her mother. For Andrew, there was something special about seeing the woman he loved with their daughter. He was somewhat surprised to see how happy Melissa was to see Torrence.

"Do you have kids like me?" Sandy asked Madison.

"No, your dad and mom are lucky to have you," answered the Texas governor.

"We're going to be on a business call now, Sandy," Julie said.

"Who is going to be on the call?" asked Sandy as she crawled on Julie's lap.

"Oh, just some people your dad and I have been working with," replied Julie.

Soon the governors of Florida and Ohio were on the call.

"Hi, everyone, I'm here with my mom," spoke Sandy. Given the anxiety in the country, they found the frivolity of a six-year-old refreshing.

After introductions were made, minus titles, the Florida governor said, "I really admire what you in Texas, Nebraska and Iowa have done. And we in Florida wish you the best. But we have the highest percent of social security recipients in the country, we cannot afford to jeopardize that federal largess in this state."

The Ohio governor asked, "Have you calculated and compared the overpayment of federal tax paid by Florida residents in your low tax state to the social security entering your state?"

"Yes, and the social security is greater."

"But then add in the extra NTE taxes to your present over payment of tax."

"I know, I know, it will then dwarf the social security influx into the state. But what can we do?"

Julie spoke, "We have been working with economists and financial experts around the country. A plan is in the works. Once we work out all the possible scenarios, let's talk about it. One question, did Florida have an Independent Bankers Association?"

Julie, Andrew, Melissa, Torrence and Sandy headed for Midland. Melissa and Torrence were left at Melissa's acreage outside of Midland. Soon many scientists and engineers who had lived for years on the ship returned to their former offices at the Atlas Transportation building. The abandoned building again became active, but not for asteroid busting. This time as the Resistance headquarters.

Julie, Andrew, and Sandy went to Julie's townhouse which was close to the Atlas building. It would become their family home, at least for a time; hopefully for a long time, but given what had been put in motion, only God knew.

Given that Austin was now secure, Governor Archibald headed back to the capitol. The governor back at her job would give people confidence. She made sure local TV crews caught her return. The governor spent the next few days at the capitol meeting with members of the legislature. She outlined a plan she and Julie had worked on. Ideas were tossed about; negotiations were ongoing until they reached an agreement and put it in the form of legislation.

Springfield, Illinois

The Illinois legislature was considering a bill that would support the president's martial law directives and urge him to fast-track the implementation of the NTE. The bill had the support of the majority. Affirming support for the president would have no consequence in the acceptance of his directives but would signal Washington that Illinois was on his side when it came time to distribute monies.

As Illinois had among the highest combined state and local taxes, NTE would not raise federal taxes for Illinois residents. Even if the new federal monies were dispersed evenly per capita across states, Illinois would be a winner. However, federal revenues were not distributed evenly. Illinois would receive more than their share. Consequently, supporting the administration was the politically prudent thing to do.

People choosing to live on government stipends had flocked to the Chicago area as subsidized housing became readily available. Another large segment of the population was non-working retired public employees. By law, they were prevented from leaving the state to retain their lucrative pensions.

Working people, whether by choice to avoid high local and state taxes, or by necessity when their jobs moved, had left the state for decades. Half the homes had been abandoned on many city blocks which took them off the tax rolls, exacerbating the state tax revenue problem. State and local governments took advantage of the situation and seized empty homes for back taxes and rented them for what the original tax had been. The state gained residents who not only replenished the lost property tax as rent but used their government stipends to pay sales taxes on other living expenses.

Legislative districts in Illinois, as had been the rule for decades, looked like pieces of a pie, the center being the Chicago metro and a triangle extending outward into rural areas. It assured state rule by the urban area. The martial law support bill was assured of passage until an amendment was offered.

The destruction of the PPU plant in Texas and Illinois's abundance of vacated manufacturing facilities offered an opportunity for the state. An amendment offered to the martial law support bill would donate an empty factory to produce the new surveillance PPUs and offer a state subsidy to equip the building. The question of where the state would obtain the money to purchase the expensive tooling was not raised.

Many legislators—who, for economic reasons, favored the martial law support legislation— bulked at the amendment. They invented several excuses for opposing the amendment but were afraid to articulate the primary reason for their opposition— fear of the plant bringing violence to the metro area as it had in Texas. They were also timid about going on record subsidizing PPU production —given public aversion to 1984 style Big Brother scrutiny—even in their state.

Damon Trotter, a state senator from Evanston who was on sabbatical from Northwestern University during the legislative session, recognized the origin of the opposition.

"Senators, whatever we may think of the PPUs either for the common good, or invasive, the fact is they will fly again. If they are not produced in Texas, it may be Oregon or Massachusetts, but they will be built. It's called progress, folks. People have stood in front of progress before and come to regret it as the tide of change rolled over them. Why not accept the inevitable and embrace progress right here in Illinois?"

When he finished his extended dissertation on the inevitability of change, he offered a sub-amendment to the amendment. It condemned the destruction of the plant in Texas and politicians and citizens there opposing the martial law edicts. The sub-amendment also forbade Texans from settling in Illinois.

When asked about the why of his proposed ban on Texans, he replied, "Illinois does not need troublemakers."

Damon did not expect the ban to remain in his sub-amendment. His intention was only to make a point. But most legislators thought him to be serious.

Enough legislators found the amendment offensive and walked out of the chambers to rob the majority of a quorum. The vacating legislators met in a hotel convention center and decided to never return to the statehouse. Representing eighty percent of the state's land mass, they would investigate avenues of secession from the state. Many argued that given where Springfield was located, it should be theirs.

Mason picked up the news that evening that a state senator from Evanston, Illinois had proposed that Texans be prohibited from moving to Illinois. He assumed it was his brother and called him after he composed himself.

"Am I to be prohibited from visiting you or only relocating in Illinois?" he asked.

"Oh, I didn't know you were that on top of the news. Don't worry about it; it was just a gesture, something to bargain away for support. That is how politics works, you know."

Playing naïve as always with his brother, Mason continued, "Oh, I understand, but what is this about an Illinois internal secession?"

"Just crazy talk probably incited by the foolishness in Texas. Do you know anyone involved in your state's lunacy?"

"Not really, just many rumors."

Chapter 14

It took twenty-four hours for the major general in command of federal forces in Texas to assess what had been delivered. He had been promised 30,000 soldiers with equipment. Delivered were 7,000 from the first night's parachute drop from Fort Bragg. Only 2,000 by parachute made it the following day and 1,200 were sent directly from the Nebraska drawdown. He had one-third of what he expected from Fort Bragg added to 12,000 soldiers from Fort Hood now south of the fort who had originally been sent to the Georgetown plant.

Federal forces under the major general's command totaled 22,000 with no armored brigades. Low numbers were only part of his problem. They were short on equipment. A combination of patrols sent out by Texas National Guard General Tate and marauding Resistance members had destroyed a considerable amount of equipment before the parachutists could secure it.

The combination of Resistance forces, under General Martinez's command, were 15,000 soldiers inside Fort Hood and two heavily armored brigades of 8,000 guarding the south perimeter of the Fort plus two Texas National Guard brigades, totaling 31,000 north of federal positions. To the south near Austin sat 7,000 soldiers under General Everett defending Austin. In addition to soldiers, unnumbered civilian Resistance members and sympathizers were willing to carry out guerrilla activities.

Long time military strategy held that for a well-defended position to be overrun the attacking force needed to outnumber the defenders two to one unless the invading forces had superior armament. The major general contacted the Pentagon of his dilemma; he was immediately transferred to the White House. He explained his position on a speaker in the cabinet room.

"I think you're over-estimating the control General Martinez has over the fort," stated the president. "It has to be common knowledge there that failure to support the commander-in-chief will destroy careers at the very least. Once you press forward, they will fall like dominos."

The CJCS spoke, "Why not give the soldiers at the fort time to reconsider what they are doing? If the major general draws his forces close and stops, it will send a message. Slowly officers under Martinez will think better, and he will have his hands full preventing his own mutiny."

"Does anyone else have ideas?" the president asked.

The major general on the ground spoke, "Mr. President, defending Austin the Resistance only has about 7,000 turncoat Army soldiers plus National Guard units on the outskirts of Austin. We have the numbers to crush the opposition, take Austin, and eliminate the head of this rebellion. Doing so would send a clear message to General Martinez."

"The success of such an operation would depend upon General Martinez leaving your rear alone," pointed out the CJCS. "The armored brigades defending Fort Hood could decimate you from the rear if they chose to follow you south."

The pluses and minuses of the three alternatives were discussed for hours before the president made a decision. "Heavy fighting in a major city is something we should avoid and use only as a last resort. I believe that the CJCS is correct. If confronted with a steadfast force, I'm confident soldiers at Fort Hood will come to their senses and this foolishness will end."

Opposing sides of a split army faced each other. They were deployed as close as a mile apart in places south of Fort Hood. Food, medicine, and supplies were dropped by parachute to what had become the invading army as Waco's airport was still out of commission and access to Austin's airport denied.

Resistance militia forces led by Mason wanted to harass the enemy supplies lines, but General Martinez and the governor opposed any such operations. Julie and the Resistance Council agreed. Now was not the time to ramp up hostilities by denying supplies to the federally controlled army.

The area between the forces was not a no-man's land. No shots had been fired. Recognizance patrols from both sides often met and compared notes. Neither side stopped someone wishing to cross the vacant area between the forces. In many respects it was like a training session with artificial battle lines drawn. The neutral mile wide zone came to be called 'all persons land'.

In the spirit of no reprisals against anyone choosing to side with the Feds, the Resistance policy was to hold no prisoners. Julie said that included spies. For a week, Zoe had remained chained to the warehouse support column inside a storage closet. Twice a day Mason brought her food, hobbled her legs for his safety, and allowed her use of a restroom. One morning Carl opened the closet door without food.

"Where is my food? You can't starve me, it's against…well, the Geneva convention."

"I don't think that agreement applies here," Carl said as he unchained her without shackling her legs and quickly backed out of the closet away from the martial arts expert.

"You didn't tie my legs. It's a mistake you could regret," she said as she smiled and stepped toward him.

"I'm not worried," he said as he nodded to Mason and Eric standing armed outside the closet door. You are free to leave, but if you are found in Texas in twenty-four hours, you will be arrested."

"You confiscated my vehicle; how do you expect me to leave?"

"I believe you are resourceful enough to find a way."

"You never bought into my ploy at all, did you?"

"No, we identified the moisture in your handshake immediately. I may be a decent looking middle-aged guy, but a 30-year-old with a model's body coming on to me? Well, it sends out red flags, I'm not stupid. And the governor is all I can handle."

"I guess I respect that," she said as she started to leave, then stopped. "You know my failure here may have ended my career. You owe me."

"You're lucky we're releasing you."

"I'm sure you've already figured out I work for the CIA. I do so on a contractual basis so they can keep me at arm's length, disavow me if needed. If I do not get work, I do not get paid. My cover is blown in Poland, so they will not send me back. Well, let me put it this way. If you people in this movement, or whatever you call it, need my kind of assistance for a price, I'm available."

Carl took her contact information.

She picked up a grape from someone in a restaurant who carelessly left it in their booth as they visited the rest room. She had no intention of leaving Texas in twenty-four hours, but her chief at CIA headquarters told her they had no use for her in Texas. Carl was right, she was resourceful— and with a permanently borrowed car made her way to Maryland. She was soon bored at her studio apartment waiting for her new grape to ring. It did not.

White House

The president was encouraged by reports of soldiers moving to the federal side. Some did, but reports exaggerated the numbers. What was not reported to the president was at least three times the number moving in the other direction. Many federal controlled soldiers outside the fort had family members living in the Fort. Territorial disputes, politics and regimental friends were often trumped by family.

"It's a good sign soldiers are moving in our direction," observed the president with false information.

"Now is the time to amplify the movement," he said to the CJCS. "Send the directive out that any soldier at Fort Hood or those taking orders from commanders not following my directives will be cut from the payroll. That shutoff will include eliminating federal reimbursement for part of National Guard salaries in states whose

National Guard have not taken pledges of allegiance to me. We'll hit them where it hurts, the pocketbook."

To clarify, the CJCS asked, "That would include the states of Texas, Florida, South Carolina, Wyoming, Nebraska, and Utah."

"Certainly," he responded, then he turned to the Secretary of Treasury, "Although the National Tax Equalization is not to take effect until the first of the year, I think it prudent to test the NTE first. The states to test it in are those which have blatantly defied federal dictates demanding the Department of Energy takeover of energy production. Adjust federal withholding taxes upward in those low tax states immediately."

The President referred to notes in front of him, "Those states include Nebraska, Iowa, Ohio, New Mexico, Missouri, Texas, Oklahoma and the Dakotas. Those governors will soon have a taxpayer revolt when voters are hit with their new tax bill."

Over the first half of the century small banks were pushed out of business by heavy regulation. The largest proponent of heavy bank regulations were big national banks. Like many industries, onerous regulations were a method to squeeze out smaller competitors. Large banks could spread compliance costs over more volume. It was an unbearable expense burden for small banks.

Eventually only three large national banks were left. But *the beast you feed can also come back to bite you.* The Department of Treasury and IRS found dealing with any privately owned banks to be a nuisance. Many executives of the large banks received lucrative federal jobs for their capitulation, and the financial industry was completely socialized.

The Department of Treasury operated regional service centers in each state, seven in Texas, two in Iowa, one in North Dakota and four in Ohio. With all citizens' financial information available at the service centers, IRS offices in the centers calculated and deducted taxes from citizens' Transaction Account Cards (TAC). Interested taxpayers could log into their account and see what the IRS deducted monthly, but without explanation unless they appealed for clarification. Many citizens were happy to be relieved of the obligation and expense of hiring an accountant or preparing their own tax returns.

The presidential moves were expected by the governor of Texas. What was not expected was his phone call shortly after she received the news.

"Governor, I'm sorry to have issued the directives, but you left me no choice. The good news is that what you have done is not irreversible. You may be able to withstand a recall effort if you retreat before soldiers in Fort Hood run out of money and come looking for you."

"What about the early implementation of NTE?"

"I'm sorry, but the wheels are already in motion. Think about your future, no charges will be brought against you if you open your energy industry to the DOE, stop this confrontation at Fort Hood, and turn your National Guard over to me. That is a promise."

"Lot to think about there," she responded.

"Remember the old cliché, he who controls the purse strings makes the rules, governor."

"I'll get back to you shortly," she answered before hanging up.

"What do you think?" the president asked his Treasury Secretary.

"I think she has no choice; you just ended her game."

Texas

The governor called an emergency session of the state legislature. Most legislators had been forewarned of the coming session and had previewed parts of the bill they would be presented.

On a call with Julie, the governor started second guessing her decision. "I know sending the bill was the right thing to do, but I have to wonder am I, are we, in this alone?"

"You definitely are not in this alone, many governors that you are not aware of share similar opinions but as they are from smaller states, they feel helpless. You've set an example and the bill passing will open the door for others to follow."

"I know the governors of Oklahoma, Arkansas and Nebraska are with me, but will they also take action, or wait until they see us succeed or flounder? And even if they do, what can four states do?"

"You'll be surprised who may act."

The Texas legislative session opened the morning following the presidential directive. Vigorous debate lasted throughout the day. Many contended that the legislation started something they would ultimately lose, an equal number argued the bill did not go far enough. It was ten o'clock in the evening when it passed the final chamber. The governor signed it before midnight.

At the governor's order, Texas Rangers and National Guardsmen had been prepositioned at the seven Department of Treasury centers in Texas. Before dawn, Texas officials including former bankers and accountants entered the seven centers. Federal workers who showed up were turned away.

Although Texas federal taxes remained higher that the national average because citizens in high tax states were allowed greater deductions, the confiscatory taxes of the NTE were not implemented. New state centric management of the centers reduced monies sent to the federal government by the amount Texas used to replace soldier payroll withheld by Washington.

Unwilling for their taxpayers to bear more of the federal tax burden and protective of their energy industry, four states joined Texas. Oklahoma, Arkansas, South Dakota, and Nebraska took control of Treasury centers in their states within a week of the Texas action.

"Well, there are now five of us," the Texas Governor said to Julie. "But will that be enough to overcome what the Feds will bring down on us? I was informed today that, in support of the Feds, the European Union has suspended all trade through the Galveston port."

"Are you telling me you will miss their overpriced wine?"

"Hardly."

"Then why worry about what countries with declining indigenous populations overrun by outsiders do?"

"A good point. The heart of Western civilization now lies here."

"I suggest you tune into your grape at 8:00 this evening, you'll soon feel better."

As Barry had feared, hacking of the media networks to air the Davis's interview and the Texas Governor's speech closed the door on hacking media feeds. Many more layers of security were added which would take technicians months, at the least, to bypass.

For an alternative, Resistance technicians working in the former Atlas facilities plant had started the Resistance information network. Newsfeeds were provided to secure grapes across the country. As the screen on the grape was small, most people carried a rollup screen which could be used for viewing. The secure grape could also be linked into a home office monitor or wall screen by pointing it at the screen. The latest shipment of secure grapes from Poland allowed a thousand more to be spread around the country. And more people with regular non-secure grapes had lost the fear of reprisals and were downloading Resistance news apps to their grapes. The Resistance newsfeeds were now watched by more with regular grapes than secure grapes.

Resistance leaders across the country, including the Texas governor, were given a heads up to watch a feed on their grapes in the evening. Many with the apps on their grapes headed to local sports bars and hacked wall mounted monitors to widen the audience.

The governor of Iowa was a ninth generation Iowan. Few called her by her given name Margaret, it was Maggie to her friends. By all standards she was considered a moderate, some just described her as pragmatic. An ancestor had been the first European settler in an Eastern Iowa county. The family had been farmers for generations. Her ancestors had been devout Methodist abolitionists who sent their sons to end slavery in the Civil War. The governor's veins ran thick with Iowa tradition.

From the governor's office at the statehouse in Des Moines, the governor addressed what she assumed were only local news stations in her address to an Iowa audience.

"Fellow Iowans, we are faced with a monumental dilemma in this country. We are at a crossroads, and a decision must be made. I have sat on the fence, moving in either direction has its dangers and benefits. After much pondering, I was leaning toward safety and security for Iowans. It, perhaps, was the easy way.

Having pretty much settled on compliance with martial law, I exited my car at the capitol yesterday morning. As you remember, it was a hot, humid Iowa day made more so by calm stagnant air. I was walking toward the capitol when I was suddenly struck by a refreshing breeze. I looked up at the capitol building. Our state flag had caught the sudden wind gust and was stretched outward in fullness. Our state's slogan was easily read on our flag, *'Our liberties we prize and our rights we will maintain.'* Some will say it is superstition or an antiquated pagan belief, but I saw it as a message. My sister advised me I should not ignore messages. For me, this was not a subtle message but a wakeup slap.

Iowa has been a leader in expanding and securing freedom since we became a state. We sent more soldiers per capita than any other state to free slaves. We gave women the right to vote before the 19th amendment and we were the third state to recognize gay marriage. As our motto has guided us in the past, so shall it today.

My grandfather often quoted a political leader in his time who said, *'Extremism in the defense of liberty is no vice.'* He was ridiculed then as some are today for standing up for freedom. 'It is archaic' and 'Freedom is not progressive,' we are told. How can you call progressive a return to the norm of past societies where class difference, authoritarian rule, and the virtual servitude of the masses was common? That, my friends, is regressive.

It was a hundred years ago that Eric Blair, whose pen name was George Orwell, wrote the books *Animal Farm* and *1984.* They were meant to serve as warnings, not instruction manuals. Orwell wrote from experience having lived through and knowing well the dangerous dual forms of authoritarian socialism, Fascism and Communism.

In the early part of this century Suzanne Collins penned a trilogy of books known as *The Hunger Games.* Perhaps you have seen the dystopian science fiction movies made of the books. Lesser valued citizens are incentivized to kill each other for the viewing pleasure of the elite. It depicted regression to the time of Romans finding entertainment in lions killing Christians. Fortunately, we are not there yet, but it is the direction we are headed. The elite live privileged lives in the greater Washington area, proper places on the coasts, or in isolated islands of proper thought. They know best for us and only they define 'the common good." We are becoming serfs in flyover country only tolerated for the goods, services, and tax money we produce. What do they produce that you can eat, drink, drive, wear, touch, or use to enhance your life? Perhaps only shackles.

I will no longer stand by idly while Iowans are bilked of tax money to pay for corruption and spendthrift policies elsewhere. Iowa followed Texas into the Union by one year, we will now follow Texas in saying 'Enough is enough!'

I am ordering the Iowa National Guard and Iowa State Patrol to seize the US Treasury offices in Des Moines and Cedar Rapids and turn the operation over to state officials and former bankers. The National Tax Equalization directive will not take effect here, and any monies denied the state will be deducted from the transfer of our money to the Feds."

Although the Iowa Governor's speech had not been hacked into media feeds, knowledge of it spread quickly. Major media ignored the speech, except one outlet that characterized the speech as a Fascist rant that immediately initiated impeachment proceedings against the governor.

Led by state representatives from university towns—enclaves of proper thought, whose livelihood depended on federal largess— a bill to impeach the Iowa governor was introduced the next day. It failed.

The following day the Iowa House of Representatives introduced a bill to rescind the governor's action. It passed the house but failed in the state senate by three votes.

In the following week, seven other states joined Iowa and the original five in taking control of the outflow of money from their states. A line of states from North Dakota to Texas effectively severed the country in half.

White House

The president had been told of the Iowa governor's speech but refused to listen to it. 'Why would I concern myself with an imbecilic speech by a governor of a no-account state?"

But seven states joining others in sending Department of Treasury and IRS officials packing did draw the president's attention.

"Let us show them what hardball is about. Suspend all social security payments and stipends to residents of states which have breached Treasury offices. And add to that states whose guards have not pledged allegiance to me. Let them deal with hordes of old people rioting in the streets."

The Treasury Secretary cautioned him. "Mr. President, that would include Florida, which has not violated Treasury offices. It could push them in the wrong direction."

"We need to send a message. And what better place than the state with the highest number of social security recipients. They have the most to lose."

To no avail, the Treasury Secretary continued to advise the president against including Florida. Within a week the Treasury Secretary was proven right when Florida seized federal treasury offices.

Florida not only failed to implement NTE, but they also replaced federal social security and stipend recipients' payments with state checks and deducted that amount from tax money they passed on to the federal government. Other states followed Florida's lead and did the same.

Chapter 15

White House

Given that suspending federal payments to individuals had not deterred the runaway states, the president had no alternative than to up the ante.

After consultation with Pentagon officials concerning logistics to Fort Hood, the president had the general in charge of federal forces in Texas on the line.

"General, I understand that all supplies destined for Fort Hood, including food, are routed through warehouse facilities outside of Waco. While you have Martinez's renegade forces tied down at Fort Hood, I want you to send a force to that warehouse facility. According to Pentagon officers, the warehouse is unprotected. If cutting off paychecks to Fort Hood will not alter their behavior, perhaps empty bellies will."

"What will we do with the warehouse once seized?"

"Hold the warehouse. Those supplies can supplement what we've been able to airdrop for your forces."

Texas

With the presidential order to suspend payroll for Fort Hood, all vendors in the supply chain to Fort Hood also had their federal funding stopped. Consequently, the supplies at the warehouse had been drawn down to a week's worth, compared to the normal month supply. Texas treasury officials were in the process of sending state funds to supply vendors, but the lag had broken the supply chain and dwindled supplies at the warehouse.

General Martinez got word that federal forces were moving toward the Waco warehouse, but not in time to defend it. Sending an armored brigade to retake the warehouse after federal forces seized it could be done but not without a major confrontation, which they hoped to avoid.

The Fort Hood Army contingent at the warehouse had an hour warning before federal soldiers showed up. They sent all trucks and delivery vans away, depriving the Feds of the normal means to move warehouse supplies. Discussion was held whether to destroy the warehouse, but it was decided that while destroying vultures was a necessity, destroying food and medicine would be an unsightly escalation to avoid. When Federal soldiers showed up, the warehouse was deserted with less supplies than they anticipated, and the forklifts in the warehouse were inoperable.

White House
The COS reminded the president, "The Chinese Ambassador will be here in an hour."

"I'm not sure why we agreed to this meeting. It's not like I don't have enough on my plate with louts on the prowl in the hinterlands."

"The Chinese Embassy said it was urgent, sir."

"What does our intelligence say? Are they up to anything? With this mess in the country, it'll be a wonder if they don't try to take advantage of the situation."

"We're not hearing anything out of line, Mr. President," said the director of the CIA. "But you realize we are somewhat handicapped as we've drawn down Asian intelligence assets for domestic work."

"Excuses, excuses, don't go down that path with me. Our general in Texas complains he does not have enough equipment; the Treasury Secretary says more armed guards should have been stationed at Treasury centers. Life is all about making do with what you have.

There are those who get it done and those who waste effort seeking justifications for their own incompetence. Which are you, director?"

The director's face flushed with the dress down. He took a deep breath and cautiously replied, "I didn't mean to complain, Mr. President. My point was to report that we have no knowledge of any abnormal Chinese activity but qualify our assessment by acknowledging that our confidence level is diminished."

"Fancier words, same meaning. I could go back through history and give you a litany of CIA failures at critical times. But perhaps you are right, diverting agents to domestic intelligence certainly has gained us no insight about these domestic dolts. Our best agent a few feet from the Texas governor's bedroom, you said, with the governor's husband salivating over her. What did that get us? Nothing but silence until she shows up with her tail between her legs in the safety of federal forces. See to it she never gets another assignment; there must be consequences for failure."

"Mr. President, the Chinese Ambassador has arrived," interrupted the COS.

It was none too soon for the CIA director, as he hurriedly gathered his intelligence briefing book and left.

The president rose from his desk and greeted Jing Fang in the middle of the plush carpet of the Oval Office. He often wondered whether Jing Fang was his real name or given to him to fit his position. *Jing,* meaning *peaceful,* and *Fang,* meaning *virtue* in Chinese symbolism. The name was appropriate if you intended to convey a desire for cordial international relations.

We have learned so much from the Chinese, thought the president. But we have so much more to learn. They have domestic tranquility and are masters at nipping any problems long before the bud starts to grow and puts on thorns. However, their history forced them to work together as a community to prevent hordes from swarming over them. Whereas this country was settled by the hordes who still liked to talk of individualism and laissez-faire.

"So glad you stopped, Mr. Ambassador. What can I do for you?"

A product of the cookie mold of Chinese training, the ambassador ignored the question and asked the president about his family.

Questions about the president's wife he could do without. After the obligatory courtesies were exchanged, the ambassador answered the question. "It is about what we can do for you."

"And what might that be?"

"It is most unfortunate that events have gotten out of hand in your country."

"I wouldn't characterize it that way. We have historically had an occasional domestic spat, but things are under control."

"We both know you are minimalizing the situation, Mr. President. Large sections of your country are in open revolt, and you are losing ground."

"Why should that concern your country?"

"Let us just say we consider your administration to be much more amicable and more in tune with our vision of the world than your adversaries would be."

"So, what are you offering?"

"The problem is upon you because you have lost control, control you've lost because you are blind without your eyes and ears. Children without oversight will run astray. And your attempts at replacing your eyes and ears have, what do you say, fizzled."

The president did not respond and waited for the ambassador to continue.

"Our citizen surveillance technology might not be at your 3.0 PPU level, but it is more sophisticated than the blind things you have flying now when they were working. And the 3.0 technology is irrelevant anyway as you cannot get them built."

"Bottomline?" the President quipped getting frustrated at the runaround.

"Such an archaic capitalistic euphemism you use, Mr. President. Hopefully, you continue to move away from such greedy mindsets. Without the archaic profit motive, we have our citizen surveillance equipment manufactured in one of our African colonies. We have purposely overproduced what we need and would be willing to share."

"I know, produced by slave labor."

"I wouldn't be so quick to criticize, Mr. President. Your country has a storied past with slavery."

"Okay, what are you proposing?"

"We can soon have 5,000 flying surveillance devices on a ship headed in your direction followed by another 10,000 in following months. They would enable you to regain control of the masses."

"What kind of compensatory payments or actions would you expect?"

"Actually, Mr. President, it would require no payment or action on your part. We would only ask your understanding when we take care of our Taiwan problem as you take care of your Texas problem. We would move to secure peace throughout Indochina. I am sure you would see that as a positive development."

"Could you be more specific?" asked the President.

"Perhaps your seventh fleet might be needed closer to California and see no reason to venture in the Pacific west of Hawaii."

"It would be granting you influence over all of Asia and most of the Pacific."

"Small price to pay for retaining control of your country. We believe your options are extremely limited. Let us know soon. The ship is loaded and ready to move in your direction at your call."

To drive an exclamation mark on the superior Chinese bargaining position, the ambassador abruptly ended the conversation, got up and headed for the Oval Office door.

The COS and Secretary of State had sat in on the meeting. The ambassador was on the way to the Chinese Embassy when the president broke silence in the Oval Office.

"Well, well," he said with a look that indicated he expected the others to speak.

"I cannot believe the audacity of the Chinese to take advantage of our domestic situation," the Secretary of State said what she thought was the obvious. Such a trade would be paramount to giving them complete control, not just influence, over Asia and most of the Pacific. You know what their definition of 'secure peace in Indochina' would mean— them seizing the area. We have spent billions in military aid to Taiwan over decades. Although the Chinese Communist

Party (CCP) would ultimately prevail, the Taiwanese would fight. The loss of life would be astronomical."

It was the COS's turn to speak. In these sessions the second to offer an opinion usually offered a counter opinion, whether they agreed with it or not. In this case, the COS believed her argument.

"I think what the Chinese want is what they will eventually have anyway. Their influence has been growing. We have not had the will or wherewithal to slow them. In 20 to 30 years, they will have what they seek now regardless of what we do. And what will we have? Perhaps not a country, but a balkanized lawless land of everyone for themselves. And I need not say where that would leave us.

But most importantly, Mr. President, you are President of the United States, notice United comes before States, rather than States before United. Your responsibility is for the common good of the United, you cannot take on responsibility for protecting the world."

After more pros and cons were laid out, the president said he would have his answer in the morning.

The SOS knew it was her clue to leave. She had a bad feeling. Once they were alone, the COS saw him glance at a cabinet along a wall. She knew from the glance he desired a highball. She moved to get one when he grabbed her arm and pulled her to him.

"You have no idea how much I rely upon your advice. Your council is invaluable."

"Is that all, Mr. President?"

He answered her by kissing her deeply.

Texas

Trucks and vans that left the Waco warehouse before the federal takeover were driven north out of the Feds' reach. Resistance members stopped inbound trucks to the warehouse on I-35 and rerouted them to Fort Hood delivery vehicles. Donation centers were opened in the Dallas/Fort Worth metro for residents of Fort Hood. They were overwhelmed.

The brief scare that Fort Hood would run low on supplies was averted. Supply routes were reestablished bypassing the Waco warehouse. Vendors were sent payments from the State of Texas, which was deducted from tax revenues sent Washington. Many in Fort Hood who were apprehensive about their opposition to the Feds were reassured with the outpouring of support from Texas civilians.

The Texas governor convened a cabinet meeting by introducing two guests. Most cabinet members had met Julie and Mason, the national and Texas Resistance leaders. All knew that the official meeting was another turning point. Julie briefed the group on what was happening in other states.

Mason updated the group on the successful efforts to supply Fort Hood. He then made a case for Texas House Bill 3489. The bill would mandate that all facilities supported and paid for by Texas taxpayers fly the Texas flag instead of the Stars and Stripes. It would include the seven Treasury service centers in Texas and Fort Hood.

Governor Archibald resisted. "I think Washington and much of the rest of the country would interpret such an act as open rebellion. What would that gain us? We are simply trying to reestablish our rights as declared in the Constitution. It is particularly the 1st, 2nd, 4th, 6th,9th and 10th amendments that we seek to be observed. Remember, we are not disavowing the principles the country was founded upon, they have. Why should we abandon what we cherish? We simply wish to reassert those principles and take our country back. Taking down the American flag would set others against us. I will veto that bill if it passes and strongly recommend that it not be considered. Julie, would you like to address the issue?"

"It is not the National Resistance's intention to start a civil war. Call it a reaffirmation of our country's founding principles symbolized by a renewed recognition of our Constitution. We have no problem with the Constitution as written, but over time it has been reinterpreted and ignored sometimes for financial interests, sometimes for pure ambition. Too often, past generations have ignored the seepage of freedom.

At the risk of getting too philosophical here, let me put things in perspective. There is a statistical term called regression to the mean. It means that any outlying data point whether it be the height of a human, a weather anomaly, or a historical measure will regress to the normal or mean. If we identify Mesopotamia as the oldest civilization of about 6,000 years ago, until the American Revolution, some sort of authoritarian rule has always prevailed. Freedom and respect of the individual is recent, representing only 300 of 6,000 years. Free societies are an outlier historically. The natural drift will be to relapse toward authoritarianism and class-based society unless we continually resist regression. However, that does not mean our struggle requires the letting of blood. If violence comes, let it be at the oppressors' hands."

Mason could sense the cabinet agreed with the governor. As Julie and he discussed earlier, it was important to show a united front. Discord needed to be avoided, and perhaps the governor and Julie were right.

"I will ask our followers in the legislature to hold the bill. But I ask your support in another area. We have prevented our supporters from going after the Feds' supplies. Unfortunately, they have not behaved mutually. After the Waco warehouse seizure, our Resistance people are insistent upon retaliation. Frankly, I am not sure I can prevent it. If I try, it will create a fracture in our organization."

Mason looked at the governor, who controlled the National Guard. "Can we count on National Guard support in guerrilla activities against their supply lines?"

Prior to the cabinet meeting, the governor and Julie had discussed the Feds' escalation. They had agreed earlier the escalation could not be ignored.

"I will instruct the Guard to coordinate activities with the Resistance, but confrontations must be avoided that would cause loss of life," the governor answered. The cabinet agreed.

It was the second trip the Fed lieutenant from New Jersey made bringing supplies from the warehouse in Waco to his federal brigade headquarters south of Fort Hood. Without trucks that normally carried supplies, he had four unarmed personnel carriers filled with food, toilet paper, medicines, and other supplies. He rode in a lead vehicle with a machine gun mounted on the roof. A similar vehicle trailed the caravan. They had experienced no trouble and did not expect any.

On a bridge across the Lampasas River south of Fort Hood, Eric and thirty members of the Resistance waited. One of the Resistance members worked for a bridge painting contractor. They hung scaffolding from the bridge bannisters that was used to support painters. This day it supported thirty armed men and women who waited on the side of the bridge out of sight.

Texas National Guard General Tate sent two armored, tracked personnel carriers to the bridge. Each carried fifteen National Guardsmen. Both carriers were hidden under a bridge approach at either end of the bridge waiting for the supply caravan.

It was a hot Texas day, only the low humidity made it tolerable. The lieutenant was on a short six-month assignment to Fort Hood and had not acclimated himself well. He had entered a New Jersey political family though a domestic partnership with the family's daughter. Politics was his future. A year stint in the military would enhance his resume and help the family, his father-in-law coaxed. Sleeping in a tent outside the Fort in the heat with no air conditioning was not what he anticipated. Hopefully, his participation in the putdown of this misfit tantrum he would someday proudly tell his grandchildren.

As the caravan pulled on the two-lane bridge, he was looking down, texting his wife in Trenton about the triple-digit heat. He looked up when he felt the driver suddenly apply the brakes. An armored carrier blocked both bridge lanes in front of them.

His rearview mirror showed movement behind them. "Get headquarters," he ordered his sergeant. The movement was another armored carrier blocking their retreat. He saw someone walking toward him on the bridge from the tracked vehicle that blocked their path. He glanced at the men in his carrier. It was his moment to show leadership; he no longer noticed the heat but felt his heart pound in anticipation. When he got up, he embarrassingly felt his back side wet, his shirt stuck to his back with perspiration. It was cold. He forced himself to walk confidently toward the oncoming officer, but his steps became hesitant when armed citizens startled him rising over the bannisters with weapons drawn. They were not in uniform—some in shorts, others in ragtag jeans— he suddenly understood his predicament.

The Army lieutenant recognized the man opposing him on the bridge was a National Guard captain. The lieutenant gritted his teeth and spoke tough to conceal his fear, "Captain, I demand that you immediately unblock this road and help me arrest these illegally armed citizens."

"Really, Lieutenant, I suggest a more prudent course of action for you would be to vacate the trucks of drivers, put them on your escort vehicles and be on your way unharmed."

"You should be aware that we have two armored platoons within five minutes which have been notified," the New Jersey lieutenant answered.

"That's odd, because the two drones we launched a few minutes ago detect you have no one within thirty minutes," answered the captain.

The lieutenant turned saying, "Let me check headquarters and get back with you."

"You have five minutes," the captain said to the lieutenant's back.

The lieutenant grabbed the phone away from his sergeant. "We are in a situation here with rebels and need backup immediately. How long before you can get us help?"

"I need to clear it with the general," said the lieutenant colonel. "Stall them."

While the lieutenant was stalling, the trailing escort vehicle with three soldiers was surrounded by Eric and other civilians.

At gunpoint, Eric ordered Sergeant Anderson, "Stay in your vehicle and turn over your weapons."

Sergeant Anderson saw National Guardsmen step out of the armored carrier behind him with weapons drawn. He looked them over, unlikely but hoping to see his brother— he did not. The sergeant was from Laredo. He had a brother in the Texas National Guard and a brother in high school who had been involved in illicit freedom protests.

The three handed over their weapons, and Anderson got out of the vehicle with his hands raised. "I told you to remain in the vehicle," Eric told him. "We are not taking prisoners."

Sergeant Anderson had been considering his predicament for some time. A corporal, he knew, had attempted to cross over and been caught. The corporal had been reprimanded to the worst duties. His lieutenant knew he was from Texas and had been watching him closely. Now was his chance.

"You don't understand, I'm not surrendering. I'm from Laredo. I'm coming home."

Eric looked deep into his eyes, then reached his hand out, "Welcome home." He was surprised when Anderson embraced him.

Resistance members were marching four truck drivers toward the rear vehicle. They were taken aback witnessing their sergeant embracing an armed civilian, then being introduced to a Texas Guardsman. The drivers were ordered to get in the rear escort vehicle, while guardsmen detached the machine gun.

A corporal, the vehicle's driver, stood back—reluctant to climb aboard the vehicle. He was from Alabama. It was known that Anderson and he were best friends. He dreaded the prospect of the lieutenant, and who knew how many other officers, grilling him about Anderson's defection. He did not understand what was going on in the country, but he knew whom he could trust.

Anderson saw his hesitation, "Don't look at me. You make up your own mind and do what you are comfortable with."

He walked to Anderson and Eric as the others found room in the escort vehicle. Members of the Resistance militia were now backing loaded trucks off the bridge and turning them around, while the rear escort vehicle moved forward in the other lane.

At the five-minute mark, the National Guard Captain ordered the rubber tracked armored carrier to move forward toward the lead Fed escort vehicle. It stopped ten feet from the lieutenant's vehicle. Ten armed members of the Texas Resistance surrounded the vehicle.

"Time is up. Are you ready to move on?" the captain hollered.

"Still waiting on orders," replied the lieutenant.

The captain told his driver to slowly move forward. The escort vehicle rocked when the track of the carrier came in contact. Its front end nosedived to the bridge floor as the track started walking up the hood. The lieutenant and the three soldiers in the escort vehicle quickly bailed.

The captain looked down the bridge and saw the Resistance had already convinced the trailing vehicle to move forward. "Now I suggest you load your people on the vehicle that is coming and be gone."

He glared at the captain and blurted, "I'm sure in the near future you will realize this day destroyed your life," while wondering what the incident would do to his own career and life.

With the remaining detail on board, the vehicle slowly traveled down the road with soldiers standing on the running boards gripping what they could. It was ten minutes before they met the column coming to rescue them. When the column reached the bridge, all that remained was an escort vehicle with its gun removed and front end crumpled and paint scaffolding hanging from the bridge.

It was a lieutenant colonel who grilled the lieutenant for hours at headquarters about the incident. What stuck in the lieutenant's mind was his statement, "You not only surrendered valuable supplies to a rag-tag group, two men under your command mutinied. You should have been aware of their inclinations. It will all go on your record."

That evening on his cot in the tent, he ignored his wife's texts. The day's activities had not gone according to their plan.

Sergeant Anderson was taken to General Tate's Texas National Guard headquarters. He was elated to find his brother with the general. He noticed his brother was holding a Bible.

"Do you wish to join the Texas National Guard with the rank of sergeant?" the general asked.

"Yes, sir."

"Then put your hand on the Bible and repeat after your brother."

"Do you pledge allegiance to the Constitution of the United States, the Constitution of the State of Texas and the governor of Texas?"

In the next few days, the Texas National Guard learned much about the Federal supply chain outside Fort Hood from a logistics sergeant.

Chapter 16

Atlas Headquarters

While Julie was in Austin at the governor's cabinet meeting, Andrew was meeting with Barry and Torrence at the former Atlas Transportation headquarters in Midland. It had now taken the place of the nearly abandoned cruise ship as the nerve center of the Resistance. It was feeling like home again to many scientists and engineers.

Barry and Torrence had been tracking the activities of NSA personnel since their headquarters and data storage facilities were destroyed. Most were still on the federal payroll, but with the facilities gone they had little to do until the new PPU 3.0s came onboard. Thanks to the effort in Texas, that was now a long way off.

They knew that twenty upper-level officials of the NSA met recently at the Holiday/Marriott in Arlington, Virginia.

"It's not that unusual, is it?" Andrew asked.

"We had the hotel they were scheduled to meet under surveillance by one of our people in the DC area. The first thing that struck her was the huge amount of security around the hotel. She saw two limos pull up with embassy plates. At least six people got out of the limos. The plates on the limos matched those issued to the Chinese

Embassy. Security would not let her in the lobby. It was late afternoon before the limos were loaded and NSA officials started leaving."

"So, it is safe to assume they met Chinese officials," summarized Andrew.

"That's not all; communication between those NSA officials and the level of officials below them has increased significantly."

"I'll talk to Julie, but in the meantime I suggest you prioritize figuring out what is happening."

Fort Hood

General Martinez planned for most any attack by federal forces except for two— air attack and bio attack. The Air Force could easily take Fort Hood out, but it was assumed the loss of life that would entail made it off-limits as would the prospects of bio or chemical attack.

High precision striking drones were a concern, however. As defense against that eventuality, he positioned the latest ground-to-air lasers around the base. The laser crews often practiced sighting in on supply parachutes being dropped on federal troops.

Given that the Waco warehouse supplies were exhausted—or confiscated in route by National Guard aided Resistance—supplies to the 22,000 federal troops south of Fort Hood had become an airlift operation. Usually in the morning, allowing retrieval in daylight, transports from bases around the country dropped supplies.

By capturing the warehouse in Waco, the Feds had breached an unspoken understanding that supply lines were off limits. The Resistance and National Guard were now disrupting federal supply lines. But they could not harass airdrops on the ground as the drop areas were heavily protected. General Martinez's ground-to-air lasers could.

The goal was not to starve federal troops but make their encampments less comfortable. To completely deprive them of food could make them desperate, perhaps endangering Texas households in the area for pilferage or cause an increase in hostilities. However, demonstrating the ability to deny the Feds supplies, hopefully would discourage an escalation on their part.

The lasers were trained on the crates of supplies as they were parachuted from the sky. It was a fish in a barrel shoot. The crates hit with lasers fell apart, scattering supplies over a wide area. Some supplies were destroyed by the laser, some by the landing after freefall. Only twenty percent was salvageable. Gathering and sorting the remains demanded many soldiers and was demoralizing.

Whenever informant soldiers behind federal lines indicated supplies were becoming critically low, General Martinez suspended laser fire. The intent was to make the Feds uncomfortable, not frantic.

Atlas Headquarters Conference Room

"We've been unable to uncover anything about the NSA meeting with Chinese officials in Arlington. Getting into NSA activities has always been tough, but it appears an extra level of security has gone up around that meeting," reported Barry.

"The extra security itself is cause for alarm. How critical do we think it is to go all out in discovering the purpose of the meeting?" asked Julie.

After discussion, it was agreed that all measures should be used to get the information. Julie said she would contact their person in Maryland.

"That person would be an amateur from the Resistance?" Mason asked.

"Yes."

"I know where we may secure a pro for the job, I'll contact Carl."

Arlington, VA

The Resistance had files on most of the upper management of the NSA. John Silvers was one who was identified attending the meeting. His specialty was the language of data storage. He had been with the agency nearly twenty years. He did not appear to have any political connections. Hence, contrary to the norm, his workaholic nature must have advanced him in the agency.

He never married his partner of fifteen years, avoiding the career harness of an outdated ritual. Long hours and fanatic devotion to data language strained their relationship. It was held together by a desire to sustain their lifestyle and lack of initiative on either's part to end their union. She had a boyfriend which he knew about but avoided acknowledging. It was okay, she complained less about his hours.

With John's office destroyed in the NSA explosion, the emptiness in his day was destroying him. His salary remained the same. Someday, he hoped, he would be needed again. Their 3,000 square foot home was a high-end four-bedroom Arlington, Virginia colonial with a pool in a community of federal employees. His status in the agency negated the otherwise strict limit on square feet of home per capita.

When his partner was at work or otherwise occupied, the house seemed as empty as he was lonesome. What had started as a late afternoon visit to a bar, now started at noon. He knew he was drinking too much but could stop anytime. He certainly would if the Chinese thing worked out.

Zoe strolled to the bank of mailboxes in her complex of studio apartments primarily for something to do. She found one envelope addressed to her without a return address. Wrapped inside was a small gold coin without a note. Private ownership of gold was again banned as it had been over a century earlier during the great depression. It, now, was one of many forms of underground currency. Within an hour, her grape rang.

"This is Carl, do you remember me?"

"Most certainly, the Texas man who destroyed my career."

"What do you think of the coin?"

"Hmm, you know owning them is illegal, but what isn't?"

"I like the attitude; would you like nine more coins like it?"

"Do my legs attract normal men? Which, of course, you are not."

It was thirty minutes of noon when John took what had become his normal seat at the neighborhood bar. John was nearing fifty years, now not quite trim since twenty pounds had found their way on him since his office was vaporized. Arriving early allowed him time for a drink before Jim, his partner in the afternoon lie and exaggeration exchange, joined him. John handled his liquor well, never once did he divulge to anyone what he did or had done for a living. When Jim asked, he said he worked on software from his home. It was not the biggest lie he told at the bar.

He was on his second drink when a good looking thirty-something sat at the bar a seat away from him. Zoe had toned down her dress two notches. She wore slacks, and less makeup than normal. She was beginning to wonder if John was going to acknowledge her presence when he asked her if she had been at the bar before. Avoiding appearing too flirtatious worked; he soon moved next to her and ordered a round for each.

In John's appraisal, this was a regular lady, not like the occasional independent businesswoman who frequented the bar seeking money for favors. He introduced himself and noticed moisture on her hand as he properly shook it.

Jim entered the bar, saw John was occupied, gave him a wink, and sat at the other end of the bar. When John nodded to Jim, Zoe added something to his drink to hasten the effect of alcohol and the other stimulant. He was on his third drink when Zoe told him she was an artist.

"What do you paint?" he asked.

"My subjects vary. Would you like to see?"

"I don't see any paintings with you."

"At my place, of course, silly."

"I'm not much of an art critic. What would I examine other than your paintings?" he asked before he caught himself feeling a bit giddy.

"I'm sure we can find something. Let's go, I'll drive. You've drank too much."

The drugs sufficiently enhanced his infatuation with Zoe that he did not notice it was a motel she took him to with her room door beside the parking spot. Stan, a local Resistance leader, held the door open for them. Zoe helped John to the bed. He pawed at her momentarily before he collapsed on the bed.

Zoe looked at Stan. "What this is about, I do not want to know. Here is a syringe loaded with the Polish serum. Wait until he starts to wake, which should be in about an hour. The truth serum will only last half an hour, so get whatever you are after fast. In another hour, he will be lucid but will not remember anything. Now what do you have for me?"

In the ongoing Cold War between the former Eastern members of the European Union and the Western members, espionage was the battleground. The previous century had seen the Western European nations dominate, but because of a declining indigenous population and unassimilated immigrants of a different culture, the Western nations were in decline. The ascending Poles, Hungarians and Ukrainians developed an effective truth serum to glean secrets from Westerners. Zoe had brought samples to the US.

Stan handed her nine small gold coins, and she was gone. Sobriety was returning when Stan dropped John off in the bar's parking lot. In familiar territory, he was not ready to go home. He entered the bar with a clearing head and sat beside Jim.

"That wasn't long. I hope you had a good time?" Jim said as a question with a devilish smile.

"Yeh, she was... just marvelous," John answered, hoping it was true, although he couldn't remember a thing.

Texas

Sergeant Anderson had met numerous times with members of the Resistance since he flipped sides at the bridge. His orders were to render information to the Resistance, but Guard members were not allowed to participate in raids unless specifically authorized. As Anderson could be arrested as a traitor, he would never be allowed to accompany a raid. His information had been the basis for raids on communication and temporary sanitation sites. An occasional explosive device dropped into a latrine made life less comfortable for those in the field.

Eric asked, "The brigade headquarters is not tapped into any electric grid. From where is their power coming?

"As part of the original equipment delivered, a self-contained dual methane or propane fueled generator was dropped. It generates electricity for communication, lights, cold food storage and the colonel's air conditioning unit," Anderson answered.

He went on to draw a crude map of the generator's location, placed 1,000 feet away from headquarters to distance the noise. Enclosed in the metal 6X8 foot cube on 4x4 runners, making it portable, was an in-line six-cylinder engine which powered an electric generator. His drawing showed the engine exhaust on the back side of the box.

"Don't think about sabotaging the generator. Two soldiers are on guard at the door to the cube 24/7. You would not get inside the door without them alerting others, and you'd soon be overwhelmed."

Kelly, a Resistance member who had been with Eric in Iowa with the railroad tie dump security detail, asked, "Where is the air intake for the generator engine?"

"It's on this side," Anderson answered pointing to the position on his drawing.

"I have an idea," said Kelly.

The moon after midnight caught Eric and Kelly crawling through grass, stopping every few minutes to listen for any danger around them. They preferred to avoid the rattle of a snake in the grass—a copperhead they could deal with. Once they heard the hum of the generator, the map on their grape was not needed. At fifty feet from the back of the generator box in camouflage clothing, they laid quietly to see if the guards periodically walked around the generator box. At twenty minutes into their wait, one guard circled the box. When he returned to the front, it was their time.

Kelly had been a long-haul trucker for years. It was his excuse for being in Iowa. Cold weather in the north presented challenges when trying to start a diesel engine. A simple aid was a can of ether, which could be sprayed in the engine intake to aid cold weather engine starting. One to two squirts of ether were usually enough. Too much would damage the engine. Diesel engines were built much heavier internally than gas or propane engines. A snort of ether would destroy a warm running lesser-built engine.

Kelly quickly crawled to the side of the generating cube, stood, and pointed his ether aerosol can at the engine intake in the side of the cube. Instead of giving it two squirts, he held the trigger down until he heard an engine knock. Unable to handle the extreme combustibility of ether, the engine noise became louder. The chatter of bent intake values could be heard as Kelly and Eric ran. They were but a few hundred feet away when the cube went silent, and lights went out behind them.

It was two days before Army mechanics figured out what happened to the generator. The engine would need to be rebuilt or replaced, parts or another engine was not high on the priority list of supplies. The heat was stifling without his AC, and the Colonel was furious. He immediately started working on a plan.

Atlas Headquarters

The information Stan had gleaned from a drugged John in a motel room was very disturbing. Stan taped the interview and the Resistance directors listened twice. The Chinese were working with the Feds to supply them with CCP surveillance drones. The first shipment will be leaving an African port in one week. The meeting in Arlington was an introductory training on the use of the African built Chinese designed drones. John did not reveal what the tradeoff with the Chinese was. They assumed he did not know.

"Stan, how confident are we John doesn't know where the Chinese shipment will arrive given he knew the approximate date?" Andrew asked.

"He didn't appear to know, and it makes sense that would be on a need-to-know basis only."

"Someone has to know, and we must find out," said Julie. "Do you have any idea who attended the Arlington meeting that would know?"

"I would guess someone higher than the technical executives at the Arlington meeting."

"Do we know where in Africa the Chinese have these things made?" Andrew asked Barry.

"No, but I'll find out." He left the conference room and was back in ten minutes.

"The Chinese have them built at a colony in Tanzania. Depending on the ship and load, the shipping time to the East Coast is around thirty days. The time is similar whether they go through the Suez or around Cape Horn."

"If they successfully deploy those things, we are back to where we were before we eliminated the NSA eyes," Andrew commented.

"We can't allow that to happen," answered Julie. "Carl, do you think your lady friend would be up to doing another job for us?"

"I'm sure if the money was right—but we would need to first figure out who knows what we need, then who is vulnerable," Carl answered.

"Okay, we've got much to do, let's meet tomorrow."

South of Fort Hood

The federal brigade colonel had planned most the night. The little sleep he got with no air conditioning gave him plenty time. A food storage shack had been placed between the main encampment and a line of trees. Patrols were in the woods behind the tree line while they were setting the trap. Five holes were dug, big enough for a person to sit comfortably in during the night. Leaves, placed on woven wire, covered, and disguised the holes. Motion detectors were placed around the shack to warn of intruders.

The first night the trap was set, the colonel did not expect any activity. There was none other than Kelly high in a live oak tree half a mile away with night vision binoculars. He did not see the men underground with automatic carbines, the holes, or notice that the closest tent held a dozen armed soldiers instead of four men sleeping.

In the morning Kelly explained what he had seen to Eric and others. "What do you think?" asked Eric.

"It looks too easy. When food is in short supply, why would you place food storage a distance from the encampment and not station guards?"

"Did you see any signs of a trap?"

"No, everything looked normal, in fact too normal."

"Let's go with your gut and leave the shed alone," Eric suggested.

The second night found no activity around the food storage shack.

The next morning while they were discussing the prior night's recognizance, Juan bragged about his Golden Retriever's nose, saying it could smell a federales a quarter mile away.

Kelly had an idea. "Didn't someone go through the feds garbage last week and find many baked bean cans?"

"Yes, what are you thinking?" asked Eric.

"Juan, if you gave your dog a sniff of an empty can of baked beans could he find full cans?"

"Absolutely, my Henry can sniff out anything."

That night Kelly, Eric, Juan, and Henry were dropped off a mile from the restricted zone around the camp. The first three wore night vision goggles. Eric had been concerned that Henry would not move with the caution required, but Juan handled him well. As always, they stopped periodically and scanned the area for any danger. They spotted a deer which was a good sign in that it had not been scared away.

Kelly was high in the lookout live oak tree with night vision binoculars while Eric stood in watch and Juan held an empty can of baked beans for Henry to sniff. Once the dog got the scent, Juan said, "Vamanos mira, Henry!"

The dog ran in a zig zag pattern, then beelined it to the food storage shack and made two circles around it. Suddenly, five men with weapons drawn jumped from underground hiding places while soldiers burst from a tent and ran toward the food shack. Henry stopped, wondering why he drew so much attention.

Hearing Juan's whistle, Henry scampered at full speed from the shed. Kelly was down from the tree and they took off. Halfway to their vehicle, Eric shot a flare over the food shack, putting an exclamation mark on the trap's failure.

They reached a road that was the mile marker which would put them out of restricted territory when they saw two Army vehicles approaching. They laid low in the grader ditch, stifling their humor at what they had pulled. The Army vehicles slowed shining spotlights across the field in which they had been but missed them.

Mason Trotter Home

Mason reluctantly answered his grape seeing the call was from Damon.

"What's up, brother?"

"Good here, I've got a steady paycheck from the University. I hope your income from the electric business remains good. But I feel sorry for those around the country who have recklessly flipped and chosen to be paid by states. Hopefully, Washington will allow them stipends when the states run out of money."

"What causes you to think states will run out of money?"

"Didn't you hear that Acme Office Furniture has pulled all manufacturing and distribution operations from states that have offered traitorous soldiers and treasury workers an alternate salary?"

"I don't listen to the news that much."

"Well, you should."

"Isn't most of Acme's business for government offices? Might they have a vested interest?" Mason caught himself before he said more.

"You were always prone to conspiracy theories, Mason. Have a good night."

Chapter 17

Torrence had developed contacts in Polish intelligence through Pawel Bartosz, the freighter captain who smuggled illegal goods into the states. The Poles had informants in Tanzania watching Chinese activities in their slave colony. He discovered that a Chinese flagged freighter was loaded in the harbor with products from a drone factory. Its destination was unknown, but it would be leaving soon.

"We must assume that freighter is headed for us," observed Julie. "The question is where will it dock?"

Barry answered, "According to the Coast Guard freighter tracking database, it historically docks in Fort Lauderdale. I think we should assume they will want the trip to appear normal and not break the pattern."

"We have three choices: destroy it before it leaves, in route, or at the harbor in Fort Lauderdale. We have many sympathetic officers in the Navy. But do we have enough on any Navy ship to target the freighter?" added Andrew.

Julie quickly answered, "No, we don't have any of those choices. US Resistance forces attacking a CCP flagged ship would either trigger a war with China or solidify support for the Feds in putting us down. Either way, it unites the rest of the country against us."

"You're right," Andrew responded. "And reaching out to China ourselves would be foolhardy as we don't have anything to offer them, and it would tip Washington off that we know of the shipment."

South of Fort Hood

The brigade colonel stood by the food shed with Lieutenant Leland. Leland had been assigned to protect the compound against guerrilla attacks. The colonel figured no one had more to gain by catching guerrillas than Leland after his bridge disaster. The colonel scanned the tree line and surrounding area with 144X zoom binoculars.

"See the slightly taller of the three live oak trees nearly half a mile away? If I were looking for an observation post for this food shack, that tree is from where I would go. Set up the trap there, curiosity will bring them back. But do not let anyone close to the tree; these people are cautious woodsmen. They can likely smell footprints as well as the dog they keep, otherwise we would already have them. The equipment I ordered two weeks ago finally was dropped yesterday. If you have any questions, let me know."

Kelly and Eric were dropped off two miles from the observation tree at a different place than before; they were cautious but also curious. Had the Feds left the food shack where it was? Had they given up luring someone to it? Once inside the mile no-go zone, they stopped four times to survey the landscape with goggles.

They took a roundabout route to the observation tree. Four well-hidden motion cameras caught their movement. The detectors were set to only catch movement above five feet and bigger than a racoon, eliminating being tripped by deer or squirrels.

While Eric checked the area with night vision goggles in a 360 degree circle, Kelly stopped ten feet short of the observation tree and studied the ground around it. He looked for any sign of disturbance. Each time he left the tree, Kelly sprayed an area around the tree with an illegal animal repellent. It assured his warning signs were undisturbed by animals. A few dead leaves he had stabilized with twigs in a zigzag pattern around the tree. They all were as he left them.

"Okay?" Kelly asked as Eric continued to scan with goggles.

"Looks clear to me," Eric answered.

"Then I'm going up."

Kelly's arm reached up to grab a low branch which he used to pull himself up. Doing so broke a laser beam guarding the branch. They heard a puff as compressed air tossed nets at them from two directions. While they were struggling to free themselves from the net, five soldiers on either side—who had been hidden under insulated, camouflaged tarps—sprung out toward them. The tarps had kept them hidden from night vision and infrared sensors. Kelly and Eric frantically freed themselves from the net only to find spotlights highlighting them. They were surrounded by federal soldiers with automatic weapons pointed at them. Their sidearms were of no use.

"Well, well, we meet again," said Lieutenant Leland, recognizing them from his bridge fiasco. "Remember the warning I gave you about your life changing? It just has. And I see we can also charge you with carrying illegal firearms."

The lieutenant walked triumphantly into the colonel's quarters. "Sir, we caught two of them. I recognize them from the bridge. Shall I bring them to you for interrogation?"

"Good work. No, I do not want to see them. I've better things to do. Lock them up until we get orders for what to do with them."

Leland, happy that the colonel was pleased, could not wait to call his partner in New Jersey with the good news. He was confident that capture of rebel hooligans would make her proud. He was disappointed. Her tone was subdued.

"So, I guess that was good, but your record will always be tarnished from the bridge incident. And that will handicap both our futures. I am no longer sure that this relationship is good for us. If something is not done, my family's political future will be jeopardized. I must let you know that I am discussing our domestic partnership agreement with an attorney."

"Let's talk about it."

"I don't believe there is anything to talk about."

The whiplash of emotions within a few minutes hit Leland hard.

Resistance protocol called for anyone on operations to check in every few hours. It was soon known Kelly and Eric had been captured or worse.

Maryland

Zoe was still out of work. Work she could get was beneath her. She was good at what she did and knew it. Because Zoe had been outed in Texas, it was assumed she could be recognized by Resistance elsewhere in the country. With no CIA assignments forthcoming outside the country, Zoe was delighted to get a call from Carl for another job. She needed the money.

The assistant director of NSA was partnered with a man but was known to have an eye for women. He pulled into the alley heading for the garage behind his house. His pathway was blocked by a car with a woman wearing a skirt. It had been months since he saw a woman in a skirt, years since he had seen one as short. She was waving, apparently seeking help with her car.

"Do you think I should drive after hitting this in the road?" she asked, looking underneath the car with a rear door open. He bent over to look, and Zoe pushed him in the open door. He fell across the back seat with her on top of him. She jabbed him in the neck with a needle and kept him pinned down until he quit squirming. Confident he was out; she drove him to the motel where she had taken John a few weeks earlier.

She offered to get whatever answers Carl needed without assistance for twice the money. Carl accepted. The man was soon blabbering all he knew about the Chinese ship.

Unbeknownst to Zoe and the Resistance, directors of critical agencies and their immediate assistants carried a chip in their arm allowing them to be tracked in case of kidnapping. The assistant director's partner found his car blocking the alley and called the agency. If not for his abandoned car, the agency would have assumed he was at the motel for a private matter. It had happened before, but unlikely this time with his car abandoned. Two FBI cars and three Maryland police cars pulled into the motel parking lot, and officers soon were inside the room.

Zoe was immediately handcuffed and taken to an NSA interrogation facility. The assistant director was taken to the hospital. His partner was so upset that he been conned by a good-looking woman again, he moved out.

After less than twenty-four hours of waterboarding, Zoe spilled everything she knew, including her contact with Carl, the Texas governor's husband. The Feds now knew the Resistance was aware of the Chinese drones. But the assistant director only knew the CCP drones were to be delivered to Fort Lauderdale. And Zoe had not the opportunity to pass on what little she discovered from the assistant director. The kidnapping and interrogation gave the Resistance nothing.

White House

"How many times have I warned you the Texans must be dealt with?" harped the VP. "It is time to use all our resources and eliminate their leaders."

"I know the governor and her husband are Neanderthals through and through." *(It was not the first time a president had called the governor of Texas a Neanderthal).* "But we can only act upon the information we have," cautioned the President.

The FBI director turned to the CIA director. "Why haven't you people identified where the Resistance is operating? We need to know where, whether it is Poland or El Salvador. Then we can use all available means to make them as extinct as their Neanderthal predecessors."

The president was furious as the others, but he did not have the luxury of flying off the handle. He needed to avoid a split in his administration, yet his response needed to be measured. With evidence the first Texas family were outright traitors with the Resistance, he would act.

He turned to the FBI director, "I want warrants issued for the governor and her husband's arrest and place them at number one and two on the FBI's most wanted list. The charge is treason. Let us also issue a million United Nations Credits (UNC) reward for their capture."

South of Fort Hood

The one-mile-wide strip between the opposing forces south of Fort Hood was now commonly called 'every person's land'. Friends from opposing sides met and talked, soldiers from the Fort Hood side often brought beer for their counterparts on the Fed side. Patrols from both sides traveled unimpeded through most of the area. However, an unwritten rule was that patrols stayed a few hundred feet from the other side.

General Martinez's patrols from Fort Hood were cautioned to stay at least 500 feet from the federal lines. He did not want any soldiers provoking the Feds or chance having them detained. The federal commanders took a different posture. They wished to convey aggressiveness and a sense that they would ultimately prevail. Hence, federal patrols were encouraged to come within a few feet of the other side.

Five members of a federal patrol were twenty feet from a sandbagged barricade that marked what they considered rebel territory. Earlier they had stopped midway in 'every person's land' and accepted beer offered from rebel soldiers. Missing beer on their side, they drank more than prudent while on patrol.

"You boys got guns loaded over there or are you too busy eating grits?" one Fed hollered mocking the other side. Usually, they soon had the insult returned. This time nothing was returned, which prompted them to push more.

They continued to taunt, "They're probably all busy sleeping with their cousins or sisters."

The five were laughing and did not notice forty soldiers who had circled around them. "Drop your weapons," a sergeant ordered them.

They turned and found themselves surrounded. "You've got to be joking, but we'll give it to you, nice ploy."

"We're serious, you are under arrest. You've violated the unwritten 500 feet rule."

The five thought the arrest was a retaliatory hoax for their taunt of a unit they assumed was mostly southerners until they were put in a cell.

Jim and Al had witnessed the verbal abuse given by the five from their platoon. They were from Arkansas and the panhandle of Florida. It was enough for them. They approached the line of sandbags their disgusting fellow platoon members had been taken behind.

"Stop there, or you also will also be arrested," came a voice behind a sandbag.

"No, we are not with the five. We want to come over."

"Drop your weapons and come."

Jim and Al were welcomed by a captain.

The next morning the commander of federal forces received a call from General Martinez. "We have five soldiers in custody who were within a few feet of our line last night. I understand you hold two members of the Resistance militia. We really don't have a place to hold your patrol."

"That is apples and oranges. The two we hold have stolen from us out of uniform. The five you hold were on patrol maybe offending, but stealing nothing."

"However you paint it, we have five, you have two."

"Above my pay grade, I'll get back with you," the commander said and disconnected.

"How'd it go?" Mason Trotter asked him later.

"I'm concerned that he brought up them being out of uniform."

"He knows the Resistance militia doesn't have uniforms."

"I know and that is what scares me."

Atlas Transportation Conference Room

The bad news kept stacking up. Zoe captured, no big deal, but the governor and her husband charged with treason. That would require guarding them 24/7 with at least a platoon of guardsmen. Not only would they be in danger of a federal patrol, but also errant citizens tempted by a million UNC.

Barry discovered that a Marine division of approximately 20,000 was being deployed around the docks at Fort Lauderdale. Another Marine division was preparing to join them. A no-fly zone with a twenty-mile radius had been established around the docks and ground to air lasers were installed. All drone deliveries in the no-fly zone were banned. Getting a bomb laden drone to a warehouse holding the Chinese vultures would be nearly impossible.

They could harass the disbursement of the Chinese vultures, but it would be crumbs while the cake was delivered. Even if they were willing to chance war with China at this point, they had no means to stop the Chinese freighter. A feeler had been put out to Poland, but the Poles were not about to risk war with China.

Julie and Andrew were particularly depressed about the fate of Eric and Kelly. They had become friends when the two traveled to Iowa offering security while they planned the attack on the NSA. Would the destruction of NSA facilities be in vain once thousands of CCP vultures were operable? Citizens, now coming out from under the heavy blanket of vulture fear, would be forced to retreat.

The president's address the prior night slammed the message home. He assured the public that stability and policies for 'the common good' would be enforced by new technologies. He insinuated that the new technology was already being deployed. Although the vultures had not been delivered, he pushed the opportunity to put the genie back in the bottle.

He also lamented his duty to serve punishment on those who would violently thwart 'the common good'. He said, "It would be easy for me to turn a cheek, but that would be violating my pledge to you. Sometimes doing what is best for the community is not pretty or easy. But we must make society the best it can be. That I shall do."

Added to all the internal bad news was international news. Although the media were ignoring or minimizing the eruption of hostilities in the Eastern hemisphere, news was getting through. A fighting war had broken out between the CCP and Taiwan. Reports were that fighting was heavy with an immense loss of life. The CCP Army was also moving into Indochina.

Barry reported, "All signs are the seventh fleet is moving east away from the conflicts. I guess it is obvious what the tradeoff is for the White House getting CCP vultures."

"Terrible as it is, unfortunately, we cannot do anything about what is happening there. In the long run, it is to the world's advantage for us to preserve freedom in America and keep the beacon of light alive. That must be our focus here."

After a long pause, Julie added, "Does anyone have an idea?".

Torrence had been staying with Melissa since their return to Midland. They had become close on the cruise ship. It was somewhat awkward living in the house that her former husband, Dan, and his former boss had built, but she made him feel at home. They filled a void in each other's life.

Torrence did not sleep well the previous night. He lay still, not wanting to deter Melissa's sleep. A dream kept reoccurring. It was of his childhood. His grandfather had taken the family on a cruise to the Caribbean. It was a good time with cousins, games, and good times. He thought of the trip the first time he got on what became the Resistance cruise ship. It all came back so vividly, particularly the anticipation waiting in line inside what looked like a warehouse to board the ship.

"I have an idea," said Torrence.

White House

Although not cheerful, the mood was somewhat better at the White House. Particularly, thought the President because the VP was not on hand to rile emotions.

"Congratulations for finally catching a couple of their marauders. Perhaps the person responsible for capturing them deserves a jump in rank."

"Mr. President," the CJCS jumped in, "The lieutenant who caught them was also responsible for losing a shipment of supplies. If anything, he just rectified himself."

"Okay, I get it, you must maintain discipline, but the loathsome cretins, we'll make an example out of them. A firing squad will send a firm message to others with crazy ideas. This is not some video game that you turn off when you get tired. Actions have consequences."

"Mr. President, may I have a word?" asked the Secretary of State.

"Hold on, we'll get to that subject later."

"Mr. President," said the COS. "I understand and agree that the punishment needs to be severe, but we should avoid an immense backlash like we caused by hanging the trio in Maryland."

"What do you suggest?" the President asked his COS while glancing at his fidgety Secretary of State.

"I believe a firing squad is appropriate, but let's not make a public spectacle of it. Have it done quietly, and just say the punishment was appropriate for high treason."

"You probably have a point. We also need to consider what we do with the governor and husband once they are in our hands. It would be unseemly to execute an elected official publicly. We would not want to set that precedent."

The SOS was even more gulled that the president, as always, catered to his COS, while ignoring her. It was common knowledge that their relationship was more than business but could not be acknowledged.

The president noticed his SOS's face change from anxiety to frustration and said, "Okay, you want to say something about our Chinese friends, what's on your mind?"

"Is it true that our seventh fleet is abandoning the Western Pacific?"

"Yes, an agreement is an agreement. I wish they would have waited until the PPUs were delivered, but they are in route. Taiwan's fall was inevitable anyway. In the long run, the sooner it happens the better for all. And let us be frank, how can we criticize them for putting their country back together when we fight to keep ours together?"

"What about our allies— Japan, Australia, the Philippines, and New Zealand?"

"I am the President of the United States, not the protector of other countries. We have our own country to save."

The Secretary of State reached inside her jacket and pulled out an envelope. "Here, sir, is my resignation. I cannot occupy this position given these policies."

She got up and left the Oval Office without another word.

When she had gone the President looked around the room and said, "If there be anyone else here of that persuasion, now is the time to speak."

The CJCS, and NSA directors exchanged looks but did not speak. In their minds, they didn't disagree with the SOS's sentiments and admired her courage, but the train was moving. They could not alter the route and jumping off was dangerous. Picking the winning side had gotten them where they were.

The FBI director spoke, "I feel more comfortable that she is gone. She has always been queasy about what must be done. If we do not break the back of these back road weasels, we will pay the price."

The President ignored the FBI director knowing the man had no limits, "Okay, now that we are in agreement. I believe the Resistance learning of the new PPUs is to our advantage. It empowered us to put Marine divisions in place. We will not be caught flat- footed. And a few renegade soldiers in Texas and some undisciplined governors here and there will fall in line when we again can monitor their every action."

Chapter 18

Lieutenant Leland had not heard from his domestic partner in New Jersey for two days. This was not their first spat, but time usually healed their disagreements. He was confident enough time had passed for her to rethink a breakup.

Their relationship checked all the boxes. For her family, it provided an appearance of avoiding another incestuous same class relationship by a well-heeled political family. For Leland, it was an opportunity to step out of multi-generational habitation in West Virginia which offered little opportunity. He was polite and ambitious; she was attractive and smart. Their passion for each other was real, in addition to the non-romantic attributes of their relationship.

They met at Princeton University. For her New Jersey family, a local Level 1 University was a good choice. It would play well with voters. Given her connections, her entry was assured. Every year Princeton accepted a few applicants from around the country, particularly if they were from disadvantaged families. It gave the appearance of economic diversity. Leland fit the obligatory bill.

Leland came from a long line of coalminers. His grandfather had been a mine supervisor before coal became unfashionable. His father seriously tried to learn computer coding but did not have the passion for it. Eventually, he came to drink too much. It was his mother who finally applied for government stipends out of necessity. Dependence devastated his father.

Young Leland overcame his family life, obtained good grades and high social scores. Most importantly, he was not socially or economically in the middle 80% of the country. He fit into a narrow window at each end of a spectrum for acceptance at Princeton. The eighty percent in the dwindling social-economic middle of the country had no window into prestigious universities.

"Hi, honey, let's just forget our last conversation. I have." Leland tread carefully.

"Yes, well, I haven't. Leland, I really wish you the best, but we are no longer a good fit. I have signed a year's lease on a studio apartment in another section of Trenton in your name and had your stuff moved there. Dad paid for it. I know mail is sporadic where you are, wherever that is, but you should soon be recieving a partnership dissolution document. Please just sign it. Let us avoid any long hassling."

"Are you serious? It was you and your dad who said military service in the family would be a political benefit and talked me into it. If I hadn't left, this wouldn't be happening."

"You can't be sure of that."

"Do you have a boyfriend?" he hesitated, "Or girlfriend?"

"It really makes no difference. Have a good life," she said followed by a dial tone.

Lieutenant Leland slept little that night. His life had been turned upside down. What would he do? He had four months left on his enlistment. A studio apartment in Trenton. He knew no one there but her family. No prospects for work. When he got out of the military, with eight months left on the lease, then what? His fancy Princeton degree was in political science. How would he get a job in his field without her family? Would he move back to West Virginia? His dad would tell him, "I told you so." His father never trusted her family. Her family's theft of his pride would have caused him to join his dad in drunkenness, if alcohol was available outside *no-persons' land*.

The next morning, he was in the colonel's quarters. He requested a leave of absence for personal reasons. Embarrassed, he explained the reason.

"I understand, something similar happened to me years ago. My wife left me for a few months. It is hard to keep a marriage, or partnership in your case, strong when we are gone much of the time. I found it helpful to give her latitude and not ask too many questions. I'll grant you a one-week leave, but I have a job for you first," answered the colonel.

Before the day was over, he received mail. As she promised, the dissolution was in a big brown envelope. It was as she said. He called her.

Twice it went to voicemail. On the third call she answered. "What?" she answered.

"I'll be there next week, and we can discuss this."

Leland heard something in the background then caught her saying, "Shhhh."

"Is someone with you?"

"Leland, just sign the document and mail it and save yourself a trip. It is over. I'm blocking your number."

There were no bars in the makeshift federal detention tent. Eric and Kelly were chained to posts. They had been there four days without explanation or charges. They often shouted at guards asking about their fate. They were ignored. Three other prisoners also occupied the tent. One for making disparaging remarks about the president, one for theft, and another for making lewd gestures to a female soldier. With nothing to occupy their time, they came to know the others. One soldier's lewd gesture was whistling at a fellow soldier. At least, the others knew with what they were charged, thought Eric and Kelly.

They protested to a guard about their sixth amendment rights. The guard was young and knew nothing about the Bill of Rights, let alone the sixth amendment. Who could blame him? It was not a topic in civics class.

Atlas Transportation Conference Room

"I understand the Feds have finally proposed a trade for Eric and Kelly, what is it? Julie asked Barry. "Why must we pry it from you?"

Barry blurted it out to Julie, "In trade they want the five soldiers held at Fort Hood released. The Resistance leaders in Maryland and Texas, the governor of Texas and spouse and you, repatriated back from whatever country you are in, all surrendered to federal custody."

"So, they think Julie is in another country," observed Andrew.

"Yes, I guess that is the only good thing."

"They obviously are not serious about a swap," said Andrew.

"We cannot ask anyone to take Eric and Kelly's place, whatever penalty they may have in mind. If only me, that would be different. The Resistance will continue with or without me," stated Julie.

Discussion continued about what else they could offer the Feds for Eric and Kelly's release. Finally, the message was sent that in addition to the five Fort Hood prisoners, all harassment of the Feds food supply lines would cease for the release of Eric and Kelly.

The reply was one word— *"No."*

Although there was disagreement, interruptions of federal food supply lines were placed on hold. The surface-to air-lasers quit targeting airdrops, and Resistance members were instructed to stand down. The hope was that unilaterally scaling back confrontation would be reciprocated.

Austin

Mendel grew up on the south side of Chicago. Competition was tough. Smart, ambitious, and keen on never bucking the flow, he knew that acquiring more power in Chicago without getting killed would require more skills and luck than he possessed. He brought the lessons learned in Chicago to a less contested place with potential. He had been in Austin 20 years building an organization unmatched in the Texas underworld. Ideology, he had none. Of all the isms, his was opportunism.

His sources of income were many. Chemists would find a new drug which would become a young people's fad before the Feds got around to legalizing it. People with low HCIs, which prevented access to life saving drugs, someway found something to illegally exchange for the drugs they needed. In a genderless society, prostitution for straight people was more of a social taboo than in religious tinted times, but the old occupation never died. The police, long since handicapped by woke correctness, were ineffective protecting people or businesses. Mendel's outfit filled that gap, providing protection citizens' taxes would not provide..

Some would say he had no scruples. But he did not force anyone to do anything they did not wish. He provided goods and services that could not be obtained elsewhere.

Arrest warrants for the governor, PPUs from a mysterious source soon to be in the sky again, and the Resistance backing down by ceasing harassment of federal supply lines— the writing was on the wall. Civil discord would soon end. The Feds would win the confrontation and extend their hold on the citizenry. Mendel was confident the president would bend marginally in a few areas to settle the civil issues. They would call it negotiation; each side would think they won. Martial law would officially end, but not in practice.

With newfound powers and the citizenry under control, the Feds would expand their reach. His organization, although savvy, was the ultimate anti-government institution. He would be in danger. With an added element of control, public officials would demand greater payoffs to protect his business. The million UNU reward for the governor's capture was not an incentive for Mendel. Delivering the Fed's most wanted, however, would earn long-term favor with those in control giving him leverage.

Two companies of National Guard soldiers and one company of regular Army under General Everett were stationed around the governor's mansion. The 300 soldiers rotated duties in eight hours shifts; no more than 100 were on duty at a time. General Everett's two brigades guarded the north side of Austin against federal invasion but were an hour away.

In addition to soldiers, loosely organized Resistance members and sympathetic citizens milled around the area day and night. It was normal for citizens to ask soldiers if they needed anything, often bringing them bottled water. It was well after midnight when Mendel's people, posing as new Resistance supporters, brought freshly baked pastries for the soldiers. The first night only a few soldiers took the aromatic pastries, skeptical of non-sealed goodies. Soon all looked forward to the delicious scones, caramel pecan rolls and bear claws delivered at midnight.

Three days after the pastry deliveries started, two hours before the normal shift change, Mendel personally led a group of thirty toward the governor's mansion. He had learned many years ago in Chicago to never ask someone to do something you would not. He always maintained this was the reason his people were more loyal than most. To avoid suspicion, he approached a barricade outside the fence at the mansion carrying bottled water.

He found five soldiers asleep. One, lying beside a half-eaten bear claw. He nudged each with his foot and only garnered a few moans. Mendel motioned to his gang. They found soldiers in the same condition in the next few barricades.

Scott was a diabetic. He had taken his blood sugar level earlier. It was high. As much as he relished the treats, he could not that night. He found the laziness of four others in his second-tier barricade near the mansion door frustrating. He could not understand their dereliction. Movement caught his eye in the adjacent barricade. *Men out of uniform, why were Resistance members allowed this close,* he wondered. Then he saw they were carrying the latest in automatic weapons. They were not Resistance.

"Stop now," he warned, looking over a sandbag.

Gang members ducked behind another barricade, but others were encircling him toward the mansion door. "Stop!" he yelled again, then directed a burst of fire over their heads.

As his gun was raised shooting above the invaders, a bullet hit the stock of his gun, ripping it from his hands. He turned to see from where the shot came and automatic fire from two guns started shredding the sandbags around him. A bullet made it through a gap in the sandbags. Although its velocity had been greatly reduced, it hit him in a bad place, the neck. Diabetes was no longer a worry.

Mason was staying at the governor's mansion that night. He met Carl in the hallway, both awakened by gunfire. At a second-floor window, they could see scurrying figures in the dark. The governor appeared in a robe in the bedroom doorway.

"What is happening?"

"We're being overrun," Carl said as he pulled collapsible stairs down from the attic. He helped his wife up the stairs, followed her, reached under blown-in insulation, and retrieved two firearms, an old Winchester model 94 lever action 30-30 and an Ithaca 12-gauge shotgun. He tossed the shotgun to Mason. They heard gunfire on the first floor. Carl put the governor on top of an old antique desk that was stored in the attic. Hopefully, the thick top would slow any bullets.

Mason crouched near the top of the attic stairs with his shotgun trained on the main stairs from the first floor. Two men cautiously came up the stairs. "Stop!" he yelled.

Their response was to send a volley of shots in his direction. Mason fired. The shot pattern was spread enough it knocked both men down the stairs. A shirt appeared, he shot, pumped another round in the chamber, and shot again before he realized it was a shirt on the end of an umbrella. Suddenly it hit him he had no reloads—how many rounds were left; he did not know.

Soon others found a second set of stairs. Five were now on the second floor looking toward the attic.

"Toss down your weapons and come down. No harm will come to you," one shouted.

Carl could hardly make out Mason's face in the darkness, but he detected a shake of his head. He looked at his wife, "We'll end up with the Feds if we surrender," she whispered. Both were thinking about the gallows spectacle in Maryland.

The gaze they shared indicated they were in agreement. It was better to go like this than on an end of a rope. To become a martyr or be humiliated as a propaganda tool of the Feds, for their mortal existence the result would be the same. For the Resistance, not so. If they asked Texans to show no fear, neither would they.

Carl aimed his 30-30 carbine from where he thought the voice came, yelled, "Come and get it!" then pulled the trigger.

An avalanche of bullets burst through the ceiling sending fiberglass insulation flying, stirring up decades old dust. They were soon coughing while Carl and Mason fired until their guns were empty. One man was hit below. Carl caught a bullet in his right calf. A bullet closely missed Mason's head but ripped his ear. The desk kept two bullets from the governor, but one made it through and grazed her arm.

Defeated, Mason tossed his shotgun down the stairs, Carl's Winchester followed. But they heard nothing.

Outside, Mendel and others waited for those inside to bring the governor out. The returning gunfire inside they did not expect, but they had superior firepower. Suddenly, one of his men was taken down with a bullet from the rear. Three Resistance fighters were firing on them from sandbags outside the gate. Their shots were sporadic, their weapons were antiques.

Why would anyone jump into the fray unless they were suicidal, thought Mendel. *What did they have to gain?* From two sides, the gang members opened on them with automatic fire. The barricade was soon silent. Mendel cautiously peered over the sandbags and saw three bodies— two motionless, one wounded breathing heavily. One had a Winchester Model 62 pump 22-caliber made for shooting squirrels. The others had an old western six-shooter called *'the peacemaker'* and a Mossberg over-under shotgun. As Mendel and three others, who had delivered the carnage, looked down upon them, the injured man reached for his mate's peacemaker laying nearby.

Mendel stepped on his hand to prevent him from reaching it and asked, "Why?"

"Freedom…" the man uttered as blood seeped from his mouth.

Realistic and analytical as always, with instincts that allowed him to survive in the most brutal of occupations, Mendel contemplated the big picture. He keyed his grape to contact his man inside. "Back out, forget them, we're leaving."

"They've just surrendered, we've finished."

"Leave them, I said."

"Why?" he asked.

"Because we were on the wrong side. Given the commitment I've seen, the Resistance will prevail."

Mendel's group and his wounded escaped before three emergency platoons dispatched by General Everett and the next shift of National Guardsmen arrived. The defenders knew of no explanation why the group had left after they had won. They left three dead defenders-one gravely injured and the governor, Carl, and Mason with injuries. The price had been heavy, but they prevailed, why they did not know.

The seriously injured man was rushed to the hospital. Guardsmen overcoming the effects of pastry were cared for; and the governor, Carl, and Mason were encouraged to seek hospital care.

Given the ordeal they had been through, the trio did not wish to leave the enclave of protection on hand.

"We don't have a doctor with us," said the Army captain. "Those injuries need treatment."

Carl said, "My sister Kate is on the way. Our injuries will be minor for a surgeon."

Doctor Katherine wrapped Carl's leg and declared it not serious. Mason ended up with a torn ear, which he would wear with pride. The governor received a few stitches.

"You three are unbelievably lucky to have received only minor wounds," cautioned Dr. Katherine. "Next time if you are not careful, I hate to think about it."

But she, as the others, knew there could be no turning back, this was literally a fight to win or die.

The pastries were laced with drugs, it was discovered. The people who brought the baked goods were not seen again. It was believed that the raiders were Feds posing as civilians, but they left no wounded to interrogate.

A few days later, Mason received a tip from an Austin gang member that the Feds were organizing a raid on the capitol building. The source surprised him. The information included location and details. The Resistance was ready and crushed the Feds in an exchange of gunfire.

Federal Encampment

Lieutenant David Leland reported at the colonel's quarters at 7:00 am as ordered. The colonel was in discussion with a major. Leland announced himself and stood quietly until he was recognized. Fragments of the conversation concerned Leland.

Finally, they broke up. "Lieutenant, the major will inform you about this morning's task and tomorrow you will be granted a week personal leave as requested."

Lieutenant Leland had given up trying to right things with his partner in New Jersey. He had come to realize the relationship was over and it was to his advantage to avoid wasting energy lamenting it. He would not go to New Jersey but with a week of free time what would he do? Perhaps, it would give him a chance to figure out where life would lead him.

Outside the tent, the major told Lieutenant Leland to find a sergeant with four dependable riflemen. Leland returned with a sergeant-led squad—three men, one woman, each carrying the latest military version of the AR15. Once assembled, the major led the group to the edge of the encampment.

"Where are we going?" asked Leland.

"See those three live oak trees," the major said as he pointed to the trees at which Leland had captured the two prisoners.

"We are going to take the prisoners to those trees and administer justice."

"What are you talking about?"

"They will be executed there."

Eric and Kelly were confident they would get some clue as to the charges against them and their future when they were uncuffed from tent poles. After being tied for days, they were halfway across the camp before their bodies adjusted to walking. The guards escorting them seemed very glum.

They approached a cluster of a few soldiers standing at the edge of the camp. It was a combination of two soldiers who had stepped away and were bending over losing their breakfasts and the sour look on the other faces that hinted of their fate. The only one they recognized turned away when he saw them coming. He was the lieutenant from whom they had taken supply trucks and later caught them in a net. The guards handed them over, said nothing, and walked back to the makeshift prison.

"Let's go," said the major as he started walking to the tree line.

Eric felt his knees start to get wobbly and compensated with sarcasm, "I think this is a party I'd rather skip."

No one acknowledged his attempt at gallows humor. It was as if he had spoken to the heavens, but they were vacant. Kelly looked at Lieutenant Leland and said, "This is what we get for stealing food?"

"We have our orders," Leland replied.

Eric and Kelly found the half mile walk the shortest they had ever taken. Funny how time travels at different speeds as a function of the time you have left. The velocity increases as the time differential between where you are, and your demise shortens. At twelve years of age, they remembered how slow time traveled as you could not wait to become a teenager. Now they found themselves at the other end of the paradox.

It was a nice morning which some would enjoy. The colonel moved a chair from his tent outdoors. He could hear a mourning dove cooing in the distance. Perhaps the mourning call of the dove was appropriate, but he had his orders. He chose to not meet the prisoners, thinking it better not to attach a face with the orders he had to pass on. More than any morning, he was glad he was not a major or lieutenant. The strict discipline he required of himself, scoring high on nebulous tests and ass-kissing had paid dividends. His rank only required him to pass on the orders.

He checked the time often on his grape. Ten minutes had passed. It would be soon. In another fifteen minutes, he was worried. His body flinched, almost knocking him from the chair, when he heard a salvo of at least two rifle shots followed by another a few seconds later. It was done. Suddenly the camp was unusually quiet. The mourning dove was silent. As if completing the task would remove it from his conscience, he raised the grape to his ear, contacted the Pentagon and said, "It is done."

White House

Within a few minutes, the president received word. He asked the COS to get the governor of Texas on the phone.

"For your information, the two traitors have received the prescribed punishment for sedition. Let it be a lesson to all who seek to overturn the will of the people. Within a few weeks we will have equipment in place to monitor all activities in the country. There is nothing you may do to stop us. It is over, admit it. But in the interest of national unity, I will promise commutation of any charges against you and your husband if you turn yourselves into federal authorities within twenty-four hours."

There was no reply. The president waited beyond what he thought prudent for a man in charge, then asked, "Did you not hear me?"

A woman spoke, he recognized her voice but could not place her. "Do you remember me?"

Silence this time on the president's side.

"We spoke while you hosted the celebrity party at the White House last fall," came the voice. The president now remembered but did not answer.

"Will you also offer clemency to me?" Julie asked.

The president gritted his teeth, a useful habit he had developed before spilling a lie. "Yes, I will. Turn yourself in with the governor. Do we have a deal?"

Julie had arrived in the governor's mansion the prior evening. Andrew and she sat beside the governor and Carl in the governor's residential office. The governor looked at Julie. Julie mouthed an exaggerated NO for all to see, then looked at Andrew, he shook his head in agreement. She turned to Carl, he followed suit. All three looked at the governor waiting for a reply.

A wily smile crossed the governor's face and her eyebrows rose on her forehead as she leaned forward to the grape on the desk and whispered at the built-in mic, "Do you want an answer now?"

"Yes," he answered, his voice following hers in lower volume. Her whisper served its intended purpose drawing the president in, causing him to listen carefully for her next words.

She took a deep breath, then loudly exclaimed, "Kiss my ass!"

They heard his fist strike the desk before the line went dead.

"That was probably wasn't..." Carl started to say.

Madison cut her husband off, "I know, but it felt good, and let's be honest with ourselves. It will not change our predicament."

Their fates sealed with an exclamation mark; the two couples did something that had been frowned upon since a virus struck the country a few decades earlier. It was a group hug that turned into a prayer that Eric and Kelly be taken care of, both here and there.

Chapter 19

Gulf of Mexico

Less than fifty people remained on the cruise ship that had once been the center of Resistance operations. Valuable equipment had been unloaded over a period of weeks. One hundred miles off Corpus Christi, two yachts approached the ship as a tanker topped off the ship's fuel tanks. Two packages were loaded on the ship. One was electronic paraphernalia which technicians wired to the ship's navigation system. The other package contained large diameter plumbing material which was installed by makeshift plumbers. When finished, the technicians left the ship.

All but four people deboarded the ship to yachts. With the yachts out of sight, the ship headed east into the Gulf of Mexico.

Outside the Federal Encampment

Eric's mind was elsewhere as he approached the live oak trees. He was remembering verses from Sunday School before churches were taxed and attendees canceled in cultural change. The verses were not verbatim, but the best he could remember. Hopefully, they were close enough to win him favor.

While Eric recited Bible verses, Kelly said a prayer and asked for the forgiveness of past sins and sins he was about to commit.

When they reached the live oak trees, Leland stepped closer to the major as if he wanted to separate himself from those who would carry out the order. Kelly thought he detected a wink from the lieutenant, but his mind was working overtime tasked with other concerns. He had decided that he would not die like a sacrificial lamb tied to a tree. When someone came within reach to tie him, he would make his move. To be shot struggling would at least give him some satisfaction, and at most shorten his life by only a few minutes.

"Tie them to the trees," ordered the major.

"Not me," defiantly said a private dropping the rope and stepping back.

"You'll be sent to the brig for refusing an order when we are back," the major said as he pulled his sidearm and commanded another private to do the job.

The next private had bent to pick up the rope when the major felt cold steel pressed to the back of his head.

Lieutenant David Leland was a political science major, but his interest lay in history. When he was stationed in Texas, he loaded books on Texas history to his grape. He was fascinated that the most famous non-native Texan to die in the struggle for Texan independence was Davy Crockett. Crockett had been from Tennessee, not far and just across the Virginia finger that separated his home in West Virginia from Tennessee.

Crockett— a frontiersman, soldier, and politician— had served as a county Justice of the Peace and a member of the U.S. House of Representatives from Tennessee. He was a folk hero. Leland learned that it was not known whether he killed a bear, that might have been someone else.

After being defeated for re-election to Congress, it was rumored he had a disagreement with his father-in-law. Nevertheless, he left his wife, Elizabeth Patton, and headed for Texas. In 1836, newspapers published the now-famous quotation attributed to Crockett:

"I told the people of my district that I would serve them as faithfully as I had done; but if not, they might go to hell, and I would go to Texas."

Crockett arrived at the Alamo Mission in San Antonio on February 8, 1836 and died aged 49 at the siege March 6. One of his most famous sayings was:

"Always be sure you are right, then go ahead."

After his partner expressed her desire to see him no more, David Leland's thoughts flipped to another David who left his wife and ended up in Texas. He had also learned that Crockett was not alone in escaping marital problems by going to Texas.

The prior evening, Leland had pondered his choices. Everyone had choices. He could go to a New Jersey studio apartment in a few months, rent paid for a year and—with his political science degree—earn a meager living harvesting votes. He could move back to West Virginia and try what his dad did without the liquor, or he could pull a Crockett and stay in Texas. But how he could stay in Texas he did not know. Texans would not look on him kindly for his capture of rebels.

The unexpected shock of the morning's assignment focused Leland's mind. Part of what he did was reflex action to an abhorrent order. Another part was a calculated use of the opportunity. He was not a Davy Crockett, but as Crockett, he was sure he was right and would go ahead.

Leland's 9-millimeter pressed tightly against the major's head. "Drop your sidearm, Major."

"What are you doing? This is crazy, you haven't thought it through."

"Oh, yes, I have," Leland answered pushing the barrel harder.

Kelly took advantage of the distraction to lunge at the private picking up the rope. The sergeant drew his weapon and pointed at the scuffle on the ground. He could have shot Kelly, but the commotion offered him an excuse to not shoot.

When another private trained her rifle on Kelly, the sergeant's side arm turned to her. The sergeant was from Oklahoma. He saw his career in shambles, letting the situation get out of control, and down deep his sympathies lay with his home state.

"Drop it," the sergeant ordered the private.

As he spoke, Eric and the defiant private surrounded the female soldier whose rifle was trained on Kelly.

"What's happening? You will all be shot when you are caught, which you will be!" exclaimed the major, now forced to drop his side arm.

Leland marched the major to a live oak tree and the private tied him to it. Kelly won the scuffle on the ground and soon his adversary was tied to another tree. Of the two privates left, the robust five-foot two inch woman from Alabama asked to join them.

"Join what?" Kelly asked.

Leland spoke for her, "We wish to desert. We helped you, can you help us out of here? Our future lies with you."

With blood seeping from a lip, his eye already starting to swell, shirt in tatters, and mud on his pants, Kelly walked to Leland and reached out his hand. "Welcome to Texas, lieutenant."

Leland looked at the remaining private, walked toward him and dragged his foot separating fallen leaves. "There is the line. Make up your mind which side you wish to be on."

Assessing the situation and unsure of the fate of those tied to trees, the private from Missouri, the *Show Me State,* had been shown. He said to the others, "Me too." And crossed the line.

With a major and one private tied to trees, Eric and Leland put a rifle burst into the trees a few feet above the men. The gun fire caused the major to lose control of himself. It was the gunfire the colonel relayed to the Oval Office.

Eric and Kelly led the five new compatriots hastily through the timber to something he had buried a mile away.

The colonel remained sitting outside his command tent. An orderly had brought him his third cup of coffee. He looked at his grape again—no messages. It had been thirty minutes since he heard the shots. They should be back. He had given orders for them to return once they had completed their task. They were to leave the prisoners tied to the trees and he would send a detail later to photograph the scene in case proof was ever needed. That detail would tag the bodies as John Doe #1 and #2 and ship them to a federal morgue. The clean-up detail was waiting in a nearby tent. He would give them another fifteen minutes to return.

Outside the mile wide 'no go zone' surrounding the federal encampment and all out of breath, Eric stopped the group in a thicket. "Seven of us are too many to hide close to the road. The rest of you stay hidden here while I retrieve my grape."

Along the road, Eric waited for a federal patrol to pass. They were not unusual to see on this road. He waited a few minutes and saw no others. Hurriedly, he scurried to the roadside bank, found a twig he had placed in the ground nearly a week earlier, and dug up a buried plastic bag containing his secure grape. He was relieved when it showed ten percent power left.

Mason was reluctant to answer his grape when Eric's name came up on the call screen. The possibility had been discussed that the Feds might eventually discover that a fingerprint matching the grape's user would open the grape and avoid its meltdown. If they did, the person's finger—attached or not—could be used to open the grape. All evidence was that Eric had been murdered. The call was too dangerous to answer.

Eric tried again, no answer. The battery was down to six percent charge. Back with the group, he explained the situation. Kelly said, "Hand me the phone once your fingerprint opens it."

Kelly dialed Mason and hung up after two rings, waited a minute and called again. This time letting it ring three times before hanging up. He explained, "Long before we had secure grapes, two rings followed by three rings was our signal that all was clear to talk."

Soon the phone rang. "Kelly, is that you? Where is Eric?"

"He is sitting beside me."

"I can't believe it. You're both supposed to be dead."

"To the Feds, I am sure, a bitter disappointment, but we are not. Details later, this is what we need before this grape dies."

As it was too dangerous to travel together and all in the same vehicle would look suspicious, they split up. Eric with the sergeant and two privates; Kelly with Leland and a private. A vehicle was to be sent for one group three miles away, while another picked up the other group two miles in another direction.

Although the sergeant had been warned to watch where he stepped, he let out a scream and Eric saw a slender appendage attached to his leg as he shook it. He had stepped on a copperhead. The snake had sought to defend herself. It was a large one, which was good, as smaller ones had more potent venom. Luckily, they were within minutes of the pickup and Eric assured the sergeant that the bite was not life- threatening. Given that the sergeant had been bitten, it was fortunate Eric's group had the shorter route to a pickup.

Kelly stopped to let Leland and the private catch their breath. Neither Leland nor the private were used to covering such distances rapidly, but both knew to tarry was to risk being captured by what they were confident would be a massive manhunt.

"Where are we going?" Leland asked as he looked in the direction they were headed.

"See that hill over yonder. Just to the right side of it is a road."

"So why aren't we headed straight for it through the field of scrub brush?" further inquired Leland.

"Because that field is loaded with hidden traps."

"So that is why our escape hasn't been in a straight line since we left the oak trees?"

"You're a perceptive guy, Leland," Kelly said in jest.

"Gee, I guess that's another reason I'm glad to be with you rather than part of a search party."

The colonel had intended to only wait another fifteen minutes for the return of the execution party. He waited twenty. He could wait no more. The clean-up crew was summoned; he would accompany them. It was his hope to avoid the messy details of this order, but sometimes responsibility required a hands-on approach. He should have supervised the original party, he now knew.

The further the colonel walked into the woods, the more frustrated he became at what the major and his crew were doing. At a distance through the brush, he caught a glimpse of two men tied to trees. Relieved, he thought, *at least they got the job done but where were they?*

Once he recognized who was tied to the trees, he was furious. "What happened?"

"They got away, Colonel," replied the embarrassed, soiled major as he was untied.

"How many did they have in ambush? How did they know the men would be brought here?"

"There were not any others. It was mutiny."

"Who?"

"Lieutenant Leland, he held a gun to my head."

"And he took all the others as prisoners, come on, Major."

"They all followed the prisoners."

"Which way?"

The major nodded the direction. The colonel graped headquarters and ordered all available personnel to close roads within twenty miles and start a thorough search of the area. He chose not to notify the Pentagon. The seven were long gone before roads were closed.

Back at brigade headquarters, the colonel's orderly brought him a glass of water and three pills. "You forgot your blood pressure medicine this morning, sir."

When his orderly stepped away, the colonel put the pills in his pocket. Three times during the day he started to dial the Pentagon with an update but hesitated. He remained in constant contact with the search parties, but there was no news except reports of soldiers injured in traps.

Four of the twelve ten-member squads sent out to search for the escapees reported multiple trap injuries. Fortunately, none sustained broken bones, only superficial injuries. Nevertheless, they would require treatment.

By late afternoon, the colonel knew the foxes had escaped. To limit further injuries for naught, he called off the search. He asked his orderly for a cup of coffee.

"This late in the day, sir?"

"Yes, I need it."

The colonel was sixty-nine. He could have retired two years earlier. Most often immediately prior to retirement, career officers received a promotion in rank. His military pension was determined by his rank at retirement. But it was more than the money. In retirement, the colonel envisioned himself hanging out at a bar or coffee shop with other retirees telling them of his exploits as a general. Last week, he foresaw talk of his participation in putting down the mini-Texas rebellion. That fleeting dream was now kaput.

The major general had all but promised when this Texas assignment was over, there would be promotions for those involved— his promotion to Brigadier General. Given this fiasco, not only was that less than unlikely, but he would be lucky to hold his colonel rank. Precedent was set thirty years prior in a disastrous retreat leaving billions worth of sophisticated weapons for the enemy that only those with a rank of general were unaccountable for incompetence or mistakes.

Past the age for retirement and with an officially noted health impairment, any worsening of the colonel's health would trigger mandatory immediate retirement. But it would take time. With certification of a deterioration in his health signed by a doctor and his signature on a voluntary retirement form, he could immediately enter retirement at his present rank.

The colonel finished his coffee and summoned the orderly, "I'm not feeling well, send for a doctor."

Three doctors in the brigade were treating victims of booby traps. None of the injuries was serious. A call from the colonel's headquarters was heeded without jeopardizing injury treatment.

"How are you feeling?" asked the doctor.

"A headache and listless," his short answer was not completely false, but likely psychosomatic.

"Wow, your blood pressure is 180/115. Have you been taking your medicine?"

The colonel ignored the question. "I suppose you better officially record your observation."

"I can come back in an hour and check again before I do that, sir," the doctor replied, hoping to do the colonel a favor.

"I believe you should follow protocol, captain. I wouldn't want anything to taint your record."

The colonel pushed a medical form toward the doctor on his fold-up desk. When the doctor leaned forward to sign it, he saw an immediate retirement form laying under the medical form.

"Are you sure you wish to do this, sir?"

"Yes."

After signing, the doctor saluted the colonel and said it had been a pleasure serving under him. Alone now, the colonel pulled the three blood pressure pills from his pocket and followed them with water.

He summoned his lieutenant colonel and notified him of the medical condition and his immediate retirement. The lieutenant colonel assumed it was forced because of the prisoner escape. He was wrong, but now in charge of the brigade. The colonel gathered his few belongings, booked a late flight, and had a driver take him to DFW—two hours away.

Julie and Andrew were still in the governor's office at the capitol when Carl took Mason's call. The serious look and squinting of Carl's eyes told all three that the call was important news. But before the call ended, his face broke into a smile rarely seen.

"What?" asked the governor.

"Eric and Kelly escaped. They are all right."

"How? What?" asked Julie.

"It seems as though a lieutenant, sergeant and three privates didn't have the stomach for cold-blooded murder and flipped to our side."

"Are they all okay?"

"Yes, the sergeant was snake bit, but not seriously."

"Get Mason back on the grape; I want all the details," said the governor.

While Mason gave details about the escape on a grape-connected speaker, Andrew checked the sanctioned news. It was now seven hours after the alleged execution, and the sanctioned media was still reporting that justice had been administered to enemies of the people.

Suddenly the governor said, "I have an idea. The Feds obviously can identify Eric and Kelly now as they can the other heroes. No reason to hide. Can you get all seven of them here by 9:00 pm?"

"What do mean by *here?*"

"The capitol building. And do not clean them up. We want them to look like they just escaped."

DFW Airport

It was a late flight the colonel was booked on to Columbus, Ohio. He changed into civilian clothes and sat in the waiting area at gate E23. It was nearly 10:00 pm, and his plane would not board for an hour. His rank gave him automatic entrance to a VIP airline club, but this evening he preferred to sit with regular people.

Earlier he called his wife and told her of his flight. She was shocked and volunteered to pick him up at the airport but seemed surprised when he accepted her offer. Their time together had been intermittent for years. Although their time, --a week here and there— was amicable, full time togetherness would require work on both their parts, he knew. He had long suspected that she had a friend with benefits; that was another matter which would need to be worked out.

It was 10:00 and CNN was giving the day's wrap-up news on a waiting room monitor hung from the ceiling. The co-anchors were dressed very much alike. The business-professional look of a jacket and tie had been shuttled years earlier as less than egalitarian, just as dresses and skirts had been lapeled anti-feminist. Two of many genders, the anchors wore different shades of the same jacket that buttoned to the base of their neck. Their hair style and length were the same. They could be distinguished separately only by his lower pitched voice and her softer features.

The colonel was surprised that word had not reached the sanctioned media when the anchors dutifully read the script before them:

> *"The people scored a sad victory today when it was necessary to bring justice to two former citizens who betrayed the 'common good.' The White House issued a statement saying it was a sorrowful day, but as his oath to the community dictated, the president had no choice."*

The other anchor continued as the camera turned to her:

> *"On a positive note, the White House said that discordant citizens were diminishing in number and national morale was increasing as more citizens come to see the error of their ways."*

The colonel noticed he was alone in the waiting area watching the CNN monitor. Everyone seemed focused on their grapes. The camera switched back to the first anchor:

"The rumor was confirmed today that the White House welcomed Tom, a Chihuahua, rescued from an animal shelter. White House residents— Bill, a Beagle and Jane, a Dachshund—were there to greet Tom. Charges are pending against the former housemate of Tom for neglect."

"Are you seriously watching that bullshit?" a man sitting near the colonel asked.

The colonel was more shocked at the public carelessness of the man's question than what he said. Attitudes had changed more than he imagined.

"What are you looking at on your grape?" the colonel asked, then spanned his eyes around the room seeing nearly everyone focused on their grapes. The man did not answer. His attention was on his grape. All was quiet until many in the waiting room started clapping, and a few travelers stood and punched the air in triumph.

"Local news, the guys they supposedly executed look fine to me," the man belatedly answered the colonel.

The colonel pulled a folding monitor from his bag, laid it on his lap, found a local TV station on his grape and backed it to the start of the 10:00 news. It was being broadcast from the Texas statehouse. The governor was standing behind a podium in the atrium of the statehouse.

Around her stood seven people, five wearing uniforms in various stages of disarray and stain. Immediately, he recognized one, it was the lieutenant he sent to carry out the execution. Then a man with his leg bandaged, yes, he had seen him; his arm showed three stripes. Three privates, one of which was a woman, he did not recognize.

Neither did he recognize two men in civilian clothes, but he knew who they were. The governor spoke.

"I have with me this evening seven heroes. Two were arrested for trying to reassert Texas freedom. The soldiers up here with me were assigned by the president the task of murdering these freedom fighters."

She walked over to Eric and Kelly and shook their hands. As she did, the colonel noticed she was wearing a skirt in public. The length covered her knees; it would be seen as scandalous, a defiant thumb in the nation's cultural nose.

Back to the podium, she continued,

> "The president's illegal decree was passed through soldiers who had not the stomach for it. Lieutenant David Leland refused to obey the order, led others in a return to ideals that made this country, and freed the prisoners. Perhaps we should take to calling him Davy because he is a modern-day Davy Crockett."

"General Everett," the governor nodded, and the general entered the view and stood in front of Lieutenant Leland.

The colonel recognized the former colonel. Only thirty days ago she commanded a brigade, as he did. He held seniority over her, but now she was a general. General or not, yesterday he would not have traded places with her; now given what he experienced over the last twenty-four hours, he envied her. She pinned a second bar on Leland, saluted him and congratulated the captain.

The governor continued from the podium,

> "This evening it is my high honor to award these seven individuals Texas Freedom medals."

She walked down the line placing a ribbon with hanging medal on each of their necks.

The man sitting close to the colonel noticed him rolling his monitor up. "What did you think? he asked.

"Amazing, isn't it?"

The colonel was glad boarding was called before further explanation was necessary.

Columbus

The colonel's wife was on time at the airport, but the flight was delayed. She parked in a grape parking lot and waited. After 45 minutes, she checked the status of the flight. It had made an emergency landing in Nashville. It was a medical emergency.

It was two hours later; she got a call that she never expected.

Chapter 20

The five federal soldiers apprehended in hopes of trading for Eric and Kelly were in the Fort Hood brig. The jail was full. Most had been locked up for theft, two for fighting in a drunken brawl, one for assaulting a female soldier.

General Martinez had changed policy from the current culture norm on thievery. It would take time before some soldiers realized that taking something which did not belong to you would not be tolerated. A few decades earlier, prosecutors around the country ceased charging people with most theft. It was believed those stealing had an urgent need greater than whomever had possession of a good. Retailers stopped interfering with those stealing as the police wouldn't prosecute and doing so invited legal liability. High losses retailers sustained from theft were passed on to customers. The cost of theft hit the dwindling middle class hardest as the connected could afford it and the poor lived on stipends.

The general also issued a new policy on the treatment of minorities. His policy was more in line with corporate policies before adherence to government regulations became more critical to the bottom line than employee performance. The promise of having the latitude to institute his "performance-based equality" system was critical in convincing the general to leave retirement in Wichita and accept command at Fort Hood.

In his performance-based equality program, soldiers would receive promotions based only upon their performance regardless of their race, gender, religion, ethic group or sexual orientation. They would not be given special treatment because of minority status if they could not perform their job. A hundred-pound five-foot female could maneuver a seventy-ton tank as well as a two hundred-pound man. But a hundred-pound woman would not be a welcome sight if you were a wounded two hundred-pound man, and a hundred-pound woman was sent to rescue you.

His new policy was intended to place in practice the dream of a civil rights leader nearly a century earlier who said people should be judged by their character, not the color of their skin. General Martinez added gender, religion, and sexual orientation to the standard.

Unfortunately, a few took the new policy as more than it was. Physical harassment of gays or women would never be allowed, as a few held in the brig found out.

However, evidence was mounting of reduced tensions between groups. No longer was it easy to blame your failure to secure a promotion because another person was taking advantage of their minority status. The person to whom you reported earned their position by performance and hence earned your respect.

The morning after Kelly and Eric escaped, breakfast was served in the Fort Hood jail. The five captured federal soldiers were eating breakfast happy that it was better than what they were eating before capture, but happier that it was not better than the previous five mornings. Steak and eggs would have been interpreted as predictive of a short future and very unsettling. Rumors circulating that the Feds intended to execute two prisoners were not a good omen for the five federal prisoners.

Other prisoners had taunted them. "I wonder what you feel when you hit the end of the rope," one said. "Do you feel your neck pop?." It was not easy for the five to ignore the harassment.

As they were eating, three MPs entered the jailhouse. Their appearance at an odd time caused the five concern. The MPs said nothing while they unlocked the door holding the five federal prisoners.

To their surprise, the MPs then started to leave. Near the door at the end of the cell hallway one stopped and turned, "Go ahead and finish you breakfast if you wish, then get out of here."

They forgot about their half-eaten breakfasts and cautiously walked the hallway to a room where four MPs sat. The former prisoners looked confused.

An MP said, "If you are turned around, make a left outside the door. 'All person's land' is about a quarter mile in that direction. Hope you enjoyed your stay."

The five headed toward federal lines, not hurrying, preferring to avoid attention, they drew none.

Once behind federal lines they found their interrogation was longer and more intense than what they had experienced at Fort Hood.

New Jersey

The head of one of New Jersey's most influential political families was livid. An editorial in the morning paper posed the question— *How could the family not know of their son-in-law's subversive inclinations?*

Leland had acquired the rank of captain, as per the plan to buttress the family's political fortunes, but his method had destroyed the family's political future. His daughter received the domestic partnership dissolution petition signed by her former partner. Below his signature he wrote, *Have a great life.*

White House

"How dare those doofuses make me look like a fool?" the president rhetorically asked no one in particular while wildly pacing the Oval Office. He appeared to be searching for something to throw. As soon as the utterance escaped his mouth, he realized how ridiculous he must look to the few advisors in the room.

His COS got up and tried to soothe him, "May I get you a cup of coffee, sir?"

"No, I've already had too much."

Seldom had his temper got the better of him as it had now. Most people who worked for him thought he was prone to lose his temper often. They were wrong. What most people interpreted as temper was actually a well scripted display of emotion intended to achieve a result. This was not, and he quickly regained control.

"We must hold someone responsible for this escape debacle. That major is obvious, what about the brigade commander? It is his ultimate responsibility to carry out an order." the president asked the CJCS.

"It is a little late for that, Mr. President."

"What do you mean?"

"Let's just say he cannot be reached."

"Oh, was that the officer I read about this morning?"

"Yes, sir."

The president had been an avid reader of newspapers in high school. It had served him well in debate and speech contests. With newspapers now gone, he came to get news online. He still skimmed a dozen news sites every morning before and during breakfast. In his early political years, reading a wide range of editorial opinions gave him perspective. Often understanding the opponent's point of view helped structure his arguments and enabled him to express his viewpoint more articulately.

However, over time, understanding other perspectives became tiresome. Other viewpoints were not something to understand, but something to discredit out of hand. Some of his supporters maintained that arguments were not to be won, but ended.

Given the trajectory of the media, his exposure to other ideas was limited. Reading a dozen sources no longer gave him a variety of opinions as it once did; it just reinforced the accepted way of looking at events. Often the same talking points were used by multiple outlets. The president's widespread reading did nothing but reinforce what he thought. Consequently, he had no understanding of the Resistants' perspective or the issues that caused their discontent.

His inability to relate to the other side was not altogether his fault. As inbreeding homogenizes good and bad genes, eliminating hybrid vigor, living in an echo chamber of ideas has a similar effect. The president traveled exclusively in academia, the Washington establishment, and entertainment circles. When free speech advocates of the '60s and '70s took over academia decades later, the first thing they did was restrict free speech. The Washington establishment had a vested interest in expanding the depth and width of federal influence. In the entertainment industry, variance from chic thoughts was a career killer.

This morning White House meeting dealt with two issues, how to characterize the condemned prisoners' escape and how to react to it.

Letting the narrative as the Texas governor framed it slide was out of the question. Collective heads in the White House would paint a different picture.

It was decided that the prisoners had been freed as a measure of good will. The false news release that the prisoners had been executed was intentional, an idea of the deceased brigade colonel. It had served the purpose of setting an example without having to hurt anyone. The lieutenant, who falsely claimed to have freed the prisoners and mutinied, was allowed to leave with the prisoners to save the hassle of his pending court martial for bungling a food shipment. The sergeant and privates were likewise involved.

The White House narrative was obediently spread by the media. Establishment Washington and the media itself were oblivious to the disregard and skepticism with which a growing number of citizens regarded their spin.

The next item on the Oval Office agenda was an extra-narrative response to the escape. The NSA and FBI director argued for a forceful response. They maintained the opposition must realize a price would be paid for the embarrassing escape. Two plans were suggested.

One option would turn federal forces bordering Fort Hood south and challenge the defense of Austin. The numbers made it more doable than attacking Fort Hood, and Austin was the center of the opposition. The other idea was to bring another Marine division into Florida from Georgia and retake the Treasury district centers in Florida. With two Marine divisions already in Florida guaranteeing the distribution of the new PPUs, another division would overwhelm the Florida National Guard and local Resistance militias. And reestablishing the federal government's first right to taxes would send a message across the country.

The CJCS and COS argued for a more cautious approach. They pointed out an aggressive response would call into question the narrative they were spinning about their benevolent release of the two prisoners. Why would we escalate when our prisoner release was supposedly done to lower tensions? With the spread of new PPUs across the country, we will regain control.

"Why draw cards while holding a winning hand?" one reasoned.

Finally, the president said, "Nice analogy, I'll use another one. We have the lead and the ball; it is time to stall. With new PPUs coming, time is running out for them."

With that subject closed, the COS asked, "Have you given any consideration to the obscene answer the governor of Texas gave to your generous proposal?"

The COS was the most brazen among the president's advisors in her switch of topics. She had been the right-hand person to the president since her internship in the House of Representatives. They knew each other in multiple ways, although not formally partners. His official partner on the second floor of the White House was but dressing on a cake. The COS knew his earlier temper outburst was real as she now knew he was rational and in control.

"Yes," the president answered, "It must be unbelievably frustrating in their position knowing they are ultimately doomed. I will admit this since I know it will not leave this room. The prime-time announcement and awards ceremony from their capitol was brilliant. I respect the stunt, even from a loser. When the governor and her spouse are captured, they will be given exception. As distasteful as their views are, we cannot breach the barrier between how public officials and citizens are treated. If we did, it could spiral into Guillotinian Jacobin France. Where would it end? Now for that derelict Cretin who calls herself Julie, it is different."

Atlas Transportation Headquarters, Midland

Torrence and other Resistance technicians, back to Midland from the ship, labored nearly 24/7 on a guidance system integrating parts of many technologies. A few degrees that way gave them three times what they wished. On the other end, speed up, speed down was slow and cumbersome. Practice, adaptation, and ingenuity had narrowly gotten them within what they considered tolerable limits of control. They had to do better.

A bigger obstacle to their plan was the appearance of an identical Chinese freighter leaving Tanzania. The only differentiating feature was the freighter's identifying numbers on the bow. The ships left the port within the same hour, and both turned the Cape of Horn on African's southern tip and were headed in the same direction. Which one carried the vultures, and which one was the decoy?

Even if they were willing to risk Chinese intervention and hit one, which one would they strike? The decision was moot anyway because they had no means to hit a moving target.

Barry hacked into government databases trying to determine which ship carried the PPUs. After exhaustive searching, they decided only the White House knew and the information was not in any federal database. Hacking into Chinese databases was beyond the former Atlas engineers' capabilities.

By tracking past voyages of the freighters to the United States, they found both freighters always docked at the harbor in Fort Lauderdale on the Stanahan River. One freighter always docked and unloaded to a warehouse near SE 35th Street. The other freighter docked at a former cruise ship dock near a warehouse on SE 20th Street. The warehouse formerly housed incoming guests and supplies for a cruise ship before they became taboo for most citizens.

Port Fort Lauderdale.

Edel Rodriguez had worked at the Port Fort Lauderdale docks for nearly twenty years and was a steward in the dock workers union for five. His grandparents had navigated the ninety-mile distance between freedom and captivity in a small hand-built raft before the turn of the century. The journey was treacherous in an ill-equipped vessel with waves higher than they envisioned, and Cuban patrols on the prowl. Nevertheless, his pregnant grandmother, grandfather and seven great uncles and aunts made it to US shores.

Edel, in Spanish, meant noble and brave. It was always his intent to live up to his name. As the United States became more like Cuba had been, and more freedom was given to Cubans, some Cuban immigrants returned to their homeland. His family did not; they were Americans. Given the opportunities they had been afforded in America, they felt an obligation to fight to preserve those freedoms. Edel was a member of the Resistance. In addition to his regular job, he attended Resistance meetings regularly and weekend training.

On the way to work, he normally presented his pass at the gate to Port Fort Lauderdale and parked his car in a lot on SE 26th street near the dock he worked. Ten days earlier, he found himself in a line of cars awaiting entry into the port. Marines were searching all cars before entry. He was asked to step out of his car while it was checked inside, and a detector was waved under the car.

Edel started leaving earlier for work. Two days prior, the line of cars outside the gate was directed to a parking lot. From the parking lot, workers were instructed to board buses which would shuttle them to their dock. The buses appeared to be retired school buses with the windows blacked out to prevent workers from observing activity at the port outside their dock.

He received notice through his cousin of an emergency meeting of the local Resistance. There were seven local groups kept separate for security reasons. The meeting was held in a church annex; it was where Edel's wedding reception had been held. The church had been closed for some time. A year previous, they would not have considered meeting at a church; but with the vultures out of commission, fear had dissipated. Now though, some were starting to believe the Feds would regain total citizen observation ability.

The rumors were rampant about the cause of a huge Marine presence in South Florida. One rumor had it that Marines would soon be boarding ships headed for Indochina to support the Resistance against the Chinese. Another said they would head to Texas to put down the mini-rebellion. Others believed the government feared a Texas style military mutiny in the area.

The local leader explained the situation. The Resistance desperately needed reconnaissance of the docks, particularly two, the one near SE 35th and one near SE 20th. With no vehicle traffic, civilian boat traffic, overhead drones, workers not allowed outside their dock area, and all worker transportation via buses with darkened windows, it looked tough. The leader asked if anyone had an idea. Edel did.

Edel oversaw maintenance on the crane at the dock near SE 26th street. It laid between the 20th and 35th Street docks. The crane lifted shipping pods to and from docked freighters.

Near noon the following day the crane operator was halfway into a two-day job unloading two seat mini-electric tricycle cars made at a Chinese colony in Africa.

Edel approached the crane operator, "Shut it down, the crane is scheduled for a maintenance exam today."

"I thought that was next week," said the operator.

"Not according to my schedule," Edel replied.

Edel was harnessing himself up when the dock shift manager approached him. "Why is that crane shut down?"

"Because it's maintenance time."

"No, we'll do it next week."

"We'll do it now or I'll call a general safety strike," replied Edel.

"Why are you harnessing up?"

"Because I assumed you'd want to be shut down for as little time as possible, I'll do the inspection myself."

"But you haven't been up there in years."

"Would you rather I sent a rookie who will take twice as long?"

"Just get it done," harped the shift manager.

Edel had heard of the secure grapes but never had one. The local leader set him up with one and programmed it with Edel's fingerprint. It was a temporary model only designed to last a few hours.

Two hundred feet in the air on the crane with little support other than his harness and grip to the ladder would have been too much for most people. But Edel felt great, not only from the refreshing ocean breeze coming in but from the feeling that he was doing something worthwhile. With the grape clipped to his harness belt, he took several photos of activity around the 20th Street dock and then moved to the other side of the crane giving the camera a view of the

35th Street dock. The grape had been previously programmed to immediately transfer the photos to the Atlas headquarters in Texas before they were erased. He did a rudimentary inspection of the crane's knee joint and came down.

"Did you find any problem?" the anxious shift manager asked.

"No, all looked fine to me."

"Great, thanks for the quick job. I owe you a drink sometime."

Little known to Edel, if the shift manager had known the purpose of the Edel's mission, he would have approved. He, too, was a member of the Resistance, although a different group. Caution dictated anonymity.

Leaving after his shift, Edel was pulled off the bus. A Coast Guard officer's attention had been drawn to a man high on a crane. His high-powered binoculars showed a grape clipped on the man's belt. They inspected Edel's grape and found it had not been turned on since morning. It was his personal grape. The spent secure grape lay at the bottom of the harbor.

Texas Capitol building

Julie, Carl, and the governor were in the governor's office when they linked into a Resistance conference call. Mason and Andrew were in Midland helping Barry and Torrence. Ten other governors and their respective Resistance leaders were also on the call.

"What do you have for us?" Julie asked Torrence.

"We've got good and bad news."

"We're still feeling good about the Texas capitol event, so let us keep it going and hear the good news first."

Andrew reported, "The media took the White House narrative of the condemned prisoners escape as an intended release to be gospel and disseminated it. Although the media push polls will show the opposite, our reliable poll service showed the public split in quarters. On the federal spin to the escape/release, twenty-five percent believed it, twenty-five percent doubted it but wanted to believe it, a quarter did not believe it but acted as though they did because they feared their future depended upon it, and a quarter didn't believe it and were willing to say so."

The Governor of Florida responded, "We know people who are still afraid will not tell a pollster anything that may return and bite them."

Andrew added, "We must remember an adage my grandfather always said, *People tend to believe what they want to believe.* And many people have difficulty reconciling their government lying to them."

"What other good news do we have?" asked Julie.

The Ohio governor spoke, "Although it is bedeviling to some of us, gang figures in Cleveland are dispatching members to provide cover for our protection of the Federal treasury offices we have seized."

"We are seeing the same thing in St. Louis and Kansas City," remarked the Missouri governor.

"We need all the help we can get. Does anyone have a problem with gangs helping?" Hearing none, Julie continued, "Okay Torrence, hit us with it."

"Our man at the Port in Fort Lauderdale sent us some great pictures. Our analysis suggests preparation is being made at two docks for PPU arrival. The security at those docks is unbelievable. The warehouses attached have been emptied and triple barricades have been placed around the adjacent parking lots."

"What is happening in the parking lots?" Julie asked.

"It is our belief they intend to ready the vultures for flight in the warehouse and launch them from the parking lot. Thereby bypassing any guerrilla activities, we plan for their distribution by truck or train around the country."

"I thought we were certain only one of the two ships contained the vultures?" asked the governor of Tennessee.

"We are confident only one does; the other is a decoy as is the preparation of a second dock."

"How do we determine which is real?"

"That is a good question."

"Realistically, have we made progress on coming up with a way to stop them?" asked the governor of South Carolina.

"We're working on it," Torrance answered, hoping to avoid more questions on the subject by quickly continuing. "But I just as well drop the other shoe. Our Polish informants tell us that the second delivery of vultures is leaving Tanzania today."

"At best, we hoped to thin their numbers a third by a myriad of small attacks as they shipped them around the country, now dispersing them overhead, what can we do?"

"Please don't be discouraged. We are working on something," Barry jumped in the conversation. "But please, ask no more."

Chapter 21

White House

"Are you looking forward to the NCLF party tonight as much as always?" the COS asked.

The National Charity for the Less Fortunate (NCLF) held a fundraising party quarterly at the White House. It was billed as a fundraiser. Invitees were expected to donate six figures to the cause. Many invitees did; others promised to consider honoring their commitment in the future. Most of those whose entry was gained by a promise had celebrity status such that reneging on the promise would be overlooked. Their contribution was attendance, which offered others the opportunity to mingle with them.

Part of the money raised by the organization helped the less fortunate, but the overwhelming portion of their budget financed lobbying efforts for the poor—primarily advocacy for increased stipends. Successful lobbying required highly qualified lobbyists with the right connections. And people with the right connections did not come cheaply, most with the NCLF had connections with people at the party. Administrative expenses were over eighty percent of the NCLF budget.

In addition to politicians, professional sports stars, Hollywood celebrities, and corporate executives who thrived on government largess frequented the event. If you were someone of consequence or aspired to be significant in the country, it was the place to be.

"Yes, I'm looking forward to the party, it will be a great distraction from the trials of the last few months," answered the president.

With a coy smile, the COS said, "I thought perhaps I had provided enough recent distraction, Mr. President."

He stepped behind her, she turned her head as if asking for a kiss, which she received. "I don't know what I would do without your distraction. That is the only positive thing about this mess around the country. It has given us long working hours with plenty of time for distraction. But you'd better go to your condo and get ready for the party. One of my economic advisors will be here shortly."

She knew the economic advisor was actually the president's portfolio manager and it was time for her to leave, "It was a year ago the party was broken up by a text from that ingrate about the imminent NSA destruction, wasn't it?"

"Yes, I don't like to think about it. She'll soon meet justice."

"If I remember, the interruption prevented you from showing the blonde Hollywood sensation of the year your personal quarters."

"Get out of here," he answered her playful jab.

The president's purported macroeconomic advisor was escorted in the Oval Office. They immediately got down to business.

"Your investments in companies building more vehicle electric charging stations has been visionary. People have been driving much more since the PPUs went down and using public transportation less. You have tripled your investment. The gain is in the high seven figures if you liquidated today."

"That is great. Now we need to reverse our posture."

"What do you propose?"

"Sell all my investments in vehicle charging and short those companies."

"Be more specific."

"Take half the profits and buy put options on those companies (*put options make money if the price goes down*). I have a feeling that the public will soon be less inclined to take frivolous trips on their own and less afraid of train and bus cameras."

"Consider it done."

"By the way, what do you think about the national economy? Given you are on a government salary as an economic advisor, you are supposed to advise me."

"It is fine, Mr. President. And I believe it is a great idea continuing to hype the quarterly GDP growth estimates, then correct it in a quiet adjustment later. The media only takes notice of the early estimate."

"Thank you, I have a party to get ready for now."

The president avoided the tuxedo he wore a year ago, perhaps he would never wear it again. He wore a new one his tailor crafted from the finest silk his COS chose. Tying the black bow tie was always frustrating for him. As opposed to the common hanging necktie of the past, bow ties were accepted. After three tries he opened his bedroom door and asked for assistance. Her title was domestic assistant, but her tasks were more that of a valet to the first family. Knowing she would be needed, she arrived earlier than her evening shift dictated. He immediately noticed the fruity perfume she wore. The fragrance was new to him.

"There, you look great now," she said after properly tying the bow.

"You mean great for a 75-year-old man."

"The mature man look is in," she replied.

He recognized the flattery immediately. He had helped many members of her large family. She was indebted to him, if only for a spurious compliment.

In was the 30-something unisex look. Barrel chested, his wide-set eyes on an oversized head, and hair showing just enough gray to look distinguished after his hair stylist did her wonders— he did not fit the unisex look. Nevertheless, he appreciated her fawning.

Her comment reminded him of his birthday. It would be soon, and he would be 76—a patriotic number, he thought. But thinking of birthdays reminded him of his birth year, 1984. Thought of the year immediately recalled the book named for the year of his birth. Why not think a book named the year you were born meant something? Dystopian, some called the book. Fear could be a good thing; it is what kept children from putting their hands on a hot stove. Orwell's book always intrigued him. It was inevitable, and if so, why not be on the right side of events?

Another person he did not know shared the same birthday, but was 15 years younger, Andrew Collier. It was later in life that Julie insisted he read the book. Unlike the president, the book scared him. Like many things in life, perspective depended upon which side of the fence one stood.

It was past time to make an entrance. Guests were waiting at the bottom of the stairs. The president pounded on the first lady's door.

"We're late."

"Soon, soon, I'm not one of your flunkies."

He stood stranded in the hallway, aware that she most likely had been ready for some time. It was a routine that he was forced to play. He played it well as hint of White House strife would be an unnecessary distraction. The first lady was twenty-five years his junior and still in the doldrums about turning fifty. She was attractive, but attractive women were not hard to find given his status. He picked her for partnership because she was great behind a podium and gracious smooching media talking heads. Her large trust fund endowment also factored into his partnership proposal ten years prior.

She stepped out of her room wearing a carnation pink silk flutter blouse and hot pink cigarette pants that clung to her long legs. She respected the taboo against wearing dresses, but the hot pink slacks were meant to draw attention— not blend with a crowd. The blouse hung below her waist and was gathered by a wide white belt tied in a bow with the ends nearly reaching her knees. Given her height of five feet, nine inches, she would never wear heels even if they were vogue. She wore open-toed flats that matched her top. Her toenail polish and lipstick matched her slacks. The president was curious what the ensemble cost, but unconcerned as she came from old money of which she often reminded him.

He leaned in and ritually kissed her on the cheek, careful not to disrupt the heavily applied make-up. "You look hot tonight," his comment part of their game.

"Well, thank you, but it isn't the fifteenth of the month, so cool it."

The fifteenth of the month had been long since set aside as a night to validate their partnership by sharing a bed.

With her arm tucked inside his elbow, they stood at the top of the grand staircase and surveyed the crowd below them. It was a maze of colors, primarily pastels, like a past Easter party gone awry. Once they had the crowd's attention, they slowly walked down the stairs to applause.

The president might have noticed one man because of his plain, drab charcoal outfit if he was not partially hidden by a Rubenesque woman wearing a sunflower yellow suit. The man was Damon Trotter, a state representative and professor from Illinois. Damon, invited because of his voting record and supportive speeches on the Illinois House floor, brought one of a handful of disadvantaged young people to the party. It was Damon's first time in the White House. A line formed to greet the president. Damon introduced the young man with him whom he did not know. The president and first lady were gracious to everyone but could not wait until the formality was over. Thankfully, a large portion of the crowd did not need introductions, as they were famous.

The blonde Hollywood sensation who the President had spent time with a year earlier approached him. She was dressed in an amethyst purple ensemble with an undersized matching skull cap which accentuated her light blonde hair bursting from the cap's edges. Only an audacious star could get by with blonde hair in 2050. The president was courteous, but she was last year's movie flame.

A bashful-acting redhead in the corner of the room caught his eye. The red was unnatural but familiar. She was the star of a new alternative western series where cowboys were the bad guys. He would meet her but would not appear anxious.

"Are you soon going to get these rebels reined in, Mr. President?" asked an executive from a quasi-government bank wearing a pea green Gothic tailcoat. The president knew the man was assuredly losing money with the state takeover of many federal treasury offices.

"We are making headway; I can assure you."

A man totally comfortable in the White House and recognizable to all by white bleached hair on either side of his head reached for a drink from the tray as the waiter passed. The news anchor for a major network took his time before stating as if all were anxious to hear.

"From my days as a reporter, I always dreaded being assigned to one of those backwater states. I swear they are full of uneducated throwbacks to less sophisticated times."

"Maybe we should just let those states go, that's what they seem to want. Without proper leadership they would soon be begging to come back and for our forgiveness," a man in an aqua outfit added.

"You must remember they produce much that we need," replied the president, feeling awkward taking a contrary position and hoping to tactfully escape the group soon. The redhead and he made eye contact again.

A bureaucrat wearing a Persian green bowler hat from the Department of Interior whose name the president could not remember jumped in. "I think someone had it right years ago, deplorable is what they are. If they had their way, they would be back in some church cult. At least through yours and others leadership we stripped them of their guns."

The president decided it better to avoid throwing a wet cloth on their banter. He was reminded of the cliché of giving a man too much rope. His eyes surveyed the room while their conversation became more vile. He saw the VP with her arms around each of her partners talking to the first lady. They had been friends since her family moved back from China after acquiring much wealth. They now lived next door to the first lady's family in Nantucket.

As always, the VP's feet were the first thing you noticed about her. To the president, they looked absurd—too large— and always in her signature white athletic sneakers with rainbow shoestrings. She thought it gave her the common person look. Nothing was common about the navy suit she wore, or the periwinkle fedora tilted on the left side of her head.

The FBI director with his trademark oversized pink bowtie joined the first lady and VP. The president was surprised by body language indicating the director and first lady knew each other. He made a note to later ask her how. They appeared to be in serious discussion but parted when the first lady noticed the president's attention. Now his curiosity was heightened.

A man with a mohawk haircut, the editor of a major newspaper, blocked the president's vision so he could not be ignored. "Perhaps the mid-landers need to be treated as we did children in the previous century, with a firm hand." His comment inspired laughter in the circle.

"Someone looks lonely," the president said, nodding toward the redhead. "Excuse me, thanks for coming everyone."

The COS saw him moving toward the redhead and knew what he had on his mind.

"Hello, fellow Illinoisian," someone said from behind her.

She turned; it was Damon who introduced himself. Introductions completed, she asked him to dance.

The first lady stood in a circle with the major league's MVP player from the previous year. They had met before. He had a way with women. With her, he would not. Soon she had a well know NFL quarterback also laughing at her jokes.

The chamber orchestra soon struck up a popular dance song. The president asked the redhead to dance. She blushed as he reached for her hand and led her to the dance floor.

"Don't be nervous, I won't bite. I've seen a few episodes of your series. You are marvelous bringing your character to life."

"Thank you," she said.

Although she was the hit of Hollywood and the envy of all in the room, the president soon determined her timidity would not be overcome in the short time he had.

He turned and saw the football quarterback was enjoying a dance with the first lady. He seemed in awe as she leaned close to his shoulder. If he only knew how cold she was, thought the president.

His COS was with a man he did not know. Later he would discover that it was Damon Trotter. They seemed to be having a good time. The new Secretary of State's wife approached him, obviously looking for a dance invitation.

As they danced, she said, "Thanks so much for appointing my husband to the position. You will not be sorry. And if there ever is anything I can do for you, let me know, anything at all."

He carefully thanked her for the dance and insinuated he would be in contact with her in the future. Leaving the door open was preferable to what she would consider a rejection. She parted with a smile, and he stepped into the hands of last year's blonde sensation.

Damon and the COS were into their fourth dance set. They had already discovered that neither were officially attached.

"Do you have family?" she asked.

"Only a brother in Texas."

"He isn't......you know?"

"Oh no, we may disagree on some issues, but he isn't crazy."

Damon could not wait to tell Mason that he was dancing with the president's chief of staff. Yes, they disagreed on most all issues but remained close. Damon had no idea Mason was involved with the Resistance, let alone a leader.

Following a sharp turn with the music, Damon's hand dropped lower than he intended, and he brought it up quickly.

"That's all right, don't be timid."

Noticing the president was watching, she reached for Damon's hand and lowered it to the curve of her hip, then turned and gave the president a smile. He smiled back; they had planned to finish a project after the party, and she was having fun tormenting him. The blonde flinched as his hand also went lower. Last year's hit or not, she interested him.

During an orchestra break, the first lady thought her social secretary had outdone herself for the evening. With her head shaved clean as always, glistening in reflected chandelier light, she wore an overly tight double-breasted pinstriped gangster suit from the previous century. But it was who that was tagging behind her that caught the first lady's attention.

"Ms. Alcott, I'd like you to meet someone."

Since the first lady and president were not married, addressing a woman as *Mrs.* was not done. Also calling a woman or girl *Miss* was considered downgrading.

"Hello, so glad to have you here, and you are?"

"Stephanie, Ms. First Lady."

The first lady soon found out that Stephanie was a guest representing recipients of the charity. She hardly appeared to be in need of charity, her top and slacks were from a designer the first lady recognized. Neither had Stephanie's hair and makeup been done by a run-of-the-mill stylist. Like the first lady, she wore pink—but bubble gum pink. On her head was a pink straw hat with a narrow straight brim, a schoolgirl hat with a white bow. Her white hat bow resembled the white silk belt the first lady wore. Both wearing pink with white bows, *it was an omen,* thought the first lady.

Although told she was a college student, Stephanie did not look old enough to have completed high school. She was adorable, although naïve.

The first lady asked Stephanie if she danced.

"Yes but.."

"Oh, don't be silly! Dancing is not just done with men."

After two dances the band broke for a break. The first lady gave her social secretary a wink and asked Stephanie if she would like to see the family quarters.

The president made sure to run into his COS during the break. "I think we can complete our work in the morning, let's call it a night."

"I suppose you're going to take the purple-wrapped blonde on a tour of the second floor."

"It's all part of the job."

The president was showing the blonde around the second floor living quarters when they ran into the first lady and Stephanie. As did the first lady, he thought it prescient that both wore pink accented with a white ribbon. Running into them was unsettling to the blonde— not because of the young woman accompanying the first lady—but being seen with the president by the first lady in their family quarters.

"Thank you very much for the tour, but people are leaving; and I have a late LAX flight to catch."

He walked her downstairs and saw his COS leaving while holding hands with the guy she had had been with most of the evening. The president told many in the dwindling crowd goodbye, then helped himself to a drink.

The first lady was back downstairs with the young woman who could have been her daughter. She was talking to her social director. The president sat his highball on a close cocktail table and could overhear them.

"I think it would be a great experience for her to spend the night in the White House. She'll have a story to tell her college friends."

Turning to Stephanie, the first lady said, "Would you like to tell your friends you spent the night in the Lincoln bedroom?"

The crowd was nearly gone. The president grabbed a fresh highball and headed for the Oval Office. In a way, he was surprised his COS was not waiting on him. He scanned the latest news for an hour before he headed upstairs to his bedroom.

Passing the Lincoln bedroom, he heard unmistakable giggles. He ignored them. Frustration came as he had trouble untying the bow tie. *What kind of knot did she use,* he wondered? *Women, they never make it easy,* was his next thought. He cracked the door and saw the family's domestic assistant standing stoically in the hallway.

"Can you help me untie this thing?"

Her family owed him. It was an hour later she left his room.

The COS invited Damon to her condo for a drink. Given who she was, he could not tell her *no,* nor did he wish to turn her down. She took him on tour of her condo. It was spectacularly decorated in post-modern motif with paintings of the latest sensations in the art world. Either she had amazing decorating skills or hired the best. It did not escape his curiosity how a meagerly paid government employee could afford such.

It was nearly two hours later when she finally poured him a drink. The thin robe she wore was anything but asexual.

"What did you think of the party?"

"I don't know; it was maybe a little surprising."

"How so?"

"It kind of reminded me of a costume party on a cruise many years ago."

"Cruise," she laughed. "Those were a bourgeois waste that we pretty well eliminated with taxes."

"Really, you think so?"

"Of course, better uses can be made of the ships and their docks, as soon will be…

She stopped abruptly, swallowed the remainder of her wine as if opening her throat would bring the words back, then changed the subject by leaning in and kissing him hard. She was not ready for him to leave.

Perhaps it was the drink— her attitude, what they had done earlier or the totality of the whole night, but he no longer felt comfortable.

"You know, I have a lecture tomorrow afternoon I must prepare— and it is late, or early, I guess."

"What are you teaching?"

"The excesses of late nineteenth and early twentieth century robber barons."

"Sounds so interesting, they were so extravagant and self-absorbed" she said, obviously disappointed he was leaving.

He realized then early twentieth century aristocracy excesses did not sound that interesting or much of an uncommon societal aberration.

Near noon, Damon sat in the airport waiting for a delayed flight to O'Hare. He called his brother, who he assumed was in Austin. Mason was in Midland.

"You'll never guess where I was last night?"

Mason could tell by the tone; it must be politically related. "Did you meet the mayor?"

"No, I was at a party in the White House."

"Wow, what was it like?"

"This is going to sound weird, but I had a feeling I was at the Capitol on the set of *Hunger Games.*"

"Hmm," Mason responded, while he thought, *if my brother characterizes it as a Hunger Games party, it more likely resembled the bar scene in Star Wars,* then he asked, "'Why?"

"A combination—the dress, the frivolity, the arrogant comments."

"Who'd you meet?"

"I met the Chief of Staff to the President."

"Did you talk long?"

"We did more than talk at her condo."

"You got to be kidding. What was she like?"

"Flippant, but with her tremendous responsibilities and workload, I guess that is a natural escape behavior.

What struck me as strange, we got into this conversation about cruises, and she belittled the people who traveled on them. Then she said a much better use could be made of their docks and would be. Suddenly, she stopped in midsentence as if someone had flipped a switch. I noticed her face flushed before she attempted to change the subject. It was like she wished to retract the conversation about cruises."

"Sounds like quite an experience," noted Mason.

"Yeah, well it was an experience."

"Let's talk about it more later, I've got to run."

Mason was pleased that Damon had, hopefully, what would be an eye-opening experience. Perhaps, all was not lost on his brother.

Torrence stepped into the room, looking glum. A revelation hit Mason.

"Remember, you told me of a strange dream about a cruise ship?"

"Yes, I know …crazy, but I've had another one like it." Torrence responded.

"I don't think so, someone is trying to tell you something. Here is why…"

Chapter 22

White House

It was 7 am. The president had been in the Oval Office since 5 am. He did not have any scheduled meetings until 9:00, but his COS was late. She was usually bringing him coffee by 6:30.

Finally, she arrived with coffee and saw that he had already finished his first cup. So much had changed in the country—but she had to wonder whether Nathan, the previous president's COS, brought Madame President coffee in the morning. He had.

"Have you been here long?" she asked.

"Yes, we've much work to do today."

"I know. I could have stayed last night."

"It all worked out. What did you think of that professor legislator from Illinois?"

"Seemed like a nice guy, but he got kind of spooked earlier this morning. You remembered meeting him?"

"No, but I did research on him this morning. Did you know he is from Texas and that his brother is still living there?"

"Yes, did you also look at his voting record in the Illinois General Assembly and discover that he teaches a college class on the excesses of capitalism?"

"Yes, yes, if his record was not good, he would not have been invited. Nevertheless, I am sure I do not need to remind you that only you, the Chinese, and I know which freighter has the goods and to which dock they will land. Workers at both docks are expecting the same shipment. The freighters will unload at the same time. For anyone that can get close enough to observe the pods unloaded, they will look the same."

"What are you trying to say, Mr. President?"

"That it is imperative that this is kept between us."

The COS remembered she had plenty to drink at her condo, but she was not impaired. If fact, she had deftly caught herself before she even dropped a hint about the freighters.

"I've been with you how many years? Have I ever betrayed you?" she asked as she walked around his desk and laid a hand on his shoulder.

He glanced to make sure the Oval Office door was closed and positioned her on his lap. He kissed her deeply. "I'm sorry, I shouldn't have been concerned."

Atlas Facility, Midland

Julie and Andrew traveled back to the Atlas facilities for work with others. They deemed even secure grapes too risky for discussing the plan. No evidence of a federal plant or blackmailed party amongst their confidants existed, but a leak now could destroy everything. Even with repatriated technicians at Atlas Transportation, all was on a need-to-know basis.

"I believe we have obtained the guidance control we need to achieve our objective," Torrence relayed.

"How about the intelligence, how confident are you, Mason?" asked Andrew.

"It is a heck of a hint. I am 100% confident that my brother Damon is not purposely leading us astray. He may be wrong-minded but not manipulative. Perhaps he could have misinterpreted the president's COS comment, or maybe we are reading too much into it, but what else do we have? It gives us odds better than flipping a coin. And without this piece of information, that is what we would be doing."

The agreement was mutual. It was all they had. A decision was made.

"How do we handle the Broward County Port Fort Lauderdale Administration and the Coast Guard? I am sure they will be on high alert. You indicated both had a hand in controlling port traffic?" Julie asked.

"We're working on a three-prong approach. And as you suggested, we are keeping all contacts in Florida out of the loop," Torrence answered.

Barry asked, "We're getting contacted by many state leaders and several governors inquiring about the federal propaganda of imminent new PPUs. Some in the public are buying it, they believe, because road traffic has declined and use of public transportation has bottomed. If we continue to ignore them, they may assume the worst."

"I understand," Julie answered. "Tell them we have a plan and what they are hearing is government disinformation. We should avoid general conference calls as it will encourage too many questions we cannot answer."

"We could just tell them for security reasons, all must be kept confidential," added Barry.

Julie shot back, obviously having thought it through, "What will it do to morale if we tell governors and state leaders, *we don't trust you enough to reveal our plan?* If I were them, I would think twice about sharing all with us. It would be an invitation for friction in the Resistance."

Andrew added, "They are hyping how soon total federal surveillance will be available. If we fail, they will have control again. And if we allege that what they are saying today isn't true, what will that do to our credibility in the long run?"

"You are right. But we need to be realistic. If we fail, it will give the Feds the advantage they need in Texas. Our numbers around the country will shrink as people scurry for cover from the IRS, FBI, ATF, HCI, VEB, PSI, and any other acronym of federal control and coercion. We have nothing to lose," she hesitated.

"Whoops, that didn't sound right. We have everything to lose if we fail. If our credibility is compromised by questioning their propaganda, we've already lost."

As leery as they were about withholding information, they needed diversions. Julie and Andrew conferenced with the governors of Florida and Georgia and their state Resistance leaders. They opted for a measure of trust.

"We have an action planned in south Florida. Please understand that it must remain secret. I would love to give you all the details, but if one of your people, perhaps three times removed from you let it slip... Let us just say our plan is 100% dependent upon surprise."

"We get it, what can we do?" asked the Georgia governor.

Julie was relieved she detected no feeling of being slighted in the governor's tone.

"We need diversions to draw attention from a plan we have in place. And your cooperation is critical to its success."

"What can we do?" interrupted the governor of Florida. "All is on the table except drawing protection away from the Treasury department offices where we must retain control."

"We need the appearance of National Guard and Resistance forces moving toward south Florida."

"What do you have in mind?" the governor of Georgia asked.

"Two ways—- first, you could move National Guard troops across the border into Florida. The precedent has been set by Iowa sending guard troops into Nebraska to liberate an ethanol plant."

"I wouldn't do that without Florida's permission."

"You have my permission, Governor."

"What is the second way we could help?"

"We need to distract the Coast Guard from the ports in south Florida. If an unusual number of watercraft were headed south along the coast, it would draw their attention."

"What would you want them to do?"

"Nothing, just be there in numbers. Do nothing illegal. And if the flotilla could be joined by craft from north Florida heading south, it would be better."

The Florida governor asked, "How far south would you want the fleet to go?"

"Only as far south as West Palm Beach. Any further south and you wouldn't draw their response far enough away."

The Florida Resistance leader spoke, "I believe we have hundreds of followers with boats of all kinds who will revel at the chance to poke their finger in the Fed's eyes without endangering themselves. I assume fishing craft, yachts, sail boats, catamarans, speed boats… all would be welcome to join. We could spread the word that it was a new annual party ritual which would bring people not with the Resistance."

"Great idea, the more boats, the more attention they will draw."

"And we could get a number to join them from the south, Miami and a few traveling from Naples."

"Not a good idea, we want the perceived threat to appear coming from the north. Flotillas from two directions may confuse them, causing them to hunker down."

Addressing the governor, Julie continued, "I realize your priority is protecting treasury locations, but whatever people you can spare, could you start moving them at least as far south as Orlando?"

"We'll do that. And I expect if diversion is the goal, you would prefer it be done as noisily as possible."

"That is right."

"I assume this has something to do with the overwhelming presence of Marines in south Florida, particularly around Fort Lauderdale."

"Draw your own conclusions, Governors."

That evening the media was filled with happy news that the Personal Protection Units (PPUs) would soon be in full operation. They did not elaborate where they would come from or how soon. It would be, at best, a few weeks before the Chinese vultures filled the sky, but the sooner the population assumed they were operational, the more fear fermented in the population and control they gained over the citizenry.

The news anchor, with hair bleached white on the sides, who was at a recent White House party, informed his listeners:

"Government officials assure us that we will soon again have the protection we deserve. The Personal Protection Units have been a major factor in reduced crime rates over the last decade. The PPUs' usefulness in crime suppression is validated by recent sad crime statistics. Without the protective units, muggings are up thirty-nine percent, vehicle hijackings up twenty-eight percent, and excessive testosterone induced assaults up forty-two percent. We need to thank all those public employees who have worked tirelessly to protect our common good. Again, it will soon be safe to walk the streets."

Statistics did show an uptick in crime. However, the numbers quoted by the anchor were an FBI exaggeration. Under direction of political appointees on the seventh floor of the FBI building, a bureaucrat in the statistics department did not need his master's degree in calculus to manipulate the numbers. His convoluted mathematical methodology was simply to enhance the numbers by a factor of ten. His larger goal was to advance his career. Muggings were actually up 3.9% since people discovered the PPUs were blind.

Although part of the population bought the security argument for the PPUs, a greater number were not comfortable trading freedom for security. They felt robbed of their identity as a person with constant scrutiny and more like malleable cogs in a wheel. But fear caused their silence. National morale moved inversely to the perceived degree of control the Feds had. Violent crime numbers diminished somewhat with total surveillance, but depression and suicide spiked.

Individuals had various reasons to fear the blanket of constant surveillance. Whether their activity flagrantly broke the law, violated a regulation of which they did not know, or lowered their social score, it struck fear into a large segment of the population.

"We are but serfs," some said. Others said slavery on the government's plantation was a more appropriate metaphor. People had a multitude of reasons to dread the return of eyes-in-the-sky.

Pleasant Hill, Ohio

Jeremy was headed to the state run grocery store with a list his wife had given him. Usually on a Saturday he was coaching soccer, but this was the Saturday players were given a respite from practice. Some called him old fashioned, being married, driving a 20 year old car, and refusing to wear unisex apparel.

He had coached at the local high school for thirty years, taught for thirty-two. He taught economics until the mandated curricula became foreign to him. They wanted him to teach social studies, but no way, he told them. For ten years he had taught geography; it was what it was. The continents, oceans and seas were what they were, and no agenda could change that.

Two state high school runner-up state champion football trophies adorned a shelf in his office. When football was banned, it seemed appropriate to remove the trophies from the school's trophy case said the school's principal. He had been soccer coach for ten years, no trophies.

In route to the grocery store he noticed four of his soccer players headed in another direction on bicycles. In his day many high school seniors drove cars, no more. You now had to be 23 to get a driver's license. The reasoning was twofold; it kept the most reckless prone off the road and it forced the young to establish the habit of taking public transportation.

Curiosity caused Jeremy to turn on a parallel street to see where the kids, whose enthusiasm for soccer had ebbed this year, were going. Three more bicycled boys were also headed in the same direction on this street. He safely dropped back and followed the bicycles. They were three miles from town when the bicycles disappeared in a timber full of walnut trees. Jeremy parked and walked to the timber to see what the boys were doing. Inside the tree line he heard voices, excited yelling nearby. As he approached the merriment, he saw boys playing in a meadow surrounded with trees.

They were playing on a makeshift field, wearing their bicycle helmets; they were playing football. On the side of the activity, he recognized dads, he had coached, encouraging their sons. Jeremy watched half hidden behind a walnut tree. In his excitement he stepped on a walnut, twisted his ankle, and fell, but quickly got up and stayed behind the tree.

One of the dads caught movement behind a tree and whispered to another. A plan was hatched. Jeremy was into the game such he didn't notice two dads surrounding him.

"Coach, it's you," a dad exclaimed recognizing his old football coach.

"Yes, it's me, may I come forward. It's been years since."

"You know what we do here must stay here."

"Absolutely, never worry about me being a snitch. How long have you been teaching the boys football?"

"Only since the vultures went down."

The game stopped as dads greeted their former football coach and boys greeted their soccer coach.

"Coach, with rumors of the vultures coming back, we soon must end these forbidden sessions," said a dad who had been a middle linebacker on one of Jeremy's playoff teams.

"I understand, but until then no Saturday or Wednesday soccer practices."

Similar changes in behavior were anticipated throughout the country.

Sophie – She took more calls and helped more citizens work through the maze of health care regulations in four days than any of her colleagues would in five. With a clear conscience, she sometimes called in sick and rewarded herself with a day shopping at the mall. She knew she would need to stop taking a day off periodically and pick up more of her co-workers' slack once the vultures started spying again. Government healthcare customer service personnel were paid on the time they spent, not their productivity.

Avery – She knew the competition at this year's lily flower show would be heightened. To compete with another potential prize-winning lily, she needed to prevent rabbits from eating the delicate shoot breaking through the soil. The animal repellent that she used was forbidden by the Federal Animal Protection Agency (FAPA). Dare she chance being caught applying the repellent if the PPUs were operational again? She was in a quandary, to apply or not to apply.

Caught in possession of animal repellent would cost her HCI points and limit her access to insulin.

Joshua – He enjoyed painting—not on canvas, but walls— roller, brush, taping; he found it all fun. His neighbor enjoyed gardening, planting, and caring for flower beds. They traded, each doing what they enjoyed and getting something done they would rather not do. Though they were happy with the arrangement, the government frowned on their bartering arrangement which avoided service taxes. If the vultures became active, they would catch his neighbor tending his garden and him carrying painting materials to the neighbor's home. He dreaded doing his own garden work again but would need to avoid the wrath of the IRS.

Jason and Mary – Mary's mother was in a federal care facility a hundred miles from their home. After years of attempting to have her moved to a closer facility, they gave up. While the PPUs were operational, twice a year they went through the hassle of using public transportation to visit her. Visiting her more than twice a year or driving themselves was considered an unnecessary waste of community energy. Upon discovering the absence of eyes in the sky, they were visiting her monthly. Accordingly, her spirits had picked up. If new eyes forced them to reduce the trips, would she again become depressed and die? — Which would, of course, save the government expense. Caught making unnecessary trips would lower the family's SCI (Social Conformity Index).

Lois – She attended Amhurst College. She knew few in her classes. A year earlier she was investigated because three times she inadvertently visited a coffee shop that an anti-government leader attended. She did not want to worry who was inside a coffee house she attended again. A reduced SCI would hamper her prospects of getting into grad school.

John and Emily – The couple lived on a hobby farm and kept eight pigs. They were properly registered as pets. However, two years prior, vultures found one missing. A search of their farm found fresh pork in a freezer hidden in the barn. They wished not to be vegetarians by force. Citizens were issued ration cards to limit meat consumption.

Circumventing those ration cards with illicit meat would negatively impact your HCI (Health Care Index).

Liam – He enjoyed a cigar a few times a year. Five years prior, a PPU had caught smoke emanating from his patio. His HCI still had a fifteen-point deduction for the cigar. Since the lapse in vulture coverage, he had a few cigars, should he never again have any? A second violation of the no tobacco law would cost him another fifteen HCI points. If it tasted better, he would consider switching to violation free marijuana.

Lucas – He was careful using a mixture of public transportation and his own car to attend Resistance meetings. Twice his car was tracked, and bus camera facial recognition put him near a Resistance meeting. He suspected the IRS audit was not random. He was right. With the skies clear, he had been attending more Resistance meetings. If he wanted to avoid audits, maintain his HCI and SCI, he would need to stay away from future Resistance meetings.

Nancy and James – Three generations had attended the small rural church in which they were married thirty years earlier. But the high taxes imposed on establishments without redeeming social value closed the church. Religious repression started when a virus hit the country decades earlier. With the vultures now blind, some had returned to the dilapidated church. Would they continue when new vultures arrived and risk a diminished SCI score which affected their HCI?

Natalie – She and her husband felt lucky being granted the right to have two children, a privilege for having a high PSI (Prodigy Suitability Index). As most children had for three generations, they loved pizza. Natalie usually ordered pizza by phone for delivery from a small local pizza place. Little did she know that Nathan, who twice was filmed delivering their pizza, was soon to be cancelled from school for anti-social activities. Given that their daughter also had a low social score, they were visited by the FBI. If the eyes-in-the-sky returned, they would worry about who delivered future pizzas.

Addison – She was overweight, but her HCI was penalized little as doctors believed it was a genetic condition. With a semblance of freedom back, she had started visiting a donut shop. If caught, her

HCI would be cut. She understood the health risks, chose to make her own decisions, and held that her life was hers and not the State's.

The question of who owned Addison's life was a fundamental difference in the underlying beliefs between the establishment and the Resistance.

Although not crudely verbalized, the predominant philosophy in establishment circles was that the State owned Addison's life. The State —defined as the community, represented by government in general— as opposed to one state. The State had invested money in her education, the infrastructure that was used to transport her mother to the hospital to give birth, the health care she and her mother received, the cost of the police force that protected her, the myriad of environmental regulations that kept her healthy, and etc., etc. That Addison and her parents paid taxes for these services whether they were desired or not was irrelevant. Because the State made an investment without which Addison would not be the person she is, the State had ownership.

Earlier in the century it was asserted by politicians that just because a person built a business it was not necessarily theirs because the State had a hand in making the business a success- built the roads for access, etc., etc. Those politicians paid no price for their clarity in expressing collective ideology. It was a small step to apply the same rationale to a person.

Backing up two hundred years in a full circle, a similar argument was made that some people did not own their own lives. Slaveowners fed their slaves from childhood, taught them how to harvest crops, provided shelter and health care—such as it was, when needed— and thus expected a return on their investment.

In short, the Resistance movement was an anti-slavery movement.

Anticipation of returning government monitors caused many citizens to engage in activities they might later be apprehensive to take. In more ways than one people saw the weekend as the last day of summer, a time to enjoy the beach before snow fell. Realistically, it was a time to enjoy life before drones squelched their fun and endangered their well-being. Road traffic was like rush hour all weekend.

Others avoided the road and took their boats to water. Non-purposeful watercraft excursions had long been discouraged. A beautiful autumn weekend all along the southeast coast contributed to the surge of boats offshore.

Resistance members with boats in South Carolina spread the rumor that a major end-of-season boat party would be held from Savannah on southward over the weekend. Many boatsmen took the day off Friday and headed south. When they reached the Savannah area, they found the harbors nearly empty of fishing and pleasure craft and boat traffic headed further south.

At high school earlier in the week, Olivia heard of a weekend boat party south of Savannah. Her parents inherited a family boat. That summer they had used the boat more than the previous five summers. Olivia loved the being out on the boat, sometimes inviting friends.

Olivia's parents Ava and Lucas had two children, including Noah in junior high. The couple had always maintained high social scores, enabling the couple to maintain a high PSI (Prodigy Suitability Index). Lucas was cleared twice to receive an antidote to the male sterilizing agent put into public drinking water. Their children were sanctioned.

The children overheard their parents discussing the prospects of a boat outing. "Let's do it while we still can," they would remember their dad saying. Their family joined a growing flotilla at Savannah headed south.

It was dark when they passed the lights on Amelia Island. Throughout the night more boat traffic joined the flotilla. The morning sun revealed a maze of hundreds, maybe thousands, of boats stretched out miles around St. Augustine, Florida. It was a thing of beauty as sailboats were joining the party.

A Coast Guard cutter near St. Augustine had prior word that a fleet of pleasure boats was headed their way. But they were shocked by the size. The captain contacted the Coast Guard's 7th District, located in Miami, Fla. The headquarters was responsible for Coast Guard activities throughout a 1.7 million square mile area including Puerto Rico, Florida, Georgia, and South Carolina. The captain was told to stop several boats and ascertain the reason for the armada's travel.

He reported back that five boats described the gathering as a season ending party. Three other boats refused to answer any questions.

Lucas cautioned the family they had gone far enough; fuel could become an issue, and with the heavy traffic, shoreside fueling stations could be without fuel. Olivia pleaded—as high school girls will—that it would be their last boat trip for the year, and they should make the most of it. Although Lucas did not discuss his concerns, he knew with new surveillance coming that next year's boat outings would be limited. He relented.

They learned from another boat they temporarily tied up with that barges further south were selling unbelievably low-priced fuel. An oil company owned by Resistance members had placed fueling barges around Daytona Beach. They were selling the fuel at a loss to encourage boaters to travel further south. If Lucas had known the fuel was subsidized by Resistance members for a mission, he would have turned around. For safety and family prosperity, he followed the rules.

By orders from Miami, four Coast Guard patrol boats and one cutter were spread out in the Cocoa Beach area charged with stopping the flotilla. It was as if five men holding flyswatters were charged with stopping a swarm of moving locusts. Lucas saw one patrol boat and thought nothing of it.

The Coast Guard had cancelled all leaves for the weekend to guard Port Fort Lauderdale. The southward bound flotilla was a quandary; did they have a mission or was it coincidental? No boats were armed. But if they drifted as far south as the Port, they would cause major confusion.

The Coast Guard did not know what the Chinese freighters carried, but they had been instructed to bar no resource to protect the freighters now in the harbor unloading. They had safely seen the freighters into the harbor. No source of concern or other anomalies were afloat. But for the safety of the Chinese freighters' exit to sea, they would ensure the armada of pleasure boats got no further south than West Palm beach. Two-thirds of the Coast Guard inventory was sent north to stop the civilian onslaught. The cutters and patrol boats blared radio and bullhorn warnings to the boats that areas south were *no-go zones*. To reinforce the message, they conducted firing exercises blocking movement further south.

The Feds were successful in stopping the flotilla, as was the Resistance in drawing Coast Guard assets away from Fort Lauderdale. The Resistance had done its job.

Chapter 23

Atlas Headquarters

Torrence, Mason, Barry, Andrew, and Julie spent the night at Atlas Headquarters. Information came in sporadically. Their presence at the headquarters was not necessary, but none of them could have slept at home. The news throughout the night was good, the flotilla off the coast of Florida was bigger than they hoped and achieved the intended result by diverting Coast Guard assets away from Fort Lauderdale.

Julie volunteered to get the group pastries and breakfast sandwiches. She needed to get out. It was policy that none would venture out to public spaces alone, and one would be armed. Andrew was busy; Barry stuffed a 45 in his belt and offered to go with her. The bakery was busy.

Julie, at an early age, wanted to be in law enforcement. Her dad steered her into private security work. He said with increasing restrictions on police, the demand for private security services would mount. Given that she was set on the field, he sent her to Israel for training by the best. The Mossad and Israel security were masters at profiling by detecting minuscule body language clues. Julie had used her training extensively, from saving Andrew at O'Hare

Airport twelve years ago to successfully directing security at Atlas Transportation. She still profiled whenever in a group of people.

The takeout shop had two lines, each four deep. Barry and Julie were third in line. Twice, Julie felt a nearly buzz-headed brunette in the other line glance at her. The glance was intended to be unnoticed; it was not by Julie. Although neutral attire was normal, the brunette was dressed as inconspicuously as possible. Her right thumb and forefinger seemed to do a dance. Her left shoulder periodically flinched. The woman was making herself keenly aware of everyone in the shop while trying to remain unnoticed. Julie's experience told her the woman was not a threat but fearful of something or someone.

The brunette picked up her bag of food first. Julie told Barry she was following the lady to see why she was fearful. They walked in the same direction in the parking lot. Julie could sense the lady's walk tightening as she noticed Julie following her.

Near their cars they started to part, and Julie asked, "Are you all right?"

"Of course, why wouldn't I be?"

"You just seem a little nervous."

"There's so much to be nervous about these days—crime up, nothing in the sky to hamper criminals. What will happen to us if the government doesn't start protecting us again?"

Julie saw Barry coming from the other direction carrying food bags. Looking back, she should have warned the lady. When he opened the car door behind her, it startled her, and all her pent-up anxiety came forward. She jumped, screamed and her bag burst on the concrete, donuts rolling every which way.

Julie apologized for not warning her that Barry was coming; the lady apologized for overreacting. Pretenses gone, the three stood and talked.

"I'm sorry, I just feel so helpless and alone with no one watching me, looking out for me. Hopefully, they will be back soon, and I'll feel safer," she stated as she glanced upward hoping to see a PPU.

Julie threw Barry a bewildering look and said to the woman, "What good comes from you living your life in fear? What is the value of life? Sometimes a person needs to take stock. Someone once told me that the value of one's life is a product. The product is the quality times quantity. Simple math taught us if either side is zero the product is zero.

Are you sure it is worth allowing fear to make your life miserable in order to infinitesimally lower your risk?"

"It is just without," she looked in the sky for a PPU again, "I feel so lonely."

"There is an entity up there looking out for you, always has been, always will be. Understanding that presence is always with us is cause for us to have no fear. Our real caretaker is not dependent on mechanical/electrical workings or the political whim of the day. It is a given. And if we allow another entity to attempt taking its place, we will be disappointed. I believe you are looking in the wrong place for comfort."

The lady was now leaning against her car in contemplation. "Sounds like you are one of those religious types." She rolled her eyes. "But you've given me something to consider. I guess I could, or maybe should, think of it that way as you religious people always do seem happier."

"Try to relax, okay, all will be well," Julie said giving the lady a hug.

"Curious, who told you of the quality, quantity product thing?"

"It was my father, three decades ago. I was in high school, but in remote classes as everyone feared a virus. That is when our protectors learned they could control us with fear.

Someone else said once '*There is a battle waging...... We must realize what is happening and enter the fray.*' You must decide whether you are content trembling and hiding under a rock, or whether you wish to overcome your fear and live your life in joy."

Headed back to Atlas, Barry said to Julie, "I bet the lady's mother wore a mask five years after that virus struck earlier in the century just because some power-hungry bureaucrat said it was a good idea. I would have told her to just think instead of being blindly led."

"Do you think that would have helped her?" Julie replied.

Barry ignored the question and replied, "By the way, if you tire of security, I can think of another profession you might try."

Port Fort Lauderdale

It had now been two days and nights the cruise ship "Tranquility" had been sitting miles outside the Port Fort Lauderdale harbor. The ship was originally designated as a large cruise ship. The 850 feet long ship displaced twenty-four feet of water and had been built to hold 3,400 passengers. It had been redesigned to carry 1,800 passengers in luxury with equal sized large state rooms throughout.

The cruise ship industry was a fraction of its earlier days. Decades earlier, a virus had crippled the industry. When it started to recover, heavy luxury taxes were imposed to discourage what many considered a Bourgeoisie excess. Those cruise ships that remained were very exclusive. In addition to money, position was a requisite to secure a reservation. The ship waiting to dock was government owned and used to reward federal employees for service above and beyond faithful implementation of the common good.

This morning, Tranquility was not tranquil. Passengers were livid. Two days they had sat with little explanation as to why. Some had children to pick up. The only consolation to those on the cruise was an announcement that all absences in agency offices would be excused.

Kevin had received accommodations for his adherence to protocol and been awarded a five-day cruise for two. He asked a co-worker to join him as a cabinmate. His domestic partner had been expecting him home from a boring out-of-town agency training meeting which he purported to dread. The training had been conducted online two weeks prior. His cabinmate's partners had also expected her back from training two days ago.

His cabinmate, Janice, was from Cambridge, Massachusetts— the city that initially recognized any domestic union between two or more people in 2021. Her household union originally consisted of three women and three men. A few years into the union, one woman strayed with another man. One of the attributes of a multi-person union was thought to be a reduction in temptations to stray from a two-person domestic partnership. It did not work out that way in their arrangement.

The partners had tried partnership therapy. With six partners, it was complicated. The union dissolution was financially many times more problematic than with two. Hence, Janice's partners kept track of her. Her absence caused them to investigate the weekend training session she supposedly was at. They could find none.

In line with the large cruise ship, many freighters could also be seen stacked on the horizon waiting to get into the harbor. The harbor had been closed to all traffic since the Chinese freighters arrived Friday night. It was expected that unloading and fueling the freighters would take thirty-six hours.

White House, Sunday morning

The COS sat with the president as information came in about activities around Port Fort Lauderdale.

"I can't believe the ineptitude of the Resistance trying to hide a boat full of explosives among an armada of pleasure boats. Did they really think the Coast Guard would allow anything near the harbor? Perhaps we've been overestimating them."

"We don't know that any of those boats held explosives. It is the time of year that people party on boats to end the summer. Maybe that flotilla is just overzealous partiers," observed the COS.

"You don't really believe that it is a coincidence they just happened to be heading toward the port, do you?"

The Oval Office phone rang. The COS picked it up and whispered, "It's the Pentagon."

"What's up?" the president asked.

The Marines had been strictly enforcing a twenty mile no-fly zone around Port Fort Lauderdale. The zone included the airport which had been closed since the Chinese freighters arrived Friday evening. Residents in the zone were unhappy as weekend drone home deliveries were not made. Occasionally, a delivery drone mistakenly entered the zone to be quickly brought down by a laser battery. Investigation determined that those few incidents were accidental.

Up to twenty miles from the port, Marine presence had all major intersections blocked and only allowed traffic through following inspection. Three of the latest design Marine attack helicopters were in the air continuously circling the harbor. The president was assured the harbor was impregnable.

Jerome's car was parked on the street leaving his two-car garage vacant. The house had been built in the early part of the century when two-car garages were common. In the mid-century, unless a family was able to secure an exemption, only one car was allowed per family. It allowed Jerome space for a shop and room to tinker.

Early this Sunday morning, he secured four-foot wings on a drone. He had the propeller idling on the drone when he raised the garage door a few feet to allow its escape. The driveway sloped down to the street. It was airborne by the time it reached the street, traveled straight through an alley, and made a right turn on the next street. Jerome lived at the border of the no-fly zone.

In a few blocks the drone rose to a couple hundred feet and headed for the port. As Jerome launched the drone, five other Resistance members living near the no-fly zone launched drones in the same manner.

"Mr. President, we want to inform you six drones were launched before 6:00 am this morning toward the Port. They were launched from near the western border of the no-fly zone. None of them made it to within five miles of the Port before our lasers dispatched them. We are searching the wreckage as we speak."

"Great work! Make sure the officers running the laser batteries get commendations. Have you been able to determine where they were launched from and arrest the perpetrators?"

"No sir, we haven't; it appears they remained only a few feet above street level away from our eyes before they rose."

"Do whatever you must. But if another launch is made, find the people responsible."

"We could divert helicopters west in the no-fly zone. But it would leave the port more vulnerable from the sea."

The president responded, "The Coast Guard stopped the sea threat, move the helicopters."

"Yes sir, we'll move two of the three."

The President looked at his COS. "Last night we stymied the sea attack, and this morning we thwarted an air attack. No way with two

Marine divisions can they get to the port by land. They've tried, but we've won."

After years of service, the COS could read the president's mind. Although it was still morning, she lifted a 24-year aged bottle of Scotch from a cabinet, poured the president a neat tumbler, and handed it to him.

"Aren't you having any?" he asked.

"You know what that does to me?"

"So, what, we have all afternoon with no appointments. After all we've been through, we deserve a celebration."

It was noon, and they were on their second tumbler when the Pentagon phone rang again.

"Mr. President, the Chinese freighter has successfully unloaded the cargo and it is leaving the harbor."

Ocean front outside Port Fort Lauderdale

Eight ships were waiting outside the harbor when the second Chinese freighter left the harbor entrance. The large cruise ship, six miles out, was closest to the mouth of the harbor and first in line. Seven other freighters of various shapes and sizes waited for notification from the Broward County Port Fort Lauderdale administration for permission to enter the harbor. Beyond the freighters was an old medium sized cruise ship.

Kevin was on the large cruise ship's deck. He had ignored three calls from his at- home partner. With time, he would come up with a plausible explanation. Suddenly, he felt the three giant propellers on his ship engage.

"Ah, at last we're on our way in," he thought.

He scanned behind the ship to see if any of the freighters had started moving toward the harbor when he noticed smoke billowing from a distant ship. The ship was gaining on them. Closer, he could tell it was another cruise ship, but a smaller one. It passed three freighters in the line at a surprisingly close distance. He was sure he could see the freighters rock from the wake of the close passing ship.

The cruise ship was approaching at twenty-eight knots, its labeled top speed at full weight. Although the old cruise ship had been partially gutted, it held an extra reservoir of fuel. The ship had not registered with the Broward County Port administration for harbor use; hence they had no way to identify it for communication. The port traffic tower stood to the south of the harbor entrance, and the fast-moving ship was passing others on the starboard side blocking vision from the tower.

A Coast Guard cutter and two patrol boats were south of the ships lined up for harbor entry. Their concern was traffic from Miami. Other Coast Guard ships were north at West Palm Beach blocking traffic from the north. Patrol boats were out of position and too slow to intercept the fast-moving cruise ship.

"All ships approaching the harbor, shut down your engines immediately!" barked the Port administration traffic controller.

The leading large cruise ship cut its engines within two miles of the harbor entrance at the Stanahan River outlet. Kevin was standing near a shuffleboard court on the starboard side when the speeding cruise ship came from behind unbelievably close.

It was almost close enough to jump, thought Kevin. But what struck Kevin most peculiar was the absence of anyone on board. He thought they had avoided its wake until it passed. Feeling the need to grab the railing with both hands, his grape tumbled into the water as he fell to his knees gripping the railing. He heard a shriek, turned, and saw his cabinmate had fallen and reached for a lawn chair which was sliding across the deck before the roll abated.

Although no one was in the ship captain's control room, Torrence was in control of the former Resistance headquarters from his Atlas office in Midland, Texas. One screen gave him propeller rpms, bearing, and speed. Another screen used GPS to show his location relative to other ships and the harbor entrance. A third screen gave the calculated ETA (Expected Time of Arrival). It showed ten minutes. The ship radio had picked up messages ordering all ships in the area to go dead in the water. They were ignored.

The last four crew members of the speeding cruise ship were in a lifeboat heading further out to sea. Earlier, they spray painted the bright orange lifeboat in camouflage. With binoculars, they tried to track their abandoned ship.

Barry had previously hacked into the fire alarm systems at the port. At the ten-minute mark, he set off fire alarms at all docks and warehouses within a quarter mile of the dock on SE 20th Street.

The Marine helicopter that remained circling the port made two low passes at the ship, then turned and opened warning fire in the ship's path. The ship stayed on course now only a mile from the harbor inlet.

The helicopter's inquiry to command received an order to stop the ship using all available fire. The ship was now a few yards from the harbor inlet. Dual fifty caliber machine gun fire was directed at the ship's quarterdeck command post to no avail. All the upper deck was sprayed with fire as the ship passed under the helicopter. Command summoned the helicopters on the western edge of the no-fly zone back, but they were minutes away.

A Coast Guard cutter was at an angle southeast of the cruise ship, unable to gain on it. They laid down cannon fire in front of the cruise ship hoping to divert it. When given the order to hit the ship, a cannon shell smashed into the port side of the cruise ship rocking it but not stopping it. Before they could send a second shell, the cruise ship entered the harbor which blocked their line of fire.

Strict government and union protocol allowed workers no hesitation vacating facilities when a fire alarm was sounded. Workers who tarried during a fire drill had been reprimanded. One hundred workers were in the warehouse assembling the Chinese PPUs when the fire drill went off. Within five minutes, they were at the far end of the fenced off parking lot. From their vantage point, they could see a cruise ship barreling toward the dock at a speed never seen inside a dock area with a helicopter hovering over it.

The huge warehouse at SE 20th Street sat adjacent to the dock perpendicular to the harbor's entry channel. Immediately inside the harbor, the cruise ship had to turn twenty-five degrees to the right. At nearly thirty knots, it was not an easy turn. Had the warehouse been deeper in the harbor, a ninety-degree turn could not have been made at but a fraction of that speed.

"Turning at this speed is the tricky part, particularly after that hit," said Torrence. He leaned toward the direction he guided the ship as if he were on it.

"There, I believe we made the turn." He blew a sigh of relief as did others in the remote-control room in Midland.

Suddenly, the ship gauges all flickered. Julie could see Torrence's expression change. "What happened?" she asked.

"I think we were just hit big time. The rudders are out, and the propellers are now gliding with the ship's momentum."

The helicopter that had directed fifty-caliber fire on the deck turned as the ship passed under it. The helicopter fired two air-to-surface missiles low on the ship's stern in an attempt to disable it.

Workers standing in the far corner of the parking lot who had evacuated the building could see the cruise ship headed for the dock and the helicopter firing at it. The ship looked like a wounded duck, listing to the port side where the cutter's cannon had torn a hole and with the stern starting to sag which raised the bow. But the ship's momentum was moving it faster than any ship would safely in the harbor. It was headed at a forty-five degree angle for the pier where the Chinese freighter recently tied.

There was a scramble to open and get through the parking lot gate. Workers knew the 43,000-ton ship striking the concrete pier at its speed would throw concrete in the air as it plowed through the pier. Most were still running a block away when they heard the deafening crunch of steel meeting concrete.

The bow plowed through fifty feet of reinforced concrete pier before being stopped twenty feet from the warehouse. Two freighter loading cranes were knocked from their moorings and collapsed on the warehouse roof.

The fleeing crowd stopped and watched chunks of concrete fall from the sky well shy of the crowd. Suddenly, they saw a stream of liquid rising in an arch and falling on the warehouse. At first, they could not believe the harbor fire patrol arrived that quickly.

Someone shouted, "It's coming from the cruise ship."

Fire erupted on the roof of the warehouse and billowed black smoke skyward. A four-inch nozzle that would be found on a fireboat continued to pour fuel on the warehouse until the cruise ship's tanks were empty.

When the harbor fireboats arrived, it was too late; and water would not deter the burning fuel oil.

"What do you see?" Torrence queried the men on the lifeboat.

"We heard a muted bang, saw some debris in the air, then flames and black smoke rising."

"Well?" Julie asked Torrence.

"Good thing we buried that fuel nozzle in an elevator until the last minute or the fifty-caliber fire might have disabled it. By what they describe, it did not. I'd say with confidence the Chinese vultures are history."

High fives were exchanged around the room. The air of satisfaction equaled the deflection of the asteroid twelve years previous and the nuking of NSA a year prior. Melissa was on hand and told everyone how proud Dan and others who were killed fighting for liberty would be as they looked down from above. All knew the task ahead was formidable, but now, at the least, possible as a return of the vultures would have doomed them.

Fifty miles out to sea, the cruise ship's former crew was picked up from a lifeboat by a Polish freighter.

Kevin and his temporary cabinmate stood on Tranquility's deck as did most of the passengers. They had been dead in the water since the smaller cruise ship raced by and rocked their ship. Now they watched black flumes billowing in the clear sky. Rumors were rampant as to what had happened. Finally, the captain's voice boomed through speakers. He said the harbor was temporarily closed and promised to relay further information as he received it. Then he added that the bars were open.

Kevin shrugged his shoulders and turned away from the harbor smoke to Janice. "I've been thinking. I think at the last minute the agency changed locations for this off-the-record training session and held it on this ship."

"Great idea," she responded. "It's amazing the sacrifices we make doing the work of the people. Tedious training sessions, boring company, and inferior facilities, what shall we do?"

"Absolutely, let's get to the bar before it becomes crowded."

White House

After the call from the Pentagon at noon that the Chinese freighter had successfully unloaded and left the harbor, the president told the weekend secretary to forward no calls and the Oval Office door would remain closed. The COS was sitting on his lap as they partied.

"Here's to a great partner in providing for the common good," the president offered a toast to the COS with their third drink among other activities of the afternoon.

"Yes, and here is to great foresight and management," she responded.

"Well, I'm told the first assembled PPUs will leave the harbor tomorrow afternoon. And they'll be all out by Friday ready for the next shipment to arrive."

"Perhaps we should think about having them filmed lifting off the parking lot and have the media frame it as our commitment to public protection?" offered the COS.

"Good idea, we might have a cartoon caricature of a masked mugger/rapist with a red slash through the figure painted on a PPU. That would exemplify the mission of the PPUs."

At 3 pm, they were interrupted by the ring of a land line phone. "I told her no more calls this afternoon," the president grumbled.

"It's the Pentagon, sir," the COS said as she handed him the phone.

It was 1:15 when the Pentagon first received word of the disaster in Fort Lauderdale. They waited for confirmation, then longer for an initial report of damages. The CJCS would have resigned if doing so would have avoided making the call.

"What?" the president barked into the phone.

"We've had an incident at the dock and warehouse where the new PPUs are, sir."

"What did protesters in inside the harbor? Have them all arrested."

"No, it is more of a problem."

"What? Don't tell me the Chinese delivered faulty drones."

"Mr. President, there has been an explosion and fire."

"What happened?"

"A renegade ship got into the harbor and crashed into the dock."

"How many PPUs were destroyed?"

"They are all gone, sir, as are the dock and warehouse."

"Where was the Coast Guard, where were the Marines, what happened to the Port Authority? Someone will be held responsible!"

By the time he was off the phone, the COS had put the Scotch and tumblers away and was in the process of tidying the Oval Office.

Chapter 24

An inspection of the harbor by the Port Authority revealed the worst. The sunken cruise ship and debris from its assault on the pier had left the north half of the harbor unusable. Clean up crews would take months clearing the channel. Most of the ships awaiting docking were diverted to other ports.

Media reports briefly mentioned an explosion at a Florida harbor without details. Years earlier they would have attributed it to domestic terrorists; now doing so would give credibility to the Resistance.

White House

"I can assure you, Ambassador, that the new location will be safe. If you can hold the freighter carrying the next shipment of PPUs up for three days, we will be ready at the new location," the President assured the Chinese Ambassador.

"Costs are incurred holding up the ship, Mr. President."

The president could not believe, given the gravity of the situation, the Chinese would want to squeeze. 'We'll pay you twice the loss of revenue."

"I'll get back to you, Mr. President."

Off the phone, he said to his assembled staff, "They will wait, what else are they going to do—take the drones back to Africa? Will the Norfolk dock be ready for the freighter?"

Norfolk Naval Station, established in 1917, was the world's biggest naval base situated in southeastern Virginia. Nowhere in the world would more firepower be available to protect a freighter in a harbor or PPUs in a warehouse from marauding kamikaze ships.

"Yes sir, we have readied a dock for unloading cargo and put an armada at sea surrounding the harbor. Airspace has been closed in a twenty-mile radius. We have two aircraft carrier groups nearby with fighters constantly patrolling the area. They have orders to sink any vessel that gets within twenty miles of the harbor without proper authorization."

"What about using the Air Force as a backup?"

"Mr. President, we are confident that will not be necessary. Beside two carrier's aircraft, the Navy has land-based fighter-bombers on the ready near the harbor."

"That's not enough. We thought Fort Lauderdale was secure also. I will not tolerate another screwup."

The CJCS did not tell the president that he had instructed an Air Force base to have bombers rotating around Norfolk at all hours. The general of the base had flatly refused the order. He would deal with the insubordination immediately. To bring it up now would cast doubt on his command.

"Can you guarantee no ship or plane will get through?"

"Yes, Mr. President, I will stake my reputation on it."

"You are, General, and more."

"The only thing I cannot guarantee is the safety of the Chinese freighter until our escort ships reach it in twenty-four hours and guide it to the harbor."

The president could tell the CJSC was holding back. "Go ahead say what else you are thinking."

"I should point out that allowing a Chinese flagged ship inside our naval harbor breaks all established protocol. The intelligence the Chinese may glean from proximity to our naval operations may be very damaging in the long run."

"Long run, hell! What does the long run amount to if we no longer have a country? If we do not get these hobbits—whose heads are popping up everywhere—under control, what difference does it make? I wish we didn't need to get the means to control them from the Chinese, but we have no choice."

"Mr. President," the COS interjected when he finished, "The VP is on the phone, and she is demanding to be put on the speaker."

"Do it, she'll like what my next move is."

"Madame Vice President, I'm glad you could join us this morning. But I must say some of the debate I have heard on the Senate floor from these belligerent states is not helpful. What can you do about it?"

"There is a move to censure them which would restrict their speaking privileges."

"I think I can help you out there. As part of my powers under martial law, I am banning all Washington representation from states whose National Guard Units have not pledged allegiance to me, states that have illegally taken over treasury offices, and states that have not complied with the Department of Energy.

Senators and representatives from those states will no longer have voting privileges until their states are in compliance with federal mandates. Any of that group who attempt entry into the capitol building or legislative offices will be arrested."

"Mr. President, that is a bold and courageous move, for which I applaud you."

A third of the senators and representatives from thirty-one states in non-compliance went home, given the martial law edict. Given that a third had more ties to the Washington area than their home states, they stayed. The remaining third refused to be silenced and were arrested when they staged a protest on the Capitol grounds.

Missouri

Whiteman Air Force Base was south of Knob Noster, Missouri, about seventy miles southeast of Kansas City. It was the original home of the B-2 Spirit bomber, called by some the batwing bomber. Although military upgrades had been curtailed for years, an upgraded B-3 was now in operation. Its stealth technology had leapfrogged the Navy's radar capabilities.

Erica Montel was the commanding general at Whiteman Air Force Base. Her husband had served under General Martinez in the army and was now retired but talked to the general often. General Montel graduated from a Dallas suburban high school in Frisco. She took all AP classes. In her AP classes was Madison Archibald, the future governor of Texas. They were friends but had talked seldom since high school.

General Montel's retired husband was active in the Resistance; although she chose to keep her distance, he kept her informed. He told her the Resistance's version of what happened in Fort Lauderdale. Her research validated it. Although she kept well informed, she chose to stay out of the fray.

The general was shocked when the Pentagon ordered her to put B-3s over Norfolk in the event they were needed. She made multiple excuses why that could not be done at the time—temporary repairs to the fleet, lack of coordination with the Navy, and reluctance to bomb anything in an American harbor. After her excuses failed, she flat out refused the order.

The evening after refusing the order, her husband said they would be getting an important call. It was her former friend, the governor of Texas.

"Madison, so glad to hear from you. I want you to know if you are ever in Missouri, this base will be a safe place for you, regardless of the warrants for you."

"Thank you, Erica, but I should make you aware others are on this conference call."

General Martinez and the governor of Missouri introduced themselves. It was a long conversation. They thanked her for her refusal to follow the Pentagon order. Both Martinez and the governors assured her that the Resistance would prevail, and that by refusing the order, her destiny was in peril with the Feds. The Missouri governor stated that Missouri would follow the Resistance, that the Air Force base was on Missouri soil, and that her pay would be taken care of by the state. After the conference call, her husband continued to make their case.

The next morning, General Montel contacted the Pentagon and asked for the CJCS. She was told her message would be delivered as soon as he returned from the White House.

Contacting the commander of Whiteman was the first item on the CJCS's agenda back at the Pentagon. With the Air Force chief at his side, he contacted her, prepared to immediately relieve her of command.

"Sir, I made a terrible error yesterday hesitating to follow your order. I know it is my responsibility to do as directed, and we will have a rotating contingent of B-3s in the Norfolk area ready in the event they are needed."

"I appreciate your better judgment, General."

Her acquiescence relieved the CJCS of the immediate problem, but he would need to deal with her hesitancy following orders when all the turmoil died down.

General Montel learned from the Pentagon conference call that a Chinese ship would be unloading PPUs in the Norfolk harbor the following Tuesday and Wednesday and out of the harbor by 3:00 pm. A rotation of four B-3 crews would alternate on standby duty over the harbor. She asked her orderly to see the rotation schedule of crews and changed the schedule so Captain Adderley and his crew would be on rotation over Norfolk from 2:00 to 8:00pm Wednesday.

One by one she summoned the crews to her office and gave them orders. Each B-3 bomber carried four bunker busting bombs, each capable of sinking a ship or destroying a warehouse.

Captain Adderley and crew were the last called into her office, her orders differed from the others. Her instructions were brief.

"I understand you know what you are called to do, if necessary. I will say no more, good luck."

Atlas headquarters— Midland, Texas

"How confident are we in Captain Adderley and crew?" asked Julie.

Andrew answered, "I talked to our Missouri leader. He said the captain has been active in the Resistance since joining at a speakeasy during the asteroid deflection ordeal. He has handpicked his crew. As the first shipment, neither will this shipment of PPUs ever fly."

"Once they are eliminated, the governor wants to move forward with the ceremony at Fort Hood."

"That is a big step," observed Andrew.

"Yes, but it will keep the momentum on our side. We are planning a major media event."

China

Fighting had been more intense than the Chinese Communist Party (CCP) anticipated. Perhaps it was hope over reality, but the CCP expected the Taiwan Resistance to fold once the outcome was inevitable. What was expected to be a week's campaign dragged on for a month. Casualties surpassed one million. The island was bombed to the extent stone age man would not have been out of place. Hopes of capturing Taiwan's economic engine intact were gone. The cost was exponentially higher than CCP planners had envisioned, and the reward was tenuous.

The CCP expected a tough fight moving armies down into Indochina. They would not underestimate the population as the French and Americans had done. Neither would they be timid in their tactics as the Americans had been. But it became a slugfest. The plan was to reinforce their armies with successful troops from the Taiwan campaign, but those forces were disseminated and needed to be rebuilt. It was now apparent to the CCP generals that the campaign could take a year.

"Of what are you the most in need?" asked the CCP chairman.

"More intelligence. They set traps we are unaware of, move their forces underground, and attack without warning, then disappear. We are too often caught by surprise. Our bombers are sent to stop a convoy and arrive to find three men pushing a cart," the CCP military commander answered.

"What would provide more intelligence?"

"More eyes in the sky," was his quick answer.

"Comrade," the chairman addressed his industrial overseer. "What is the status of the freighter carrying our drones to the US?"

"It has been sitting for two days in the mid-Atlantic—1,000 kilos from their harbor, waiting for an American escort into their harbor."

"Turn it around. We need those drones."

"But we have a deal with the Americans, Comrade."

"Our interest is paramount to any deal, and what will the Americans do? Complain as always? They may bark, but seldom bite. Perhaps, in the long run it will be better for us with them divided."

White House

"It's the Pentagon, sir," the COS said.

"Does your escort have that Chinese freighter in tow yet?"

"No, Mr. President, it was not at the prescribed location."

"Where is it?"

"The latest satellite feed shows it has turned around."

"Get the Chinese ambassador on the phone," he barked at the COS.

"Mr. Ambassador, I understand the second delivery of drones has turned around. Is there a problem with the ship?"

"No, Mr. President, but Beijing has determined we have need for the drones. We will have another batch in production soon and should be able to deliver them late next year."

"That was not the deal. We have an agreement. The 7th fleet moved east of Hawaii as we agreed. Now you must hold up your end."

The president didn't think a response was coming from the ambassador until he finally spoke, "Perhaps your Navy should also have complied with the deal. Your Pearl Harbor base is on an east island, but a Navy cruiser twice circled on the west side of Coconut Island."

"That is a preposterous overly strict interpretation of our agreement."

"Interesting that you accuse the opposition in your country with the same language about your Constitution," retaliated the ambassador.

"Given that our agreement has been breached, perhaps we should send the 7th fleet to the South China sea."

"That would be most unfortunate for your Navy, Mr. President."

"Are you really considering moving the 7th fleet, sir?" asked the COS after the call.

"How dare the Chinese lecture us about our loose interpretation of the Constitution? But back to your question... perhaps, we should think about getting involved in the South China sea. We need not enter the fray, but thousands of American sailors close to the first major war of the century would divert national attention away from hooligans here. Uniting the country would be worth the risk."

Media outlets that had downplayed the bloody slugfest in Asia began giving updates on the fighting and misery imposed on Indochina. The president held a press conference and affirmed American's resolve to stand up for those under attack. He assured the public that Americans would not participate in the fighting, but our presence would give those involved reason to reconsider their aggression.

The clandestine Resistance news service had been giving detailed reports about the demise of thousands of would-be eyes in the sky. The grape app to the alternative news service was illegal to possess. Citizens were liable for heavy reprimands including loss of HCI points if the app was found on their grape. But a new Resistance news app developed by technicians at Atlas bleached itself from the grape when not in use. Aware that the new app could not be found on their grapes, more people downloaded the app.

Before the media switched their focus to Asia, the Resistance news service had been giving reports about the horrific Asian war. Mainstream media now covering the war only validated the Resistance news early reports. The mainstream media's conversion to accurately reporting the events in Asia also brought credibility to the Resistance media's version of what happened at Fort Lauderdale.

Atlas Headquarters

To give authenticity to their reports, communication personnel at the Atlas facility lobbied for a Resistance leader to interview. Andrew was chosen. Julie insisted that he be anonymous in the interview. In a makeshift studio, Andrew sat in front of a white curtain. He wore a mask that covered half his face and fell over his neck. Under the mask was an audio device that altered his voice frequency. His script, crafted by committee, was scrolled on a monitor before him to read.

The unseen anchor's voice stated, "This evening we have a leader of the Resistance with us to give us their perspective. Can you give us a summary of recent events in this country, including the fire at Fort Lauderdale?"

> "Heroic liberty fighters sabotaged a shipment of Chinese made PPUs at Port Fort Lauderdale. All precautions were taken to give warning, and fortunately no one was killed in the attack. It is our goal to restore basic freedoms as provided for in the Constitution, without the loss of life. Every day more people are coming to see the stifling effect government control has on our lives. Are we to be slaves controlled by our own fears and manipulated by the government?"

Suddenly, Andrew paused, words scrolled on the monitor in front of him, then stopped and retreated to where he quit reading. Andrew felt the stoical sterility of his message. It took courage for citizens to betray their government, a government that had come to control most of their lives. What was he portraying by appearing anonymous? He was depicting fear. Fear of government repercussions was the biggest obstacle to the reestablishment of freedom. The optics of his interview was substantiating the government's most powerful tool.

He reached for the mask clasp behind his head, held the mask in front of him, then tossed it to the side. Without the mask, revealed an average looking middle aged man, not the handsome Hollywood look of the normal anchor. His hair was gray and thinning, obviously untouched by color or surgery, and his face was somewhat shiny, devoid of heavy makeup. He hesitated, looking somewhat nervous, not purposely, but it focused viewer's attention on him. He avoided the script in front of him and spoke from the heart.

> "I'm willing to cut the pretense if you are. What they call Personal Protection Units or PPUs, most of us call voyeur vultures. Their purpose is it to keep you under their thumb all wrapped in the charade of 'the common good'.
> My name is Andrew Collier. I am a member of the Resistance board of directors. Some of you may remember

my name as having identified an asteroid back in '38. At the time I was apolitical— no, apathetic would have been a better description. I was never a troublemaker, but neither a mover in elite privileged circles, nor of a group whose votes were depended upon.

I had a bad knee, and like many non-status citizens, it required I leave the country for the fix. Sometime after we deflected the asteroid, my name was besmirched. I learned firsthand the dangers of government gone awry. I have been a Resistance leader ever since.

Fear is the first and most effective tool in the controllers' toolbox. It is used to control and convince you to relinquish liberties for security. It was used decades ago when a new virus strain hit the country from a totally population-controlled country. From fear, people wore masks like the one I took off. They did even after being vaccinated for a virus that was not much more deadly than the common flu. It was not rational, but fear has a way of distorting our choices. Ultimately, tens of thousands of independent businesses were ruined or became dependent on government, fitting the goals of would-be overseers.

Today people fear the reappearance of those voyeur eyes in the skies peering at our every movement and the repercussions if we act as individuals rather than carefully sculptured cogs in their machine.

Yes, and some people fear that without the protective vultures, crime will rise. Crime numbers are exaggerated. It is a way to force you to live in fear. What price are we willing to pay for an infinitesimal reduction in crime?

I am here to tell you there will be no more vultures in the sky. You have newfound liberty. Hang on to it. The conflict in Asia is not our concern, but a distraction to draw your attention from the freedom movement in this country. Over a hundred years ago a president said, "All we have to fear is fear itself."

Andrew leaned forward toward the camera; his eyes peered into the lens. He held the view in silence until his audience was not only curious but concerned about what he would say next.

"FEAR NOT."

Some citizens watched the alternative news out of curiosity. But many citizens who had discreetly watched the alternative news, took a defiant step. They downloaded the interview before it was bleached from their grape. They shared the download with friends and family.

White House

The COS reported, "Mr. President, that renegade excuse for news last night had an interview with a leader. He identified himself as Andrew Collier. I've got the interview on my grape. I think you should see it."

"No, I won't waste my time. But that name sounds familiar."

"Yes, he's the guy who was involved in the asteroid thing and harassed NASA in its successful response."

"Where did he operate?"

"He was from Boise, but later worked for a private space vehicle launching company in Midland, Texas."

"Get the CIA director on the phone."

Midland, TX

Torrence turned on Ridge Road off highway 349 South of Midland. At the first stoplight he saw a man, clothes in disarray, standing beside the highway. It had been some time since Torrence had seen a beggar in the area. The man held a scrap of cardboard with a message. It read:

Partner left for Oregon… for more stipends.

Help me, I want to stay in TX.

The man could have been looking for vouchers to menu approved fast food outlets, but more likely liquor vouchers. Torrence avoided eye contact and pulled into the Atlas parking lot a half block away.

The next morning the man, cleaned up and dressed in appropriate unisex clothing, entered the reception area in the Atlas

Transportation building. He buzzed for a receptionist. While he waited, Torrence and a technician entered, stood at the second door, put their thumbs on a pad, and then waited. The man, appearing uninterested, noticed their irises were also being scanned before the door clicked, allowing their entry. As Torrence walked through the door, he turned and glanced at the sitting man.

The man sat for another five minutes before someone, who did not have the demeanor of a receptionist, appeared behind a sliding glass window panel.

"May I help you?"

"I'm wondering if I could talk to your HR department, I'm looking for a job."

"We are not hiring."

"I can do anything, I'm good at janitor type work."

"Sorry, I understand the factory two blocks west is hiring."

"Thank you," he said as he turned, nearly bumping into Andrew Collier entering the building.

Torrence entered Julie's office for a morning meeting, "There's a man in the reception area who I recognize as yesterday's street corner beggar."

"Perhaps he has cleaned up and seriously wants a job. Good for him, hopefully he'll find one," Julie replied.

"Something about his posture didn't strike me as someone down on their luck," replied Torrence.

Torrence had grown up in a rough Baltimore neighborhood. He developed street savvy long before he acquired enough software education to ignite his self-learning passion. Julie trusted his judgment.

"When he leaves, check out his departure on the tracking cameras."

When the meeting concluded, Torrence viewed the digital recording. Cameras programmed with facial recognition software to identify employees encircled the building. Anyone not recognized was tracked by cameras— including hidden cameras in driveway lights at the end of the long entrance road to the building.

The man was not parked in the visitor lot. He walked the length of the driveway. Cameras used their far vision lens to follow him crossing the street, walking a block to a convenience store parking lot.

In the lot, he got into a small black sedan and drove away. The plate on the sedan's rear read RVU-3495. Above the number were smaller letters, US Government.

Torrence showed Julie the information. "The license number is from the government motor pool in Odessa, it is not driven by a Fed stationed here."

Julie believed it was her calling to act as quasi-leader of the Resistance, but administration was not her forte—security was. She had been Director of Security at Atlas Transportation before the asteroid ordeal. The security cameras and software system she designed and installed. It was Julie, not a burly bouncer type, that Barnmore sent to Chicago's O'Hare to rescue Andrew from Federal arrest.

"We've been made. Let's implement Plan B at once. Motor pool car… that means he was sent here. Get a list of all the motels, hotels and B&Bs in the metro area. We will divide up and find that car tonight."

Over the next two hours, Atlas personnel calmly vacated the building. Leaving the building, they followed driving instructions Julie had issued. Their routes were designed to lose any non-professional tailers. At prescribed places they parked, walked blocks, doubled back and eventually drove another vehicle home. Until notified otherwise, they would work from home. Explosives throughout the building were set, in the event security was breached.

While the man slept at 2 am, others combing Midland-Odessa lodging facilities got a text from Andrew. He found the Fed car and bugged it.

The man had worked for the CIA fifteen years. He was not comfortable being transferred from international espionage to domestic. The work was outside the original mission of the CIA and what he had signed up for. But he heard rumors of what happened to Olivia Bidwell— alias Zoe Barnett—whom he had served with in Poland. Accordingly, he did as instructed.

Chapter 25

Whiteman Air Force Base

The rotating B-3 flights over Norfolk had been abruptly stopped by Pentagon orders. General Montel was offered no explanation why. Through her husband's Resistance connections, she found the rerouted Chinese ship eliminated the need for security at Norfolk harbor. Whatever the reason, she was relieved.

Her relief was short-lived when she received word from the Pentagon to have a crew ready for a special mission. When inquiring of the mission, she was told that it was of utmost secrecy and could not be discussed on any electronic medium. The Air Force service chief would arrive at the base and personally inform her and direct the crew.

She did not know what was coming but summoned Captain Adderley and told him that a distasteful mission might be in the works. They were soon in contact with the Missouri governor and Resistance leadership now scattered around the Midland-Odessa area outside of Atlas headquarters.

"General," the four-star Air Force service chief saluted as he boldly walked into her office.

"General," she returned the salute.

He immediately got to the point of his arrival, "We have been ordered to take out the Resistance headquarters located in Midland, Texas. A few bunker busters from a B-3 should do the job. It should be done exactly at 1100 hours CDT tomorrow to assure a full house of undesirables are on hand. Our mission is complete elimination of their leadership."

She struggled but did not express any reservations to his surprise directive.

"As requested, I have my best crew ready, sir."

"And who would the captain be?"

"Captain Adderley—his crew is the best we have, sir."

The service chief had gone over the crews assigned to provide backup support for the Norfolk naval base. He remembered that Captain Adderley was assigned the shift after the Chinese ship had been scheduled to leave. It would have been the most critical time. He also expected some pushback or at least reservation about the order from General Montel. There was none.

He pulled the Norfolk crew rotation list from his pocket. "No, let's use Captain Bartlett and his crew."

"But sir, Captain Adderley is our best."

"Get Captain Bartlett, that is an order."

"Yes, sir," she replied and stepped out of her office.

"What is taking her so long?" the general asked an orderly after her fifteen minute absence.

"Probably trying to locate Captain Bartlett, sir."

She entered her office followed by four others.

"Is this Captain Bartlett's crew?" he asked, wondering why one of the men had an MP emblem on his sleeve.

"No, this is Captain Adderley. And you are under arrest."

"This morbid joke is not funny."

"Neither is implementation of an illegal, unconstitutional order to murder civilians in violation of the sixth amendment," said Captain Adderley.

He ignored Captain Adderley, "You, General—woman or not— will be shot for this insubordination!"

Although the service chief's public demeanor was politically correct, General Montel had heard rumors of his hands-on treatment of women.

"I detest that sexist remark. And shot by whom, General? As of now, this base is property of the state of Missouri."

"So, you are a member of the Resistance?"

"No, I am not; however, my first allegiance is to the Constitution. If the Resistance happens to agree, so be it."

Under protest, the Air Force chief was taken to the base hospital and sedated. As the service chief was being discreetly cared for in a hospital bed, General Montel connected with Resistance leaders and the governor.

Atlas Headquarters

As the development was being discussed at headquarters, Torrence entered.

"The White House has announced a press briefing to take place in the Rose Garden at 12:30 EDT. Rumors are flying that the announcement will be major."

"What a coincidence! Immediately after they planned to kill us," Julie observed.

"I have an idea," added Andrew. "We could use this opportunity to spike a silver nail in their credibility."

At 9:00 am CDT, 10:00 EDT, Captain Adderley lifted a B-3 stealth bomber into blue skies over central Missouri. The runway headed him west. He saw nothing but blue sky over the horizon. The Pentagon-ordered mission was two hours distant. Fifty miles west of Whiteman, he turned his batwing bomber one-hundred eighty degrees for a destination the same distance. To the East was heavy cloud cover. An appropriate sign, he thought.

General Montel received a call from the Pentagon. "We've been unable to reach the service chief, is he there?"

"No," she told the CJCS. "The general has taken ill and is in the infirmary. But his order is being carried out. The bird left five minutes ago."

Her declaration was confirmed by a report from a CIA operative on the ground outside of Whiteman who saw a batwing takeoff and disappear into the western sky.

White House

The White House press secretary had been ready to move the briefing inside, but unexpectedly the cloud cover raised enough to allow it to be held in the Rose Garden. A great sign that the country was soon to be relieved of an annoying virus, thought the president.

As required, Camila and Grayson presented their press credentials thirty minutes before the Rose Garden announcement and press briefing started. They attended the same prestigious journalism school. Each had started as a roving reporter for a local TV station and worked themselves up to White House reporter for different news outlets. Although their outlets competed for audience, they always compared notes before a press briefing.

"What is the top question on your list?" Grayson asked Camila.

"I want to inquire about the first family's decision to send their adopted daughter to Harmony Prep instead of Equalitarian Academy where she attended last year."

"Well, that's a good question, but it might not be received well, pointing out she is attending a non-public school," observed Grayson. "I'm going to stick to something less controversial. Since the season is approaching, I'll ask if the president will be presented a broccoli sprout or a cauliflower head from vegetable farmers for Thanksgiving."

"I suggest you call it the fall festival," cautioned Camila.

"Yeah, good idea."

Atlas Headquarters

"Are you sure you don't want me to go with you?" Andrew asked.

Julie was down to her bra and was pulling a bullet proof vest over her head. "No, remember it was I who rescued you at the Chicago airport, not the other way," Julie replied as she picked up an old AR-15.

"I know, but please be careful."

Tracking showed the Fed motor pool car a mile from the Atlas facility. From a quarter mile away, Julie and two Atlas men identified the federal agent with binoculars. He was parked at the edge of a wooded area, hoping the location would be inconspicuous. It was his mistake.

Julie and one man were dressed in camouflage clothing, the other in commonly worn workout clothes. The agent in the car saw an older guy leisurely jogging. He saw the jogger slow to a walk, then head towards him. Abruptly leaving could raise suspicion. The guy looked friendly. He pulled his sidearm and held it inside the door as he lowered the window.

"How's the jog?" he asked the old man.

"Wonderful, great day, isn't it?"

"Do you jog here often?"

The agent was startled by a thump on the passenger window, turned and saw a woman in camouflage gear pressing an AR-15 barrel against the window.

"Drop your handgun on the floor, raise your hands and step out of the car," Julie demanded.

The agent hesitated until he turned forward and saw another AR-15 pointed at him from the front of the car. The jogger opened his door and said, "Please step out now."

He stood outside the car while his hands were bound with plastic ties. Julie reached into his pocket and found his grape.

"I'm just doing my job," he said.

"Yeah, and we're doing a greater job," replied the man holding him.

It was ten minutes of noon. They waited. He asked questions but got no answers. At a minute till 12:00, Julie turned on his grape, stepped behind him and reached for his finger.

"No," he protested trying to hide his fingers.

"We'll open your grape with your finger either attached or not—your choice," said Julie.

The jogger now holding plant shears left no doubt of her intent.

She found his last text exchange. It was a government number. At one minute after 12:00 she texted:

Big explosion, building gone, full parking lot was full— all must be present.

To support the message, the alternative news feed went silent at noon.

White House

The president was seen exiting the White House and walking the porch to the podium set up in the Rose Garden as media cameras focused on him. It was a walk many presidents had taken. His purposeful walk always set the stage and built drama for his remarks.

The round presidential shield more than covered the podium. The shield with an eagle on a blue background surrounded with stars and a white border had grown larger through the years; the growth emblematic of powers that the president had acquired.

"Fellow citizens, I have great news and disturbing news to report today. First the troubling development, the ongoing war in the East we can no longer ignore. Casualties are mounting at an unheard-of pace. We cannot stand idly by while the carnage continues. I am ordering the 7th fleet to enter the South China sea. Hopefully, their mere presence will allow cooler heads to prevail. But in the meantime, we must unite as one country and support our service men and women who may be in harm's way.

On a very positive note, the strife in this country will soon be ending. The traitorous leadership of the unjustified discord in the country has been silenced permanently. We can thank many patriot men and women for coming to the defense of the common good...."

Captain Adderley was approaching the Washington metro area from the south less than a thousand feet above the ground. The few radars in the area that could detect the B3 stealth batwing aircraft recognized his signal as friendly.

He had throttled the bomber back to only slightly above stall speed. When he crossed the Anacostia River, the engines thrust to full power. Doing so sent loud thundering sound waves out in front of his batwing plane. Although the plane was moving below the speed of sound, it's speed concentrated the vibrations in front of the batwing. It was the ultimate announcement of his coming presence.

The president continued,

"Without misguided leadership, we expect this counter-progressive group of discontents to wither on the dying vine…"

The assembled dignitaries, the White House press corps and viewers around the country could see the president's lips continue to move but could not hear him. The rumble was deafening. All eyes, including the president's, turned to the direction from which the noise came and saw the batwing bomber barrel over them. Windows shook in the White House. Vibrations toppled one camera spotlight. Many tried to take cover, all felt the aircraft's wake. Secret Service personnel quickly scurried the president inside, then to the emergency underground bombproof catacomb.

North of Washington, Captain Adderley made a left turn and headed for Missouri at full speed. Upon word from the White House, fighter aircraft were dispatched, but the batwing was long gone.

Whiteman Air Force Base

General Montel entered the hospital room of the Air Force service chief. He was cuffed to the bed, awake and obviously aggravated.

"Are you going to jail me or shoot me? The consequences for you will be the same."

She turned to an MP, "Uncuff him."

Then to him, "Neither. Your plane and pilot are ready. My car will take you to the runway. Have a great day." She ignored his obscene retort as she left the room.

"Get me out of here as soon as possible," the chief said as he boarded his plane.

"As soon as the incoming clears the runway, General."

From the window, the chief saw a B-3 taxi near his plane and wondered where it had been. He would later find out.

Media news programs that evening focused on a child abduction in Maine, reports of brush fires in California, the pending landfall of a dangerous hurricane in Florida and fall crop prospects in the

Midwest. The insinuation was clear that PPUs could have prevented the child abduction. Naturally, the cause of brush fires and disappointing crops was manmade. The hopeful-faced reporter on a Florida beach warning of a potential hurricane was largely ignored as another wolf warning.

Media viewership was unusually high as some tuned to discover what happened in the abbreviated press conference. Others were curious to see what spin would be put on it. Both groups were disappointed as no mention was made of the press conference or the interruption. The media was on hold waiting for direction. The president and staff, now out of the catacomb, were in a quandary how to spin it.

The alternative news app from the Resistance was back up reporting the day's events.

Torrence commented, "Can you imagine how easy our job is compared to their media?"

"Yes, it's very straightforward reporting the truth, without waiting for a group to formulate the spin," answered an Atlas communication technician.

And report they did—to the biggest audience on the app to date.

White House

The president still refused to watch the alternative news feed. Although no one would know, he would not dignify them with his attention. "What are they saying?" he asked his COS.

"It is pretty simple, that Whiteman Airbase was ordered to destroy the Resistance headquarters and murder its leaders, but Whiteman refused. And instead sent the batwing east to buzz the White House."

"That's it?"

"Well, a little more than that."

"Let's hear it."

"You should see first-hand, sir."

She pointed her grape at the large wall mounted monitor and played the feed.

Julie and Andrew sat behind a desk and introduced themselves.

"She's certainly no beauty, she'd never turn my head," spouted the president.

"Really, Mr. President, do you have any idea the problem that comment would cause if overheard outside this room?" The COS usually called him *sir* and only *Mr. President* in the company of others... or when perplexed with him.

He waved her off with his hand as the video continued.

Julie and Andrew went into detail about the order from the White House to destroy the Atlas facility and everyone inside. Having no reason to conceal their whereabouts, they showed an aerial of the Atlas facility and explained that it was from this facility the successful deflection of the asteroid was planned and orchestrated twelve years prior.

A video clip was shown of the CIA agent being released who was sent to find Andrew and verify the destruction of the headquarters. Julie explained how she sent a false destruction text report on his grape which the White House assumed was genuine.

Another video was of Captain Adderley and the crew who had buzzed the White House in response to the illegal order, followed by footage of the Air Force chief being escorted by MPs to a plane.

Then Julie looked into the camera and said, "Among other constitutional guarantees that have been violated, the intent of today's presidential order violates the Sixth Amendment."

Julie read the amendment as the video feed switched to a printed copy:

> In all criminal prosecutions, the accused shall enjoy the right
> to a speedy and public trial, by an impartial jury of the State
> and district wherein the crime shall have been committed,
> which district shall have been previously ascertained by law,
> and to be informed of the nature and cause of the accusa-
> tion; to be confronted with the witnesses against him; to have
> compulsory process for obtaining witnesses in his favor, and
> to have the Assistance of Counsel for his defense.

Then she continued, "We will not be silenced or cease our pursuit of liberty until there is a reaffirmation of the protections guaranteed the people in our Constitution. You, Mr. President, have until noon tomorrow to address these concerns."

Mason Trotter home

It was after midnight, and Mason Trotter was ready for bed when his brother Damon called from Illinois.

"Did you hear that diatribe the Resistance put out this evening?" he asked.

"Yes, I had no idea you followed them."

"You need to get people in your state together and pound some sense into those rebel heads."

After prolonged no response, Damon asked, "Did you hear me?"

"Yes, I heard you, and I have a confession. I am a member of the Resistance. We no longer have reason to hide, and neither will I."

"I knew you had some wacky ideas, but... how long have you been with them?"

"I am the Resistance leader in Texas."

"Oh, my God!" Damon responded before hanging up.

Mason took his brother's response as anything but negative. An avowed atheist had just acknowledged the existence of God. Hope prevailed.

Texas

Former CJCS and commanding General Martinez at Fort Hood sent a regiment of 1,500 soldiers— including laser air defense batteries— to Midland to protect Atlas headquarters. It was a similar unit that aided national guardsmen protecting the capitol in Austin. Only the B-3s could evade the radar guided lasers, and all B-3s were at Whiteman under General Montel's command.

General Everett's two brigades of 7,000 soldiers who had held defensive positions north of Austin were readying for a move north. The general had been waiting and hoping for the order to squeeze the Federal force's rear — or spank their bottom as she put it. She was a history buff and enamored by WWII General Patton's colloquialisms.

The major general who commanded Federal forces continued to lose soldiers. The 22,000 soldiers under his command had dwindled to just over 20,000. Morale was terrible and declining. Most had been living in tents for months. Only cooler fall weather lessened their anguish. The locals were not helpful, but hostile to their presence. They faced 27,000 soldiers under Martinez's command immediately north at Fort Hood and Everett ready to approach their rear. His pleas for reinforcement were ignored.

White House

Morning was a mad house at the White House. The cabinet had as many ideas as people filling seats. *That is all most of them did,* thought the president.

Finally, he threw up his hands, "Out, everyone out, it's up to me to come up with a plan to save all our butts."

They picked up their notes of bureaucratic dribble and filed out. Before his COS left, he hollered at her, "Not you."

Given all that had transpired, she would not have been unhappy to have left.

"Did you hear anything that sounded believable or worthwhile?" he asked her.

"No, did you?"

"Every idea I heard would be less effective than nothing."

"How can we do or say nothing? It would lend credibility to their version," the COS responded.

"How do you answer a charge that you are a witch? You do not. Answer it, and you appear defensive. We'll simply say we do not respond to fanatical diatribes."

"So, you plan to ignore the deadline?" It was now mid-afternoon. "Absolutely."

"Mr. President, Mr. Hollister is on line one." The presidential secretary had been told to put him through if the cabinet meeting was over.

"Yes Hollister, you heard me right. Sell stock in electric charging stations and buy stock in any company based in the midlands that actually makes something."

The COS's grape buzzed with a text, while the president was on the phone with Hollister, his financial advisor. The text sender was identified as Julie Collier. The COS had no idea how the Resistance had found her number. Neither she nor Damon Trotter knew that while on a call with his brother, Damon's contact list was scanned.

"It always makes sense to hedge your bets," the president told Hollister. Then he could tell from the COS's look something was up and covered the phone receiver with his hand. "What!" he exclaimed.

"I just received a text message from Julie Collier. How she got my number I have no idea."

"What was the message?"

"She asked for your response."

"Well, I still remember the response they gave me when I offered to settle this thing, 'Kiss my ass.' Send it just like that."

Lights were on late at the White House as they were at Atlas headquarters sixteen hundred miles away. Confident that the danger was past, Atlas headquarters was again bustling with activity. In the White House, it was the president and COS alone who contemplated their next step.

"That's enough, I'm exhausted and headed upstairs," said the President.

"I'm staying to finish this press release for morning," responded the COS as she turned to accept the president's good night kiss. It did not come.

As he stepped on the second floor, the president saw the first lady haplessly wandering around in a plush imported fuchsia silk robe. He remembered that his COS had picked it out for her birthday last year.

"Kind of late for you to be up, isn't it?"

"How can I sleep when you can't manage affairs? The atrocious sound and vibration of that awful machine! Are we safe here?"

"Perfectly safe."

"So you say. I know tomorrow is the fifteenth, but for my safety, I no longer feel it prudent to stay here. I am leaving to visit my family home in Nantucket tomorrow morning."

"Have a good trip," he said as her bedroom door closed behind her.

The president turned, knowing sleep would not come easy. He opened the Oval Office door.

"Good, I see you're still here."

"Did you forget something?"

"Yes."

Chapter 26

Early in the morning, the White House released a press statement. Written by the COS and approved by the president, it spelled out the administration's position in a simple one sentence statement.

"This administration will not respond and legitimize illusionary, fabricated stories by people bent upon circumventing the will of the people."

Fort Hood, Texas

Given the president's response, the Resistant's next step was initiated. Few really believed that the president would be open to dialogue; but they tried, and it was a necessary hoop for the public support.

Gathered in General Martinez's headquarters at Fort Hood were Julie, Andrew, Mason Trotter and the governor with her husband—along with other Texas elected officials. The governor briefed all about the speaking order and the optics.

The prior evening after the president's terse reply, all media outlets were informed that a major event would take place at the main entrance gate to Fort Hood. Perhaps out of curiosity, some came. Alternative Resistance news was set up with newly purchased top-of-the-line cameras. One major media network, upon seeing Resistance news openly covering the event, left before setting up.

Before the two o'clock event, the group proceeded to the Bernie Beck Main gate at the entrance to Fort Hood. Facing the entrance to the fort on the left side of the gate was a huge American flag. On the right side of the gate hung the same sized Texas flag.

Julie was surprised that in addition to media cameras at least a thousand Fort Hood soldiers were waiting in front of a stage elevated three steps above the crowd. On the left side of the stage stood an army band on a set of aluminum bleachers. On matching bleachers to the right stood an army choir.

The group from General Martinez's headquarters filed onto stage. Andrew, Julie, Mason, and General Martinez stood on the left side of the podium. To the right stood the governor, Carl, and state elected officials. The Resistance leaders would not speak but be introduced.

"So much for anonymity," whispered Andrew to Julie.

"What a coming out party!" she whispered back.

General Martinez welcomed the crowd and media outlets to Fort Hood. In succession, he introduced the railroad commissioner, the lieutenant governor and attorney general. They each spoke for five minutes. Then the governor took the podium. She summarized the events of the year and said that given federal obstinance to negotiation, Texas had no choice but to adhere to the Constitution alone if need be.

She then turned to her right and introduced Julie and Andrew as leaders of the national freedom movement and residents of Texas. Mason Trotter was introduced as leader of the Texas freedom movement and an Austin businessman. Julie and Andrew were both surprised when a cheer went up with his introduction.

All was quiet as a pair of soldiers moved formally to both flag poles. A drummer beat a cadence when both flags were drawn down. Each pair of soldiers held their respective flag high and marched to the opposite pole crossing before the podium.

The star-spangled banner was attached to the right pole and hoisted up but stopped ten feet short of the fifty-foot pole while the band played the national anthem and the chorus sang.

Next the Texas flag was attached to the left pole and ran to the top as the band played "Texas, Our Texas" and the chorus sang the words Julie and Andrew had never heard.

The governor then said all personnel stationed at Fort Hood would have Texas citizenship and paychecks from Texas unless they chose otherwise.

She then addressed the federal soldiers positioned outside Fort Hood, "For all federal soldiers stationed on Texas soil, we welcome any soldier under Pentagon command to join us. If you come from another state sympathetic to our movement, you may keep your citizenship in that state, maintain your rank, and join our mutual cause.

Any soldier on Texas soil who remains compliant with the president, Pentagon and unconstitutional government is asked to leave Texas soil immediately. No recourse will be held against you."

White House

"Mason Trotter... wasn't that professor you were with at the party named Trotter?" the President asked his COS who was busy on her grape researching people named Trotter in Texas.

"Yes, and Mason is his brother," she spit the answer out as if it were vile.

Before he could say more the COS called Damon, "You told me your brother wasn't in the Resistance."

"I didn't think so and only found out yesterday."

"Did you give your brother my personal grape number?"

"Absolutely not."

The president signaled her to end the conversation by drawing his hand across his throat. "Forget it, water under the bridge. We've more important things to do."

Off her grape, she quietly took a sip of coffee and sat the cup down careful to not make a sound as she could tell he was mulling a plan in his head.

"What do you do when you're playing monopoly and getting beat?"

"I don't get it, sir."

"You upset the board; nothing to lose at that point. It is time to upset the apple cart. We must shake things up to alter where the country is headed. Get the Pentagon on the phone."

"Yes, Mr. President," the CJCS answered.

"Our forces in Texas have sat long enough. It is time to move."

"Are you considering pulling them out, sir?"

"No, absolutely not, we attack."

"But, sir, we're outnumbered and outgunned."

"You will order an attack immediately, or you will be replaced as will any officer who hesitates."

"But sir…"

"Don't but, sir, me. How do we really know they will fight back and it's not a grandiose bluff?"

The president added, "And turn the 7th fleet around and send them to the Gulf of Mexico. Let it be known that we plan to lay waste to ports in any states not in compliance with federal mandates."

"Sir, it will take weeks for them to get there."

"So be it, perhaps the imminent destruction of their ports will give them second thoughts."

Atlas Headquarters

Mason was in a meeting when he received a call from his brother. When finished with the meeting, he stepped into another room and reluctantly returned the call—- skeptical, but hopeful, his brother and he could maintain a relationship.

"I guess you were not exaggerating when you said you were a Texas Resistance leader."

"No, brother. I never told you because I didn't want to jeopardize our relationship."

"Well, you've done that big time, brother. I just got a call from the dean. I suspect they have no tolerance for a professor with a Resistance leader brother. And the majority leader of the legislature is trying to reach me."

"I'm sorry about that, Damon."

"Well, sorry will not suffice when I lose my job, political position and friends."

"You are always welcome in Texas."

"That's not even funny. Have you ever studied history? Do you know what happened the last time some renegade states started a civil war? It was disastrous for them and took the South decades to recover. The power, wealth, corporate structure, and influence resides in northern and coastal states. We control the education, news and entertainment industries without exception."

Mason had heard enough, "Perhaps it is you, Professor, who has not kept abreast of changes in the country. Where does the nation's food come from? What states do most all manufacturing? Where are most of the military bases in the country? As trust funds in the wealthiest enclaves are tax exempt, in which states do people pay the most federal taxes? Which states produce energy— be it fossil fuel, wind or solar? And it is not the South vs. the North. We split the country all the way through Kansas to North Dakota.

And if you want to talk about a potential civil war, do you know most people in the military come from states inclined toward more freedom, not less? Before guns were made illegal, Texas and Florida had nearly 1.2 million guns registered. New York, Massachusetts, Illinois, New Jersey, and Connecticut had only 400 thousand. That disparity is exaggerated now, as I'm sure residents of those five states are more inclined to follow government edicts than they are in freedom loving states. I do not think you people should desire a shooting war.

You should also consider where do most people live who are dependent upon stipends? Where do the most people live who produce nothing other than bureaucratic harassment for producing people?

You brought up education—which states have schools with the highest test scores? Which states actually have a middle class?

And if you wish to compare the civil war two centuries ago with this conflict in an inverse way you are right. The North was fighting for the rights of all citizens to live in freedom. Our great something grandfather fought for the North in that war, and I am proud of it, as I thought you were. As the North fought for freedom and breaking the yoke of a social hierarchy and slavery, we in the Resistance fight to remove a dictatorship of the elite. Your group is not our betters, and we will slave for you no more."

Damon timidly answered, "Well, I guess we both spoke our minds."

Later in the day, Damon was placed on non-paid leave at Northwestern University. The following day he was censored by the majority caucus in the Illinois legislature. Home with nothing to do, he loaded the Resistance app on his grape and scrolled through a month of broadcasts. That evening, he watched the movie classic *Hunger Games* and was reminded of the White House party.

Fort Hood

The general in command of federal forces in Texas had his orders. He would grudgingly follow them. His plan was to call off the attack at the first sign of heavy resistance. No one would accuse him of refusing an order. As he reluctantly prepared to order an attack on Fort Hood, an orderly delivered him a message.

"Sir, we've received word General Everett is on the march and approaching our rear."

"Do we turn and defend against her attack?" asked a colonel on his staff.

"No, we have our orders. Begin canon bombardment of Fort Hood's defenses in thirty minutes."

"But sir, our rear is open, she will run unimpeded through our ranks."

"I said we have our orders," replied the general.

General Martinez was notified that the federal forces were preparing for attack. He picked up his grape.

The federal orderly reappeared, "General, you have a call."

"I'm kind of busy at the moment."

"It is General Martinez."

The federal general eagerly took the call. A call at this point before hostilities from the opposing general could only be a good sign. The federal general was cordial, "General we haven't spoken for some time. The last time, I believe you were my superior."

"Yes, and now we face each other, but let us end this now. Do you know where that former high school football field is on the east side of 'no person's land'?"

"Yes."

"Appear there at 1800 hours with your senior officers as will I under a flag of truce."

"We'll be there."

The federal general was elated. Flag of truce indicated a desire for a truce, tantamount to waving a white flag. The general called off the artillery barrage and notified the Pentagon of the good news, which was quickly relayed to the White House.

"Shall I break out the scotch?" the COS asked.

"No, I've been bamboozled enough into early celebration, not this time," the president responded.

The federal general approached with his senior officers from the south side of the field. Senior officers included ranks of major, lieutenant-colonel, colonel, and general. General Martinez was waiting at what had been the fifty-yard line before the game was banned with his officers behind him.

"Too bad they banned this game. It built character," said General Martinez as the federal general approached.

"I won't argue with that," he replied.

"Well, let us end this confrontation before bloodshed begins."

"I couldn't agree more, could you open a corridor for us to move into Fort Hood?"

General Martinez responded, "I don't think you understand, General. I'm trying to save the lives of men under you. If you initiate hostilities, we will retaliate in force and many under you will be killed."

"What the hell! You invited me here under false pretenses."

General Martinez waved his hand, and a stadium loudspeaker barked what he had previously recorded.

> "Officers and enlisted men under federal command, thirty-one states have reached an agreement to sanction military forces under their joint command. Representatives of those states are meeting in Kansas City as we speak to

finalize a constitutional document to guide those states
until the remainder of the states see fit to honor the original
Constitution. We are open to any officer or enlisted person
who wishes to join our cause. You will be welcomed back at
Fort Hood. You may signify your desire by stepping forward
and we will welcome you on our side of the fifty yard line.
If you choose otherwise, you may leave this and any of the
other thirty states immediately without harm. If you choose
to stay and follow orders from Washington, you may return
to your units— and may God have mercy on your souls."

Another voice then listed the thirty-one states that had agreed to leave the Union if the Constitution was not resurrected as consequential document.

"Alabama, Alaska Arkansas................West Virginia,
Wyoming.

"This is blasphemy," the federal general spat.

"Blasphemy to whom, your God in Washington?" General Martinez replied.

The federal general turned and addressed his men, "Any man who crosses the fifty-yard line will be shot as a traitor."

For decades, the top ten states in military enlistment per capita were Georgia, South Carolina, Idaho, Alaska, Texas, Arizona, Virginia, Alabama, North Carolina, Florida, Oklahoma. The only state not among the thirty-two was Virginia, in which a secession movement to join West Virginia was underway.

The bottom ten in military enlistment per capita were, Pennsylvania, Connecticut, Minnesota, New York, Vermont, Iowa, New Jersey, Rhode Island, and Massachusetts. Except Iowa, they all were non-seceding states.

For decades, forty-four percent of military recruits came from the South. The Northeast was the most underrepresented region of the country for military recruitment.

The senior officers standing behind the federal general were representative of the greater military demographics.

On the federal side of the field, a colonel whispered to a major, "I'm tempted, but I don't want to be shot."

The major pointed out that all firearms had been left behind for the conflab. The major then stepped forward from the thirty-yard line. He was even with the general at the forty-five yard line when the general reached behind him and pulled a hidden sidearm.

"Not one more step, Major."

At that time, a dozen enlisted men behind sideline barriers rose, weapons trained on the general.

"So, you set a trap," the federal general said to General Martinez.

"They are only here in case you cheated by bringing a firearm, which you did."

The major crossed the fifty-yard line and was congratulated by officers he knew and had served beside.

The colonel with whom he had whispered followed the Major. One by one other officers crossed the line until an avalanche started. Eventually the federal general was left with ten percent of his senior officers.

General Martinez spoke, "Now you have a choice, leave the state in peace or organize what you have left and fight—it is your choice. But you should know this message was broadcast to all your junior officers and enlisted men in the field."

Kansas City

Word spread quickly of the federal capitulation in Texas. Julie was asked to chair the meeting of thirty-one states but only agreed to do it temporarily until a publicly elected leader was agreed upon. The governor of Texas was unanimously elected as permanent chair.

The first matter of business was adopting a constitution. It was moved by the governor of Arkansas and seconded by the governor of Iowa to adopt the original constitution and the twenty-seven amendments to the constitution pending the addition of other amendments. After affirmative arguments by most governors, appealing to their home constituencies—which took hours—it was passed unanimously.

Four other amendments were on the table. The first, to be the 28th amendment stated simply:

The first ten amendments, known as the Bill of Rights, will be interpreted as originally written. No variance from those amendments will be allowed by an opinion from a court or legislative action. Any variance in those ten amendments will require a constitutional amendment properly passed by a supermajority of the states.

It passed.

The proposed 29th amendment caused considerable debate before it was passed. It called for federal term limits of two terms for a senator and six for a representative. It also prohibited any retired elected federal official from holding a federal job after retirement or lobby for any organization. Additionally, it forbid any retired public employee from employment at a company who conducted business with the government.

The 30th amendment set into the Constitution strict antitrust laws. It stated any corporate entity that achieved over fifty percent market share in a given industry would be forced to divest itself of holdings. It was argued that mammoth corporations used government regulations to stifle competition, had undue influence on government and would willingly bend to government desires to avoid harassment. The amendment also forbid any public traded corporation from spending more than one percent of its total revenue on lobbying efforts. The amendment passed 20 to 12.

The most vigorous debate centered on what was called a 'reconciliation resolution'. It carefully defined the actions of the thirty-one states as a separation, not a dissolution. It set conditions for the reestablishment of the Union. The resolution terminated the separation of the thirty-one states once the remaining nineteen state legislatures ratified the 28th through 30th amendments. Some states desired retributions from the remaining nineteen states for past overpayment of taxes by low tax states. The majority deemed the idea as unnecessarily vindictive.

After considerable debate, the question was called for. Governor Archibald said a vote would be taken, when the governor of Iowa asked for the floor. Although it violated Robert's Rules once the vote was called for, the governors had discussed the Iowa governor's proposal.

"Today is September the 16, tomorrow will be the 17th, the 262nd anniversary of the signing of the original Constitution of the United States. It is 7:00 pm, I propose we establish the United States 2.0 tomorrow morning."

The revised constitution was passed the next morning unanimously.

It was decided that the states needed to designate someone to negotiate for the states if the need arose. The governor of Texas was first to say that the person should not be an official from any state as that would raise conflict of interest claims. Julie only agreed after it was stipulated she be appointed as a spokesperson, not the leader.

Delegates left Kansas City taking the three amendments and the reconciliation resolution to their respective state legislatures for ratification.

Fort Hood

The commander of federal forces in Texas, General Hammel, and his remaining senior officers moved against the flow returning to their headquarters. Enlisted men and junior officers were moving toward Fort Hood—some riding, others on foot. It was not an attack.

"We should notify the Pentagon," said a colonel at headquarters.

"And tell them what? That we have no effective force left? That we let it slip through our fingers?"

"What do you suggest, General?" asked the colonel as he was packing gear, obviously assuming they would be leaving.

"Send the message, *We have been defeated.*"

It was the best spin he could think. There was some dignity in fighting and losing. But now attacking would be idiocy, and who would follow him if he gave the order? Better to leave out the details until he considered various alternatives. Soon the Pentagon would know the truth. Where would that leave him?

"I assume we are leaving," stated the colonel as if he had not decided.

"I guess so."

"Shall I pack your things, sir?"

"Not yet, but go about yours."

General Hammel was from Georgia, although he had not lived there for decades. He would be ruined—the general who would not fight allowing his men to desert him. Although he felt no allegiance to Georgia, it would be assumed his home played into his performance. There were no easy choices.

General Martinez's number was on his grape. He stared at it.

"Can I get you something, sir?" asked the colonel.

The general did not answer. He could go back to Washington in humiliation and become a mockery of jokes for generations, or he could use the nine-millimeter he pointed at the major. At least then he would not hear their scorn. Would it show courage or be evidence of guilt? But he had another choice. He struck dial.

"Yes, General," answered General Martinez.

"Are you still accepting all comers?"

"Certainly."

"I'll be there shortly."

"General, there is just one thing. To assure no harm comes to you, I suggest you carry a white flag."

It was a bit of humiliation, but General Hammel had no choice. He pulled the sheet from his cot and left his field headquarters on foot.

White House

"Mr. President, the VP has been trying to contact you for days. May I suggest it might be a good idea to talk to her before she hears of the disaster in Texas?" the COS offered.

"Good idea, get her on the phone."

"Mr. President, I want to congratulate you on your decision to turn the 7th fleet around. We have no business meddling in affairs over there. Sources tell me they are headed to the Gulf of Mexico. May I ask the purpose?"

The president knew that a politician praising your action most likely had an ulterior motive. He also knew she would sympathize with whatever the CCP did, but nevertheless, praise seldom found its way to him.

"I'm sending them to make waste of the ports in the states that are rebelling."

"It is about time, Mr. President. You have my wholehearted support."

"What do you think that call was about?" his COS asked.

"She's up to something. Her 'sources' tell her. Of course, she has sources, but why point it out to me? And her sources also know why they are being sent to the Gulf, so why ask me?"

Chapter 27

White House

Everything was falling apart for the president. The remaining senators and representatives from nineteen states on Capitol Hill were in an uproar. Many were blaming the country's discord on him. They were focusing on his inability to end the strife. Many alleged the president lacked a firm hand.

The president's level of concern rose when a senator had asked him if the first lady was sympathetic to the rabble-rousing vice president. Often some level of truth underlies such questions— the president knew from experience.

The first lady had been gone ten days. People talking would be expected. They loved to gossip about celebrities' domestic affairs. The first couple's relationship was anything but normal, whatever that was. To allay anxiety in the country, things needed to appear normal at the White House.

"Is the first lady there?" he asked a house employee at her family home in Nantucket. The sounds of a party were obvious. He was taken aback hearing one unmistakable voice among the partiers.

It was at least five minutes before the first lady made her way to the phone.

"We need to talk," he said.

"You are right about that, but I'm busy. I'll call you in a couple hours."

"That didn't sound like it went well," said his COS.

"Not particularly, and the VP was there at whatever kind of party it was."

"That's the best news we've heard all day. If the VP is there, she isn't causing trouble on Capitol Hill."

"How many senators do I have left on my list to call this evening?"

"Four, sir."

Senator Temple of Wisconsin was first on his list. The President hastily scanned the file on the Senator his COS handed him.

"How is your son with diabetes doing in school?"

"Thanks for asking," the senator replied, knowing his son's health was the least of the president's concerns.

"You've always been a great supporter. I hope I can count on you."

"I'd really like to, Mr. President, but I was at a campaign fundraiser in Madison yesterday and… well… there was concern about where the country is headed. Perception is that you've allowed the misfits out of the cage."

"What would you have me do differently, senator?"

"I don't think it is a matter of what you've done, but where we are."

"Hopefully, the Chinese source of money can be inconspicuously filtered into your campaign away from the eyes of ethics investigators from as it was six years ago," said the president playing his last card.

"Yes, the VP has assured me it is taken care of."

It was four hours later, nearly midnight, and he was ready for bed when the first lady called back.

"I'd appreciate it if you came back to the White House. Tongues will start to wag if you remain away."

"Well, they are already wagging, dear…and I left because it was embarrassing living there while you let the country get out of control."

"The vice president was at your party?"

"Yes, she was. She has some great ideas about putting the hordes back in the box. You should try listening to her."

"We are in this together, you know."

"Now, are we? I would appreciate it if you gave the movers I'm sending no trouble packing my things. My attorney says it would be in our best interest to do this amicably."

"I had no idea."

"Neither did I have any idea you would be so incompetent running the country. Our friends here are all appalled at what is happening. Bumpkins are running amok. Thirty-one crazy states, who would have believed it? It is embarrassing. At my favorite latte bistro yesterday, people spoke in whispers away from me. I can imagine what they were saying.

It would be better for all, including yourself, if you quietly stepped down and let the VP straighten the mess out. Some are talking about invoking the—what is it? — 25th amendment. You certainly have been incapable."

The president could hardly contain his ire, "You have absolutely no clue what the real country is like, do you? Living in your enclave of privilege and reckless disregard of how most people think, live, and work—you have no idea how ridiculous you sound!

It is ironic that those you call backwater know nothings know much more about your elitist lives than you do theirs. Hollywood and the media focus on your groups and they habitually portray middle American as hillbillyish, immoral nincompoops. It is you and your kind who is ignorant about the rest of the country.

Although I have opposed the Resistance every step of the way, your group makes me wonder. Perhaps, the resistance has a point."

"Well, I guess we now know whose side you are on. Did you get that soundbite captured, Camille?"

Rehashing his conversation with the first lady, the president couldn't believe he said what he did. He had to wonder from where some of it came. Although he had never publicly uttered such thoughts, he knew they spoke the truth.

Sleep did not come easily for the president that night which was not bad. Insomnia often let his mind explore scenarios uninterrupted by the commotion of the day. Most the major decisions in his life came through meditation in the middle of the night. He could see the country and himself going one of four different directions. He game played each out as far as he could in his mind. Two led to disaster, one was very unlikely. He had to wonder if the peace that came to him was from the ghosts of the White House or a greater entity. Perhaps all were connected.

His first order of business the next morning was contacting the Pentagon.

"Where is the 7th fleet now?" he asked the CJCS.

"They've come as far as Hawaii, sir,"

"Instruct them to remain at the base there. I'm aborting the Gulf of Mexico mission."

Mason Trotter home

It had been a productive but grueling few days in Kansas City. Mason planned to spend a couple days at home and in his business before traveling to Midland.

Before he hit the garage door opener, he knew something was amiss in his house. A timer randomly turned the lights on and off in the kitchen to create the illusion someone was home. No timer was hooked to living room lights, yet they were on. He circled the block once and noticed a car with Illinois plates parked across the street. Professional hit men from Illinois possibly, but they would not be so careless to leave a car in plain sight, he thought.

Mason approached the living room window and saw a man sitting on the sofa with his back to the window. One man, Mason could handle. He quietly made his way into the house through the back door and announced himself with his old Colt Combat Commander leading the way.

"Don't move and keep your hands where I can see them."

The man turned, "That's a heck of a way to greet your brother."

"Damon, why didn't you call, and how did you get in?"

"I wanted to surprise you, and just like our parents you keep a key under a rock behind the second rose bush."

"I'm glad to see you, but why are you here?"

"Let's just say that while you and I will continue to disagree about much, the 30th amendment passed by your confederacy, or whatever you call yourselves, impressed me. You know I have been teaching about the early twentieth century robber barons for years. I have been advocating breaking up powerful monopolies in the college classes I teach. Amazingly, with all your wrongheaded ideas, you people have one right."

"And that is the only reason you are here?"

"The White House party I attended—- it really woke me up about how the social and economic classes in this country are more estranged than they ever were in the last century."

"And that's it?"

"Well, I thought it would be good to spend some time together."

"And?"

"Okay, they canned me at the university, and I was censured in the Illinois legislature. I made a statement supporting the 30th amendment. They then assumed I was sympathetic with other Resistance issues. I attended a faculty meeting last week, and you would not believe the attitude and comments made about the Resistance.

Many of my former friends are afraid to be seen with me. The homeowner's association in the Gold Coast Condo complex where I live suddenly found I was in violation of obscure covenants. My longtime coffee shop group broke up and left when I joined them. Whether they were appalled at my family or just feared associating with me, I do not know— but the result is the same.

Being on the inside, I'd never realized how intolerant they are about any deviation from proper thought. I was thinking, might a university in Texas want a professor with a different perspective?"

"Yes, brother, we believe in free speech."

Mason reached out to his brother, drew him in a hug and said, "Welcome home, brother."

White House

"I understand you talked to the first lady last night?" the COS carefully asked the president.

"Yes, how do you know?"

"It was recorded, and they are circulating your statement, 'The Resistance may have a point' around Capitol Hill."

"That's out of context."

"I'm sure it is, but it doesn't sound good and certainly is not helpful."

The COS picked up the phone. "It is you economic advisor slash investment broker," she informed him with her *should I leave the room* look.

"Stay here," the president said.

To his broker the president said, "From this point on you are to manage my portfolio without any advice from me. As that will take much of your time I am relieving you of any responsibilities as a presidential economic advisor. You may replace your salary with commission fees from my investments."

Obvious something had changed in the president's attitude, the COS asked, "Are you okay?

"I'm fine. Didn't you say the vice president is to be interviewed on CNN now?"

Sitting near the vice president was the first lady. The VP was animated in her answers. Her characteristic oversized white sneakers vibrated as she talked.

"There is no doubt the failure of this president to effectively use the Air Force and other tools at his disposal is impeachable. It appears from the sound clip we have heard that he is sympathetic to the national mutiny."

The president turned the monitor off, "What do our numbers look like this morning?"

"We've lost the House, no doubt. They will pass articles of impeachment later today. Of the nineteen states with thirty-eight senators, we need sixteen to vote against impeachment to deny them sixty percent. The four senators you spoke with last evening, you secured the one from Pennsylvania; we now have thirteen."

"Where will we get another three?"

"It doesn't look good, sir. That interview will not play well for those on the fence. The media is playing over and over your quote and is characterizing it as sympathetic— if not supportive—of the Resistance. And of course...."

The president interrupted her, "I know, I know… the first lady sitting beside her. It looks bad. So, we've lost control of the media?"

"Looks like, at best, they are trying to play neutral between you and the vice president. But as always they love to agitate."

"Now I know what a walnut feels like when the nutcracker starts to squeeze. Thirty-one belligerent states on one side and an out-of-touch elitist community on the other—clueless about the rest of the country!

If she becomes president, her bluster about the Air Force is not a bluff. Although not the Whiteman base, she will find bombers to carry out raids, and the Resistance will retaliate in kind. Clueless, she will be hellbent on making this a real civil war. A war in which thousands will die before the country is permanently divided.

Let me be frank, about what will happen. I have played this scenario out in my head often the last few months. We have played our cards for all they are worth, but our bluff is over, kaput.

In the 2020 census those thirty-one states had fifty-four percent of the population. Now those states have nearly two-thirds of the population. They will do fine without the other nineteen states.

When the thirty-one states win—which they will— they will not want to reattach to the other states. They will come to see the nineteen states as a non-productive drain on their prosperity. Unless there is a tremendous upheaval in the nineteen states, economically they will become third world. The elitist mob will be dragged kicking and screaming into reality."

The president stood looking out the Oval Office window. He had said it. No longer could he ignore the obvious; that is, obvious to those who chose to live in the real world.

Cautiously the COS stated, "If we agree that your chances of surviving impeachment are dim at the moment, there is a way."

"I know, I know. As distasteful as it is, I must do what is best for the country. Get that Julie, whatever her name is, on the phone."

"Mr. President," answered Julie.

"At least you still call me *president,* and your last name? What should I call you?"

"Collier. Call me Julie, Mrs. Collier or Ms. Collier, whichever you are comfortable with."

"Okay, Ms. Collier, let me be as straightforward as I can. It appears that I will be impeached; and with the vice-president in charge, she will be unrestrained in her response to what came from your Kansas City conflab. She will find military units to fight. All it will take is one or two bombers, and well… we can both imagine where it will go from there."

"The alternative is?"

"I could rescind the martial law proclamation banning lawmakers from your thirty-one states voting in Congress."

"And you would expect them to oppose your impeachment in order to prevent Washington going from bad to worse?"

"That is not how I would put it."

Julie continued, "Thirty-one states have carved out what we want. What would we have to gain?"

"Avoiding bloody civil war. Some agreement would need to be reached barring both sides from any military action. We both have our perspectives, but we have a moral obligation to avoid the destruction of the country."

"I'm sure part of any agreement along those lines would require your commitment to not seek reelection next year," stated Julie.

"That could be part of the agreement. But the agreement would need to address and make provisions for rapprochement."

"There would be many details to work out. It would take time. Time that you don't have," cautioned Julie.

"Here is the bottom line, I'm going to preemptively rescind the martial law edict banning representation in congress from the thirty-one states and immediately release those elected officials arrested at the capitol. I have aborted the 7th fleet attack on Gulf Coast harbors. If an agreement cannot be reached, your representatives can always proceed with impeachment without the 19 states."

"You don't have a choice, do you, Mr. President?"

"No, I don't."

"Go ahead, and I'll contact the states. But I can make no promises."

The three constitutional amendments and the reconciliation res-olution had been introduced in thirty-one state legislatures but not yet acted upon by any, although passage seemed imminent. Julie laid out the president's position to thirty-one state governors and Resistance leaders.

Capitol Building, DC

The president contacted the director of the FBI and informed him of the decision to rescind the edict barring representation from thir-ty-one states and instructed him to send a complement of agents to notify the vice president in the Capitol building.

The director said that with a shortage of available staff, it would be later in the day. The president answered, "Now!"

Hours later, the president was informed the impeachment vote easily passed in the House, and FBI agents were blocking the return of legislators from the 31 states.

His first call was to a Marine contingent that had been detailed outside the Capitol since the national discord began.

His second call was to the FBI director. His message was short, "You are fired."

House members carried the impeachment bill to Senate chamber and presented it to the vice president, who was presiding over the Senate. She laid it in front of her and stated that debate would com-mence within an hour.

"Madame President, are any copies available? And if so, how can it be read in an hour?" asked a senator.

As vice president, she was president of the Senate; but the word now had new meaning as she was about to become the country's president.

"We all know what is in it, Senator."

Four senators from the banned states arrived. Although they could not vote, she welcomed them. They had chosen to remain in Washington as it was home. The states they represented were but a necessary foreign place to travel every six years. They would sup-port her because coming out on top trumped adhering to antiquated principals. With a wink, she ignored them.

Before she could call for debate, her chief of staff informed her of the president's recension of the ban on senators from 31 states.

Hearing commotion in the halls, she instructed the sergeant-at-arms, "Close the doors to the chamber. No one else is to enter."

A senator from Massachusetts was recognized on the floor. "I move we dispense with hearings on the impeachment bill before us and call the question."

"Do we have a second?"

"Aye, Madame President," yelled a senator from Oregon.

Suddenly, the door burst open, and a Marine MP team entered followed by previously banned senators. The VP ignored them. "The question has been called for. Proceed to vote electronically."

Only ten senators had their votes recorded before the electricity failed.

Recognizing what had happened, the VP then exclaimed, "We will voice vote. All those in favor of the impeachment bill say, Aye."

The chamber was filled with previously banned senators. Although she did not ask for the 'Nay' vote, it was overwhelming.

"The Ayes have it; the impeachment bill has passed," she ruled.

"Madame President, I call for a division of the House," three senators yelled from different positions on the floor.

She glanced at the parliamentarian. The returned sour look and shake of her head gave the VP her answer. She jumped up and promptly left the chamber quietly in her white sneakers. Later, the articles of impeachment were defeated.

Washington DC – Midland, TX

"Our senators kept our end of the bargain, Mr. President. You know though, they may change their minds if we cannot agree on something substantial," cautioned Julie.

"Yes and thank you for that. I am sure we saved many lives. When can you be here for negotiation?"

"My team is not coming to your backyard which, given the behavior of the FBI, even you don't control well," stated Julie.

"And here I thought less control is what you people were after."

"You understand what I meant. I suggest we meet in Indianapolis."

"That is your territory, perhaps neutral ground— Pennsylvania, perhaps Philadelphia. It would be emblematic working something out where the Constitution was framed."

"I think Pittsburg would be more neutral territory."

"You drive a hard bargain, Ms. Collier. I suggest you send an outline of areas for discussion beforehand as will we."

In consultation, the Resistance states worked on a compromise proposal to submit to the president. Some states preferred to forgo any serious attempt at rejoining the other states. Others desired a settlement but realized that negotiation would whittle at their proposal, so it needed to be bold. In the end, agreement was reached but some states considered the proposal a take it or leave it offer, to others it was subject to compromise.

Julie and Andrew were chosen to negotiate on behalf of the thirty-one states. However, any agreement would need to be ratified by at least twenty of the thirty-one state legislatures and signed by their respective governors.

The proposal was nearly finalized when they received Washington's outline for reconciliation. The president offered an end to martial law and implement the National Tax Equalization (NTE) only by constitutional amendment. It called for the return of all military bases and local treasury offices to federal control and limited any future surveillance data collected or stored on citizens to only activity outside the law.

Some saw Washington's offer as a gain in the preservation of liberty over what had existed prior to martial law, although they were skeptical about the enforceability of limits on surveillance. The majority of the thirty-one states maintained that this was not a time for halfway measures.

White House

The COS entered the Oval Office, "They have made their proposal public."

"Public, so much for confidential diplomacy. Doing so makes talks more difficult," responded the president.

"They preceded the release with a plea for transparency."

"Put it on the screen, let's take a look."

The thirty-one-state proposal called for the end of martial law, the scuttling of any attempt to implement National Tax Equalization, and autonomy of each state's National Guard. It also required adoption of the 28th-30th amendments to the Constitution as passed by the breakaway states.

It called for elimination of the National Security Agency, the Departments of Energy, Information, and Education, and the Voter Empowerment Bureau (VEB). It required the CIA to limit themselves to international intelligence and for the FBI to terminate all management personnel on the 7th floor of the FBI building. The proposal called for a ban on any federal surveillance of civilians by drones or other means without a properly obtained court order.

The compilation and issuance of a Prodigy Suitability Index, (PSI), Social Conformity Index (SCI), and Health Care Index (HCI) for citizens was forbidden.

The document stated the original purpose of a District of Columbia without representation in congress was fear that government employees would gain undue influence over citizens. In order to allay that concern, given the growth of the federal government, it called for all counties in Maryland and Virginia bordering the District of Columbia be moved into the District of Columbia.

They had hardly finished reading the proposal when phone lines lit up.

"Vice president on line one, the dismissed FBI director on line two," the White House secretary said on the intercom.

The president picked up the VP's call. "As ridiculous as your capitulatory proposal was, theirs is so far out, it borders on fantasy. Do these people think we are living in the nineteenth century?"

"Calm down, it is all about positioning."

"Well, your position is too radical to start with. We will not give away the means to contain these mid-continent misfits we've worked so hard to contain," demanded the VP.

"Ms. Vice President, you played your hand in the Senate and lost. Get a grip on yourself."

"I'll have you know that many stand with me, and this will not be tolerated."

"Give my domestic partner my hello, and have a nice day,"

On the other line, the COS tried to ignore the fired FBI director's rantings. He stated he was obligated to remain until another director was appointed.

"It's the FBI director," the COS whispered to the president, with her hand over the receiver.

He shook his head. She replaced the receiver.

"What do we do about him?" she asked.

"Ignore him for now; we've bigger fish to roast."

Back to the proposal, the COS said, "Obviously, most of their demands are ridiculous and will never be seriously considered."

The president did not respond as he read the proposal again.

His response was subdued, "Their demands may seem outlandish now, but what happens when people in the nineteen states must have their food imported at prices they cannot afford? What happens when their lights go dim or they become hot or cold because solar, wind, and fossil fuel sources are from the other thirty-one states? What happens when the car or washing machine breaks down? They are all made elsewhere. Where will the tax money come from to support the unproductive with stipends? And with two-thirds of our citizens gone, what purpose do multilayers of bureaucrats serve, and how will they be paid?"

"You are serious, aren't you?" the COS realized.

"I'd call it realistic."

Chapter 28

Vice Presidential Mansion

The vice president, senators from Massachusetts, Rhode Island and Connecticut and the FBI director greeted the envoy from the European Union at the U.S. Naval Observatory—home of the vice president. Envoy Aimee Garnier came at the invitation of the senator from Massachusetts. She had known this group well from parties on both sides of the Atlantic.

Ms. Garnier got to the point, "It brings us great sorrow to witness the discord within your country. However, we have never thought those areas from here south and west, the pioneer hooligans in the rest of the country, fit well with your refinement. We fear that many in the hither regions of your country hold to the idiot opinion expressed nearly a hundred years ago by a politician when he said,

"Sometimes I think this country would be better off if we could just saw off the Eastern Seaboard and let it float out to sea."

The vice president interrupted her, "The cowboy was defeated soundly; that is long past. What can you offer us today other than an embargo of exports to Texas?"

"Our embargo can be extended to thirty other states, and we will deny entry into our union of visitors from those states. Perhaps we may send a few naval vessels to Florida, if you in turn show us more support against the Polish and Ukrainian separatists."

The FBI director nearly choked at the suggestion thinking…*A European naval fleet couldn't conquer Iceland, let alone discourage Florida.*

"We have a plan in the works," offered the FBI director.

"We wish you the best but know if it does not work out your Northeast complement of states is culturally a much better fit to our union than theirs," the envoy offered.

"It is not their union; it remains our union as it will stay," the VP shot back firmly.

White House

The president's secretary buzzed the Oval Office, "The first lady has arrived and is on the second floor."

"Excuse me, I won't be long, Erica," he said to his COS.

Erica, his chief of staff, missed neither him calling her Erica or the look the president gave her as he left. Although they were in the midst of the most turbulent time any president had ever seen, his demeanor this morning was not hostility or reservation to failure, but business like tranquility.

A porter stood outside the first lady's room. The president knocked once and entered before she could reply. He found her folding clothes into a small suitcase, much too small for her extensive wardrobe.

"Well, did you finally come to gather all your things?"

"No, just temporarily picking up a few garments." She gave him a look, obviously insulted by the degrading tone in which he spit out things."

Her use of the word *temporarily* confirmed what he already suspected. "I know about your agreement with the VP—for you to remain first lady after she was sworn in, but that possibility is over now. You just as well clear completely out."

"I wouldn't be so confident; one never knows what the future may hold."

With both palms up, the President sought to avoid confrontation as he backed out of her room. "Go ahead, live in a dream world if you choose."

He then stopped himself. "Let's cut the facade, this is the best for both of us. I'll sign whatever papers you serve me. I wish you the best."

The resignation and comfort contained in his last statement startled the first lady.

"That was quick," observed Erica as the president entered the oval office.

"Yes and satisfying."

"Is she leaving or staying?"

"She is leaving. I agreed to any terms she desires. It is for the best."

"Are you sure you are okay?"

"Absolutely, I'm uncomplicating my life. Now I need a hug from my best friend."

Midland, TX

Most of the Resistance team gathered at the former Atlas headquarters wishing Andrew and Julie well as they left for Pittsburg. The Texas governor and Carl arrived via the governor's plane, which the Colliers' would take to Pittsburg.

All knew that the meeting only represented a start in the process of reaching any agreement, but it was a start. The meeting itself was a victory. It represented a joyful culmination of hope over fear and hard work over despondent compliance.

The couple had been gone only minutes when Torrence burst into the Atlas conference room with intelligence. The tip couldn't be confirmed and wasn't solid enough to cancel the meeting but merited checking out. The governor offered a Texas National Guard jet. Mason, Eric, and Kelly immediately left for Pittsburg. They passed Julie and Andrew in the governor's plane somewhere over southern Indiana.

Vice Presidential Mansion

The vice president sat on a long ornate sofa between her domestic partners. On a chair sat the former FBI director. The first lady and a sympathetic member of the Supreme Court, who was there for a later ceremony, sat on a facing sofa. In the first lady's hand, she held a vial of eye irritant.

"I only left the White House temporarily so as to not distract my husband from doing his job," the first lady said to no one in particular.

"Save the grieving widow speech for later," the FBI director said.

Outside, a media camera crew waited after receiving a tip of a pending news development. The first lady also had her personal photographer outside the mansion.

Pittsburg

In a suite on the fourth floor of the Holiday/Marriott Hotel, FBI sharpshooters sat with pillows on end tables in front of windows to stabilize two H-S Precision HRT (Hostage Rescue Team) .308 sniper rifles. An FBI helicopter sat on the hotel roof supposedly to provide protection for conference attendees—in actuality, to provide an escape route.

Timing for arrival at the conference had been carefully staged. The president and Erica arriving in the presidential motorcade. Julie and Andrew arriving in a Lyft rideshare from the airport. It was the image each side wished to project—the president highlighting his power and position, and Julie her commonality with citizens. Their differing desires for imagery was emblematic of the country's divide.

With all forms of media encircling them, the two couples exited their vehicles on opposite sides of a grand walkway that had been covered with red carpet leading into the convention center. Julie and Andrew had been informed of the tip and would advise the president when they met.

Dumpsters sat on both sides of the alley service entrance to the Holiday/Marriott across from the Pittsburg Convention Center. Two FBI men were posted around the door. The lead FBI agent had stepped outside with them.

"Is everything okay out here?" he asked.

"No unusual activity," an agent answered.

Suddenly they heard a bouncing garbage truck headed toward them in the alley. The agents assumed it was regular garbage pickup day. It was not. An FBI agent stopped the truck and held his badge for the driver to see.

"Come back later today."

"Can't, we are across town then, union rules prevent us from altering our route."

The agent stepped up on the truck's running board and peered inside the truck's cabin. "You are alone?"

"Yes, only me; it's a shame that lift on the back put many of us out of work."

The smell from the dumpsters was ripe; the agents would be glad to have it removed. "Okay, get it picked up fast and get out of here."

The three agents watched closely as Mason maneuvered the hoist arm and attached it to a dumpster. They seemed fascinated with the process, which was good. Mason reached for another lever, and the crushing end gate of the truck rose. The first thing the agents saw in the truck were Eric and Kelly holding short barreled automatic weapons pointed at them. The lead agent started to reach inside his jacket when he felt the silencer on Mason's 45 poke him in the ribs.

"What do you want?"

"What room are the snipers in?"

"What are you talking about?"

Mason ground the silencer into the agent's ribs.

"I'd be shot if I told you that."

"Have your choice, shot then or shot now and compressed with the truck's garbage."

The lead agent turned and saw Eric and Kelly had the other agents pushed against the garbage receptacle on the back of the truck. Their faces showed fear.

"Can't do it."

The loudest noise heard was a yelp in reaction to the silenced 230-grain bullet traveling at 830 feet per second from Mason's 45 obliterating the agent's kneecap. Mason soon had him gagged and thrown in the back of the truck.

Mason stepped in front of another agent.

"No, not me. They're in room 424. Don't blame us, most agents want no part of this. It's all the political cronies on the 7th floor in Washington."

"Get in."

"No, we told you what you asked."

"We're not going to crush you, but we don't have time to tie you up and hide you."

With three FBI men in the compaction chamber, Mason momentarily studied the three hydraulic levers and hoped he remembered which was which. The first lever shut the gate. The second lever which crushed the contents he did not touch.

Kelly and Eric tucked their weapons under their jackets and stepped through the service entrance door behind Mason. They drew a few looks from service personnel until they found the service elevator. Eric pushed the up button on the elevator. Immediately they heard cables moving the elevator down. Eric noticed Mason looking at an adjacent door marked *stairs,* knew what he was thinking and said, "Elevator will be quicker."

Something about the elevator gave Mason a wheezy feeling, "Yes, but the stairs are more dependable."

"Splitting up might be a good idea," offered Kelly as he headed for the stairs.

"We'll see you on the fourth floor," Mason agreed.

Although Eric pushed the fourth-floor button, the elevator stopped on the second floor. Elevators had been programmed to stop at the second floor for a security check. Three FBI agents awaited the occupant of the elevator, each with a gun pointed at him.

"Where are the other two who were with you?" an agent asked.

"They went to the lobby," answered Eric as he was being handcuffed. Pushed into a room where two agents held two other handcuffed prisoners, Eric asked, "What are you going to do with me?"

"It is not good," answered the handcuffed woman.

Eric recognized the woman as former CIA agent Zoe. The man he did not recognize.

"What are you doing here?" Eric asked Zoe.

"They brought me from prison and," nodding at the man in handcuffs, "this is Tom, your Resistance leader in Pennsylvania. We are about to be arrested for assassinating the president and your leader, Julie Collier."

An agent stepped in front of Zoe. "We've heard enough chatter from you. If you don't shut your trap, I'll gag you."

Zoe had been vocal distracting the agents. Any well trained CIA agent kept a pick embedded in their backside waistband for these predicaments. Zoe whittled one in prison. As she talked, she picked the handcuff lock on her left wrist.

She broke her return glare at the agent in front of her to the window. It distracted the agent as her right hand swung the empty left hand cuff to his temple. A one hand detached handcuff was a dangerous weapon.

As the agent fell to the floor, she lunged at the other agent. He was reaching for his handgun when the Pennsylvania Resistance leader kicked him in the midsection knocking the wind from him. Zoe quickly had her handcuffs wrapped around his neck.

For Eric, Zoe's quick turning of the situation validated her reputation. "Mason and Kelly are headed for the fourth floor, room 424. We've got to get there."

With the others uncuffed, Zoe opened the room door with a bang followed by two bangs in one motion she directed at agents guarding the door.

Mason and Kelly waited at the elevator until they knew something had gone awry. At the door to room 424, Mason held the universal hotel door key card Torrence had given him against the door card reader and heard the unlocking mechanism click.

The president walked confidently to the juncture of walkways that was brightly lit to eliminate shadows in vivid 8080 definition TV feeds. Erica was only a step behind, and three men Julie assumed were secret service agents surrounded him. Standing at the end of the red carpeted entrance were two men with FBI badges hanging from their jacket pocket. Julie showed a slight hesitation scanning the crowd as she stepped from the car. Andrew whispered something, and they walked together toward the president. Within a couple steps of the president, Andrew took half steps allowing Julie to take the lead.

The president was gracious, but straightforward as Julie approached him, "Well, I cannot say it is a pleasure to finally meet you under these conditions."

"Given your honesty, my hopes have risen for this conference," Julie responded.

Her peripheral vision caught movement. The two FBI men were briskly walking away, trying to leave inconspicuously. Her Mossad security training kicked in.

"Down, Mr. President!" she yelled.

In response to the warning from Julie, a secret service man stepped in front of the president as a sniper squeezed the trigger. The trajectory of the bullet from the 4th floor entered the secret service agent at the top of his shoulder blade and exited after destroying his right ventricle. The deformed bullet then plunged into the president's arm at his elbow.

Andrew instinctively jumped to his wife's side at her warning. The second sniper's bullet hit Andrew from behind. It traveled between his body and arm toward his wife.

The hotel door mechanism click to room 424 was followed by the unmistakable report of two high powered rifles. A swift kick from Kelly dislodged the security chain and they burst into the room. FBI snipers were at each window in the suite with their eye focused into a Bushnell match pro 6-24 riflescope as they re-aimed.

Before they could get a second shot off, their bodies shuttered in involuntary muscle reaction to a barrage of bullets from Kelly and Mason.

Zoe, Eric, and Tom heard two high powered rifle blasts followed by semi-automatic fire as they reached the fourth floor. Like Mason and Kelly, they were too late to stop the carnage. Mason pointed his gun at Zoe.

"No, she's with us," Eric exclaimed.

"Who is paying you?" Mason asked.

"No one, your cause is mine now."

Vice President's Mansion

It had been quiet until the FBI director, hopeful for reinstatement, read a news bulletin on his grape. *"Shots have been fired in Pittsburg."*

A satisfied look came across the vice president's face as she glanced in relief at her domestic partners.

"Should we invite the cameras inside?" asked the anxious, would-be grieving domestic partner widow.

A picture of the grieving first lady nearly a century earlier cemented her stardom as an iconic figure in the country's history. Although only figuratively blood stained, this first lady saw herself in the role of perpetual first lady of the nation.

"Let's give it five minutes until we get confirmation," answered the FBI director.

Pittsburg

With notification the plan had failed, the remaining FBI agents in the hotel scrambled to the roof helicopter. Agents in front of the convention center reverted to plan B and escaped by car. Mason, Tom, and Kelly stayed in room 424 to secure the scene and from the window watched four bodies loaded on ambulances. Eric and Zoe went to the hotel lobby. The secret service was not letting anyone out of the lobby. Zoe recognized a secret service agent she had served with in the CIA. She waved frantically until he noticed her.

Vice President's Mansion

It had been quiet until the FBI director eyes rose from his grape. "No word yet."

"Did something go wrong?" asked the VP.

"Don't know. I'll contact our lead agent."

Trapped in the back of the garbage truck, the pain in the lead agent's knee had not subsided when his phone rang.

"What's happening there?"

"Don't know, sir."

"Why not? Where are you?"

The lead agent thought better of continuing the conversation and disconnected.

"What is happening?" asked the uneasy first lady.

"I think it best if we dispersed until this is sorted out."

As they prepared to leave, none of the group knew what to make of the sirens they heard approaching.

The bullet intended for Julie traveled, impeded only by a jacket between Andrew's arm and body until it hit the 357 he carried in a holster inside his jacket. The gun's metal frame fragmented the bullet into pieces which entered Andrew's torso and Julie's backside. The gun had absorbed most of the bullet's energy, and injuries from the fragments were not serious.

The attempted insurrection caused a secret service agent's passing to the next dimension. The president would never regain use of his left arm. Some later believed the arm loss symbolic.

Andrew and Julie and the president with Erica at his bedside were in adjoining rooms on a vacated hospital floor. A Marine company stood guard on the floor while a battalion surrounded the hospital. After they recuperated, it was decided the seclusion of the hospital was a good place to work on a settlement.

On the third day of negotiation, Julie and Andrew entered the president's room to find Erica sitting on the bed with him.

"Shall we tell them?" he asked Erica.

She nodded yes.

"You two are the first to know we have decided to form our own union."

"That is great that you've decided to partner, congratulations," offered Julie.

"No, not partners. I've had enough of those. It will be a marriage."

Within a week, an agreement was reached including amendments to the constitution. They were submitted to all fifty states for ratification.

Epilogue

Of the nineteen states not sided with the Resistance, eight soon approved the amendments constituting the USA 2.0 in hope of holding the Union together. Seven states—Rhode Island, Delaware, Connecticut, Massachusetts, New Hampshire, Vermont, and Maine— soundly defeated the amendments and began negotiations with the European Union before they would reconsider remaining in a USA 2.0.

The president used his authority under martial law to overcome opposition from local authorities in Massachusetts and Nantucket to the arrest of the first lady and vice president.

Zoe was appointed director of the FBI. Her first job was to clear out the 7th floor of the FBI headquarters. Upon arrival she found the floor empty, and the former director had fled to Europe.

The President rescinded martial law within a month and finished his term.

California and Illinois initially defeated the amendments, giving steam to the states' secessionist movements desirous of inclusion into USA 2.0. At the request of Illinois downstate residents, Iowa, Missouri, and Indiana were on the verge of carving out 90% of Illinois making Chicagoland an unsustainable island, until Illinois legislators reconsidered and ratified the USA 2.0 amendments.

Citizens blockades prevented state legislators from San Francisco and Los Angeles entering the capitol in Sacramento and threatened food boycotts of the cities until California ratified the USA 2.0 constitution.

Adoption of the 2.0 constitution narrowly failed in Maryland and Virginia initially. But when both states voted to exclude counties surrounding the District of Columbia with vested interest in federal largeness, the new constitution was ratified..

The seven holdout northeast states remained in turmoil. USA 2.0, now comprised of 43 states, left the seven states to make their own decision. They spent years pondering whether their culture was closer to Europe's or American's. As they pondered a decision, their economies collapsed.

Without electors from those seven states in the new USA 2.0, Madison Archibald, the governor of Texas, was easily elected president with the Governor of Iowa as vice president.

General Martinez was convinced to return as CJCS for two years under the condition that he have complete latitude cleaning out incompetent generals and admirals in the Pentagon.

Within a year Captain David (Davy Crockett) Leland, now dependent upon his abilities and work ethic rather than inlaw family connections was promoted to Major.

Erica and the former president remained in Washington as a married couple and became valuable advisors to the new administration.

Mason Trotter was elected governor of Texas. His brother, Damon, obtained a teaching job in the history department at the University of Texas. His perspective on history had changed.

Governor Trotter asked Eric and Kelly to manage Trotter Electric in his absence.

The Atlas News Network, ANN, was formed. Torrence was selected as CEO. Many corporations no longer guided by fear of the government eventually owning or running everything moved their advertising to ANN, causing many other alphabet networks to fold.

After deflecting an asteroid, stopping an invasive bloodstream device by nuking NSA, and making possible USA 2.0, Julie and Andrew were ready to leave the spotlight as much as possible and spend time with their daughter. President Archibald offered them positions in the administration. They respectfully declined.

Andrew used part of the Atlas headquarters to restart Collier Robotics. An engineer again, he also took up his former hobby, astronomy.

Julie directed security for ANN and Collier Robotics. She was overwhelmed with requests for security consulting work around the country. She had the luxury of being very selective.